I dedicate this book to Gloria—her humor, intelligence, intuition, love, loyalty and compassion make each day a marvelous experience for me, and everyone she meets

Cradled by the Waves

A Collection of Short Stories

DYAN D. QUINN

Cradled by the Waves

Copyright ©2018, Dyan D. Quinn

ALL RIGHTS RESERVED.

ISBN: 978-0-692-62358-9

This is a work of fiction. Names, characters, places and incidents are products of the author's imagination or are used fictitiously. Any resemblance or reference to institutions, authors, businesses, events, locales, or persons, living or dead, is entirely coincidental or fictional.

Published by

Fideli Publishing, Inc.
119 W. Morgan St.
Martinsville, IN 46151

www.FideliPublishing.com

Table of Contents

On the Island Cradled by the Waves

Squeezed into the Chevy with all our worldly goods, Mom and I were headed for Richards Avenue in Portsmouth, New Hampshire. Mom's relatives lived there and her bother's newspaper had offered her a job. My mother's Aunt Maud, a single, retired music teacher, had invited us to come and live with her. We made the trip from Denver in three days, stopping only to eat and sleep. I had my twelfth birthday on the trip.

Dad was my go-to guy for problems in math and explaining weird things boys or girls said or did. Mom worked on a lot of causes and never had much time to talk over my issues. Dad's leaving tore my world apart. I blamed Mom for not trying harder to prevent the divorce. I hated leaving all my Denver friends to go east.

Aunt Maud hugged me. "The house won't seem so big with you here." I moped around a lot, wondering, *Did I spend too much money on clothes and stuff or fail to do my chores? Maybe I didn't tell them I loved them enough?* These thoughts churned constantly in my mind and my guilt got heavier and heavier with every miserable day.

Mom was frazzled and unhappy. The newspaper work had a steep learning curve and not much pay. Besides, she had to get me settled in a new school and Aunt Maud had health problems. Maud listened to my school questions, like dad used to, but she had been out of the loop a long time and couldn't give me math help or explain street-talk. To cheer me up, she always brought me a bracelet or necklace when she went shopping. "I thought this would look

1

good on you." Our tastes were different, but I appreciated her kindness and generosity.

My A-student record in Denver went to hell. I argued with Mom and my teachers a lot. I was just skimming by in school. I felt like I was on my own and drifting, drifting…

I joined the rest of the skimmers; an entirely new species compared to my Denver friends. The new boys and the girls dreamed of great futures, but didn't have a clue how to achieve them. They thought of school as an obligation, not education. They were pretty loose. I learned to dance to rock music, ride a Harley and broadened my street-talk vocabulary. I used to think a hump was a bump in the road.

Mrs. Sixberry, the school counselor, called my mother. Whatever she said upset my mom. We had a loud fight that left me crying, because I hated her, and didn't want to. I shouted, "I know I was too much trouble. It was my fault Dad left."

Mom said, "Oh my! Is that what you think?" She began to cry and held me tight. "Your father *wanted* to leave. He loves someone else." Then I felt even worse than before, but for a whole new reason. *He didn't love me like he said or he wouldn't have done that.*

Mom sobbed, "Please forgive me for not talking with you about the divorce. It's very difficult for me to do, but I should have done it. None of it was your fault, ever." It felt like there was a vacuum where my heart should be and air was rushing in. The pain was awful.

Mom and Mrs. Sixberry suggested I get involved with one of the school clubs to meet others my age with real plans for their life. I joined the Drama Club. I found pretending to be another person, a dog, a vampire, a ghost or whatever, made me temporarily forget the wind tunnel in my chest. I was pretty good in the plays and even got the lead in some. It surprised me how I could step out of myself and be cocky, comfortable and controlled on a stage.

Aunt Maud came with mom to every one of my performances. They, and the drama coaches, told me my curly black hair, blue eyes, smooth, delicate skin and gentle smile made me movie material, and I believed them.

I loved Allen O'Neil. He was more than a great drama coach. I wanted him to love me. I was disappointed when he joined the Navy.

I edged my way through high school. After some special events I try not to think about were over, I ignored my mother's warnings and left New England for the west coast with orders to call or come home if I was afraid or unhappy. Mom gave me $500 and a bus ticket. It was all she had. Aunt Maud slipped me $800. I was eighteen.

I'd decided to go to Los Angeles because, for me, all movie action seemed to start there. Being young and naïve, I was sure I could act as well as the women I had seen in movies and on television. I was as good-looking, too, and taller than many of them.

I practiced greeting people and listening more than talking, like Dale Carnegie described in his book *How to Win Friends and Influence People*. This worked for me. I made acquaintances easily and later it helped me get waitress jobs in several trendy restaurants on Sunset Boulevard.

In LA, I changed my name from Kathleen Marie Stevenson to Katelyn Marie Stevens. It seemed more "Hollywoody." Entering a drama program at the University of Southern California, I found the tuition was too high for a waitress and what they were teaching was old stuff to me. I read about an audition for a comedy movie in *Variety,* tried out, and was offered a job as the male lead's heartthrob in a science fiction, comedy film. At nineteen, I left the university and never looked back.

Associating with older actors, I discovered the potholes in my education and began a vigorous catch-up plan. I went to free lectures at museums, read books recommended by librarians and asked questions of nearly everyone I met. I think my youthful appearance helped.

Solicitous actors, directors and staff were generous with advice. I had to be careful though. Some men saw a young, naïve country girl as a target. I did a reverse of my Dale Carnegie training. If they asked about me, they were usually legit. If they talked about themselves, I dodged them. It wasn't 100% foolproof and some older, glib guys expected sex in return for advice. I made sure I was never alone with them. Usually their advice wasn't any good, anyway.

Despite all my bravado and film success, I still needed acting to turn off the wind tunnel in my heart. Yoga and meditation helped a little but I often cried myself to sleep. As soon as I could afford it, and on advice from another budding actress, Sarah Gabriel, my roomy, I connected with Dr. Lily Rhodes, a psychiatrist. She was just the right physician for me. Soft spoken, she told me I was not alone and many children, especially teenagers, had my feelings after a divorce. She reassured me I would get better, though it might take a while to shake off the onus. When I fell back into my old fears and hates from time to time, she helped me regain my self-esteem.

So I, Katelyn Marie Stevens, am a person of value, ability and strength with a sense of humor—most of the time. I love Los Angeles and it loves me, within the limits of the ferocious competition for film jobs. Two thousand twelve is my twelfth year as an actress in movies and television. Helen Alford, my agent, finds auditions for me, and I'm rarely idle. I fill any gaps with interviews, posing for ads or signing autographs at film festivals. I know what "blow your own horn" means, and I do it well.

"Helen, why don't I get chosen for leading roles in A-list, big-money, romantic films?"

She told me what her casting director friend said, "Katelyn knows the film business inside-out, but she can't make love to the camera. You know how a girl looks at a guy, and without a word lets him know she likes him just by her mannerisms and expression? She can't do that. If you want her to play a strict or worried mother, a doctor, teacher, crook, detective or someone like that, she'll be fine.

"She isn't afraid to take off her clothes for nude scenes, but even then, her face doesn't fit the theme well. She might be a good director, but she's a little obsessive-compulsive and might drive everyone on a set nuts. Do you think she's a lesbian? She doesn't seem to be fond of men."

I don't agree with her description. I like men: the honest, amiable, respectful men with a sense of humor.

Helen works around her friend's assessment of me, but still has me try for the starry-eyed parts. I've never gotten any so far, so maybe her friend is right. I'm somewhat standoffish with kids, too. Helen steers me away from jobs where I have to act with young children. Dr. Rhodes tried to help me understand this quirk, but I still don't. Maybe that's my fault.

Driving down South Beverly Drive Friday morning on June 15th, 2012, I could see heat waves radiating from the tarmac for the first time in a month. The smoke from the burning trees in the San Gabriel Mountains was finally blowing east, though the campfire-smell still hung in the air. In my office, I mulled over a film shoot to be done later that day. My concern was the end of a movie in which I was an abused wife.

In the scene, the writers had me kissing and jumping into bed with Harvey Alston, a fop with bad breath who liked to be called Stud. *How the hell am I going to make this look real? He makes me want to puke.* I welcomed the interruption by my secretary, Terese. "Katelyn, Helen wants to send over Mrs. Zimmer from ART Films. She wants to talk with you about a new film."

"Great. Ask her to set a time and send over the script."

"Mrs. Zimmer just wants to discus something with you. It's not about casting. Her office is just around the block. She can come right over now. There's time before you have to leave."

"Okay. Let's do it."

"Ms. Zimmer, pleasure to see you. I think we met before at a film festival in Vancouver." I extended my hand.

"My! You have a marvelous memory. That's correct. Is it all right to call you Katelyn? I'm Rachel." A small, thin woman with shriveled skin and sharp cheekbones, she had a voice that went up and down in pitch and volume like a trumpet player with asthma. As she spoke, her gaze darted about, looking at the office and tracing me from shoes to hair with laser precision. I had to smile and decided, *This lady is a hawk on steroids.*

"Sure, Katelyn's fine. Terese said you have a new film in the works. How can I help?" Cosmetically prepared for the day, Yoga-trained, slender and tall with homegrown black hair to my shoulders, I was Rachel's physical opposite.

"Here's the first-run script. The character givin' me a fit is Brian, a male, but that's not why I'm here. There's another problem. Let me explain."

I was thumbing through the script. "But, this character is in the whole film. I'd need a brush-cut, mustache and a double mastectomy to look like this guy. You need a male actor."

"I don't want you to act. I want you to direct."

I stared at her, speechless, and then my disbelieving smile exploded into gigantic grin. "Really?"

"I need someone who has a deep feeling for nature and oceans, who is well read and dotes on the truth. I think that's you."

"Rachel, one sentence. What is this movie about?"

"It's based on a book by an American guy, Dan Darrigan. The title is, *Maguire's Plan for Life, Luck & Love.* He lives part time on Prince Edward Island in Canada." She handed me a book. "Read the book. See if you like it. It's well written. He's published several books. He teaches at a university. Creative writing, I think."

I flipped through the book pages. "There's no photo of him on the fly-leaf. The bio says he was born in New Hampshire." My brain gave me nudge. *I know that name. Where did I hear it?*

"Yeah. I think he is a backwoods kind of guy. Never met him. We bought the movie rights from his lawyer over the phone and fax machine. Can you believe that? He never does book signings, according to my author friends, but his books sell. He sure knows how to get people's attention. I'll bet he's a good teacher. Let me know what you think of the book by next week. We have the pipeline to three producers and you can help me there, too, if you'd like."

"Okay."

Rachel gave me her business card and we shook hands. I was studying the book's contents before Rachel was out the door. She was smiling as she left. She had my interest, and knew it.

The first paragraph hooked me:

  I remember my dad taking me to hear my mother sing or
  act in plays. The only other memories I have are her tickling

or hugging me, and that she smelled like flowers. Then she was gone. I learned later that I was three then, and we lived near the ocean. We still do.

My father worked at home as a writer-editor for a magazine. Occasionally he made trips to Boston and left me with the Howell family next door. Their daughter, Sara, was my age. Except for school, my father and the Howells were my world. Nearly every school soccer game Sara or I played, my dad and Mr. and Mrs. Howell were there. Mr. Howell even refereed some of the games.

Gray-haired Mrs. Cassidy, our cleanup lady, sometimes made us food and put it in our freezer. She often told my dad, "That boy,"—she always called me that—"needs a good meal cooked by a woman." Dad would hug her and roll his eyes, looking over her shoulder at me, making me laugh.

We each had our house duties and followed the rules about washing dishes, making our beds, emptying the trash and mowing the lawn. From there, we would go to our homework. Dad was great at explaining things or could always find a book on his shelves for me to read about a question.

By eight, I could use the dictionary, encyclopedia and write stories. Dad showed me how to make stories interesting. He'd asked questions, as if he didn't know the answer. "I wonder what would be better word for dessert?" If I said ice cream, he would hiss, yessss, and hug me, and then get us both some ice cream. At his suggestion, I tried out my stories on Sara. She was my friend and told me exactly what she thought.

By the time I was ten I was an experienced fisherman. My father and I went fishing nearly every Saturday or holiday. "We'll go out into the ocean until we're out of sight of land," he would say. When I was older I wondered if he was trying to forget the land existed, or that what went on there was too painful to think about.

When I asked him about my mother, he would say, "She is a famous actress and singer and has to be in a place where people make movies and give performances." If I asked when she would return, his voice became kind of scratchy. "She won't be back. We have to take care of each other." It was the same each time I asked, so I stopped asking.

On a Saturday early in October, we went fishing as usual. The sun was bright and the water calm, but a cold north wind prompted us to put on our long johns and warm jackets. We went out the usual distance, just "out of sight of land" and caught a sea bass and two blue fish in a couple of hours.

We were about to start home when Dad suddenly grasped his chest, hit at his left arm with his right fist and his face went white. He tried to stand and fell overboard at the stern. I screamed and tried to reach his leg to pull him back. He was floating face down in the water and made no effort to swim. I grabbed the boat hook but wind was moving the boat too far away for me to reach him. I started the boat motor and circled around trying to see his checked coat, but the wind was picking up and waves made it difficult to keep him in view.

I was afraid of hitting him. I kept circling and circling, but he was gone. I shut down the engine and turned on the emergency radio and started yelling, "May day! May day!"

The swells became stronger and I could tell the boat was drifting northwest. I tried to start the engine again, waiting briefly between tries, as Dad had taught me to do. I tried again and again, but it wouldn't start.

After a few seconds a crackling, stuttering voice said, "Where... are... you?"

"About a mile east of Portsmouth. My dad fell overboard, and the engine won't start. Drifting northwest."

"Hang...in...there.   ...We...are...on...the...way. Throw...out... the...sea...anchor."

I tried starting the engine again. No luck. I threw out the sea anchor and used a mirror to flash an S.O.S. at a plane gaining altitude after taking off from the Portsmouth airport. I had no idea if they saw it. I sat on the bait box and cried.

At dusk, the Coast Guard found me. I didn't hear them at first. I was laying on the keel wrapped in a blanket, shivering and half asleep, clutching a flashlight with dead batteries. When they pulled along side, I was surprised—the Captain of the Coast Guard cutter was Sara's father, Mr. Howell. I didn't know he was in the Coast Guard.

He asked, "What happened to Mike?" I told him about Dad, how his face turned white, and something made him fall overboard. How he didn't try to help himself, and my trying to pull him back aboard and losing sight of him.

"You drifted about two miles from where the plane spotted you."

"Did you find my dad?"

Mr. Howell shook his head slowly no. "Come with me, Brian. We need to get you warm and take you to the doctor. We'll tow your boat." He held out his hand to steady me. The boat was rocking and my legs felt like rubber when I tried to stand.

The first thing Monday morning, I asked Terese, "Would you see if you can find a phone or email contact for this author? Maybe the publisher will provide information." I handed her the book. "Give it back to me after you take notes."

Terese returned the book and I'd just started chapter three when she entered again to say, "I can't get any information. His name doesn't come up on any of the social media sites. The Boston University Publishing Department acts as his agent and publisher. They don't have any information except what's on the flyleaf. Summers, he teaches writing at the University of Prince Edward Island and Boston University in the winter. The book is for sale by the biggest sellers, but for details, they refer me back to BU. "

"Call Rachel Zimmer and ask for the contact she used when they bought the movie rights. If she asks why you need the info, tell her I want to talk with the author to get a sense of his personality and cooperation."

An hour later Terese returned. "Here is the phone number and address of his lawyer. Ms. Zimmer seemed quite elated to hear you wanted to talk to the author."

I laughed. "I'm not surprised. See if you can get the lawyer on the phone."

Ten minutes later, Terese entered again rolling her eyes and frowning to indicate, I wasn't going to like what was coming. "Mrs. Alexander, Mr. Darrigan's lawyer is on the line."

"Mrs. Alexander, I'm Katelyn Stevens in Los Angeles … I know you're busy. I just need five minutes. Okay… You and Mr. Darrigan sold the movie rights to his book, *'Maguire's Plan for Life, Luck & Love,* to ART Films. I've been asked to direct it and would like to ask a few questions. …

Well, can you give me a phone number for Mr. Darrigan? We don't know how to reach him. So, this is the number for the English Department number at the university?" … *She hung up on me! Can you believe that? It's like they don't give a damn if this movie gets done or not.*

I buzzed Terese. "Terese, this is the number of the English Department at University of Prince Edward Island. Please call and see if I can talk with Mr. Darrigan."

Twenty minutes later, Terese reported, "Dr. Darrigan is teaching a class. I left a message with the secretary that you would like to talk with him about his book and gave her our number. I asked the secretary for information about him and she gave me the University of Prince Edward Island's website." She handed me a note with the website address. "I looked at it. I don't think it will tell you much about him. It's just about academic qualifications."

"What's he teach?

"Creative Writing. He graduated from Boston University with a B.A. and M.F.A., and has a Ph.D. from Brown. Teaches at Boston University, too."

"Well, that explains a little. Um … If he doesn't call us back in the next day or so, call the secretary again. See if you can get an address or home phone number. In the meantime, do a website search."

I resumed reading:

Captain Howell wrapped me in a thick blanket and sat next to me all the way into the harbor. When he first sat down, he said, "Sorry about your dad. Good man. Good friend to me and my family. Sorry." We were both silent from then on, even on the trip to the hospital in his car. I'm sure he saw the tears on my cheeks, just as I saw his eyes glistened.

After a couple of hours in the hospital emergency room, getting my temperature up, checking my blood pressure and feeding me water, I was pronounced good-to-go. Suddenly it came to me, *Where do I go? I don't have a father or mother. Our house is empty. What will happen to me?* I began to sob and shake; and tears poured down my face. Without a word, Captain Howell squeezed me tight against his chest with his huge arms. The emergency room physician gave me a pill to swallow and handed a bottle of pills to the Captain.

While I knew from the minute Dad went overboard I'd be alone, I guess I didn't realize what it meant. The bottom had dropped out of my life and I had no idea where I'd land. After a few minutes, Captain Howell grasped my shoulders, pushed me back a little and looked down at my face. "It's going to be all right, Brian. Trust me." I tried to smile. He saw the effort. "I have to talk to the Social Services lady for a few minutes. Come with me."

I wiped the tears from my face with my sleeve as we walked down the hall and entered a door marked Social Services. Inside, there was a small waiting area and another door straight ahead. The name Sally Gould was painted on the rippled glass. Captain Howell and I had just sat down when the glass door opened and a big, black-haired woman with a friendly smile came out.

Her voice was soft and she spoke slowly. "Brian, I'm Mrs. Gould. I need to talk with Captain Howell. Will you be all right here for a few minutes?" I nodded yes and they both went in the other room. I sat in one of the chairs near the glass door. I could hear some of what they were saying, especially when Captain Howell got excited.

"Sally, the boy's mother and father divorced when he was three years old. He doesn't even know her. She has never seen him since the divorce. Michael Maguire's sister lives in Illinois, has four kids and has a souse for a husband. Mike's older brother died ten years ago. I'll try to reach the mother and the aunt tomorrow. The grandparents are deceased, at least on the father's side."

"Paul, that makes him a ward of the state."

"No, no, no! Don't do that. Get your evaluation team off their butts and have them investigate, inspect, and whatever else they have to do over at our house, tout suite. He's going to stay with us. We don't want foster child money from you. We want the boy in our home. He's had enough trauma. Don't make it worse. We have the room—Gwen went to college last month. I haven't talked to Ann yet, but I'll bet you $100 she'll agree without a blink. I'm going to talk to Mike's lawyer, Marian Roberts, tomorrow."

"Paul, you know I have to go through the ritual."

"I don't care what you do on paper, just don't give this boy more grief. Please! Mike had a will. Marian will have it. He's given us guardianship. Go slow on the reports. Take a vacation or something."

"You really love this boy, don't you?"

"Brian is the same age as my Sara. They've been friends since before they could say goo."

When Captain Howell came out the door, I was crying. He didn't know the tears were now a mixture of sadness and relief. He put his arm around my shoulders. "Let's go home now."

The black-haired lady stood in the door of her office smiling and waving.

Early Wednesday afternoon, Terese opened my office door to announce, "Dan Darrigan is on the phone."

I swiveled around in my chair, reached for the phone and, in my effort to pick it up quickly, fumbled the receiver and dropped it on my desk. "Mr. Darrigan, sorry about the noise. I dropped the phone."

"That's okay. I do it all the time, sometimes on purpose." I grinned. *His voice is strong and clear, like a veteran public speaker.* He asked, "What can I do for you?"

"First, I'm Katelyn Stevens in Los Angeles. Pleasure to meet you. I'm enjoying your book, *Maguire's Plan for Life, Luck & Love.* Rachel Zimmer, from ART Films, purchased the movie rights. She's asked me to direct the movie."

"Great. It's going to be difficult to help you over the phone though, especially if you keep dropping it." This time I laughed. Dan paused a few seconds. "Will you be shooting it in the East?"

"Too early to answer that. It would be nice though, to use the original scenery you described."

"It's hot in LA. Why don't you come up here? I'm here all summer. Can you get away? I can show you around and we can get photos for you to show Mrs. Zimmer."

"How long do you think it will take to do that?"

"A lot depends on how much time it takes for us to agree on format and theme. Can you stay two or three weeks? If you can, I think we can work through tough decisions on locations. I'm teaching a one hour class twice a week, but I'm free the rest of the time."

"I'll have to think about that. Before I forget, please give me a phone number and an email address. We had a terrible time trying find you."

"Sorry. I'm out a lot. Like the outdoors. Here's our number: 902-344-6171. The email is: ddarrigan@bu.edu.

"Can you recommend a place to stay?"

"The Holman Grand and Dundee Arms downtown are best, I think. They have fine restaurants. Near the airport there's the Royalty Maples Motel and near us, across the bridge, is the Southport Motel. Will you and your husband be bringing children with you? Give me a call or, better yet, send an email."

"If I come up, I'll come alone. Will I need a bodyguard."

"You can use mine."

I laughed again. "Thanks, bye. You are a helluva writer."

"You're a helluva an actress."

"How did you know I'm an actress?"

"Come on up and I'll tell you."

"You are also a fox."

I called Rachel Zimmer. "Rachel, I just had a conversation with Dan Darrigan. He's willing to help and wants me to come there to explore scene ideas. He teaches writing, summers at the University of Prince Edward Island. He seems to know a little about me. Did you tell him I'm an actress?"

"I may have. Don't recall. What's he like? Can you work with him?"

"Seems normal. Outdoor guy. Not phony. He says we can get a theme start in two to three weeks. Does that seem right to you? I haven't read the whole book yet."

"Probably means he wants to be involved. Final approval is up to him. It's in the contract. Can you get away for three weeks?"

"Yes. He recommended the Holman Grand or the Dundee something."

"Good. When do you want to leave? I'll get accounting to schedule the flight and book the hotel accommodations."

"I better check with him again about the best time. I'll call you."

"Fine. Will you be taking anyone with you, like a secretary?"

"I don't think it'll be necessary. I'll keep notes and take stills."

"Let me know if you think of anything else you will need."

I decided to wait a couple of days before calling or writing Darrigan. I wanted to read more of the book and didn't want to give him the impression I was easily persuaded to make the movie on the East coast. I continued reading:

> As we drove home, the sun was beginning to rise. I turned toward Mr. Howell. "Thank you for saving me."
>
> He didn't speak for a minute or so, and when he did his voice sounded kinda static, like the boat radio. "You're wel-

come." After a little period of silence, he added, "Would you consider living at our house? We need another man around."

"My dad is dead, isn't he?"

"Yes."

"I heard some of what you said to the lady. My dad liked you, Mrs. Howell, Gwen and Sara very much. I do, too. I'd choose being with you over anyone else I know."

"I'm glad. Now, when we get to the house, the girls are going to be crying and asking if you're all right. It's okay to feel sad and cry with them. We're a family. Gradually we will all feel better and honor your father with our bravery. Okay?"

"Yes, Sir."

It happened just as he said it would. Mrs. Howell ran out to give me a smothering hug, almost before the car stopped. "You *must* be in our family now." Gwen and Sara hugged me too, tears pouring down their cheeks to join mine. Mrs. Howell had breakfast prepared and a bed turned down in the spare bedroom where I usually slept when my dad went to Boston.

Mr. Howell went into his den and stayed there a long time. When he came out, we were still sitting at the table. "Brian, your Aunt Patricia can't come over. She lives in Illinois and has four children. She's going to call you soon. I know you've only seen her once or twice, but she's your dad's sister and loved him, just like you. She's having a tough time of her own right now.

Father O'Hara is organizing a memorial service at St. Patrick's for your dad. Why don't you get a shower and some shut-eye, before you keel over." He grinned and came around the table to tousle my hair.

Sara stood up. "I'll get you a toothbrush and paste," and ran out of the room. Gwen and Mrs. Howell began clearing the table and I helped.

I slept until Sara knocked on my door, opened it a crack, and asked, "Can I come in?" Her arms were loaded with my clothes. "I went to your house and got these. Supper is ready. Come down as soon as you can."

She put the clothes on a chair, started to leave, then turned back. "Brian, I'm sorry about your dad."

"Thank you."

"Welcome, Hotshot." That was the name she'd given me after I'd beaten her at basketball in the driveway three weeks earlier.

At dinner that evening, Mr. Howell described his failure to reach my mother. "Maybe your dad's lawyer, Mrs. Roberts, will have better luck. Lawyers seem to be good at locating people. She'll clarify your dad's wishes about a lot of things. You and I will meet with her soon. Anything you want to ask about?"

"Do you think my mother will come here? I don't even know what she looks like. Can she take me away?"

"No. Not a chance. Mrs. Roberts already told me your dad appointed us to take care of you, and that we will do. Don't worry about it." *The ache in my chest eased a little.*

After dinner, we watched a New England Patriots football game on television and talked. Gwen, a whiz at math, and a first year engineering student at Maritime University, teased her dad about being "old-fashioned" in his Global Positioning technique. She planed to return to college after the memorial service.

Mrs. Howell said, "Now, stop bothering your father. Do you have enough warm clothes to wear to school, Gwen? How about you, Brian?"

Gwen laughed and hugged her mom, "Worrywart!"

I said, "I'll be fine, Mrs. Howell. Thank you."

Captain Howell turned off the television sound and held up a hand. "Okay, hear this. Except at work, I'm known as

Howie or Dad. If you're angry with me, do what Mom does and call me Paul. Your mother is called Ellie or Mom. If you're angry with her, call her Ann. But you better watch out if you do that and she has a broom in her hand." I knew he said it for me, but everyone laughed, including Mrs. Howell.

The memorial service slid by in a blur. I didn't know my dad had so many friends. They came from New York and Boston, as well as throughout New England. Mrs. Howell had everyone sign a register so they could be thanked later.

Some of the visitors stood up and talked about my dad. They told many stories of how he made them laugh. One speaker said Dad was the Donald Westlake of Boston. Gwen whispered to me that Westlake wrote a series of funny crime novels. Some of my dad's books were called the Steve Stonebreaker Series. They're about a bumbling thief who gets into ridiculous situations.

Later, I went to the bookshelves in our house and found the whole top row held Dad's novels. He never mentioned to me that some were made into movies. He was always cheerful and kind with me, and as I listened to the speakers I began to cry. Howell arms squeezed me tight.

Learning about him from other people made me sad. I wished I'd asked him more questions. We did talk a lot, but mostly about school, soccer, fishing, camping trips to Maine or vacations on Prince Edward Island. He really liked the story of Green Gables.

His childhood never came up in our conversations. He never took me to see my grandparents and never talked about them. I thought they were dead.

Hearing all these things from others made me wonder, like the "out of sight of land" thing, if there was a big gap in his life that was too painful to discuss. I decided to ask Aunt Patty questions when she called.

Mr. and Mrs. Howell and I went downtown to Mrs. Roberts' office. I was uneasy about calling them Howie and Ellie, so I just turned toward each one when I had a question. We learned from the lawyer that Dad left two thirds of his estate to me and one third to his sister Patricia Maguire. He'd asked the Howells to be my guardians and use the estate for expenses in caring for me.

The lawyer had the paper they had signed together years ago and read it to us. As Mrs. Roberts read, Ellie smiled at me. Howie put an arm around my shoulders and said, "Marian, will you please write a formal letter about this to Sally Gould at the Social Services Department? She's struggling with regulations about children without relatives."

"I'll take care of it, Paul." Sara told me later her father and Mrs. Roberts were classmates in high school.

The rest of the stuff about the house, royalties and banks I didn't understand except that, when I was twenty-one years old, I could make my own decisions. Dad had directed what he left to Patricia was to go into a bank account in her name only.

In my new home I was immersed in whatever was going on in the family. I had my duties, like every other member, and took the good-natured heat if I was derelict in my work. If I was mopey, Sara threw a basketball at me, or kicked a soccer ball my way.

Sometimes, Howie would decide to paint a fence, wash the windows or build Ellie a new bird feeder. He had tools for every kind of job, and I learned to use them all. Sara and

I helped him coach the Little Leaguer's soccer team in the summer.

Ellie insisted I learn to cook. "Every boy should know how to make a good meal." We had a garden behind our house. We raised tomatoes, beans, peas, cucumbers and a few other plants. I learned to plant, cultivate, harvest, throw-out duds and cook vegetables. I wasn't the Boston chef I saw on TV, but I was pretty good. I had great teachers. I belonged.

"Professor Darrigan, this Katelyn Stevens in LA."

"No Professor Darrigan here. There's a Dan Darrigan, also known as just Dan. Would he do?"

I had to laugh. "Okay, Just-Dan."

"How may I help you, Madam?"

"If I come up there Sunday, will that work out all right with you?"

"Fine. Do you want me to meet you at the airport?"

"No. I'll leave here Saturday night, have an hour layover in Toronto, if I'm lucky, and get to Charlottetown near eleven in the morning on Sunday. I'll be wiped out by then. I'll take a cab to the Holman Grand and get some sleep. How about meeting me in the hotel restaurant at seven o'clock?"

"Great. We'll be there. See you then."

"Okay." Hanging up, I frowned. *Who is 'we'? Will that curt lawyer be there, too? God, I hope not.*

Flying, I mulled over what I was doing. *I'm going 3000 miles in the middle of the night to meet the author of a book. This may be the dumbest thing I've done. We may not even be able to convert it into a movie script. It's an excellent book, but I'm not sure it can be a good movie. He doesn't seem too enthusiastic, either. I may be misreading him though. Being in Canada will be a change from the summer heat in LA. Haven't been to Prince Edward Island before. We talked about it when I was a kid. It is sure going to be different than my trips to New York City or Vancouver.*

Arriving at the Holman exhausted about 11:30 a.m., I collapsed on the bed without even unpacking. It was five o'clock when I awakened; it would've been later if I hadn't asked for a wake-up call upon checking in.

Hanging my clothes, trying to shake out wrinkles, I considered what to wear that night. *Most of the hotel guests I saw were casually dressed.* After showering, I decided a professional look was best, and put on my gray business suit, silver earrings, necklace and a bracelet, all with small onyx stones to match my black shoes. I added a narrow, red scarf on my neck for contrast.

I entered the hotel restaurant just before seven o'clock and asked the maître d', "I'm meeting Mr. Dan Darrigan. Is he here?"

"No, Ma'am. Let me show you to a table. I'm sure he'll be here shortly. He's always on time."

"You know him then?"

"Yes, Ma'am. We both coach local soccer teams. Good athlete, good man. I guess you haven't met him before."

"That's correct. Thanks for the information."

As he turned back toward his station, he exclaimed, "Here he is now," and hurried to the entrance.

My gaze followed him and I saw a broad-shouldered man with a tanned face, about six feet four in height. His sandy hair was neatly combed and he was wearing a brown sport coat and darker brown slacks. No professor's beard, pipe or horn-rim glasses, as I had imagined. *He does look like an athlete.*

I watched as he and the maître d' joined in a conversation that was a mix of words and laughter. I heard him call the maître d', "Charlie."

Next to him stood a trim, young boy whose height was just below his shoulder. He also had neatly combed hair, but it was black, like mine. He joined in the repartee. Dressed in a blue sport coat, gray slacks and maroon tie, I judged him to be sixteen years old. When he smiled, his white teeth contrasted with his tanned face and reinforced the sincerity of his greeting as he shook Charlie's hand. Still laughing at something Dan said, Charlie motioned them both toward my table.

"Katelyn, pleasure to meet you in-person. I'm Dan Darrigan." He extended his hand.

"Thank you. Pleasure to meet you also."

"Meet my son, Jed Darrigan, the world's best soccer player."

Jed smiled and offered his hand. "Don't believe anything he says. It's all fiction." I was amazed, *His grip is as strong as his father's.*

I had a flash sensation that the boy's hair color and facial features were familiar, and all other thoughts in my mind were snuffed out for an instant.

Dan seemed to notice my hesitation and broke the spell. "How was your flight?"

"Long, and the time-zone changes have twisted my orientation."

"I understand you grew up in New Hampshire. Have you ever been to Prince Edward Island before?"

"No. Certainly is beautiful from the air." *How does he know I grew up in New Hampshire?*

"I told Jed you were here to research scene locations for a movie based on my book. Jed, tell Katelyn what you told me."

"There isn't much action in it."

Somewhat surprised, I paused, wondering how to answer. "Don't you think people's troubles are enough action?"

"I didn't think of that. Today everyone likes explosions and stuff."

I glanced at Dan who had an amused look as he awaited my response. *This may be tougher than I thought.*

Then, seeing the concern on my face, he said, "Let's order." He motioned for the waiter.

"Good idea. What's special here? I'm famished."

"Me, too. Order what you like. It will be good. Everything is local, fresh and prepared well."

The waiter was a wiry young man about Jed's age, with neatly trimmed hair, glasses and a clean white coat that diverted attention from his obvious youth. "Hi, Coach. Hi, Jed. Are you ready to order?"

Dave said, "How's your dad, Eddie?"

"Better. Thanks for asking."

Jed turned to me. "Is it all right for me to call you Katelyn?"

I nodded yes, smiling at his decorum. *Long time since I met someone his age who is instinctively polite.*

"Eddie, meet Mrs. Katelyn. She is a movie actress and director from California."

Eddie bowed his head slightly toward me. "Nice to meet you, ma'am."

"Pleasure to meet you, Eddie. Tell me, do these two," I pointed at Dan and Jed, "know everyone in this town?"

"Yes, Ma'am—even my dog, Romeo. May I take your order?"

"How come you're so well known here, and I'm told, you never do book signings?"

Dan thought a few seconds. "We've been coming to the island every summer since Jed was two. We're pretty active in sports and events. It's easier to do here than in Boston—less traffic, shorter distances. I figure, if my books are good, people will read them. If they're not, no one knows I'm a dud. I know, coming from Hollywood, the capital of hype, that sounds stupid. But I like to live in a world of reality with my feet touchin' the ground. Tell us what you would like to see or explore here. Jed and I will be happy to show you around."

Jed put down his water glass. "When one of my friends comes here from the city, if their interested, I give them a little island history. Most them know Lucy Montgomery's book, *Anne of Green Gables,* but not much else."

"I'm in that category. Fill me in. What a great idea. How did you get so smart?"

"I have a smart mother," Jed said, giving his dad's shoulder a light punch with his fist, making Dan laugh.

"Okay. The Native Americans, the Mi'kmaq, were here first. It's pronounced mic-mac. They used to hunt in the winter and fish in the summer. They named the island Epekwitk. That means 'cradled on the waves'."

My eyes locked on Jed's face. "What a lovely name."

"Jacque Cartier was the first white man to come here in 1534. He claimed the island for France and made it part of Acadia, the French colony that included the Eastern Canadian Maritimes, some of New Brunswick, Quebec and the state of Maine. The iron-red soil was excellent for agriculture, and being near a large body of water, the fall temperatures stayed up, so crops were protected from freezing until harvest."

I could feel Dan watching my face to see if I was really listening, and glancing over I saw him slip a proud smile behind the menu.

Jed went on. "In 1755, just before the seven year war between France and England, the British invaded and drove the French from Acadia, separating the women and children from the men. Some French people stayed in New Brunswick and Quebec. Others went all the way to the new French colony of New Orleans in Louisiana. The people there turned the name Acadians into Cajuns. The Cajun customs, music and food originated here.

"You probably had to read the poem *Evangeline* by Henry Wadsworth Longfellow in school. It's the tale of Acadia and an Acadian girl's search for her lost love, Gabriel.

"The British re-named some of the maritime land Nova Scotia and this island's name was first changed to Saint John's then to Prince Edward Island. Prince Edward was the father of Queen Victoria. The island became a seaside resort for wealthy Victorian nobles who dared to make the Atlantic crossing in the 1800s."

I was impressed. "You're somethin' else. Great introduction."

"Do you remember how, when school starts in the fall, the kids are antsy having to sit all day?"

I nodded yes.

"And, to calm everyone down, the teachers ask them to write an essay on what they did during the summer?"

Again I nodded yes.

"I wrote this. We have a new teacher every year. I've been using this same story for three years. I got two A's and an A+."

I couldn't help it. I let loose a squealing blast of air, like the air brakes on a bus, put one hand over my mouth and waved apologetically with the other, struggling to control my laughter.

Dan turned to look squarely at Jed. "I didn't know you did that." His face was serious, but not angry.

"You don't need to know everything."

I erupted into laughter again. When I recovered, I told Jed, "I did the same thing with a story on Shakespeare."

Dan took over. "The eastern, Atlantic end of the island has many fishing ports. Some on the north side, too. The central area is called the Blue Heron Belt. It's a bird-watcher's heaven and there are beautiful farms to see. That area has theaters, museums, Green Gables, Province House and the Center for the Arts. There are parks, beaches and camping areas everywhere.

"The city of Summerside is the entrance to the western, Prince region, known for its flowers. Some call it the Lady Slipper County. There is a paved bicycle trail that runs across the whole island. Megan, Grace, Jed and I like it. Its a great way to see and feel the beauty of the place."

Jed added, "Mom and Gracie will be here Friday. I'll bet they'll have ideas. Mom's a cineaste."

My fork paused between the plate and my mouth. "Am I interrupting your family vacation?" I'm sure an anxious look passed across my face and my fork went down to the plate. "I don't want to do that. Please, don't let me do that!"

Dan waved away my concerns with a hand. "We enjoy having family or friends visit us here. We do it all the time. It makes us happy to introduce others to a calm, laid-back summer life, show people the many things they never knew about the sea, and the history of North America. Relax. We'll have a good time, and so will you."

Jed asked, "Do you like soccer? You can come to our games. We're pretty good."

"I like soccer. I learned about it when I was doing a movie in Spain. I'd like to see you play." Jed smiled when I added, "You know, that fits into the book-movie plan. It could be part of the 'action' you said the book lacks, but," I warned, "probably best you don't say anything about that right now. We don't want get something going we can't deliver. Right?"

Jed nodded his assent and held his smile. Dan's expression was the opposite: anxiety.

I saw it and decided to talk with him privately later. "So, your mom is a film buff, huh?" All the time I was thinking, *How would a 16 year old know the word cineaste?* I decided to change the conversation's direction. "Dan, did you go to Boston University?"

"Yes, for undergrad. Megan was at MIT. We were married when we were both in master's programs. Jed came to us a year later. Megan has a doctorate in biomedical engineering and is working with the CRISPR technique to change genes in people with hereditary diseases."

"What is CRISPR?"

"It stands for Clustered Regularly Interspaced Short Palindromic Repeats. The name won't help you understand the process unless you know genetics. That's why my master's and doctorate are in scientific writing to help non-scientists understand the literature and help researchers write grant applications. I'm teaching academic writing to the veterinary students in the marine biology department here. There are a number of sea farms near the island."

"Whoa! What's a sea farm?"

"Sea farmers grow Sugar Kelp, oysters, scallops and mussels. The farmers are always looking for ways to keep the ocean healthy and producing oxygen."

"Can I come to a lecture?"

"Sure. There's one at 8 a.m. tomorrow. I'll pick you up out front at about 7:30. The college isn't far from here."

Jed laughed. "Man, is he goin' to snow you."

"Hey, wise guy," I replied, "I got a brain."

Dan's laugh bounced along between his words. "You better be careful, young man. You've met your match!"

He and Jed walked me to the elevator. Dan asked Charlie for a map of the island for me. "This will give you some ideas of places Jed and I can take you. Probably it's best to take one section at a time, unless you can pinpoint something of special interest. Pleasure to meet you, Katelyn. Glad you could come up."

"Likewise. Good to know you both. Thanks for dinner. It was superb."

Jed took my hand. "Sorry I was tough on you about the lecture. Guess I was remembering the last time I went to one."

I squeezed his hand and said in a deep voice, "As Crocodile Dundee would say, 'No worries, Mate,'" and I disappeared into the elevator, leaving them laughing. Ten minutes later I was at my laptop reading about sea farms.

The next morning, Dan was on schedule. Dressed in jeans and a blouse to try and fit in with the students, I sat in the rear of the lecture hall. *The students look so young.*

After Dan finished the class, students pressed forward to ask him questions and it was twenty minutes before he approached me. "You're a good teacher. I like the way you played dumb to make them think. You're a regular Jane Austen. It got them involved. Good job!"

"Thanks. Could you follow the gist of it?"

"Pretty well. You have a special vernacular for your work, just as we do in film, and that tripped me a lot."

"You're right." Dan seemed impressed that I recognized his teaching methodology. "Let's go have some breakfast and pick up Jed. Have you decided where you'd like to go today?"

"I've been thinking about that. When you dip back into the story, what scenes mean the most to you? I think that is going to be critical."

As we drove, and on into breakfast at a diner, Dan talked enthusiastically of memories. *What I'm hearing doesn't all come from the book. I'm certain. There's a change in the tone his voice when he describes the favorite places of Michael John Maguire and the Howell family. They have a sentimental effect on him. Why is that?*

After picking up Jed, we visited the Coast Guard station on Charlotte Harbor, then traveled north to Green Gables and North Rustico beach. We had a lobster lunch, garnished by deep-fried mussels, in the village of Stanley Bridge then stopped at The Preserve Company in New Glasgow. The flavors and varieties of jams and jellies were so unique I ordered boxes shipped to my house and to friends in Los Angeles and Rhode Island.

Dan pointed out the Confederation Bicycle Trail as we crossed it.

Jed asked, "Mrs. Katelyn, do you ride a bike?"

"Just Katelyn, Jed. It's my first name. And yes, I do ride, a lot."

"Mom, Dad, Gracie and I have ridden the whole trail. Not all at once. It's 175 miles long. There are bike races all summer, too. I like the ride up to East Point and Singing Sands best. Fine beach, and nice breezes. It's cooler ridin'. That's on the east end of the island."

"Then I think I would like it, too. Let's do it." *I like this boy.*

"Can we, Dad?"

"Sure. Let's wait 'til Mom and Gracie get here though. They like it there too, and having everyone together will be great."

The rest of the week was occupied by lectures, soccer practices and short trips in all directions from Charlottetown. Comfortable there, I wandered about the harbor, taking photographs of the fishing boats unloading, the hospital, a school and typical homes, all like those described in the book. I realized they were not exactly like the ones in Portsmouth, New Hampshire, but they fit the words.

Together, the three of us pedaled on the bicycle trail from the outskirts of Charlottetown and west through Milton almost to Greenvale and back. It was a thrill to ride unchallenged by motor vehicle traffic. The clear air was scented by flowers and the shades of color in the fields of clover, corn and canola were spectacular. *There's no such thing near where I live in LA.*

Friday evening, Dan brought Megan, Grace and Jed to the Holman to meet me and have dinner. Megan walked right up to me and hugged me. "So nice to see you again. Glad you came 'Down East'."

I was stunned. *How does she know me? I hope she isn't a film critic.* "When did we meet before? My memory is failing me."

Megan stepped back, her hand over her mouth. "I'm sorry. I thought Dan told you."

"Told me what?"

"We rode the same school bus together for a year. You were about 11 or 12 at the time. We were seniors. On the bus we were probably kind of ... irrelevant to you. You lived about six blocks down from our house. My name was Megan Cameron then. Yours was Kathleen Stevenson."

My memory rushed into action. *That's why the name Darrigan seemed familiar. Is she giving me a zinger about my name change or my recognition failure?*

"Megan, I'm sorry." I gave Dan a semi-withering glance, making him shrug his shoulders with his hands palms up, while struggling to suppress a laugh.

"That's okay. Dan likes to surprise people. Meet our daughter, Grace."

In my mind I had pictured Megan as an engineer—pale from sunlight-deprivation, with thick glasses, unkempt hair and no lipstick. Instead, Megan was my height, slender, with strong, supple arms, and beautiful. The hair that curled from under her blue hat was light brown, and undoubtedly an older version of the blonde hair of her daughter, Grace, standing next to her.

Megan's eyes, two shades of blue, sparkled with enthusiasm and curiosity, just like Grace's. They both had the same delicate facial features and sweet, humble smile. Each wore a cocktail dress, but with different colors and flower patterns. Both had belts that matched their shoes and one color in their dress.

"Hello, Grace. I've heard so much about you from your dad and brother, I feel I know you already."

"Really?"

"Really. You have fans, too. At Jed's soccer game, several boys came over to ask when you were coming to the game."

Grace blushed, hesitated, then stepped up to me and extended her hand. "Glad to meet you, Ms. Stevens."

Standing behind Grace, Dan was grinning, inflated with pride. I found out later he and Grace had talked about confidence and self esteem, and until this moment, he wasn't sure she was listening.

"I hear you're quite a soccer player." *She's tall for a twelve year-old.*

Jed jumped in. "She's good. Dad said she has ambidextropedia. I don't know what the words means."

"Wow! I don't either. What is it?" *I was truly astonished.*

Grace explained. "He makes stuff up. It's not in the dictionary. It just means I can kick equally well with both feet."

Dan hugged Grace and laughed with everyone else. Jed added, "Is that all? Let's order. I'm hungry."

A rare tingle of pleasure coursed through me. *What a joy it is to be with people just being themselves.*

Megan, the cineaste, couldn't hold back her questions any longer. "Katelyn, you've made more than fifty movies for film or television. That's a lot of work. How did you decide to become an actress? Do you have actors in your family?"

"No. No actors in the family. I started in school plays, and pretending to be someone else just seemed to come to me. I guess I was pretty good at learning lines and keepin' my cool on stage. I just kept getting more and more jobs."

"You had to pretend to be someone?" Jed gave me quizzical look.

"Yes. That's what acting is all about. You try to become the other person, just for the movie. That's the art."

"Man! I could never do that. I like being me." He got the premium laugh of the night.

Grace changed the subject. "Would you like to go to Fisherman's Haven Park near Tignish? It's on the Gulf of the St. Lawrence and we might see some whales."

"You know, wherever you would like to go, I'll go, too." *We're going to be friends. The smile on Grace's face confirms it.*

In the next two weeks I got a grand tour by auto and bicycle. Crossing on the ferry to Nova Scotia, we visited the Alexander Graham Bell Museum near Bell's home in Baddeck, and followed the breathtaking Cabot Trail to the end. We attended a play in Summerside on Thursday and went to a festival that included music, every imaginable type of seafood, paintings and jewelry made from pebbles and shells polished by the sea.

During this time, I witnessed a family image I'd rarely seen among my multimillionaire friends and co-workers in Los Angeles. It was priceless, and had nothing to do with wealth or celebrity. *It's a communion of life. A mind-song with words and actions flush with understanding, honor and intimacy; bound together by notes of respect and admiration. This is important—and it's missing in my life.*

On Friday of the second week, Grace's team played the New Glasgow soccer team and she made two goals. "One with each foot," Jed said. After lunch, we went to nearby Cavendish beach. Grace and two girlfriends from her team wandered down the shore, scouting out the boys and laughing. Jed sat near the water's edge, making little trenches in the sand and watching the water flow back when waves filled them.

I asked, "Jed, what are you doing?"

"I like water. I like to see how it behaves when it moves and how it can change what I make."

"What do you think you'll do when you're older?"

"I'd like to be a water engineer. I read how the Dutch people learned to hold back the ocean. Did you know the Bay of Fundy has tides of sixty feet? That's a lot of energy. Engineers have already built some underwater turbines there to make electricity."

"You know, you're a pretty smart guy. It's hard to believe you're only sixteen years old."

I learned later, that Dan and Megan, who'd been sitting nearby, heard our conversation.

Megan's eyes were closed. Dan leaned over and touched her arm, but didn't speak. She opened her eyes and he motioned toward Jed and me. Then he put a finger to his lips, as if to say, don't speak, listen.

"I'm not sixteen, I'm fourteen."

"No way!"

"Way. I'm fourteen."

"When's your birthday?" My voice had a new tone: a fragile, compressed sound, almost drowned out by the waves. On this warm summer day, a shiver went through me.

"December 12th."

Dan and Megan told me later they saw the color vanish from my face, despite the tan. I tried to speak but my mouth closed over the words. Dan said my breathing seemed to stop, and I looked away, toward the sea.

After a pause, I stood up and looked toward Dan and Megan, who seemed to be sleeping. "I'm going to walk along the beach a little. You want to come?"

"Sure."

We started west, me on the sand and Jed jumping in and out of the water, looking for shells. I'm sure the waves pounded the shore, hissed as they withdrew, and the seagulls screeched overhead, but I didn't hear either one.

On the way back to Charlottetown, I helped Grace pick out some cool shorts from a catalog. We talked about where to get them locally. I showed Jed how to accentuate the iridescent colors in the clam shells by changing how the light hit them.

I was quieter than usual. The children sensed it and perhaps thought I was sad because I had to leave the next day. They kept asking me questions, trying to make her feel better. "Do you like the Los Angeles?" "Does the sun always shine there?" "Where do you walk your dog?" "My mom said you used to ride a motorcycle. Do you still ride one?" I answered each question gently and forced a smile.

Dan asked, "Katelyn, instead of changing clothes to go to a restaurant, why don't you come to the house and I'll grill some steaks or salmon. Okay?"

"I'd like that."

I felt like more than a guest at the house by the bay. It was a strange, unexplainable feeling of belonging. Megan sensed my ethereal mood and tried to reify it. "I think you like it here. I think you like being with us. I'm glad." We were working on the salad, beverages and desserts, while Dan grilled, and the children set the table.

"Oh, I do. I do! There's something you have, I've never had. I guess I'm feeling sorry for myself. I know that sounds stupid coming from a grown woman." *I wonder what Megan thinks of me.*

"Not at all. We all have hang-ups of some kind. You'll be comfortable here. Jed and Grace are very fond of you. Dan and I are, too. Will you stay overnight with us?"

"I- I don't want to impose."

"You won't be. Everyone is tired tonight. It's been a long day. We'll sleep where we fall. We have two guest rooms. Jed likes to sleep on the back porch. He says the singing frogs lull him to sleep and the night air smells special. I tell you, that boy is a gem."

"Megan…" I started to speak, then stopped as a tear rolled slowly down my face. *I need to tell her something, but I'm afraid.*

"It's okay, Katelyn. Everything is going to be all right." She put an arm around my shoulders, held on for a minute, then returned to her food preparations. "Now, let's get this tribe fed." She handed me a head of lettuce.

By nine o'clock dinner was over. The day's events had been deliberated, and Grace and Jed were yawning as they helped complete the clean up. "You two better hit the sack," Dan said. "You're making me yawn." He went to the kitchen and returned with three glasses and a bottle of white Zinfandel. Grace hugged Megan, Dan and me, offering a sleepy, "'Night." She received a forehead kiss from everyone. Jed followed, duplicating the hug and wish, and received the same affection, except for a headlock from Dan.

As Grace started up the stairs, I heard Jed say, "Good game today, Sis. You know, with two right feet, you'll probably walk like a duck when you get older." That earned him a poke in the ribs.

Dan poured a sample of the Zinfandel for me. "Try this. It's made on the island. If you don't like it I have others."

"I like it. It's gentle."

"Good." He filled my glass, Megan's and his own. "Megan and I have a story to tell you. Fourteen years ago, when we'd been married only two years, Megan had a miscarriage. We were devastated and Megan had terrible postpartum depression. She wouldn't eat, read or walk and even withdrew from the master's program she cherished. I was scared. Dr. Jamieson, our family physician and Dr. Redfield, the obstetrician, tried everything."

The name Redfield startled me. *I'm sure my face is red and they both can see it.*

Dan kept speaking, quietly though, as if what he had to say was important and mustn't be delayed or go unheard. "After a month of frustration, Dr. Redfield called me. He had an unmarried, teenaged woman about to deliver a child, and she wanted to give the baby up for adoption. He thought it might be just the thing to help Megan. He asked us to meet him after the delivery in the newborn nursery at 11:30 p.m. I bustled Megan into the car—against her wishes—and we were there waiting, hugging each other, when Dr. Redfield and a nurse came to us carrying Jed. That was December 12ᵗʰ, 1999. We loved him then, we love him now, and we always will."

I was crying but managed to say, "He was born at 10:48. He was my son."

"No, not *was* your son, *is* your son. He's our son, too." Megan was adamant. "When you called and said you would come up, we were ecstatic. Today, when you asked Jed his age and birthday, we saw how his answer startled you. Seeing how you reacted, we were convinced Jed's DNA-link defining you as his mother was correct. You just confirmed it; he's your son. No one but a mother would've remembered the exact time a child was born after 14 years."

"Megan… Dan…," my voice was scratchy and uneven as I continued, "I watched from the doorway of my room that day. You were holding each other and talking softly. I didn't recognize you. When the nurse let you hold him, you both looked so happy. You each bent and kissed his head and a perfect little hand reached up to touch your face. I remember it like it was yesterday."

I paused, my head was bowed and my hands were clenched in my lap. I looked up at them. "I've been seeing a psychiatrist for ten years. It took that long for me to get over thinking my parents' divorce was my fault. I never told the psychiatrist about the baby. I should have. Every minute of every day I've worried, wondering if he was happy, healthy and loved."

Megan spoke again, tenderly and slowly, considering each word as it arrived. "There's something else, Katelyn. Dan and I will be forever grateful to you. You and Jed pulled me from depression-hell. We're so glad you came here so we could thank you for helping us. Also, we wanted you to see that Jed is a wonderful, strong, smart boy filled with sensitivity and humor. Your courageous decision at such a young age was right in every way, and you should hold no shame or remorse. Jed only knows we adopted him, nothing more. No one will know he's your child unless you tell them—it won't come from us.

"If Jed asks about his mother someday, and he's old enough to understand and assimilate the fear and despair you suffered, we'll ask you what to tell him or let you answer him. Knowing him, we can assure you—he will hold you in his arms and thoughts, without anger or sadness, only with love—as he does with Grace, Dan and me. Grace is our biological child, as I'm sure you can tell from her appearance. There isn't a doubt in my mind that you gave me the courage to try again, so you had something to do with her being here as well."

I knelt down on the floor in front of Megan and Dan as they sat on the sofa and pulled them both into my arms. When I could speak, I released them, but held each of their hands. "In my whole life, I've never met two people I admire as much as I do you." I kissed the back of each hand.

I think Dan felt he had to say something. The best he could do was, "Let's finish this wine."

At breakfast the next morning, Dan was director. "Okay, here's the plan."

Grace leaned toward me, whispering, "He's always got a plan," and we laughed.

Dan pretended he didn't hear us. "First, we take Katelyn to the Holman and help her pack her stuff. Second, we get Katelyn to the airport an hour before her flight at 11:20. Third, we tell Katelyn how much we enjoyed having her with us and ask her to come back soon."

Megan cut in. "Enough 'plan', Dan. You can't tell us, 'no hugging or crying'. It won't work."

I was thinking, *I don't think I've ever felt this good and bad at the same time in my whole life.*

Jed touched my hand. "Did you like it here?"

"Very much, especially being with all of you."

"Can Gracie and I call you Kate if we phone or send an email?"

"I don't care what you call me, as long as you call or write. Be sure to send photos."

Jed and Grace said in tandem, "We will." I put my arms around them both.

Dan continued. "Fourth, from the airport we will go to Howie's Hog Heaven for lunch before the soccer game."

This brought a deluge of responses. "No way!" "That dump stinks!" "You're out of your mind."

I was laughing and only stopped when Dan added, "Then it's a good thing your mom made a whole basket of cold chicken, salad and chips. We'll have lunch at the picnic area near the soccer fields. Okay let's move. We don't want Kate to miss her flight to the City of the Angels."

At the hotel, a steady conversation was going on between Megan, Grace and I, while I changed and packed my clothes. Dan and Jed carried the bags to the car as we shoved them out the door. I gave Grace and Megan hairspray and some cosmetics prohibited on planes and answered their questions about why I liked each one.

On the way out of the Holman, I handed three envelopes to Charlie. One was addressed to him, the others to Eddie, the waiter, and Sadie and Holly, the maids. Charlie said, "Ms. Katelyn, you don't need to do this."

"I know that, Charlie. But I'll be back sometime and I want see your smile when I come."

"Thank you, ma'am. We'll remember." I heard later Charlie told Dan I gave each of them one hundred dollars and he responded, "She's a class act, Charlie."

Arriving at the airport on Dan's schedule left only time for thanks and hugs before I entered the boarding area. Megan held me in an embrace and whispered in my ear, "So glad you could come. You're a special person in our lives for many reasons. Come to see us anytime, here or in Boston. We'd love it. Please call Dan next week, even if you have nothing to say."

I said I would, but was puzzled by the request. Grace, Jed and Dan also asked me to come again soon, then released me to the flight crew, waving as I left. I was delighted. *Of all the flights I've taken, this was the first one when a family, my family, came to see me off.*

Airborne, I wrote myself a note concerning Megan's unusual request, then dosed off, only to be awakened by the landing announcement on reaching Toronto. The long second leg of the journey to Los Angeles gave me time to ponder how various places visited on the trip might fit into the story. I looked at my photos and re-read several sections in Dan's book.

I'd been at it for an hour when it I suddenly realized why Megan wanted me to call Dan the following week—Dan is the child Brian in the story. His mother abandoned him to go to Hollywood. It isn't fiction; it's real. *Megan thinks my leaving will make him sad and wants to soften those memories for him.*

Meghan must be Sara. She fits the character of Sara. They have loved each other their whole life. I can feel it. Jed couldn't be in a better place.

I turned to look out the window so the passenger next to me wouldn't see my tears. I began reviewing the story in Dan's book. *There are hidden elements. Sara grew up with Brian. They were like brother and sister. How did that change into husband and wife?* I wondered if being separated for college and meeting others made their feelings for each other blossom.

It must have been some day at the Howell house when they asked for a marriage blessing. From his description of the Howells, I'll bet they expected it to happen. That must have been one happy time. A deep, deep feeling of joy came over me.

I arrived at the office at noon on Monday. "Good morning, Terese. Anything important come up while I was away? "

"Nothing urgent. I put a list on your desk. "

"Thanks. How old are your son and daughter?"

"Peter is 11 and Janice is 15."

"What kind of gifts do they like best?"

"Let's see… They both play basketball like their dad, so T-shirts or caps with the names of famous players are always good."

"I was thinking of something more exciting."

"They like to go to college or pro games, but that's pretty expensive."

"Thanks for the tip. Which teams do they like most?"

Terese hesitated… "I'll ask Jack. He'll know."

"While you're at it, see if you can find out which colleges and universities in the Boston area have the best soccer teams, and if there's a pro soccer team there. Do the same with basketball, hockey, lacrosse, baseball and football. I just need the names for now."

"Will do."

Terese's was wearing a "what's goin' on in her head" look. *I'll be she's baffled. She knows I'm not a big sports fan. I'll bet she's thinking I must've had some trip. Wonder if she thinks I met a guy?*

Thursday evening I called Dan. Grace answered the phone and I asked, "Grace, how are you?"

"Fine. How was your flight? I got those shorts we talked about. I love them."

"I'm glad. Someday, you and I will go on a shopping trip. Flight was easy. Is your Dad there? I need to talk with him a minute."

I could hear Grace yell, "Dad! Katelyn's on the phone."

"Hi. How was the trip?"

"Smooth. I have some questions."

"Shoot."

"When you're in Boston, what sports teams do Jed and Grace like to see play?"

"We all like hockey. Basketball, too, but Bruin's hockey is our favorite."

"Do you have season tickets?"

"No. Little out of our budget. Why do you ask?"

"I know a guy who knows a guy who can get a bargain price. You got one minute to tell me if you would like to have them, then we move on to question two."

"Sure. We'd love to have them but—"

"Question two. Do you have a college plan set up for Grace and Jed? If so, can I contribute to it?"

"We have one. You don't need to—"

"Dan, I have a vested interest. Check with Megan to see if it's okay. It will make me happy to help. You don't want to take that away from me, do you?"

"No."

"Then talk it over with Megan. If she agrees, send me the details so I know what to do. Please?"

"Now I feel like a dud."

"Why?"

"I just sent the movie money back to Rachel Zimmer and cancelled the contract."

"I knew you were going to do that."

"How'd you know?"

"Because your book is a true story. You're Brian, and Megan is Sara. Am I right? Your adoption of Jed puts me in the story, too. You want to protect us.

It's too personal. I agree with you, and I admire you, Megan, Grace and Jed more than words can say."

Dan's voice lost its professional tone and his words stumbled with surprise and emotion. "Yes. … You're right. Thanks." Regaining the oomph in his voice, he added, "Megan and Jed want to say hello, too. You know … you're a special person. Bye".

Megan took the phone. "Katelyn, so glad you called. Having you with us this summer made the vacation a gem. Hope we can do it again sometime. Thanks for calling Dan. Whatever you said has him sort of stunned, in a good way. We share everything, so we'll talk things over. I think you understand why I asked you to call him, don't you?"

"His book isn't fiction. Losing contact with his mom when he was three was a terrible blow. You're a very sensitive person, Megan Darrigan. It's easy to see why he loves you so much. I enjoyed every minute of our time together."

"Thanks. You're great at understanding people. That's why you're such a good actress. Hang on. Jed has something to say."

"Kate, have you ever been to The Netherlands?"

"Yes. Why do you ask?"

"I read about how they pushed the ocean back to make farmland. Did you see it?

"I probably did, but didn't know what I was seeing. I should have had you there to explain it to me. Maybe we can all go there sometime, say in the spring, when all the tulips are in bloom?"

"Great. Bye!"

"Bye."

A week later, as I entered the office, Terese covered the mouthpiece of phone to say, "Rachel Zimmer is on the phone. She's hot about something."

I picked up the phone. "Hello?"

"What the hell happened up there?"

"What do you mean?"

"Darrigan sent back our check. He even sent a check to pay for your flight there and the hotel. He's withdrawing the movie rights to his book."

"Can he do that?"

"Yes. It's in the contract. What did you do to him?"

I was smiling, but made sure my voice wasn't. *I'll give her just enough information to quench the fire.* "I didn't do anything to him. His wife and children were there, we toured the island for locations and talked over many ideas. They're wonderful people. I found out the story isn't fiction. It's based on Dan's life. He just changed the names. He didn't say anything about withdrawing the movie rights while I was there.

"I suspect he, and his wife, Megan, are concerned a movie will veer from the truth and add drama, sex or twists to make money for investors. They don't want a film that will distort the facts, remove the beauty and depth of their feelings, or trivialize them. I don't think they can accept that. I didn't know enough about your plans to reassure them on any of these concerns. Had you talked with Dan about them?"

"No. The scriptwriter would do it during the re-write. It never occurred to me that it's a true story. I should have asked." Her voice was softening and I gave myself a virtual pat on the back. "Sorry you made a trip up there for nothing."

"Well, it wasn't wasted time. It's a beautiful sea-side setting and the family was very gracious."

Rachel sighed. "I'll call you if I hear of any changes."

"Thanks."

"Terese, are the best seats for Lakers games in the middle section, about halfway up?"

"Yes. That's what Jack says, anyway."

"Okay. We're going to need four of them for all the home games, that is if the games aren't on a school night. You may not want to take your children if they have school the next day. I'll leave that up to you and Jack."

"What? The tickets are for us?"

"Yes. Before you order them, maybe you should discuss with Jack what will work best for the family. Also, call the Boston Bruins Hockey office and order four tickets for all their home games. Probably sitting closer to the front in the center would be better for hockey. Ask the agent which seats are best when you call. They're for the Darrigan family I visited earlier."

"Yes, ma'am! Thank you. My kids are going to love this!"

"Good."

"Oh! I almost forgot. Your art museum friend, Marco Davilla, called from Rhode Island. He's coming to Los Angeles for two weeks and wants you to have dinner with him. Please call him. Do you have his number? He seems nice."

"I will. I have the number. He *is* nice." *I think this is turning into the best summer of my life.*

I went into my office, closed the door and dialed the phone. "Marco, you're coming to LA? Next week? Great. Are you helping the LA Museum with some restorations? Oh. Student lectures. I have a pile of things to tell you. Just doing a few ads and auditions. Big let down here with all the misogynists in shackles. Can you bring me some info about the film department there? I'll tell you why when you get here. So, Tuesday at seven. Right? Did you get the blackberry jam I sent from Canada? Good. Isn't great? Some liqueur in it, I think. Miss you, too. Bye."

Tuesday, I bought a green, patterned cocktail dress and shoes to match because Marco likes the color. I went through my jewelry and found a set of earrings, necklace and a simple bracelet with green sapphires. As I went through my date preparations, I was singing to myself. Anticipation took over my thoughts. *Marco always makes me sing. His laugh and his ability to see the shiny side of every problem makes being with him priceless. I laugh like a teenager every time I think of the day we met at the Los Angeles County Museum of Art. Standing at the sign-in table for a lecture I turned around pinning on my name tag and bumped into him. He dropped the book and folder he was carrying, and papers went flying all over. I apologized and helped him recover them. He was very gracious. When the lecture commenced, I found he was the honored guest speaker internationally known for his ability in art restoration and teaching at the Rhode Island School of Design. His first words were, "If my talk seems a little uncoordinated," he held up the pages we gathered from the floor, "there is beautiful reason. But I won't tell you what it is." I squeezed down in my seat.*

I stood in line after the lecture to apologize again and he asked me to come with him to the faculty dinner that followed the talk. Among the accidents in my life, bumping into him was the best one I have ever had. I hope Jed and Gracie will get a chance to meet him some day. When they hear he was once a member of the Spanish Olympic soccer team, they will ask him hundreds of questions, and he will answer every one.

I was ready when Marco arrived carrying a bouquet of my favorite Shasta daisies.

He gave me a beaming, loving smile and put his hand over his heart. "Be still my heart." He pulled me into his arms and held me a long time. "You are absolutely gorgeous."

I returned his embrace. "You, too. Look at that tie!"

"You gave it to me."

"I know. Thanks for the daisies. Great minds think alike." We laughed.

His dark eyes sparkled with joy.

"I made a reservation at Tamino's. Is that all right?"

"Fine. So, why are you here? What's the lecture series about?"

Our conversation continued in the taxi.

"New class starting to learn restorations. Dr. Cuyler and John Anderson asked me to come. It's more a round table discussion. Informal."

"How long will you be here?"

"Just two weeks. Tell me about your trip to Prince Edward Island. Is the book going to be made into a movie?"

"No. The author withdrew it."

"That's too bad. Does he know what he's done to his income?"

"I think he made the right decision."

"*Really?* I can't believe you said that. Tell me about him. Is the book poorly written or something?"

We entered Tamino's and, as frequent customers there, greeted many employees and other patrons before I could answer his question.

"No. The book is excellent. Actually, better than most." I described the Darrigan family, their work, their play, and my tour through the Maritimes with them. My enthusiasm and the word pictures of Prince Edward Island and the Darrigans fascinated him. He was silent, listening to every word. "They have two lovely children. Grace is twelve and Jed is fourteen. He's adopted. Grace is their biological child. They are so smart and likeable I hated to leave." My voice trembled a little.

Marco studied my face. "This must be a wonderful family to effect you this way."

"Remember we discussed my broken-family guilt trip and how acting the part of another person gave me temporary relief? I've never felt real love—not like I did with this family. When I'm acting, it's difficult for me to show artificial love to children or men. I see them as actors, not people. I think that's why I'm always type-cast as the stern mother, boss or tough co-worker, and never a lover."

"Kate, that's behind you now. It was never your fault. You know it."

I took a deep breath. ... "You're right. But, I live in a vacuum here. I know many people, but few who would come if I called for help—except you." Marco embraced me with his eyes and smile.

The arrival of dinner briefly interrupted our conversation. I continued. "I'd like to go back to college and learn film-making from the director's standpoint. I like creating a painting, a sculpture or photograph and seeing the final product. The bits and pieces in acting are like putting a bolt into an auto frame on an assembly line and having no idea what the finished car is going to look like. It's a job. The director has to visualize the whole film, the art. Will they take a thirty year old student at the Rhode Island School of Design?"

"Of course. With your background in film and art, the school would treasure having you. I'm on the admissions committee and they'll listen to my recommendation. There are many colleges in California with good programs, too."

"I want to be with you."

Marco was startled. He waited for a laugh, assuming I was teasing him. He looked away, then back. My face was serious. He said, "Over the three years I've known you, I've proposed to you three times."

I smiled, and interrupted, "Four."

Marco grinned. "Are you saying you'll marry me?"

I nodded, sending big hope in his direction.

Marco kissed me gently.

"Marco, I've wanted to marry you for two years, but I was afraid you wouldn't take me if you knew…" my voice faltered. "Jed, the Darrigan's adopted son, is *my* son. He isn't aware of it; but Dan and Megan are. I had Jed when I was seventeen. They adopted him right after he was born. The guilt I've hidden all these years has nearly been washed away by seeing how happy, healthy, and smart Jed is, and that he's in the loving hands of such wonderful parents. I worried you would, or will, reject me because of my history. If you do, I understand. I'm stronger now. I made the right decision years ago and the Darrigans are my friends now."

Speaking softly, Marco held my gaze and both of my hands. "We've all made mistakes, especially as teenagers. You made the perfect choice for your son; and I'm proud of you. In fact, I'm proud of you in many ways—how you think, what you say, what you don't say, how you've educated yourself despite your fractured life, your enthusiasm, your dedication, your humor, your gentleness—millions of things. I'd like to meet Jed, too, and watch him grow up along with you. I'll do anything that makes you happy. All I ask is that you be with me."

The Banana Peel

The banana peel fell on the grass in front of Mark. He jumped up quickly from where he and Katy were sitting in the shade of a tree, picked it up and cleaned it on the front of his shirt. Dividing it carefully, he gave half to Katy. They sat quietly eating the yellow banana skin. Brian, who threw it down, was stunned. Open-mouthed, he watched them eat the peel and a jolt of shame robbed him of interest in the schoolyard games going on around him.

Mark and Katy arrived at the rural elementary school in September, joining a group of one hundred fifty students. In June of that year, a local farm family, the Halls, had taken them as foster children. Mark was eleven, the same age as Brian. He was the same height too, but with thin arms and thin legs looking too frail to hold him up. His light-brown hair, deep-set blue eyes, lean face, and high cheekbones made him look older than his age.

Katy, age eight, was a copy of Mark, except for size, finer facial features, and longer hair. She was very quiet. Their clothes, the same every day, fit loosely, as if made for larger children. Staying close to each other, they rarely spoke and never smiled. Everyone believed they were shy or uneasy about the new surroundings and people.

Mrs. Hawley, the principal, put Mark in the sixth and Katy in the third grade sections based on what they told her and their sketchy, rambling school records. They had been to nine different schools in their short lives. They responded politely to questions, but never volunteered answers in classes. Their answers to direct questions were usually correct and the teachers in those classes told Mrs. Hawley her class assignments were accurate.

At recesses or lunch, Mark and Katy didn't join in games. It was not that they weren't asked; they just shook their heads no, or tried for a little while and had to rest. Talking quietly to each other, they ate their lunch of two slices of bread spread with lard and two soda crackers carefully, not losing a crumb. Mark would lift Katy up to drink from the fountain before drinking himself.

Evelyn, Brian's mother, met him at the door each day after school. She was surprised when he ignored the routine cookie and glass of milk that day to blurt out, "I threw down a banana peel and Mark and Katy ate it. They're really thin, Mom. They can't even run around much. They get tired real easy." It had been boiling in his brain all afternoon. He had a terrible feeling about what happened. He was ashamed and concerned it was his fault. He was crying as he spoke.

Evelyn pulled him to her. "It's not your fault, Brian. Tell me more about them."

"Their clothes are kinda loose and their shoes are pretty worn. They wear the same things every day. When Mrs. Byrnes asks Mark questions, he gets 'em right—he's smart."

Evelyn, an elementary school teacher before marriage, saw a red flag. She called social services. Mrs. Reeves, Mark and Katy's social worker, told her Mark and Katy were brother and sister, and wards of the state. Evelyn described her concerns.

Mrs. Reeves drew in a quick breath. "I'll call the foster parents and schedule a site visit. Can you come with me? I'm new here and recently assigned to Mark and Katy's care. I don't know my way around very well."

"Of course. Can I bring Brian along if school is closed for a conference that day?"

"Certainly. He can occupy the children while we talk."

Broken fences, unpainted barns with doors askew, emaciated cattle, and fields unprepared for winter lay before them as they approached the Hall farm. The house was similarly neglected. Evelyn and Mrs. Reeves exchanged a look, both with raised eyebrows. Mrs. Reeves' study of the records had found two previous female foster children placed there had run away. The girls had a history of running away, and the recorded investigation absolved the foster parents of blame. Mrs. Reeves considered whether the foster-care program was a source of income for the Halls. Evelyn had already reached this conclusion, but kept it to herself.

While Mrs. Reeves, Evelyn, and the Halls were talking, Brian, Mark, and Katy stayed outdoors. The Halls' biological children were away visiting relatives. Mark gave Brian a can-I-trust-you look. Deciding he had to, he led Katy and Brian to a barn and a bin of potatoes from the fall harvest. In a hushed voice he told Katy, "Take the small potatoes and put them in your pockets. Not too many though, or they will see the bulges." He did the same.

Brian didn't understand. "Why are you taking the little ones?"

"Because they won't notice they're gone."

After filling their pockets, they each took a final potato, rubbed it semi-clean with their hands, and ate it raw, and rapidly.

"Do you like them?" Brian said.

Mark stared at him. *Is he mocking me or doesn't he understand being hungry?* He didn't answer Brian at first, pondering how to respond. "… Do you want one?"

Brian held back a gag-face. "No, thanks. What do you do here?"

"I feed the chickens and pigs, and get hay for the cows. I have trouble lifting the hay bales. Bernard, the oldest Hall boy, laughs at me and won't help." He didn't tell Brian he thought about braining Bernard with a shovel someday, but had held his temper so far. He feared being sent to reform school or labeled a troublemaker and being separated from Katy. He had heard such stories. "Katy helps make meals, wash dishes, and clean the house. Mrs. Hall shakes her sometimes. Katy's scared of her." Brian saw bruises on Katy's arms.

"Why are you eating raw potatoes? Don't they give you food?"

"After they eat supper at night we eat the leftovers in the kitchen while they watch TV. Sometimes they don't leave much. I'm glad your mother came." Mark glanced about as if afraid of being overheard. "Maybe they will blame her for the visit and we won't get a lickin'."

"Are we going to move again?" Katy looked worried. "I cleaned the house the best I could."

Mark took her hand. "I think so. I know you did."

Brian was frightened. "Is it my fault? I don't want you to go. I'm sorry."

Mark studied him a few seconds. "It's okay. It's probably best we go. Maybe the next place will be better than the last three, and this one." His voice was weak, like him, but had authority, as if used to making decisions.

Katy began to cry quietly. Mark put his arm around her shoulders.

Evelyn called Brian to come to the car. He looked at Katy and Mark, feeling like a traitor in his gut. Sadness and guilt followed. Mark waved goodbye by raising his right hand waist high, palm up. Brian shifted his gaze to the ground, said, "Bye," and walked slowly to the car, scuffing the dirt.

Both Mark and Katy had learned long ago not to expect much from life, and stood with stoic faces, watching him leave.

Mark wished for the thousandth time—*If I was older I'd take Katy and run away to the south where it's warm. We could sleep outdoors if we didn't have a place or warm clothes. I'd find a spot where no one would find us and I could work in a McDonalds, or somewhere. I'm not sure how to do it. We have never been on a bus and I don't have any money.*

Sadness flooded Katy's voice. "Is it my fault our mother or father won't come to get us?"

The nights of terror lying in bed listening to their parents scream and throw things at each other were still fresh in their minds. One night their father left, slamming doors, and never came back. Their mother was lying on the kitchen floor with blood on her face when Mark called 911. He comforted Katy through her nightmares for three years, and when he screamed at night, she held him in her arms until he woke.

Mark reassured her softly, as he had done many times before, "It's not your fault."

"Do they love us?"

"I'm sure they do."

"Then why don't they come to get us?"

"There must be some important reason, but I don't know what it is, Katy. Now we have to take care of each other."

He explained, "Some foster parents can't take two children. We might not be able to stay together. If any foster parents or their children don't give you food or clothes, hit you, make you do hard work, or you are sick, you have to tell the social worker or the school teacher, even if someone at the foster home says they will beat you if you tell."

"Mark, please stay with me!"

"I'm going to try, Katy. If I can't, I'll talk to you on the phone or visit you every week, if I can. We need a code word so you can let me know if anyone is hurting you. Do you understand?"

"Yes, what will it be?"

"Remember the banana peel from last week?" Katy nodded. "Just say something like, 'Do you like bananas?' or 'Are all bananas yellow?'"

She was crying louder now. "Please, Mark, don't leave me."

That night he held her until she was asleep, just as he had done each night since she was one, turning his face away so she wouldn't see his tears.

On the way home, Brian decided Mark was right. They should go. He whispered to his mother about the potatoes.

"Can they come to our house? Please!"

Surprised, she whispered back, "I'm proud of you. We'll see about the coming to our house part. It may not be possible."

Evelyn asked him to tell Mrs. Reeves about the potatoes. He did.

Mrs. Reeves gave Brian a startled look, and then frowned with suppressed anger. "I'll pick them up tomorrow."

Mrs. Reeves arrived at the Hall's farm at 10 o'clock the next morning in a sheriff's car with Deputy Rogers. She had Mr. Hall sign some papers, then asked Mark and Katy to get their things. She told them gently they were to come with her. "You will stay at the Children's Center for a while, like you have done before, and go to the school nearby."

They brought their peeling, bruised cardboard suitcases, toothbrushes, two pairs of socks and underwear, and the clothes they were wearing.

Mrs. Reeves expected them to have warmer clothes. "Where are the winter coats, boots, and other things given to you?" Mark shrugged. When they got in the sheriff's car, she turned to look at him in the back seat and asked again.

Mark started to speak, but Katy cut in. "They gave them to the other children." Deputy Rogers looked at Mrs. Reeves. He knew the reasons for the visit. Her eyes glistened, and his as well. They quickly turned to look forward.

By December Mrs. Reeves had all the interviews, inspections, and approvals needed. The new family had never cared for foster children. She and the family had discussed whether they had enough room, the skills needed to raise the children, and a host of related issues. It was ten days before Christmas when she brought them to the new foster home. As they came toward the house, Brian ran out the door and hugged both Mark and Katy. Looking dazed, their lips parted in a trace of joy from his welcome. Evelyn got down on her knees and pulled both of them to her. There were tears in her eyes. Ken, Brian's father and Evelyn's husband, offered his hand as they were introduced. Mark and Katy didn't know what to do. No one had ever shaken hands with them before. Ken's doubts about the banana peel and potato stories evaporated as he stood back watching all the faces. He smiled, grateful as always for his Evelyn.

Wiping her eyes, Evelyn took Katy's hand. "Come on, I want to show you your room. I painted it some, but waited to finish so you could help decide colors, curtains, and other things we need to make."

"I have a room?" Evelyn took Katy's suitcase and they ran up the stairs. Katy's legs weren't as thin now, but she stumbled some and Evelyn held her hand tight.

Ken, proud of his wife and son, joined in the greetings. "Mark, with two boys in the house we had to double up. We put in bunk beds. You will be in with Brian. Bring your suitcase and we'll show you around. Brian and I thought a coin toss should decide who gets first choice, top or bottom. That okay with you?"

"Yes, sir," he answered, thinking to himself—*Please, God, let this be real.*

Christmas was a joyous time. There were gifts, simple and practical, for everyone. Both Evelyn and Ken decided Katy, without even knowing it, was the leveler. They believed Mark probably would have rebelled against everything and everyone by then if he didn't have Katy. And Katy had survived a living hell because of Mark. They discussed this, and Ken said, "Their dependence on each other saved them."

"Probably," Evelyn agreed. "They're smart, but they are still going to have some tough times. If we are fair, steady, and honest with them, perhaps we can give them back a real life."

"They're easy to love." Ken was watching every move and expression. "Look at those faces."

The smile on their son's face, and the surprised looks from their two new children delighted them.

Every day the family had their evening meal together. Mom, the teacher, gave each one time to tell about their day, or something they wanted to talk about. She would smile and raise a finger to stop interruptions. At first Mark and Katy listened and rarely spoke, but laughed at the give and take. Everyone agreed to rules about making their own beds, setting the table, helping with the dishes, shoveling snow with Ken, working with Evelyn in the garden, and always telling Evelyn or Ken if they were going far from the house.

Saying goodnight to the boys one Friday night in April, the excited tone in Ken's voice told them he had something cooking. "Did you guys see the fish hatchery men putting trout in the lake last month?" Heads shook 'no.' "Let's get up early tomorrow. Brian, that new fishing pole I bought is Mark's. Show him how it works. Ask Mom for a can of corn and a can opener."

"I have my own pole?"

"Yep. Ever been fishin'?"

"No. What's the corn for?"

Ken explained, "The fish hatcheries feed corn to the fish. Most fishermen don't know it, and use worms or lures. We are going to catch the fish!" And to Mark's utter amazement, and joy, they did. Brian showed Mark how to clean them.

It took until the third Christmas for Mark and Katy to shed their worst fears. Before then, Brian would often hear Katy crying quietly after Evelyn tucked her in and kissed her goodnight. Mark would go to her room, kneel by the side of the bed, and hold her in his arms.

They would talk softly, "Will we move again?"

"I don't think so, Katy."

"Do you like it here?"

"Yes."

"Me too."

It was soon apparent, with nourished bodies; Katy and Mark were eager students with limitless curiosity. This made Evelyn and Ken smile, and Brian buckle down on his studies. Until Katy was in the fifth grade, they had nightly story time. Evelyn or Ken would read a story or chapter from a book they all liked. As the boys got older, if it was a 'girl' story Mark and Brian pretended not to listen. With time, sports-talk, school activities, television and movie stories needing explanation or homework replaced the reading.

One night, when the boys were thirteen, Ken came to their room for his usual, "Goodnight, fellas."

Mark asked, "Why do you think our parents abandoned us?"

Ken sat down, paused, and then leaned toward him. "Tough question. I don't know the details, Mark, but understand they were very young; your mother was only two years older than you when you were born. She, and your father, got addicted to drugs. People taking drugs often need more and more. I think the drugs took over their lives, and the police and social workers thought you and Katy were in danger."

"Do they love us?"

"Oh, I'm sure they do."

"Why don't they come and see us? Are they dead?"

"I don't know if they are dead. The last time Mom and I talked with Mrs. Reeves, they had separated, been in and out of rehabilitation centers, moved away, and couldn't be found."

"They won't be coming for us, will they?"

"Probably not. It's too bad, because they missed knowing two very special people."

There was a long pause in the dark. "…Can I call you, Dad?"

There was an even longer pause, and when Ken answered his voice was husky. "Of course you can, and I'm proud you want to. I consider it an honor."

"Katy wants to call Evelyn 'Mom', and so do I. Will that be all right?"

"You couldn't do anything that would make her happier. I can't wait to see the look on her face when you do. Goodnight, son. Goodnight, Brian."

"Goodnight, Dad," Mark and Brian said in unison and rolled over.

After Ken left, Brian whispered, "See, I told you he would say that."

Mark, who had been a 'father' since he was four years old, burst into tears and deep, wrenching sobs he tried to stifle with his pillow. Brian didn't know they were tears of relief and happiness because he and Katy had crossed over into a family: into a life of safety, caring, and reason. The despair and fear crushing Mark was beginning to fall away. Brian had never been where Mark had been, but he was his brother. He jumped down from the upper bunk and put his arm around Mark's shoulders. "It's going to be all right, Mark."

Two days later, Brian was alone with his father for a few minutes. "Dad, Mark cried his eyes out after you went to bed the other night. Remember, he asked to call you Dad, and Mom, Mom? I think it was because he is glad to be here." Surprised, Ken put a hand on his shoulder. "Thanks for telling me that. I'm going to talk with Mom about it."

At dinner that night Ken asked, "Mark and Katy, Mom and I would like to adopt you so you are in our family forever. Would that be all right with you?" Two startled faces stared at him, and then broke into huge smiles. Both got up from the table to give Evelyn and Ken long, tight hugs. Some watery eyes were involved, of both the adult and the child variety. After a few minutes Ken continued. "As far as Mom, Brian and I are concerned, you are already in this family forever, but there is legal stuff that has to be worked out. Mom is going to call Mrs. Reeves tomorrow and get that started. It takes awhile." Evelyn and Ken were delighted by the discussion and questions that followed.

It was almost a year later, near Katy's birthday, when Ken, waving a letter, announced, "You are now officially Mark Barrett and Katy Nanette Vaughn!" When the cheering subsided, Brian turned on music and started to dance around the room with Katy.

Mark quietly wandered off. Evelyn found him sitting in the dark on the front steps, bent forward and clutching his knees. She sat down beside him, put her arm around his shoulders and pulled him to her. He looked up at her and then back into the night. After a few minutes of silence, he looked up at her again. "...I love you very much. I don't mind that my mother and father never come to see us. I just hope they are safe and have some happiness, too."

Evelyn was overwhelmed with admiration for this child who had suffered so much. He wanted to share his happiness with his ill parents. Such kindness seemed impossible, yet there it was. When she spoke her voice was soft and choked by emotion. "I'll call Sheriff Rogers in the morning. If anyone can find out about them, he can. I love you too, ...very much." She was still holding him when the rest of the family found them and pulled them into the dance.

Mark and Brian competed in everything when they were fourteen. Swimming at the lake one day, Brian set a challenge. "I can swim across this lake and back. I'll bet you can't."

Brian had a tendency to jump into things without thinking them through, and Mark knew it. "Prove it, big mouth."

When Brian took the bait and dove in, Mark pulled the rowboat into the water and rowed silently along behind him. Halfway across the lake Brian was struggling and his progress slowed rapidly. Mark turned the boat around and rowed backward so he could see Brian constantly. In few more seconds Brian was in big trouble. Mark moved to the stern, grabbed Brian by the hair, and pulled him into the boat where he lay, weak and struggling for air. By the time Mark rowed back to shore, Brian could talk. "Don't tell Mom or Dad about this, please."

"If they don't ask, I won't tell. If they ask, I'll tell. Use your head. You have to build up your swimming strength gradually. Swim out to the buoy over there and hang on to it until you're rested, then swim back. When you can go out without getting tired, then you try going out and back without stopping. When you can go out and around it ten times without stopping, about the distance across the lake, then you may be able to swim across. You've got to pace yourself. Your energy has to last the whole distance."

Brian lowered his head. "Okay, bro."

Mark smiled. What made him happiest however was what occurred when Katy was fourteen. Katy wanted to swim across the lake, but Brian wouldn't let her go unless she agreed he could row the boat along beside her. Mark thought, *Being in the action makes people remember things. Just having someone tell you something, or reading it, isn't nearly as effective. I gotta remember that.*

On the way home after a lacrosse game when the boys were sixteen, Ken said, "Mark, I know that guy from Adams fouled and cursed at you, but you shouldn't have taken the bait and yelled back."

Brian jumped in. "He was nasty, Dad."

"I know. But when somebody does that, they are usually just a lousy player and trying to cover it up."

Mark wanted to know, "Are you saying I shouldn't do anything?"

"No. You should do something. You should turn your back and walk away; that makes them even madder. Just like you did with the Hall kid. You probably wanted to brain him, but you didn't."

"How did you know I thought that six years ago?"

"Didn't, but it was exactly the way I would have felt."

"No kiddin'?"

"Wouldn't have done it though."

"Why not?"

"Wasn't his fault. Nobody taught him right from wrong. The key in sports is to practice, practice, practice, and at the next game, win big, then walk the line and say 'good game,' meaning—'you were good, but we were better!'"

Both boys were laughing, enjoying a bump up in their already considerable respect for Ken. Mark no longer had broom-handle limbs. He was a formidable player, six feet tall already, and would play every minute of every game, if the coach would let him.

The boys and Ken were raking leaves on the front lawn one fall day. Katy brought lemonade and all four sat on the front steps.

Brian turned to Ken and asked, "Dad, ...when do you become a man?"

"Wow! Great question. Where did that come from?" Katy got up to leave. Ken patted the steps near him. "Katy, please stay." She sat down.

"You know red-haired Paul who drives the school bus?" Brian asked.

"Yes, I do."

"Amy Curtis is in first grade. Last winter when we got to her house the snow was blowing and deep, so he got off the bus and carried her to her mother waiting on the other side of the road. He did it for each of the little ones. No other school bus driver ever did that.

"What do you think of him?"

Mark didn't hesitate a second. "He really likes kids and wants them safe."

Brian agreed. "Yeah, he knew her mother would be worried."

"He's a kind, gentle man," Katy added, her voice almost a whisper.

"You are all right. Mark, you were already a man when you came to us."

"Why do you say that?"

"Because you cared for Katy since she was an infant. You fed her; you washed her; protected her; cried with her; loved her: and made her equal to yourself without the slightest hesitation. It takes a real man to do that."

Ken continued, "Brian, you were on the way to manhood when you told Mom about the banana peel and potatoes, and asked if Mark and Katy could come live with us.

"Katy, you are a real woman. You have accepted all that happened to you without bitterness or complaint. You haven't let the past break your spirit, stop you from learning, or take away your affection for others. I'm proud of each of you. Always be like Paul with everyone, if you can. There are times when it is difficult. You may have to defend yourself with actions like walking away, words, or a physical response—but only if you must."

Ken paused, and then said, "Some men are not respectful of women, and occasionally, the opposite is true. Women may be smaller in size or not as strong as men, but they are just as courageous and smart—maybe smarter."

Katy grinned and poked Brian in the ribs. Ken saw the poke, and smothered a smile. He admired her self-confidence. He continued. "Women are just as capable as men and can do things men cannot, like make a new human being. Being important, educated, strong, wealthy, or good-lookin' doesn't come close to the qualities you saw in Paul—his are the ones to be a real man, or woman—you all have them, and your reputation will go ahead of you. Do you know what I mean?"

Katy's answer was quick and accompanied by a huge smile. "The word gets around when you are a good person."

"Right!"

Katy was gorgeous by fifteen. She was as tall as Mom—trim, with white teeth, and hair and eyes the color of the sand and the sky on a perfect day at the beach. Even sourpuss Mr. Bates, the high school principal, couldn't stop himself from returning her smile. The best part: she had humility, every trait Ken talked about, plus she was an information sponge. She could hold her own in any subject in school, and with her brothers at sports, including fishing. She held the attention of boys and girls equally. It was her nature to get others to talk about themselves.

At dinner one summer night when Katy was sixteen, she asked, "How do you know if you love someone?" drawing nervous laughs and 'come-on's' from the boys—even though they wanted to know too, but couldn't muster the courage to ask.

"Mom, how did you know Dad was the one for you?"

Evelyn explained she and Ken were friends in high school. "We were in the same classes, went to dances, worked on the yearbook, and sang in the chorus. We chose the same university, but rarely saw each other there. Ken was in civil engineering and I was in elementary education. Sophomore year, there was a big dance, and a popular football player asked me to go. Two days before the dance, he broke the date to go with someone else. Ken overheard him tell his teammates and thought he was rude.

"Ken called and asked me to go to the dance. He didn't mention the broken date. I found out later he knew and realized my happiness was important to him. We danced every dance and shared our ideas on classes, professors, and the future. We laughed together the whole time. We talked over everything. I found what I valued, he valued." Everyone had stopped eating, their eyes fixed on her.

She paused, reminiscing. "When we got to my dorm, he didn't try to kiss me, but I kissed him. Not just because he made the night a memory, but also because I saw a gentle, honest, humble, strong man who didn't need alcohol or drugs to have fun or be special. He already was; I knew it, and I had overlooked him."

As she talked, Ken held her with his eyes, and she smiled at him. Mark, Katy, and Brian saw this, heard the tenderness in her voice, and saw how it fit nearly everything they did or said with each other, and them.

Evelyn had their attention. "It takes time to know a person. Sometimes you will be convinced right away a boy is the one for you, but that is just the time to remember what makes a real friend, and a real man. If a boy is rushing you to have sex, then he does not have those qualities or love for you."

"Wow, I never thought of it that way," Katy said. "Some of the girls at school say that is the way to get a guy."

"You know the biology. Only women can have children, but the man has equal responsibility for that life. A child should be conceived with love, not just sex. A child born where love is weak or missing doesn't have a fair chance at a happy life. You know that better than anyone. If the subject comes up among your classmates, boys or girls, don't be afraid to tell them what you believe— they'll listen to you more than a teacher. It's your decision whether to tell them what happened to you and Mark. That information is a powerful tool, if you elect to use it."

Evelyn and Ken coached, sympathized, corrected, cheered, and cried with all three of their children over the next few years, swelling with deserved pride the whole time. Truth be told, they would have sold the furniture to give each the education they sought, and almost did. Brian's struggles to keep up with his siblings academically paid off. He received a scholarship to undergraduate school, excelled, and received another to graduate school. Mark made the athletic scholarships come to him. He was Most Valuable Player in lacrosse for two years and salutatorian of his class. Katy just breezed on through smiling, saying little, loving everyone, and everything around her. She was offered scholarships at five universities.

Mark and Katy have done research for ten years on the quality-of-life in young adults from broken homes. They have published three articles on the results, and made a documentary film called *Life in the Not-So-Fast Lane*, which was used by high schools and colleges for instruction. Mark received a Ph.D. in physical education, and teaches, and coaches women's lacrosse at his alma mater. He found Halle and they have two daughters and a son.

Katy is a pediatrician. She supervises the pediatric and neonatology units at the hospital where Brian works. She will get a Ph.D. in public health this year. Brian calls her, 'Sis.' In her Franciscan order they call her 'Sister Anne,' after the patron saint of mothers.

The dedication in all their publications is the same:

> To Brian, Evelyn, and Ken—
> You reached out your hands,
> Pulled us from our despair,
> And pressed us to your hearts:
> An act never to be forgotten,
> Creating a love never to diminish.

Extracurricular Education

I was sliding in the soapy water from one end of the tank to the other, twisting in mid-passage so my feet hit the ends first to cushion the blows. Sometimes, as the tank turned, I would slide halfway up the side like a snowboarder in a half-pipe and had to twist hard to get my feet in position for the next dead end.

I could hear shouting and laughter coming in through the open hatch and understood what was happening. When the motion finally stopped, I grabbed the pail that had been ricocheting around the tank with me, scooped up all the water and suds I could capture, and positioned myself on my knees near the open hatch. The tank was long, but only five feet high and even a fourteen-year-old boy couldn't stand in it.

Suddenly all the merriment I heard through the hatch stopped, and I smiled. Maybe they were worried they had injured me with their prank of driving the tank truck around the parking lot with me inside.

The first idiot to stick his head through the hatch got a face full of frothy water from the pail and slid down the outside of the tank, fingers dragging along the stainless steel side in a desperate effort to hold on, nails screeching like they were being dragged across a blackboard. He landed on his ass on the tarmac.

Soaking wet and boots half full of water, I stood up in the hatch. The laughing and hooting resumed, but now it was directed at the tarmac-guy, whose eyes were on fire from the soap. Someone threw a pail of clean water in his face.

I launched a variety of curses at my crewmembers, covering stupidity, ugliness, self-coitus, and illegal birth. Included in the tirade were questions about the sanity of family members going back two generations.

Pencil climbed to the access hatch, handed me the hot water hose and soap, and I went back into the tank to finish the job. Pencil, named for his slim frame and elongated face, like a photo over-worked vertically in Photoshop, slid through the hatch.

"Soap, I'm sorry. Are you all right?" he asked, calling me by my work nickname.

"Yeah. I'm fine. I'll bet Charlie set this up. He's been on my case since I was ten!"

Pencil grinned so broadly the corners of his mouth disappeared around the sides of his face, happy to confirm my suspicion without having to say it. We finished the job together, did another tanker as well, and punched out for the day.

This wasn't the first new-guy test I'd received. Two weeks earlier, I was locked in a 'powder room'—a two-story sized box as big as a small house, where powdered milk is made. The windowless room, lined with sheet metal, was heated to two hundred degrees. Milk that was sprayed in near the top of the box was powder by the time it hit the floor. After the powdered milk was removed from the box by the mechanized rakes and augers, my job was to scrape and wash the caramelized milk from the metal sides.

It was still one hundred five degrees when I crawled in with my tools. I was worried about the heat, so I made sure to note the location of the emergency button, and it was a good thing I did. Somebody not only locked the door, but also turned off the lights while I was inside. As soon as the lights went off, I dove for the button, tripping over my tools and fumbling in the dark.

I couldn't hear it from inside the box, but was told later that the alarm went off not only outside the box, but in the main office as well. Shade, the shift foreman, promptly got me out. He was worried the plant supervisor would come down and chew him out if he heard of the antic. The whole crew got a lecture from Shade, garnished with expletives clear enough for a first grader to understand, and at a decibel level that was truly admirable. The whole crew had to help me clean the box that day. I thought the lecture had smartened 'em up. Maybe the tank truck treatment was retribution.

I got my first work permit at fourteen, and the summer job described above at the Hudson Milk Processing factory that year. Because I was summer help, and new, the less desirable jobs fell to me. I didn't complain. The money was the best I had ever made. After the tanker incident showed I wasn't a wimp, I really became one of the crew, except I was too young to get into O'Reilly's after work.

Sometimes, I would go with the guys and sit on the back steps out of sight. Shade would come out the back door, sit down, and pull a cold bottle of beer for me from one of his gigantic back pockets. Shade, six foot three with a thick chest and arms as large as my legs, was nicknamed Shade because, even after he shaved, his face still had a shadow.

Occasionally, just to showoff, he would take out the bridge replacing the front teeth he lost to a hockey puck, put a bottle of beer in the gap, tip his head back, and empty the bottle, no hands. He could pull an eight hundred pound wooden barrel of sweetened-condensed milk on edge and roll it up a ramp from the loading dock into a truck like it contained air.

After the tank truck incident he asked, "You want me to take care of Charlie?"

"No. I'll do it."

"I knew you would say that," he answered, and slapped me on the back with a ham-sized hand that knocked me right out from under my cap. "He's not a bad guy, you know. Just screwed up."

"I know. My mom told me."

My first encounter with Charlie at age ten was still vivid in my mind. We were playing touch football after school. Charlie purposely pushed down a receiver to intercept a pass. He was three years older and a head and a half taller than the rest of us. He had failed a grade or two. When I objected to the dirty play, Charlie hit me on the nose. I knew I wasn't going to win that fight and went home holding my nose to stop the bleeding and crying all the way. Crying, not because it hurt so much, but because I was ashamed I wasn't braver and stronger.

When I got home, my mom put ice on my nose and I explained what happened. She talked and I listened. "Charlie's mom left when he was two. He and his dad live in two rooms in the back of his gas station. His father gets drunk sometimes and beats Charlie. I think the way Charlie acts with classmates is his way of fighting back. When he won't play fairly, just walk away. The other boys will eventually do the same, and maybe Charlie will re-think his behavior."

As always, she made me feel better. I started lifting the heavy crowbars in our barn twenty-five times each day, first with both hands, then one hand at a time—just in case ignoring Charlie didn't work.

When I was sixteen, there was no summer work for me at the milk plant. I got a job in the local meat market, cutting up sirloin and grinding it into hamburger or putting round steak through the cubing machine. I swept floors, scrubbed the chopping blocks with salt, stocked the shelves, and waited on customers. I knew nearly everyone who came in and could ask them about their families or things we had in common.

Somehow, I got the owner's attention. The job turned out to have a great perk. Wag, the owner, had no kids, so he took to treating me like a son. When he learned I didn't have a driver's license, he taught me to drive his Oldsmobile. He even sat in the back seat for the road test with his favorite huge, stinking, black cigar in his mouth. He said, "It will let the driving test guy know we mean business." He didn't need to do that. I was good.

Wag's generosity glowed through his gruff exterior. I never forgot his kindness and went on to try to mirror his efforts.

I kept it to myself, but I had decided not to spend my life working at the milk plant or the meat market. I liked the guys and the camaraderie, but I wanted something beyond the same daily ritual. I began to study more and tried to imitate my brother, Sam. Sam's mind was like Velcro. He took in every subject and it stuck. He wasn't distracted from his studies, even if the study hall was in a total state of giggles, screams, laughs, and spitballs. He graduated from high school with a four-year average of ninety-eight percent.

The summer before I left for college, I got work at the milk plant again. The stainless steel pipes used to pump milk to different locations had to be disassembled and washed each day. One of my jobs was to take each ten-foot pipe from a trough of soapy water, push it onto a long, rotating steel rod with a wire brush at the end, pull it off, and put it on the drying rack. Once, a loose rag hanging from my back pocket caught in the rotating-brush when I bent over for a pipe. The brush wound up both the rag and my overalls like spaghetti on a fork before I could hit the shut-off button. In fact, I could no longer reach the button because of the tightening wedgie. It was Charlie who saw what was happening, jumped to hit the button, and helped me get untangled.

"You gotta be careful 'round here."

It was my own fault and we laughed over it together. I made the mistake of saying, "That damn brush almost turned me into a eunuch." Then I had to explain what a eunuch was. It earned me a change in nickname from Soap to Unick. I begged, "Please, don't call me that outside the plant." I got no promises, just laughs.

Sitting on the back steps of O'Reilly's after work on my last day, I was surprised when it was Charlie who came out the backdoor to bring me a beer.

"Whatcha goin' to study at collitch?"

"Not sure," I said. "Kinda feelin' my way. When I was bitten by Wiley's dog on my paper route and had to have rabies shots, I went to the doctor every day. The doctor and the nurses really knew what they were doing. I liked the way they went about things."

"Aw, you just liked that pretty nurse there."

"Yeah, I did. But I liked what they did, too. I been thinkin' about that a lot."

"…Charlie, why do you think most everybody at work has a nickname but you?"

"Never thought about it."

"I don't want you mad at me, but I think there's a reason, and you oughta know it. I think maybe you *have* thought about it."

"What are you sayin'?" His voice sounded like he was about to take a bite out of a steel bar.

"I know you've had it rough with no Mom and your dad drinkin' and whackin' you around."

"How do you know that?" he snapped.

"Charlie, everybody in this town knows that. It's a small town."

"So what?" he said, his eyes on fire.

"Well, sometimes you treat people the way you were treated: not good. What I'm sayin' is—and it isn't easy to change—if you started treatin' people the way you would like to be treated instead of the way you were treated, people would be happier to be around you."

Charlie slumped forward and looked at the ground for several minutes. His breathing stuttered a little. I was sure I saw some drops of water scatter the dust near his feet.

"…I know you got a good side. When that wire brush was eatin' me up at the plant, it was you who jumped to help me."

There was a long pause. Then Charlie grabbed my collar behind my head and stood up slowly, dragging me up with him. I was thinking—*I've gotta learn to keep my mouth shut.* When we were both standing, Charlie wrapped his big arms around me and squeezed, long and hard. Then he let go, straightened my cap, and walked slowly away down the street without a word. I was startled, relieved for myself, and sad for Charlie all at the same time. As I turned to watch him go, I saw Shade, Pencil, and the rest of the crew standing silently in the open backdoor of the bar.

The Book Signing

The engine suddenly quit on Mirror Lake Drive near McKinley and the rental car rolled to a stop, eliciting a vigorous, "Oh, shit!" from Dee Ibarra. Trying to restart it three times without getting even a sound led to, "Shit, shit, shit!" and a blow to the steering wheel. She turned on the flashers and dialed auto assistance. Given Dee's location, the cheery operator informed her a repair vehicle should get to her in ten minutes. She wondered, *What the hell am I doing here? It'll probably snow and I'll be here a week.*

Twenty minutes later, a tow truck showed up. As the mechanic got out, Dee instantly recognized Lenny Haus, the jerk who tried to have sex with her in his father's pick-up after a high school prom. She had grabbed his Y-chromosome marker and twisted it, then jumped out, and walked home in high heels. *The bastard! Maybe he won't recognize me; it has been twenty years. Damn it! He will as soon as he sees my driver's license.*

As Lenny ambled to the car in his baggy, grease-stained coveralls, she rolled the window down. Seeing her face, he looked puzzled. "What seems to be the trouble, ma'am?" he asked, talking through his nose. Dee thought she had flushed the memory of his ridiculous voice from her mind long ago, but there it was.

"Rental car. Just quit on the way in from the airport. Won't turn over when I try to re-start it."

Now Lenny had two puzzles wrinkling his greasy brow. "Please open the hood," he instructed. She did, and he disappeared behind it.

Dee was tempted to blow the horn, but opted out in favor of getting to the hotel faster.

Lenny appeared at her door again. "Battery's down. I think the generator is bad; could be the starter, too. I'll have to tow you to the garage."

"Can you leave me at the Crowne Plaza on the way?" Looking at her auto club card and driver's license, Lenny suddenly broke into a big grin. Dee grimaced and swallowed a couple of her best curses.

"Now I recognize you. You're Dee Ibarra. Well, how about that? This time I get to give you a ride and get paid for it."

"Well, if it isn't Lenny with the twisted dick," Dee fired back.

Lenny didn't laugh. "Hey, that's not funny. Yeah, I'll drop you. I heard you were comin' back. Somethin' about a book, right?"

Lenny is right, she reflected. *I've got to concentrate on this book signing, the village award, and the media so there is good publicity for the rest of the signing tour. Damn! I hate it when a dumb-ass like Lenny brings me down to earth.*

While Lenny attached the towing gear, she got out of the car, giving Irving hell in her mind for his crappy idea of doing the first book signing in her hometown. *Half the people here probably don't know me, and the other half, like Lenny, don't care to know me or don't read. Just because the book is about a hometown girl who works in movies and television doesn't mean you have to do all this memorabilia crap. Everybody has to come from somewhere.* By this time she was in the cab of Lenny's truck and he was ready to go.

Lenny smiled. "Doesn't this bring back memories?"

"Don't get any ideas, Lenny, or I'll twist it right off."

The half-mile to the Crowne Plaza went by with only a brief weather report by Lenny. "It's gonna be nice all week."

There were no other vehicles at the hotel entrance, so Lenny drove right up. A bellhop came running out and Dee made sure he found everything. She turned to Lenny. "Do you have a card with the phone number of your garage?"

Lenny fumbled in the glove compartment of his truck and came up with a bent, greasy card for Lenny's Garage that assured, "The Best Service in Town." Dee rolled her eyes thinking, *What a myth,* but out loud asked, "Lenny, are you married?"

"Sure. I married Delores Witcomb. You remember her? We have two girls."

Dee took the card. "I'm going to call the rental place at the airport. They can decide if they want you to repair the car or if they will do it themselves.

The automobile club will pay you, but here is twenty bucks to buy your girls a surprise. Say hello to Delores for me."

That's sad, she thought. *Two girls and both parents with the bare minimum of Betz cells.*

Dee checked in and was surprised every hotel employee knew her name. She called Marge O'Neil at the library. The book copies had arrived. Marge asked, "The village plans to honor you the day after the book signing. Can you stay and speak to the high school students, teachers, and parents? They're really looking forward to it."

Dee was pleased. "Yes, I can, but I don't have anything prepared."

"That's all right; they don't expect a speech. They just want to meet you."

After hanging up with Marge, Dee wondered how the people of Lake Placid would remember her. *Will they recall my free-style teenage behavior? Have I written anything that will offend anyone? Will my family be embarrassed? Is the book any good? Will it sell? Is it worth the hard work I put in it?* The flight, the car, and Lenny had done her in. She unpacked and took a nap.

It was dark when she awoke. *It sure gets dark early near the Arctic Circle,* she mused, chuckling at her own joke. She was reminded of the clock radio she had as a teenager. Every winter morning, she awoke in the dark to hear it was twenty-five degrees below zero at Chazy Lake. She shivered thinking of it.

During a light dinner via room service, Dee decided she was being too serious about the book. Putting on a sweatshirt, running leggings, and shoes, she left the Crowne and walked a circle up Main to Saranac, down Lakeview and West Valley, then back to the Crowne. The cool air smelled clean and fresh, so different from New York City and Los Angeles. Taking deep breaths, her lungs felt fully expanded for the first time in months. A good hot soak in the tub after her walk helped put her concerns behind her, and sleep came shortly after.

At eight-thirty the next morning, Dee ran two miles on the nearby Olympic Center track, trying to decide what to say to the students as she went. Choosing to tell them a little about her own high school years and career, then let them ask questions, she relaxed and enjoyed the fresh air, the freedom, and the bright blue sky.

There were several other runners there. One man, about her age, with light-brown hair, broad shoulders, and a great tan, passed her twice. Slowing down so he would go by again, she decided, *Good looking guy. He has a runner's butt. I wish mine looked like his.* Then she sped up and passed him, just to show him she could.

Returning to the hotel, she showered, had breakfast in her room, and dressed for the library book signing session that would start at noon. She chose sand-brown tapered slacks, a white blouse with an oversized collar and cuffs, brown shoes the same color as her coat buttons, and no jewelry. A camel-colored walking coat completed the outfit. She decided it went just right with her black hair and blue eyes. *I'm going to be a Christmas tree in the desert in this combo!*

Judging by the gaping mouths she encountered in the lobby as she left, she was right. At five-feet-ten-inches tall, a posture as straight as a steel beam, and a constant Mona Lisa smile, she was a striking woman.

The desk clerk asked, "Should we get a cab to take you to your meeting, Ms. Ibarra?"

"No, thank you; I'll walk. It's a beautiful day."

As Dee approached the library, there were reporters, photographers, and videographers clustered around the entrance. She answered questions, staying in the book-box, parrying expertly personal responses about herself or co-workers. She told the group, "Marge, the librarian, will give you a copy of the book if you show your credentials. Remember, you have to get signed releases from anyone other than me who appears in your photos, and the parents, if you include children."

She noticed Kris Joseph from the *New York Times* in the crowd. His clothes were disheveled, his face gray, and his hair like a shag rug.

"Kris, did you come up this morning?"

Even his response was fatigued. "Yeah. Got up at three and the damn rental car died comin' in from the airport."

Dee laughed. "Mine, too."

Kris added, "You should feel honored. The book editor put the screws to my boss to pay for a charter here. He has only done that twice before in the ten years I've worked there. I'll see you back in the City."

Dee grasped his hand and locked her eyes on his. "Thanks for coming."

It was twelve-thirty before she got to Marge O'Neil at the signing desk.

Marge was beaming. "We haven't had a turn out like this since I started working here. Thank you so much for coming."

"Thank you for having me. Are all these people here for books?"

"They certainly are!"

In mid-afternoon, Brad paddled his canoe across the lake and pulled it up on the sandy beach at the village park. He walked to the library a block away. The library faced Main Street and had large windows on the back, overlooking Mirror Lake. A line of people extended a hundred feet down the street from the library entrance. He passed along the line to the far end, exchanging greetings with friends as he went.

It was nearly four o'clock when he was close enough to see Dee ahead of him. *Wow! She is so much more attractive in person than in movies. Maybe this isn't such a good idea.* Her black hair, blue eyes, and inquisitive demeanor held his attention like a photograph by the famous Yousuf Karsh.

She greeted each person with a friendly remark, asking his or her name. With children, Dee took more time, asking questions about books they liked, favorite subjects in school, and sports. Each person, adult or child, had her full attention as they came to her.

New copies of her book, *The Ibarra Chronicles,* were piled high on the table to her left. Marge stood by the stack and passed books to Dee for signing. Marge saw Brad when he was third in line, and greeted him with a cheerful, "Brad, how are you? We haven't seen much of you lately." She tossed her hair slightly, held her smile, and stood up straighter.

He returned her greeting with a wave and a grin. Since Marge had been pretty much silent until that point, the exchange caused Dee to look up. She signed books for the next two readers and before her stood the tall, tan, sandy-haired runner from the Olympic track. His eyes were as blue as her own, and joined his lips in a warm, friendly smile. Somehow, his attention made her feel she was the only person in the room, and momentarily unsettled her composure.

His voice was steady and confident. "Thank you for coming to Lake Placid, Ms. Ibarra, and for starting your book tour here. That kindness is consistent with the many stories I've heard of your early life in the village." She detected sincere gratitude, not the fawning flattery she heard so often.

Dee blushed a little. "I hope you only heard the true ones. What would you like me to write in your book?"

"Well, you don't know me yet. Can we change that? How about: 'To Brad, a friend in the making?'"

Dee smiled. "Sounds good to me," she answered and transcribed the note, adding her signature.

Before Brad turned away, he pointed out the library window behind Dee toward his canoe. She turned to look. "I'll be there reading when you leave. When you are done signing, if you can, please come down so we can talk'."

As soon as he left, Dee turned to Marge. "Who is that man?"

"He's Brad. I don't know his last name. He's a professor somewhere, I think. He writes and takes great photographs. He donated many of the photos on the library walls. Everybody likes him. He trains, sometimes, with the Olympic athletes. Kind of handsome, don't you think?"

"Yeah! Did you ever ask him out?" Dee gave her an impish look.

Marge's face reddened, "Please … I'm married."

"Come on. I saw you fluttering your eyelashes at him."

"Stop that. Get these books signed." The words were mixed with giggles.

By the time everyone had a book, it was past five-thirty. Dee looked out the window toward the lake. True to his word, Brad was sitting on a bench near the canoe reading *The Ibarra Chronicles*. She thanked Marge for all her help, got details on the next day's events, and they agreed to meet again before she left town.

She walked down to the bench where Brad was reading and he stood up, extending his hand. "Brad Nolan."

"Dee Ibarra. Pleasure to meet you. Can I call you Brad?"

"Please do. Can I call you Dee?"

"Sure."

"Joan Martin at Greene Publishing called yesterday and asked me to assist you here, if I'm needed."

"How do you know them?"

"I've worked for them off and on for five years."

"Do you live in Lake Placid?"

"I have a summer place across the lake. I write, edit, and take photographs. I taught screenwriting in the drama department at Toronto University, but gave it up to freelance. I winter over in Toronto, New York City, or Los Angeles, depending on where my work takes me."

"Oh, that's nice. So, what did you want to talk about?"

Brad motioned for her to sit down on the bench with him.

"I would like to know how a girl of seventeen had the chutzpah, courage, and skill to leave home and jump into the whirlwind of Hollywood, movies, television, and stage plays. How did you do it? I've seen many of your performances and read what you have written, but don't think they tell the whole story. How did you obtain such a marvelous vocabulary and education with so little time at a university? I've had very few students with your command of writing, even in their senior year of college. So far, this book only serves to deepen my curiosity. Will it answer my questions? The bio said you are also a sculptor, painter, and producer."

Dee paused, thinking about her answer, but before she could start, a swarm of mosquitoes attacked them.

Brad was slapping at the pests. "Mosquitoes stay near shore. Twenty feet off shore and they are gone. Will you join me in the canoe?"

Dee looked steadily into his eyes for perhaps fifteen seconds. *Can I trust this guy?*

He anticipated her concerns. "I will not harm you; in fact, the opposite is true."

Somehow she believed him, not quite sure why. "Let me run up to the hotel and put on some jeans."

She was back in about forty-five minutes, wearing a white, long-sleeved shirt, sandals, jeans, and a matching baseball cap. She could smell citronella and thought, *He must have sprayed his clothes.* "Let's go."

Brad's face was serious. "Can you swim?"

"Hey, I was brought up on this lake. Three things I learned were swimming, fishing, and ice skating."

Brad smiled, nodded, and moved the canoe down on the beach until the bow was floating. He steadied it by the gunwales while Dee waded in the shallow water to get in. *She is careful to step only on the keel. She knows something about canoes.*

"Since you are on board as my guest, Madam, you don't have to paddle." He had a backrest against the forward thwart so she could sit facing him. "The cushion is a flotation device. I don't take chances with precious cargo."

"Shove off, sailor. The mosquitoes are having me for dinner."

They moved out into the lake and, just as he said, the mosquitoes were gone. He passed her a windbreaker with a faint smell of citronella. "It will be a little cooler on the water."

Now, there is a thoughtful man, she decided, surreptitiously studying his face. Dee pointed toward the library. "You know, Marge has been watching us from the library window. We are going to be the talk of the town, maybe the county, by seven tonight." They both laughed.

"About your question from before, the book will provide answers, at least to the level I want on public display. It reads easily and makes me look good because I have an excellent editor." While speaking, she rubbed her cold, wet feet together. Brad reached behind him and pulled a towel and a shoebox from the stern.

"May I?" He slipped off her sandals, dried her feet, and replaced the sandals with soft leather moccasins.

This guy is something else. What's he got in mind? "They feel so comfortable. How did you know my size?"

"Joan Martin from Greene Publishing, again." He grinned.

Brad paddled slowly and steadily, straight across the lake. The sun was at his back. He saw the sunset fascinated Dee and she was studying the sky and water. True to its name, Mirror Lake was reflecting a masterpiece, a magnificent abstract as the ripples in the water frolicked with the colors in the light.

Dee had already decided, *I'm going to paint this scene someday: the sunset, the canoe, and the man.*

As the colors started to fade, Brad said, "Since the book answers my first questions, I'm going to ask a tougher one."

Dee smiled at him. "Do you have to?"

"Well, I would like to ask the question. You don't have to answer if you don't want to, but if you don't, I won't take you to the fine dinner Georgio has prepared for us."

Dee looked puzzled. "Where?" He pointed with the paddle toward the lights they were approaching.

"Okay, what's the question? I'm starving."

"That worked pretty well," Brad commented aloud to himself, eliciting a chuckle from Dee. "Here is my question: in entertainment and other public occupations, people often develop a hard shell and seem to be 'on stage' even when they are not. How can they enjoy the sights, smells, and sounds of our planet enough to relax and be happy when they feel somebody is watching them all the time? How do you do it? To me, it appears you are the servant of everyone. Who takes care of you?"

Dee frowned and remained silent. *What is he getting at? I don't need anybody to take care of me.*

Brad saw wrinkles form between her eyebrows, and a flash of defiance cross her face. "Let me re-phrase that. Is there ever a time you can just let your guard down and simply enjoy life? I saw you at the track this morning, and for a short time, you looked serene and relaxed."

"You were watching me?"

"Tried not to let you see me. You looked so happy, I didn't want to disturb your pleasure; and you are a damn good runner, by the way."

"Really? … I just love being outdoors. For me, it's quality time. Last night, I took a walk around the village. The air smelled so good! I miss that smell and the rush it gives. Some of my city friends consider themselves outdoors if they drive with the car windows open."

Brad erupted into a lively laugh that was probably heard across the lake. *He has a great laugh,* Dee decided, smiling.

Brad slowed the canoe. "Isn't it great how smells, sounds, and views we took for granted as kids lodge in our brain and come rushing back when we experience them again?"

The moonlight was reflecting so brightly from the water the dock ahead appeared to be in a spotlight. He pulled up to the side of it and held the canoe tightly against it with his left hand. He gave Dee his right hand as she stepped onto the dock. The strength of his grip startled her. Pulling the canoe onto the sandy beach by the dock, Brad grabbed the shoebox with her sandals. "Let's go see what Georgio has made." He took her arm.

Crossing the front deck of the cabin, they entered a great room with a high ceiling and fireplace made of rough-hewn, jet-black rock. Studs of deep red garnet protruded from the stone, some larger than a fist. A fire sent flickers of light onto the knotty-pine walls of the room. A stairway on the right led to a balcony above the great room with multiple doors on the opposite wall. To the left, in the great room, was a dining area with large windows providing an overlook of the lake. A table with candles was set for two. The opera *Don Carlo,* accompanied by a booming voice singing in Italian, poured into the room from an open door near the dining area. Dee and Brad both smiled.

Singing, a handsome man about Brad's age in a white chef's jacket and cap came through the door, carrying a bottle of wine. Seeing them, he put down the wine and approached.

Brad held out his left hand palm up. "Dee, meet Georgio Amoroso. Georgio, author Dee Ibarra."

"It is indeed a pleasure, Madam. Brad has told me of you. His description was very complimentary, but obviously inadequate."

Brad added, "Georgio and his family have a cabin a little way down the road."

"Ms. Ibarra—"

Dee held up her hand. "Please, call me Dee," then took his hand.

Georgio made a shallow bow. "Thank you. When Brad told me he was going to try to win your heart, I volunteered to cook for him. You would probably be getting Spaghettios if it weren't for me. I like your clothes, except for the moccasins."

Brad explained, "He saw me buying them and is trying to rock my boat."

Dee turned to look at Brad. "So, you are trying to win my heart?" This created a premium blush that showed right through his tan.

Georgio grinned amiably at Brad's discomfort, and Brad rushed to change the subject by saying, "Georgio is the chef at Lattanzi in New York City."

Dee was impressed. "I've been there many times. The food is marvelous."

Georgio bowed again. "Thank you, Madam … uh, Dee. I know you are both hungry. Everything is ready."

While Dee freshened up, Georgio instructed Brad on what he had prepared and how to serve it. When they were seated at the table, Georgio brought in the first course and poured the wine. "The lake trout you are having was caught by your host this morning. It is native to Mirror Lake, a body of water free of all mercury, PCB's, and any other things with names so long only the initials are used. The wine is from a small upstate winery. It is not Italian but … Brad likes it, and actually, so do I. Don't tell anybody; I'll have to deny it," he commanded as he scowled with fake seriousness. "I hope you like it, too. I'm going to leave now and let you enjoy each other's company, and my food."

Brad and Dee blurted in unison, "Thank you, Georgio," and then laughed at themselves.

The dinner was delicious and the conversation flowed freely. Brad asked, "What made you want to be an actress?"

"At thirteen, I was tall and dorky. That got the attention of upperclassmen that thought I was older than I was. I was just as smart as they were, and could hold my own in the banter. I got more confidence, began to speak up in class, asked questions, and got into activities inside and outside school, including stage plays.

"My mother worried I was growing up too fast, and we had many arguments about things like riding motorcycles, smoking, drinking, sex, and how right and wrong don't overlap. My respect for my mother was, and is, steadfast, and I follow her advice, even if it's sometimes reluctantly."

She paused and looked at Brad. *I think he's interested and wants me to go on.* "I read every celebrity magazine I could buy, borrow, or steal, especially ones about Geena Davis. I avoided required reading when I could, but loved books where the characters' thoughts and qualities were revealed. Jane Austen novels were my favorites. Sometimes, I pretended to be someone else for a day, to the amusement of friends and the irritation of my mother and teachers.

"A quote from Macbeth "…told by an idiot, full of sound and fury, signifying nothing…" was all I wrote for a two hundred word essay on a poem by Edgar Allan Poe. It got me two things from my teacher: a reprimand letter to my mother and an introduction to a drama coach. What people would think, say, or do in different situations became my art."

Brad was smiling now. He was undecided whether he admired her more for her brain, honesty, or perseverance.

"What are you smiling about?" Dee asked, with a frown. "Are you mocking me?"

"No. No. It's not applause you cherish; it's the satisfaction of bringing words and actions into a believable story. It's the same reason I write."

Now Dee was smiling, too. "Are you sure we aren't related?"

"If we are, you shouldn't be here now."

Dee smiled, and then paused, her smile fading. She looked away, and spoke softly. "Sometimes, I wonder if my art jeopardizes making strong relationships. I never seem to form a bond strong enough to get really close to anyone."

"I doubt that. You have kept friends and family close for years."

How does he know that? Wary, she hesitated, but decided to continue. "Drama teachers told me I had the determination, independence, smarts, amiability, and looks to go further. I didn't think I could fulfill my dreams here in Lake Placid and by seventeen, the urge to be like my idol overrode my anxieties about leaving." Dee's voice grew fainter and went down a pitch.

Brad sensed the change and detected a far away, frightened look in her eyes. *I think she is re-living the big step of leaving home so young.* He reached across the table and took her right hand in both of his.

"… I'm being too nosy. I'll tell you about me." Dee looked at his hands, then at his face. She realized he was purposely diverting her thoughts away from the old fears. She was grateful, and surprised that he seemed to know her thoughts and wanted to ease her feelings.

"Unlike you, I was not getting attention at thirteen. I think I was a dork a lot longer than you. I was into track and lacrosse in college." Dee had seen some of his trophies on the great room balcony and knew he was being modest. "My confidence came from sports, I think. Interest in writing came from a great English teacher and my parents. Both have written novels. My father is the editor of a newspaper and taught me how to put people's feelings and intentions into words and photographs. When a person created news for the paper, my father and I would have a contest between us to see who could make up the most ridiculous excuse for the person's poor judgment or amusing predicament.

"Bringing that experience to college led me into the fantasy world of making characters say, and do, the right thing at the right time to tell a powerful story. I got an M.F.A. in creative writing and Ph.D. in literature, and they asked me to stay and teach.

"I was engaged in grad school, but it was a mistake. She loved nature, but was glad God put it outside. The freelance thing started a few years ago. I needed to see the world. I needed to meet people like you."

"Brad, you asked earlier about the shell around people in entertainment. It's true. There are many reasons: fear of saying or doing the wrong thing that will hurt your career, protecting yourself from dishonest or obsessed people who masquerade as friends…" her voice trailed off.

Brad sensed her sadness. "It must be difficult to make real friends, especially if both are in a shell profession."

Dee overpowered the sadness and regained her voice. "It is. Finding real friends who make you happy when you are sad, stronger when you are weak, or you can trust when the competition is fierce sometimes seems impossible."

Brad was quiet for a few minutes, and then spoke softly. "Friendships are built slowly. Both parties will test a friendship-in-the-making often as it develops. If it flourishes, it gets stronger every day. When each one puts the other's well-being before their own, or feels, say, the happiness and sadness of the other like it's theirs too, then I think that person is your friend. What do you think?"

Dee studied his face. "You really are after my heart, aren't you?"

He smiled. "I am. But that's not why I said that; I believe it."

After dinner, Dee helped Brad carry things to the kitchen. "That Georgio is something else, and a great chef."

"He is a good and loyal friend. Wait until you meet his wife and kids. Would you like to go out on the deck, look at the stars, smell the night air, and listen to the silence?"

"I'd like that."

Brad picked up a double sleeping bag and opened the door to the deck. On the left side there was a large inflated air mattress.

"You really are a devious, confident guy. You had this thing already blown up, didn't you?"

Brad explained, "You better get in this sleeping bag and netting or you may need a blood transfusion in the morning. The temperature is dropping and you are warm mosquito bait."

They got in the sleeping bag fully clothed and zipped it up. Brad put a mosquito net over their exposed faces.

They were silent for a long time enjoying the sounds of the night and the stars. "Ibarra is a Basque name, isn't it?" Brad asked suddenly and, not waiting for an answer, added, "Do you think that is why you are so intelligent, confident, and independent?"

"Man, you really are workin' to win me."

"Should I stop?"

"No, keep goin', Romeo."

"The view of the big dipper is great tonight." He pointed skyward. "The traveler's companion, the North Star, Polaris, is there. That larger, brighter evening star not far above the horizon isn't a star, but the planet Venus, the Roman Goddess of love and beauty."

Dee sighed. "It's so peaceful here." They let the quiet surround them awhile.

"Would you like to hike along the Au Sable River tomorrow or go up Van Hoevenberg or Whiteface to see the leaf color?"

"Sure, either one … but I have to go to a meeting at ten first. They are going to put a plaque up at the school and want me to talk to the students. Will you come with me?"

"Of course." Brad was pleased she asked.

"Can I introduce you as ... say, my editor?"

Brad chuckled. "That's a good idea. Most people in town probably think something risqué is going on after Marge's rumor machine started tonight."

"Some of the older people who knew me as a teenager probably thought I would be in jail by now. I can't wait to see the looks on their faces."

"It will be worth a week's wages to see Marge's face."

Whenever they exchanged looks, they burst into laughter. Gradually they allowed the quiet of the night to return. For a time, only the subtle hiss of the waves running up and down the sand and a coyote howling far, far away penetrated the silence. The air had a faint aroma of night-blooming daylilies and honeysuckle. Eventually owls hooting, fish jumping, frogs croaking, and cicadas singing joined the symphony.

Brad said quietly, "Dee, I have to tell you something."

Suddenly Dee had an empty feeling. *Damn! Here it comes. He's married or has eight kids, or both. Why the hell can't I get a break?*

She struggled to keep unhappiness from her voice. "What is it?"

"Dee, I *am* your editor."

Dee bolted upright and exploded, *"What?* You are not! Irving told me the editor's name was Chad Morgan! That's you? I've been calling you Chad for two years. I pictured somebody very patient, very understanding, very bright, very professional, and very married."

Brad interrupted, laughing and trying to talk at the same time. "I am not married. I may not be any of the other things either. All our communications have been by phone, email, or on paper. We have never met in person, mostly because we were never in the same place at the same time. Irving has been taking great pleasure in his, possibly intentional, naming error. He plans to introduce us at the book release party in New York next month."

Dee blurted, "That son-of-a-bitch!" She struggled for words. "... But I swore and screamed at you over the phone a lot of times. You never yelled back. Now I'm embarrassed."

Brad took her hand. "No need to be. You remember Mallo Cups when we were kids? You're a Mallo Cup—kind of hard on the outside, but all soft, sweet, and gooey on the inside. When I was right, you always gave in. When I was wrong, you explained carefully why, once you calmed down—you are 'Elinor, be Elinor', like in Jane Austen's *Sense and Sensibility*."

"I said that; it's in my journal!"

"I know. I've read all the journals you sent to Greene Publishing from the beginning to the present. I know more about you than your parents do. I want you to know, no matter how our personal relationship unfolds, that information will never be revealed, except by you."

Tears ran slowly down Dee's cheeks. *How could I not know this lovely man before now?*

Brad saw the tears glisten in the moonlight, but kept silent. *They belong to her, and only she can share their meaning.*

Dee couldn't believe the tears herself. *No man has ever made me cry because he cares for me.*

After a few minutes she said, slowly and quietly, "Brad, thank you for editing my book so beautifully. You have made it say everything I wanted. I'm proud of it, and will be, even if no one reads it."

Brad understood and cherished the depth from which those words came. He knew this wasn't in-the-shell talk. Her humility instantly doubled his respect for her. "Don't worry, Dee. It will be read—and it will teach. You did all the hard work, keeping those journals since you were a teenager, and pulling out the best information. Thank you for letting me do it. You are a talented person in many, many ways and a person I will always admire."

Dee, amazed and grateful, rolled toward him and gave him a long hug, thinking, *This is turning out to be one magical trip!*

Brad was tempted to kiss her, but did not. He didn't want a gratitude kiss, but something more. He feared closing the shell and shattering any chance she might care for him as much as he cared for her. Then it happened.

Dee said, "There is a suicidal, dive-bombing mosquito inside this sleeping bag. Let's get off this air-trampoline."

Brad agreed. "Okay, but do I have a chance at being your friend and maybe more?"

Dee put her face close to his. "You know that question you asked me earlier, about what makes me relaxed and happy? You have done that for me, and much, much more—and not just today—also every time we have talked or written since the book was started, and I just now realized it. I have known you, and treasured our work time together for two years, Brad Nolan, but I just met you today. Yes, I cherish having you as a friend. We'll see about the 'maybe more' part." She smiled. "You only know the paper me, though. I want you to know the everyday me, and I want to know everything about you. The question is—can I make you my friend, or more—forever?"

Brad's chest felt like he had just run a mile at top speed. He studied her face and saw just what he wanted: the same look of tranquility and pleasure she had when running in the sunshine at the track. "You know, you're so smart it's scary. Let's go."

They squirmed out of the sleeping bag, teasing each other about their clumsiness. Brad took Dee's hand and they ran through the cold for the cabin.

Just inside the great room door, in an almost continuous motion, Brad dropped the sleeping bag, dimmed the lights, and turned on a recording. He extended his arms and Dee stepped into his embrace. They danced, drifting gently with the music—

An International Incident

A female voice singing "All the Things You Are" pushed through the open doors of the Toronto hospital auditorium as Ted walked down the corridor. Pure tone, perfect control, and lyrics with feeling made him stop in awe at the entrance. He wasn't surprised everyone else at the rehearsal had stopped to listen.

By uniform, the vocalist was a nurse. Her voice, poise, and skill commanded attention. She had a scrubbed look, fair skin, and blue eyes. Her blonde hair, in a chignon, and a graceful neck accentuated her youth. The blue uniform and starched white collar couldn't hide her attractive figure. He was mesmerized. The music director didn't stop her once to comment or correct an error.

When she finished singing, chatter resumed in the room. Ted looked around. He saw only one nun. As he moved toward her she was describing lighting for the stage in the jargon and detail of a seasoned professional. As soon as she was done talking, he approached.

"Sister Grace?"

"Yes, I am."

"Father O'Leary asked for volunteers for the hospital's pediatric fundraiser at morning Mass. I'm Ted Stuart, a student at the university. May I help?"

"You sure can."

"I've worked on production of plays in high school and community theaters. I overheard your discussion about stage lighting. How do you know so much about it?"

"I had a double major in college, nursing and drama, plus a year as an understudy in New York. That was all before I took this gig." She laughed, and

Ted had to smile. He thought, *What a pleasant person. She has a smile full of joy and her green-blue eyes are just loaded with self-confidence.* Except for her hands and face, the rest of her was obscured by a wimple and black habit reaching to the floor.

"Sister Grace, who was that singing?"

"Pam Bligh, the lead in our show and a student nurse here. She has a beautiful voice, don't you think?" Ted nodded in agreement.

"Would you like to meet her?"

"Yes, ma'am."

Sister Grace introduced them and told Pam that Ted was going to help with production.

"I enjoyed your song. You have a beautiful voice. I'm a student at the university. What year nursing are you in?"

"Thank you. I'm glad you like my singing. I'm a junior. You can tell by the stripes on the hat. See?" She pointed to her cap.

"I thought maybe you were a sergeant or a lieutenant."

Pam laughed. "We better get to work or Sister Grace will be on our case. Will I see you again?"

"I hope so."

"Me, too." Pam smiled.

Pam and Ted talked whenever possible at rehearsals. They also met leaving church after morning Mass each day during Lent. Walking to class together, talking about music, school, and future plans, he found she was very sweet and reserved. She had a lively imagination, enjoyed her life, and looked forward to being a nurse. He was fond of her, becoming more so daily.

He finally got up the courage to ask her, "Would you like to go to a movie sometime?"

"Yes, but I can't for a few weeks. I gave them up for Lent. Can we go after Easter?"

"Sure."

On a day Pam was going home instead of to class, Ted walked her to her door and she introduced him to her parents. They didn't return his smile. They shook his offered hand, but said nothing except for hello and goodbye. He thought they were being protective of their daughter, but got no opportunity to reassure them of his respectful intentions.

A student in a university football team jacket rode by them on a bicycle as they were walking the last three mornings of Lent. Ted had noticed Pam's eyes follow him, and her conversation halted as he passed. On the third day, the rider stopped beside them, addressing Ted like an old friend though Ted didn't know him and the biker didn't know Ted's name. He struck up a conversation with Ted and Pam, but focused his attention on Pam. He walked along with them pushing his bike for a short distance, and then offered Pam a ride. She jumped on the crossbar without a word to Ted, and never looked back.

Ted stood in a puddle of disbelief and disappointment—the air had been sucked from his life. The warm, sunny, fragrant spring morning, filled with joy because he shared it with Pam, disappeared like a hat in a hurricane.

At the next rehearsal, Ted tried to talk with her. "Pam, are we still friends?" No answer.

"You barely know this guy. Did I do something to offend you? Why are you ignoring me?"

She looked at him sternly. "He's captain of the football team and he likes me."

"Do you think I don't? No answer. "Pam, please tell me what's wrong."

She said something in a firm voice that startled him. He had never been called that before. Turning, she walked away. He could feel his heart thumping against his ribs and hear his pulse in his ears. He sat down and stared at the floor. It had never occurred to him that the respect and affection he thought they shared was his alone. *Maybe she likes the spotlight so much that being with the captain of a football team is as deep as she gets. I thought she liked me. What's wrong with me?*

He felt weak—an eerie feeling of inadequacy—like facing a question on an important exam with a complete mental block. After fifteen minutes, he went to Sister Grace and gave her the completed paperwork on seating, deposits, advertising, and revenue expected. He wished her luck.

"Ted, why are you leaving us?"

Ted lowered his eyes; he had never lied to a nun before. "I'm sorry, Sister, but I have to spend more time on qualitative analysis." He looked up then and saw her frowning at Pam, who looked a little frightened. Sister Grace had heard their conversation.

"Sister, I'm sorry, but I can't be around her any more."

Sister Grace reached up and grasped his chin, pulling his face down to look straight into his eyes. "You are a good man, Ted Stuart. It's not your fault, and don't you forget that."

He hugged her and walked out. He never saw Pam Bligh again.

Ted applied to five medical schools, including the university he was attending. At two hundred dollars a pop, it was a struggle. The Dean of the College of Medicine and the Registrar of the University called him in for an interview after receiving his application. It was a brief meeting, more of a declaration on their part. He was told the medical school could not admit him. He went to the registrar's office and got his two hundred dollars back. As soon as his last exam was done he left. He didn't attend graduation.

Father O'Leary came out of the sacristy at dusk to prepare the missal for morning mass at six. As he entered the darkened church, he saw a lone young woman in a pew near the front. Approaching, he recognized Pam, and saw she had been crying.

"Pam, what's wrong? Is someone ill in your family?"

"No, father. I've done something bad. ... Do you remembered Ted Stuart?"

"The young man who helped with the pediatric fundraiser?" Pam nodded yes and tears welled up in her eyes.

"What happened?"

"I was rude to him. I tried to call him several times to apologize, but they said he was out. I went to his rooming house today and the landlady said he left a week ago. Graduation is next week. I think it's my fault he didn't stay to attend it." She began to sob.

"Oh my!" he said, holding her.

Ted entered exam room four of his New York office—and time went into reverse. Before him Pam, now Pam Murdock, her husband, Robert "Bob" Murdock, the bike-riding football player, and their son, Dave, sat grim-faced on the edges of their chairs. Despite twenty added years, Pam had the same lovely face he remembered, but her eyes were filled with fear and anxiety.

The whole undergraduate time of joy and disappointment he had experienced washed over him, threatening his professional composure. Struggling with his thoughts, he quickly shook hands with Pam and Robert Murdock, introducing himself as Dr. Stuart. They gave no sign of recognition, so he did the same.

He turned to Dave in the examination chair and grasped his hand. "Dave, I'm Dr. Stuart. Dr. MacDonald tells me you had a fight with a baseball." He did not let go of his hand but pulled Dave toward him turning him to his left to look at the remnants of bruising and swelling around his right eye. He released Dave's hand and asked, "What did you do, try to short-hop a line drive?"

Dave smiled. "How did you know?"

"I've seen this injury before. I used to play baseball, too. When I tried to do that, I usually caught the ball with my nose; that's why it's so crooked."

Dave laughed, and exhaled, expelling anxiety with the air.

Dave was fourteen years old and the youngest Murdock. Ted reviewed the story of his injury, past illnesses, the usual checklist of allergies, review of systems, and brief examination findings collected by his admitting nurse. Since salicylates make injured tissues bleed more than usual, Ted asked, "Dave, were you taking aspirin before the injury, or have you since?"

Dave looked at his mom to answer for him. "No, he hasn't had aspirin," Pam replied.

Ted asked Robert and Pam about eye or blood clotting problems in their families. There were none. A series of tests: pupil responses, eye pressure, color identification, and peripheral vision integrity; were followed by drops to dilate his pupils. Vision in Dave's right eye was reduced to light perception and the view inside the eye was totally obscured by blood. Sound wave testing revealed a retinal detachment, blood in front of, but not under, the retina. The left eye had 20/20 vision and was healthy in all respects. Ted dictated the findings as

Dave, Robert, and Pam listened, and then brought them to his office by a connecting door.

He sat down face to face with Dave. Using a model of an eye he explained details about eye anatomy and how the blood was affecting his vision. "The blow from the baseball broke blood vessels. Exactly where, I can't tell yet. The retina, the film in the camera, has been displaced. When the film is wrinkled, the pictures are wrinkled. That adds to the poor vision caused by the bleeding. Understand?" Dave nodded a yes.

"The best chance of improving vision is going to come from an operation. Waiting for the blood to clear will take too long. There could be irreversible changes if we wait. The longer the retina remains detached, the less likely good vision recovery will occur, even with successful surgery. It has already been four weeks, and I don't think we should wait longer. You must have questions."

"Will the operation hurt a lot?" Dave was struggling to look brave.

"Some, but not bad. Let's talk about that in a minute. I want to be sure you, and your mom and dad understand why I'm advising you to have surgery. Okay?"

Pam, an experienced nurse, asked the critical question, "What are the chances of getting back Dave's vision in the eye?"

"I'll be able to answer that best after clearing the blood so I can see the extent of damage. The ultrasonography gives us gross details but I will only be able to see the fine details after clearing the blood in the operating room. I think there is a reasonable chance of improving vision, but right now, I can't tell how much.

"Dave, there will be pain in and around your eye, especially the first three or four days after surgery. It will not be severe and medication will relieve it. It is important for you to tell the nurses if you are having serious pain. Being brave doesn't help. The medicine works best if used before the pain is severe."

He waited for more questions, and hearing none, continued. "After surgery you will wake up in the recovery room. Both eyes may be patched temporarily, and that can be scary, but a nurse will be with you all the time. The patching means only one thing: I don't want your eyes to move for a little while. It isn't an indication of success or failure. I will probably put a gas bubble into your eye to help hold the retina in place, like a splint used to hold a broken bone steady until it heals.

"The bubble won't last as long as a cast or need to be removed. It will dissolve in about two weeks. Keeping the bubble in place up against the retina after surgery requires you to sit or walk around with your nose pointing toward the floor. Can you do that for me?"

"Sure."

Ted turned to Pam and Robert. "I have to see a post-op patient. It should take me about ten minutes. Think of other questions and decide if you want to go ahead with the surgery. If you want another physician to see Dave for an opinion, I'll arrange that for you and provide all my information to him." He left the room.

Pam looked at Dave. "What do you think?"

"I like him. I think he'll fix it."

"Me, too. What do you think, Bob?"

"Pam, you're the medical expert in this family. He seems very thorough, and Dr. MacDonald trusts him."

Pam got up and walked around the office. A photograph on Ted's desk showed two blonde girls with soft smiles and sparkling-blue, impish eyes. The youngest seemed Dave's age. They were cheek to cheek with a woman she presumed to be their mother. They all had the same smile. Pam had a feeling she had seen the mother's face before.

When Ted returned, Pam told him their decision was to go ahead with surgery. Ted called his nurse in. "Trisha, please make arrangements for Dave to be admitted. See if you can get him in the room with the two boys operated on yesterday. Check the operating room schedule for time tomorrow. We will need about two and a half hours. Mr. and Mrs. Murdock will need the names of nearby hotels."

Dave's surgery started at 9:20 the next morning. In two hours and twenty-minutes, Dave was in the recovery room. Ted went to see Pam and Robert. He described the findings and reported, "I'm optimistic about Dave's vision. I'm going back to the recovery room to check on him, and then operate on another patient. By the time I'm done, Dave will be in his room upstairs, sleepy but able to talk with you. I will be up after I finish here. The nurses will get him settled in and positioned. I didn't need to patch his left eye."

Pam had a little more color in her face with this news and was able to force a small smile.

"Oh … I almost forgot. Just now in recovery, Dave gave a double thumbs-up sign when I asked how he felt. He told me to tell you he loves you. That's the meds talking. I can assure you, he will be a normal teenager by morning."

Pam laughed. Robert looked puzzled.

"Inside joke, Robert. Pam will explain it."

Ted kept Dave in the hospital three days. The first post-op day, Ted warned, "Dave, the vision in your right eye will seem like you are underwater because of the bubble."

"I already see more light, Dr. S."

Dave was discharged home with instructions, medications, a follow-up appointment, and some polycarbonate safety glasses. "These glasses stop minor flying things but not big stuff, so avoid sports right now, and don't aggravate your brother so he pokes you in the eye. Okay?"

"Yes, sir." Dave smiled.

Ted chuckled and tousled his hair. Turning to Pam he said, "Please report promptly if he is having more pain instead of less, if the eye looks more inflamed, or if you are worried about his progress. Encourage him to use the positioning."

He shook hands with Pam and Robert. Pam flashed a smile almost like the ones he remembered so well.

At the first post-op visit, Dave was excited. "Dr. S, when the bubble moves out of the way, I can see great!"

Ted smiled. The retina was in normal position and the laser treatment was doing its job. Dave's visual acuity in his right eye had improved to 20/40 and the gas bubble was half its previous size. "See you in two weeks. By then the air bubble will be gone. Use the positioning while the bubble is there. Once you hardly notice it, you can stop the nose down thing. When you return, if everything is good, I'll send you back to Dr. MacDonald. Okay?"

"Okay!"

Two weeks later Pam, Robert, and Dave were chatting and smiling as he entered exam room four. The bubble was gone, the retina was intact, and the visual acuity 20/20. Ted brought them to his office. Instead of sitting at his desk, Ted pulled up a chair in front of the family and handed Pam a folder.

"Here are copies of all our records on Dave, except for today's, including the operative note and correspondence with Dr. MacDonald. He already has them all; these are for you. I'll send you a copy of today's notes also. You will need to call Dr. MacDonald's office for an appointment in about two weeks."

"Thank you." Pam's smile was the one he remembered from years ago.

Dave broke in, "Will I be able to play football, Dr. S?"

"Dave, I've seen patients with injuries worse than yours who did not get a retinal detachment. You have no family history or findings to suggest vulnerability, but I'm concerned you may be more susceptible than others. What do you think about other sports where there is less chance of a blow to the eyes or head?"

"Like what?"

"I was thinking, track or swimming."

"But Dr. S—girls don't cheer for guys who do track or swim!"

Ted hung his head and sighed. "I know. Well, you will need to talk this over with your dad. He is the sports authority, but you should wear good eye and head protection for rough sports. Whatever you do, I know you will do it well and I'm looking forward to hearing everything about you. You, Dave Murdock, are on your way to being a great man."

Ted stood up and looked at Dave. "Can I ask you to wait outside a few minutes? I need to talk to your mom and dad. It's not about you. It's about when we were in college together."

"You were in college together?"

"Yes, we were." Dave moved to Ted and gave him a hug. Pam and Robert looked at each other in utter disbelief. He had never done that to anyone.

Dave locked his gaze on Ted's eyes. "Thanks for fixin' my eye, Dr. S. How did you get so smart?"

"You know, my daughter Staci asked me that same thing when I blocked her shot at a basket in our driveway last night. She usually beats me." Dave was still laughing when he walked out the door and closed it after him.

Pam went to Ted and took both his hands in hers. "Thank you for helping Dave. Sister Grace was right. You are a good man. What happened was not your fault." She kissed him on the cheek.

Ted motioned for them to sit down. "Twenty years ago, I would have given up food to have you do that." Pam blushed.

"I didn't think you remembered me. There are several things I would like to say. First, I'm happy for you both and for the splendid family you have raised together. I know only Dave, but suspect his siblings are also delightful people anyone would be pleased to know." Pam and Robert smiled.

"Pam, I'm not sure what you mean by 'not your fault.' But, since you quoted exactly what Sister Grace said twenty years ago, I wonder if you remember what you said to me that day?"

Pam replied, looking somewhat uneasy, "No, ... I don't."

"Well, it made a big difference in my life. You said, 'You are an American.' I felt being an American somehow made me a person of no interest to you." Pam and Robert both drew in a quick breath and looked at the floor, like something unspeakable had been spoken.

Robert bristled, "I don't think Pam meant that."

Ted ignored Robert's attitude. "I always wondered why Sister Grace said, 'It's not your fault.' I thought, if two people liked each other, that a boundary between two countries couldn't be important. I don't know if she meant it did with us. Robert you weren't there. The only people who know what was implied are Pam and Sister Grace, but Pam, I don't want you to tell me what you think, because it makes no difference to me now. Please hear me out.

"I applied to five medical schools. My first choice was to stay right there and perhaps see you again. At the university interview, I was advised they only accepted Americans if their fathers graduated from the medical college. I knew this was not true because two men in my class from my home area, one a football player, the other my roommate sophomore year, were admitted and their fathers were not physicians. They did not say my grades were unacceptable or that they had a quota for foreigners. Four other medical schools accepted me, including McGill in Montreal. I took the scholarship offered by an American university.

"I want to thank you for telling me the truth by rejecting me. It forced me to confront reality. You, and the university, got me on an educational path to learn skills in five different American universities I could not have achieved in Canada at that time. Those are the skills I've used to help your son, and many others."

He paused, considered stopping there, but could not. "Twenty years have passed and sentiments may have changed. I don't know if there are still anti-American feelings in eastern Canada. I only know what I experienced."

Pam started to speak, hesitated, and then replied, "My parents were not happy when I told them about you. They were not very gracious when they met you, and I'm sorry for that. Sister Grace understood. Being young, I was naive and a captive of my roots. I don't think it was … is … right, but I didn't have the courage to rise above the prejudice. Then I didn't have to, because I met Bob. How the university treated you doesn't surprise me. Bob, do you have anything to say?"

"I'm disappointed one of their own graduates couldn't get an honest answer why he was rejected. To have a good football team or get professors, they often override their prejudice."

Pam quietly added, "I hope we'll be friends. If we are, good, and if not, I hope we can still count on you for help if we need it."

"Of course you can."

Ted stood up, picked up the photograph on his desk, and held it as he spoke. "You won't receive a bill from me for Dave's surgery. Please consider it a late wedding present from Kylie, Staci, Meg, and me. You may recognize the children's mother in this photo as the woman you knew as Sister Grace."

Pam had her hand over her mouth as she stared wide-eyed at Ted. She took the photo from his hands and sat down heavily, studying it like a dedicated detective on a murder case.

"…But, how did that happen?"

"Sister Grace's mother became gravely ill and was admitted to the American hospital where I was an intern. As the only child of her widowed mother, she asked her Mother Superior for leave to care for her. She refused. As a result, Sister Grace left the sisterhood and returned to being Nurse Kylie Alison McGuire. We passed in a hallway and she recognized me. I had never seen her without a black habit and was as surprised then as you are now. Let me rephrase that: very pleasantly surprised, because she was not only the effervescent, joyful person we both knew earlier, but a very beautiful woman with more generosity, affection, and intelligence than I had ever seen in one person. Our two daughters are just like her."

"She agreed with me, a boundary between two countries should not interfere with matters of the heart."

A Stitch in Time

"He's a crotchety old fart," Scott, age seven, told his mother.

"Enough, Scott Nathan Brownell!" Elizabeth said quietly but firmly, making a mental note to talk to Jack about what he said in front of the boys. "You go to confession Saturday and ask for forgiveness. Don't judge so quickly or you'll make big mistakes in life. Remember that!"

Scott was looking at the ground, not sure he was wrong, but bowing his head to say he was sorry. She often asked him to bring food to the sour old man across the street, and he never said thank you, not even once. Scott frequently put the food down, knocked on the door, and ran. He knew him as Mr. Koerner, and thought he was scary.

Mr. Koerner lived in one of the twenty houses behind the maple trees lining both sides of the single village street. The trees supplied shade in summer, maple syrup in spring, and a windbreak in winter. The village, near the Canadian border in upstate New York, was a remnant of a once larger community that originated around a gristmill and brickworks. Both located there to use water power from a millpond, now called St. James Lake, that settlers made by damming Pleasant Creek.

The Stage Coach Hotel was gone, burned to the ground years ago. Walt's grocery store was near the lake. The grocery was actually the first floor of Walt's house, and it doubled as the post office. Included in the village were a dairy farm, a Quaker church, and an elementary school. Mr. Koerner's house was the fourth one east of the store on Main Street. The stone schoolhouse was across the street from his house. Scott lived next door to the school with his mom, Elizabeth; father, Jack; and bothers, Ben and Dennis.

The Koerner house was a weathered gray two-story wooden box with shutters hanging at strange angles, clapping against the walls in the wind. A single-level kitchen was attached to the back. A barn behind the house and to the left matched the house in color and condition. Neither had ever seen a coat of paint. There could've been a vegetable garden behind the barn, but Scott wasn't sure. He didn't snoop around; Koerner was too scary. In winter, smoke curled up from the chimney in the kitchen, filling the air with the acrid smell of burning wood.

Mr. Koerner was rarely outdoors, or seen any place other than at home. Scott never saw him drive a car and there were never any tracks in the driveway snow. There were no lights on at night. Nobody visited. The few times Scott saw him at his mailbox and said hello, Koerner never responded. The perpetual look of sadness and anger on his face didn't invite conversation.

He was slim, about five feet nine or ten inches tall, and stooped a little forward, his looks made Scott worry he'd pounce on him and drag him off to a dungeon. His older brother Ben used this worry to tease him.

Koerner's clothes were always the same: old scuffed brown work boots, dark gray pants, and a light gray shirt—the same color as his skin, beard, eyebrows, and remaining wisps of hair.

Scott took advantage of the dormant playground swings one fall day when school was closed for a teacher's conference. At age seven, his lofty goal was to go higher than anyone dreamed possible—to see over the big steel pipe anchoring the chains of the swings. He was fully involved in that endeavor when he heard someone yell, "Boy! Boy!"

He looked around to find where the voice was coming from. The rattle and squeak of the chains, exaggerated by his bold attempt to defy gravity, masked the sound of the voice. Dragging his feet on the ground to slow down, he heard it again, "Boy! Boy!" It was coming from across the street. Mr. Koerner was sitting on the front stoop of his house, holding his leg with one hand and motioning for Scott to come over with the other.

Afraid, he "sucked-it-up," like Ben told him to do when he cried, and headed that way. Approaching gingerly, Scott could see blood on Mr. Koerner's hands and pants. His face was white and his lips were in a tense, thin line. He was pressing a bloody towel to his left leg. Hearing him speak for the first time, it came out gruff and mean, just as Scott expected, except it was also weak.

"Hurry, Boy! Get your mother." Scott bolted for home, scared of and scared for Mr. Koerner.

"Mom, Mr. Koerner's cut off his leg! He told me to come get you." Elizabeth looked at his face. It might have been paler than Mr. Koerner's. She pulled the first-aid kit from a kitchen drawer and they ran across the street. Together Elizabeth and Scott helped Mr. Koerner into his kitchen. She had him sit in one chair and put his left leg on another.

Taking out scissors to cut open his pant leg brought a vigorous protest. "No, no! I'll have to buy new pants; roll up the pant leg."

Apparently the large tear in the pant leg and the blood had not made the pants unusable. She did as he asked.

There was a gaping six-inch cut on his lower leg, oozing a steady stream of dark red blood and an occasional bright red spurt. "Axe slipped," was his terse explanation.

Elizabeth cleaned around the cut quickly with alcohol, put two sterile pads from a package on it, and wrapped gauze tightly around his leg. The bleeding seemed to stop after that, or at least it didn't bleed through the bandage.

"Mr. Koerner, you have a big laceration." Elizabeth gave him a serious look. "You need stitches and maybe an x-ray. Jack will be home with the car at 5:30, and we'll take you to Dr. Sylvester in Black River. I'll call his office."

He wouldn't consider it. "No, no, no! Get the sewing kit in the closet, put water on to boil, and get the brandy from the kitchen cupboard."

She complied without a word. Scott thought Koerner should do what she said; it always worked for him. Elizabeth asked Mr. Koerner what he wanted to do. Scott didn't understand the conversation, but was fascinated. He'd never seen any injuries except for scratches, bruises, and poison ivy on himself or his brothers.

Mr. Koerner downed two shots of brandy and told Elizabeth, "Thread that large needle with black thread, tie the ends of the thread together, and hold both in the boiling water a few minutes." He pointed to a shiny metal clamp-like thing to hold the needle. Waiting for the water to boil, Elizabeth put a clean towel under his leg, removed the gauze placed there earlier, and wiped the skin around the cut with alcohol again.

She won the argument with him about washing and putting alcohol on their hands. "I won't help you if you don't." He grumbled something inaudible, then held out his hands to be washed and flushed with alcohol.

When the needle was cool enough to touch, Mr. Koerner leaned forward and put fifteen stitches in his own leg with Elizabeth's assistance, and only an occasional flinch. Scott didn't know brandy could numb your leg. With each stitch he made two passes. The first one passed deep under the cut then back through the edges to where he started. Elizabeth tied and cut each stitch.

These weren't just any stitches, they were special—the wound closed into a fine line and the bleeding stopped. Elizabeth stood up. She'd been on her knees beside his leg, helping pass the needle when he faltered. "There. That looks good. Have you ever had a tetanus shot?"

"Thirty years ago."

"Let's hope it's still working."

She washed around the wound again with alcohol and bandaged the leg. Scott heard her whisper softly to herself, "Please, God, don't let him get an infection." Then louder to Mr. Koerner, "Let's get you on the sofa. I'm going to send Scott over with some ice in a plastic bag. You hold it on the bandage as much as you can, and keep your leg elevated on the pillows so it doesn't swell up. I'm going to send some food with him, too. You stay put. I'll be back later to check on you."

Mr. Koerner nodded he would do what she said. He seemed more placid now, willing to take orders. Was it the brandy, loss of blood, fatigue, or did he appreciate her? Scott thought he saw Mr. Koerner give his mother a brief smile. Whether he did or not, she gave him one—a big one, full of reassurance and caring like she gave her boys when they needed it.

Scott was proud of her. He lacked the words to tell her, but on the way home he took her hand. She looked down at him and smiled, understanding—as mothers do.

When Scott returned with the ice and food, Mr. Koerner was asleep. He placed the ice on the bandage, as his mom told him to do, and Mr. Koerner awakened momentarily to murmur something unintelligible. Scott placed a kitchen chair next to him for the food and the bottle of Carling's ale Elizabeth knew he liked.

When Elizabeth and Jack went to bring more ice at seven o'clock, he had some color in his face. "The pain isn't bad. I think the ice helps. Thanks."

"You want me to get you some crutches?" Jack asked.

"Don't need 'em."

The next morning when Elizabeth and Scott arrived, his face was washed and shaved. He had on clean pants with the left leg rolled up, a clean shirt, and was making breakfast. He offered them scrambled eggs.

Every day, when Elizabeth and Scott changed the bandage, he was stronger. He asked Scott to feed his chickens and be sure they had water, and then collect the eggs.

Scott and Ben found there was a marvelous vegetable garden behind the barn and, wonder of wonders, four old cars covered with tarpaulins in the barn. One had the name Stanley on the radiator. Another was named Franklin.

Mr. Koerner didn't even limp after a while. Six months after the injury, Scott told him, "You're the only person I know who sewed his own leg back on." It was the first time he ever heard Mr. Koerner laugh.

One day, Mr. Koerner surprised Elizabeth and Scott by saying, "Please, call me George."

He began to talk to them, a little at first—then like a dam had broken. He choked up and his voice became a soft whisper. "My wife, Nicole, was a beautiful young woman in every way, and I loved her more than life itself. She died trying to have our only child. The child died, too. The doctors said amniotic fluid got into her bloodstream. Her family was devastated and her brothers blamed me. I don't know how they could've felt worse than I did. It *was* my fault."

Elizabeth talked softly to him, like she did to Scott and his brothers when they were upset. "George, you can't be blamed for loving your wife and wanting to have a child with her. That's a natural thing for people to do." At first Scott couldn't tell if it helped George like it did when she talked to him.

Elizabeth studied George's face. "Tell me about Nicole." He showed them pictures and knew exactly where and when they were taken, as well as the identity and relationship of each person in the photograph.

From the day of the injury on, George thanked the Brownells for food or any act of kindness. Seeing any of the Brownell boys outside, he would ask whether their mom needed eggs or vegetables.

He and Elizabeth also began to share gardening secrets, and he had many. For example, he advised, "Don't fertilize the plants until you see little green tomatoes, otherwise you get all top growth and poor fruit." He asked Scott or his brothers to feed the chickens occasionally and laughed when Denny, Scott's youngest brother, got them to eat from his hand or was chased by a rooster.

Scott asked, "What kind of cars are those in the barn? I've never seen any like them before." This brought out a completely different kind of smile from George, like he had been waiting for the question, maybe for years.

"I'll tell you what. You help me get them cleaned up and ready to go and I'll give you all a ride like no one around here has had in sixty years." They spent hours working on the Packard, the twelve-cylinder Duesenberg with the fold-up steering wheel, the Stanley Steamer, and the Franklin.

Despite being immobile for such a long time, the cars responded to George's touch. He knew every detail and had stored them meticulously. The Stanley Steamer was Scott's favorite. Once the kerosene-fired boiler was ready to go, George would release steam to the pistons and, with a gentle hiss, they would glide down the street. No noise, no shifting gears, just a gentle glide. To speed up, George just gave more steam to the engine. He drove fast over a bump in the road to make it feel like they were flying.

George and the boys laughed together and toured about. "We can't go too far," he said. "There's no license on the cars and I don't have a driver's license anymore." Scott learned George's hobby as a young man was restoring old, discarded cars deemed beyond repair. The interest of the Brownell boys brought it all back.

Over the next eleven years, the Brownells and George Koerner remained friends. Elizabeth coaxed into him coming for dinner on Thanksgiving, Christmas, and an occasional Sunday. It turned out George was sixty-eight years old, not seventy-eight as Scott surmised at first.

George slid into a happier state of mind. With Jack's help, he got historical license plates for all four of his vehicles. Jack drove the antique Packard to take George and Elizabeth to the boys' lacrosse, soccer, and baseball games plus concerts and graduations. George was astounded by how interested people were in the old vehicles and answered every question he got about them.

In the spring of the ninth year of their friendship, after attending one of Denny's lacrosse games, George asked Jack and Elizabeth, "Do you have time to take me to Northland Bank? It'll take an hour. Could you go to the mall or something?"

"Of course, George." Jack said, subtly pleased he was re-entering the world.

When they picked him up, he handed Elizabeth an envelope, "Please read this together when you get home."

"What is it, George?"

"No big deal. Just some things I'd like you to know."

After dinner, the boys busy outside, Jack and Elizabeth opened the envelope to find a letter and a key.

> Dear Elizabeth and Jack,
>
> If you will, please be co-executors of my will. The key is for a Northland Bank safety deposit box and either of you may open the box when the will is activated. Keep the key in a safe place.
>
> Should anything happen to me: lock down the house and barn (the autos are valuable and included in my assets) and call Sidney Carpenter at Northland Bank (422-1356). He has my will and all the details about my assets, and will help you. He is honest and fair.
>
> Your friendship means everything to me,
> George

When Scott was a senior in high school, George Koerner went to be with his Nicole. Elizabeth found him lying on his bed, holding Nicole's photograph on his chest. She made arrangements for his burial and sang the High Mass at Saint Mary's. Only Father O'Brien and the Brownell family were there. No relatives could be found.

As a freshman at Colgate, Scott struggled academically at first but survived, bolstered by new friends and inherited diligence.

During his sophomore year, his closest male friends were former hockey players. Gordy Donahue was their point man. "We can rent the ice for an hour at six a.m. on Saturdays for ten dollars, if you guys kick in a buck apiece." Scott had only frozen-pond hockey experience, but joined them, mostly for the exercise and friendship. Playing five on five for about six weeks, they were convinced they were pretty good, but were getting a bored.

Gordy, sensing the mood, told them, "I've set up a game for us with a real team. Saturday morning at 6:30. Don't be late."

"Who we playin'?" Howie asked.

"You'll see. Be there."

Gordy was a thick-chested, former Canadian junior hockey player, addicted to practical jokes. Some healthy skepticism swirled in the group about the upcoming game. They wondered if he'd have them playing against a team of chimpanzees or something.

With a pudgy face, constantly on the verge of laughter and a visible beard even after a shave, Gordy was the best skater in the group, by far. He'd given up on pro hockey, not because of poor skills, but because he was just too short and constantly got pummeled by six foot four guys. Lost teeth, a broken nose, a fractured collarbone, and a concussion changed his goal from hockey to an education in marketing.

Tiny was puzzled. "We don't have a goalie."

"You're it," said Gordy. "Borrow a mask and some pads from Jake, the varsity manager. I already talked to him. He doesn't have pads for the rest of us though."

Tiny was their best choice for goalie. His barrel shape almost filled the net. His major problem was he couldn't stand up on skates and move his arms at the same time. If he moved his arms to stop the puck, he fell down.

Gordy instructed him, "Stand still and let the other team try to hit the small slits on either side of you or between your legs. I got Mongo to play, so we'll have eleven guys. It'll be a short game: two ten-minute periods."

It was even shorter for Scott. He was at the blue line near the boards in the first period, awaiting a pass from Hairy Holmes (famous for his giant moustache), when an opposing skater—at full speed—knocked him into the boards from behind, twisting his right leg. Falling back, his head hit the ice with a thud, creating an explosion of fireworks in the darkness before his eyes.

Unsure if the pain radiating from his leg to his head or the pain from his head radiating everywhere else took precedence, Scott lay there wondering, *Should I get up? Can I get up?* Gordy came over and straightened his twisted leg. There were no referees and the game only stopped long enough for Scott to drag himself off the ice.

After the game, Gordy and Howie took him to the university infirmary where he reported 'a fall on the ice.' Howie told him, "If you say you were boarded by a girl hockey player, you'll be campus wuss-of-the-year."

The game Gordy had arranged was with the fully padded and helmeted university women's varsity hockey team. Scott's fractured fibula required a cast. His throbbing and swollen skull was intact, except for a two-inch laceration.

The following Wednesday, Scott, with a cast and crutches, made his way slowly along the cafeteria lunch line at the student union. Pushing a tray in front of him, he reached the cashier, paid her, then stood puzzled about how to get the tray, the crutches, his legs, and the rest of himself to a table without an accident.

The cashier saw the dilemma and came around the counter. Her slim physique, long black hair, high cheekbones, intelligent green eyes, and friendly smile gave Scott's heart a twist. She picked up his tray, and pointing to a nearby empty table asked, "Will this be all right?"

He nodded. Checking her ID badge, Scott said, "Thank you, Sara." Adding, "Are you a student?"

"Yes, geology-engineering. I better get back," she replied, pointing at the students waiting to pay.

"Would you like to meet sometime to talk?"

"Sure. Before you leave, come up and I'll give you my number."

While Scott was eating, a group of eight girls sitting together across the room were intermittently gazing his way and laughing loudly. He ignored them, until one, a tall Neanderthal of a woman with trim hips, straight blond hair down to her broad shoulders, and a proportionately broad face, came over to his table. She stood looking down at him, her arms crossed on her ample chest.

He didn't recognize her, but knew immediately who she was when she spoke. "All you guys think you can play hockey, but you found out you can't the hard way, didn't you?" she goaded with a cocky smirk that spoiled what was an otherwise pretty face—for a giant.

"Are you the one who boarded me?" The helmets had prohibited facial recognition during the game. "What's your name?"

"Ellen. Yeah, I boarded you, and it was easy." As she said it, Gordy, Hairy, Shane, and Howie joined Scott at the table.

"You do know hip-checking a player without the puck isn't allowed, right?"

"So what?"

"If you do that in league play you're going to spend a lot of time in the penalty box, might even get ejected if you injure a player like you did me." As he spoke Scott handed her a fork.

"Who cares? What's with the fork?"

"If you impale my hand to the table with the fork you'll probably get a big laugh from your teammates," motioning with his head toward her friends across the room.

Ellen's face turned crimson, she threw the fork on the table, glared at him, and walked away. Scott's friends went into a fit of uncontrollable laughter, making everyone in the cafeteria look, and buzz, trying to find out what was going on.

When the laughter subsided, Scott turned to his teammates. "When I was a kid, I was taught to walk on the street side of a woman, take off my hat in an elevator if a woman entered, and open doors for them. My mother said nature made most men bigger and stronger than women—not smarter or more skilled—just bigger and stronger. She said men were made that way for a reason: to provide respect and protection for women and children. It's getting' harder and harder to remember that."

Scott ate hurriedly. "I'm going to be late for class. Crutches double my travel time, and I keep forgetting to adjust for it." Scott stood up. "See that pretty girl at the cash register? I'm going to get a date with her." The others watched in awe as Scott approached Sara, got a smile, a laugh, and a piece of paper with her phone number. Passing them on the way out he said, "I told you."

Gordy's chronic smile went limp. "A sympathy date. Why didn't I think of that?"

Sara and Scott met frequently to walk, talk, go to sports events, see concerts, and share their thoughts. Six weeks after meeting, Scott, without crutches but still in a walking cast, took Sara to a dance. When he arrived to pick her up, she was ready: black hair in a chignon, sparkling eyes, arched brows, subtle makeup, and a flowery dress with a matching belt, "for spring."

"You're gorgeous!" Then he saw she was wearing hiking boots, and he gave her a quizzical stare.

Sara saw the look. "I don't want my toes crunched by your hoof." Scott had to sit down. It was either that or fall down, he was laughing so hard.

They had a wonderful time, made many friends, and didn't miss a single dance. Instead of Scott taking Sara's hand to twirl her, she twirled him, pivoting him on the cast. They got laughs and the band even asked them to join the drummer for two numbers by stomping the beat on the floor.

Scott was on a scientific track in college, without a specific goal in mind. It just seemed the correct path. All through the first two years, in every course, a question was building in his mind, *How can this information help people?*

Summers he worked on the surveying team in his dad's engineering firm doing menial tasks like equipment transport, holding the rod, and recording data. His dad's firm concentrated on bridge building or bridge re-building. As he worked he was thinking, *These engineers really have to go for the facts, like the strength of materials, speed of vehicles on curves, how much weight a bridge will hold, and whether the towers can withstand a hurricane or high water. I wonder if their kind of analysis would work for people?*

That summer he struggled through two books: *Studying a Study and Testing a Test* by Richard K. Riegelman, and *Clinical Epidemiology* by David Sackett.

Before returning to Colgate for his junior year, he asked his dad, "Can your fact-finding statistics programs be applied to people?"

"That's over my head, Scott. Maybe, but I think you should talk to someone who teaches biostatistics." Jack was busting-his-buttons proud that Scott had learned the importance of having the facts before making decisions. He told Elizabeth about Scott's query, and she asked, "Do you suppose George was right? How could that be?"

"We just have to wait and see. He was a foxy old bird." Jack shrugged his shoulders and lifted both hands in the air palms up to signal 'who knows'.

Arriving home for Christmas vacation his junior year, Scott folded his mom in his arms, and suddenly realized, *The day she helped Mr. Koerner suture his leg I was proud of her. I was looking up at her. Now I'm looking down at her, and I'm still so proud of her.* The whole event came rushing back to him. *She's a teacher, not someone trained to do surgery, yet she helped him with his leg, and later pulled George from despair giving him some happiness before he died. She has a different skill; not everyone has it—one that's really special. Could I do that?*

Returning to Colgate after Christmas, he sought out an adviser and applied to take the Medical College Admission Test.

At spring break, Scott broached the subject with his mom, dad, Ben, and Denny. "I'd like to go to medical school after graduation, if I can get in, but I don't think I can make enough money doing construction in the summer for the tuition unless I get a scholarship."

"Wonderful!" Elizabeth said, and Jack nodded approval. "We have the money to help, don't worry."

"But I don't want to take away from what Ben and Denny need."

Jack turned to him. "You won't. We have a story to tell you. We've been waiting for the right time." He went into his office and returned with a bank box.

"Remember George Koerner?" Elizabeth was excited. Something she had held back a long time was about to be revealed.

"Sure. Who could forget him? He nearly cut off his own leg," Ben said.

Elizabeth emptied the box. "He left everything he owned to us."

Denny was puzzled. "But he didn't have anything, except chickens and some old cars."

Elizabeth couldn't wait to tell the story. "Oh, but he did. By the time he was thirty-two, George Koerner had become an assistant editor at the *New York Times*. One day, he interviewed a young Columbia graduate for a proofreading position. Her name was Nicole Gabriella Stratford. One year later, they were married. Two years later he was here, in his hometown, his life destroyed by the death of his wife Nicole and their daughter. You know the rest of story, except for his will.

"George had life insurance, owned his parent's home across the street, the old cars, some land in Florida, and oil stocks he purchased fifty years ago. He left everything to us so you boys could get educated, start a business, or whatever you wanted to do, provided your dad and I agreed with your choices. This is in the will, and you may read it yourself."

She passed the handwritten will to Ben. "Scott, you'll see in there he says, 'So Scott can go to medical school.' We didn't understand why he wrote that—but he did."

Jack added, "Ben and Scott, George Koerner has been paying your college tuition and there is no monetary reason you cannot go on to grad schools. You will need to work summers, and perhaps part-time jobs at school, for some of your room, board, and books. Denny, we have money for you go to college, too. The remainder of the money, after you graduate, goes into a scholarship fund for other students from your high school. Since we're contributing to the fund also, it's going to be called 'The Koerner-Brownell Scholarship Fund.'"

"I never thought—," Scott was looking at his mom, who, though silent, was smiling at him, eyes wide, brows up, anticipating his reaction. Scott could hear her saying—'Don't judge so quickly or you'll make big mistakes in life.'

Denny pointed at a loosely bound folder about four inches thick. "What's that pile of papers?"

Elizabeth picked up the bundle. "This is the manuscript of the book Nicole Stratford was writing when she met George. It was never published. I've started to read it, and it is very good. She titled it, *Life Begins With Love*. Dad and I are going talk to a publisher about it. If it is published, any money it produces will go into the scholarship fund, too."

All the way back to Colgate, Scott mulled over George Koerner's life and the news he'd just received. He wondered, *Why would he be a recluse for all those years? Being a hermit is just a step shy of suicide. Did he see something extraordinary in Nicole? Was he missing a love so grand, that the vacuum left by her death sucked every bit of joy and feeling from him? Maybe there was more to it; like she wanted to be a writer, had potential, and she was robbed of the opportunity by death.*

I don't think even Mom knows why George took such a nosedive after Nicole and the baby died. If it was all love, I hope I find someone to love that much. Sara may be the one. She has a great sense of humor, is easy to talk to, likes to do the same things I do and … I hope she feels the same about me.

Sara and Scott shared their free time all through their senior year in under-graduate college and on into the first year of medical school for Scott, and graduate school for Sara. They often spent weekends and holidays together, and the next two summers. They became experienced rock-climbers and mountain-bikers.

On a Sunday at Southwick's Beach in July of 2014 Scott asked Sara, "Do you have claustrophobia?"

"No."

"An engineer neighbor and long time friend of my family has invited me to go down in a lead and zinc mine where he works, and I can bring you."

"No kiddin'? I'd love to do that."

The following Friday, Scott introduced Sara to Hugh Collins at the St. Joe Mine in the foothills of the Adirondack Mountains. A tall, jovial man with a big smile, broad shoulders and strong arms; he was dressed in jeans, a plaid shirt, and a hard hat with a headlight.

Hugh, about eight years older than Scott, was a graduate of the same engineering department as Sara. "Pleasure to meet you, Ma'am. Scott tells me you're a geologist. That's good. I'm looking forward to hearing what you have to say about my rock pile." He laughed at his own joke. "Let's get you both outfitted. Glad to see you wore hiking boots. We don't have the linoleum down yet." This time Sara and Scott joined his chuckle.

Sara and Scott got a lesson in mine conditions and safety. They were fitted with hard hats with headlights and instructed about their small backpacks filled with survival gear. Hugh described the mine briefly. "We will be down 3,000 feet. The mine extends out under Sylvia Lake. The temperature is a steady 57 degrees, the yearly average for this area. Ask any questions you want."

They rode the elevator down with Hugh and a group of stoic miners, who gave them the semi-sardonic, visual pat-down applied to all interlopers. Stepping out of the clanking and groaning open-sided elevator at 3,000 feet, they entered a huge cavern filled with drilling machines and loaders being repaired. Tunnels extended off in multiple directions.

The lid flew off Sara's question box. "How do you get these machines down here? Why aren't there braces on the walls? How do you survey underground when you can't see ahead of you? Where is the air pumped in? How does the ore get to the surface? How do you follow a good ore vein?"

Hugh was grinning now. He answered each question, patiently pointing out details as they moved about, headlights reflecting off the walls.

Scott listened, absorbing the answers. He was ecstatic that Sara was showing so much enthusiasm. They spent the whole day learning about hard rock mining. On the way home, Sara thanked Scott and gave him a soul-stirring kiss unlike any that had preceded it.

Three weeks later, Scott took Sara to The Cornell Plantations. Since she worked outdoors as a geologist, he thought she would be interested in learning which poisonous and medicinal plants to avoid in the wild.

Reading about an Emergency Room patient gave Scott the idea for the trip. The patient was a nurse who arrived disoriented, with a temperature of 104 degrees, slow heart rate, and low blood pressure. According to a friend, she had been fine the day before.

She recovered quickly after intravenous fluids. Nothing else was needed after it was discovered she was an avid gardener and growing a genus Datura plant called Angel's Trumpet. The large white flowers, spikey seed pods and leaves contain scopolamine, and she had been rubbing against it.

Scott started to explain to Sara why he brought her to Cornell. "You may have contact with some of these dangerous plants outdoors in your work. This is Angel's Trumpet. Pretty, but don't touch it. It's poisonous. That tall dark-blue flower is Monk's Hood. It contains aconitine, the stuff our ancestors used to make poison arrows. The juice can paralyze a person. Over there is milkweed. The monarch butterflies love it. The milky sap doesn't bother them, but predators leave the monarchs alone because they have the poison on-board."

Yawning, Sara's eyes were barely open. Scott paused, *Let's see if she is listening at all.* He pointed. "If you eat that little yellow flower, your right leg will twist a 180 degrees. Then, when you take a step forward with your left foot, the right one takes one back, and you go nowhere."

Sara murmured, "That's nice. Let's go to the beach."

"I've never seen you so distracted and tired."

"Out late last night. Your friend, Hugh Collins, took me to dinner again."

Her statement took away Scott's breath. "…He's married! Again! Again?"

"Not anymore. He told me his divorce came through last week."

On the way to Southwick's Beach Scott asked, "How long have we known each other?"

"Nearly three years. Why?"

Scott didn't answer and was quiet for a long time. "What is your opinion of marriage? Just curious."

"Marriage? Haven't thought about it much. Haven't been to Australia yet."

"What's Australia got to do with marriage?"

"I'm going to do my Ph.D. thesis on some peculiar rock formations in the Lake Gordon area of Tasmania. Probably be there a year."

"When were you going to tell me?"

"I just did. Where are we going? This is the way to my house, not the beach. Are you mad I went out with Hugh?"

"Let me take a wild guess. You did more than go out with Hugh. And Hugh is going to Australia, maybe to avoid alimony and child support. Right? I know him better than you do. I can't believe he'd do this. I can't believe you'd do this. Again? I thought we were—"

Sara didn't respond.

Scott was silent until they reached Sara's residence. "I'm not angry—just feeling stupid and disappointed."

He got out of the car and went around to open the passenger door for her. "I wanted to be the man you could love enough to marry." Scott's feelings for Sara were honest and strong, and he didn't want to hurt her. He spoke sincerely and softly. "I hope you have a happy life. Goodbye, Sara."

She looked at him, started to speak but stopped, turned, and walked away.

Scott drove home slowly. His sad, pale, stunned face alarmed Elizabeth. She quickly produced a chocolate milkshake, his favorite. "What is it Scott?"

"Sara dumped me. She's going to Australia with Hugh Collins."

"He's married!"

"He told her he got a divorce." Elizabeth was speechless. Sara had been at their house many times, and she was fond of her.

Scott looked at his mom. "Am I boring? Does goin' to med school make me a dork?"

"Sit down, Scott." He was pacing around and around the room. "You are *not* boring or a dork."

"But you're my mother; you're supposed to say that."

"Not true."

"Am I just in med school because George Koerner thought I should be?"

"George never thought that. He wasn't clairvoyant."

"What?"

"He just thought you matched a character in Nicole's book who became a doctor. The way that manuscript was worn, George must have read it a thousand times or more. He probably had it memorized."

"I'm a character in a book?"

"No, silly. You had the qualities Nicole wrote about. Her father was a physician. She patterned the character after him. He was curious and asked questions about everything. What he didn't know, he tried to find out, especially about people, their illnesses and how to prevent or cure them. He wanted to know the facts, the truth. Now, who does that sound like?"

Scott was staring at her unable to speak.

"Dr. Stratford took great joy in curing a patient's disease or saving a life. He understood their suffering and was compassionate and tenacious when looking for ways to help them."

Elizabeth paused, smiling because of something she remembered. "George loved answering your questions. I can still see you sitting in that old Stanley Steamer, just your head visible above the door, asking him questions about what made it go. You had a smile of pure pleasure as you rode along, and so did George, probably for the first time since Nicole's death. You have every characteristic Nicole described to make a great physician. George saw that. Your dad is proud of you, too. He thinks you ask better questions than some of his engineers."

"You think I have those qualities?"

"I know you do. I've lived with you your whole life." She handed Scott a new copy of Nicole's book. "Read what she wrote and you'll understand. There's something else you need to know. The book says it, too, but it's better I tell you from my own experience. It's about life. I probably should've told you this sooner. Please forgive me."

"Of course. What is it?"

"If a man or woman loves their work, it's sometimes difficult for a person to marry them and accept being the second love in their life. But remember, love of a job and love of a person are two distinct things, and they can mingle a little, but not much. When you're with the person you love, the conversation has to be about topics you share. And listening will often be more valuable than talking, especially when you want to know that person.

"I know you mean well, but I wonder sometimes if you spout information that doesn't interest Sara because of your enthusiasm or you're trying to convince her you're smart. If I were her, I'd much rather talk with you as a companion, a person in whom I could confide and explore plans, ideas, or problems. Being such a confidant is never boring and is likely to make Sara your best friend, and maybe more."

"I- I thought Sara and I had a start a relationship like that. But, I guess not. It might be my fault she's leaving."

"Again, don't be too quick to judge. Things down-under, and I don't mean Australia, may not be as great as she thinks. If she returns, and you can set aside the hurt and forgive her, perhaps the two of you can make it work."

Scott gave his mom a kiss on each cheek and a hug. "I gotta go!"

"I made some cookies for you to take with you." She handed him a bag. "Your dad's going to be sorry he missed seeing you. Call him tonight."

He waved and called over his shoulder as he ran to his car. "Okay. Thanks. You're the best. I love you."

Before he could start the car his phone rang.

"Sara?" She was crying. "Sara, please don't go. It's my fault all this happened. I'll be there in twenty minutes."

"Scott, I made a big mistake. Please, forgive me."

"Sara, I'll be there shortly. We have to talk. Wait for me!" She hung up.

When Scott arrived at Sara's house, both her parents answered the door. They looked worried. "Mr. and Mrs. Darcy, is Sara all right?"

Mrs. Darcy took Scott's right arm with both hands and pushed him toward the stairs. "She's locked in her room, Scott. She won't come out. Please see if she'll talk to you."

Scott bounded up the stairs and knocked on Sara's door, yelling her name. The door flew open and Sara threw herself at him. She was crying and put both arms around his neck.

"Are you all right?"

"No. Let's get out of here." Sara washed her face, dried her eyes and they went down the stairs. Both parents hugged Sara.

"Mom and Dad, Scott and I are going camping for a few days. I'll call you."

Scott was surprised by this announcement, but didn't object. *We need to talk and what could be better than a quiet spot in the woods. Why does she have her camping gear and three suitcases packed?* He loaded everything into his car. As they drove off, waving to Mr. and Mrs. Darcy Scott thought, *They seem relieved by Sara's quick recovery.*

Sara turned to him. "Let's go to Lake Placid."

"… Okay." *I think she's really mixed up. I don't think she even knows where Lake Placid is.* "It'll take two hours to get there. Are you all right?"

"Never better. I booked us a room at the Crowne Plaza."

"What?"

"Stop. Pull over." He did. To say he was surprised would be the understatement of the year; but what followed couldn't even come close to that. "Do you want to marry me?"

"Yes. Absolutely. I love you. I have for a long time, but wasn't sure how you felt." She gave him a kiss that almost set his pants on fire.

Then it hit him. "You set this whole thing up. Didn't you?" Sara had an impish smile. He'd seen that smile many times before, but never so saturated in happiness. "Were your parents in on this? My mother? You'd better call Hugh Collins' wife to tell her—" Sara's smile became a laugh. "They were in on it, too? Did you guys take an acting class?"

"When I told you about the 'affair' with Hugh, I knew you loved me. You didn't get angry. You couldn't hurt me; even verbally, or even shout at me. Your face told me you were devastated, but you wanted me to be happy. I was a little worried you might punch Hugh in the face, so Helen kept him out of sight. Your mom gave me the work-love-person-love talk while I told her my plan and we packed your clothes. You didn't stand a chance, young man. Drive on. The wedding is five days from tomorrow at the Crowne. We have to get ready. Everybody will be there."

Sara's eyes were teasing. "…That little yellow flower would make my right leg twist 180 degrees? If I took a step with my left foot, the right would go the other way and I wouldn't move? That's ridiculous!"

"You heard that?"

"Are you kiddin'? To keep from laughing, and blowing my whole plan, I had to hold my breath so long I thought I'd faint."

"You are a devious woman, Sara Lyn Darcy. Every day with you is a new experience and I don't want to miss a single episode."

It was a little while before Scott could drive. His arms and lips were busy telling Sara how he felt about her.

Bandit

New snow had been falling day and night for a week and the village of Ansted was buried in white frosting. Eight miles from the Saint Lawrence River and the Canadian border, Ansted was home to about a thousand souls. Houses and maple trees lined the streets. Small businesses, a fire station, a library, two schools, four churches, and a food processing plant completed the community at the crossing of two major roads and a north-south railroad line that split the village in half.

Swept by the wind, huge drifts formed in the hedgerows and across highways. Plow drivers struggled to push the snow off the roads, even making double passes with the plow wings high to knock the tops off the roadside banks to make room for more snow. Temperatures hovered at zero, dropping way below at night: minus fifty degrees at times.

The quantity of snow and temperature were not the biggest problem: it was the poor visibility. Anyone duty-bound to be out took risks walking or driving. The sidewalks were buried; walking in the road was the only choice. The flashing lights of snowplows or headlights of vehicles often burst out of a white haze in an instant. Snow in the air dampened sound and, combined with poor visibility, doubled the danger. Even on bright sunny days, wind sweeping across open fields drove the snow in a dizzying frenzy over the high banks along the roads as if hell-bent on filling in the snow-tunnels made by the plows.

On the third Tuesday in January 2004, the snowfall stopped temporarily, but not the cold. Without snow in the air to muffle the sound, the shrieking whistle of the southbound train was louder than ever. It was behind schedule and the engineer was trying to make up time. The thermometer on the railroad station wall read minus forty degrees. Flashing red lights and clanging bells at the crossing signaled the train's approach, adding to the cacophony from the rising pitch of the approaching whistle, the squealing brakes, the rattling metal cars, and the deep rumble of the diesel engines.

Thirteen-year-old Ryan Brady could've beaten the train to the crossing, but didn't try. He liked to watch the huge black engine as it passed, towering over him belching smoke, and the giant wheels grinding 'round and 'round. The clouds of gray smoke rose and swelled like gigantic balloons filling the air with the smell of hot oil.

The whistle and other sounds bounced back and forth off the walls of the station building and nearby houses, and Ryan covered his ears. He didn't understand why the engineer blew the whistle when the locomotive was already in the crossing. *What good could that do, except wish somebody clobbered by the train a nice trip to heaven?*

Five days a week, the three Brady children and others walked a mile to and from school over the crossing. Each weekday afternoon, Ryan made two extra crossings. Depositing his books at home, he would slurp down a glass of milk and fold a slice of bread around a large gob of peanut butter. Grabbing a canvas newspaper bag, he would head back uptown to start his paper delivery route, eating the bread as he went.

The sixth day, Saturday, he only made the paper route trips. This day, waiting for the train to move on, he was on his way to the post office. The bundled *Times* was fired off a moving delivery truck there about four o'clock: usually into a snow bank.

Crunching under his feet, the snow was somewhat musical and he could almost tell how cold it was by the sound. Ten, twenty, or more degrees below zero all had their own notes and let him know his feet were still there, even when he couldn't feel them.

The train stayed only long enough at the little station for the stationmaster to throw on a few boxes, a mailbag or two, and get two or three people aboard. In five minutes, the engineer, trying to break inertia too fast, made a frantic racket spinning the wheels on the slippery steel. Soon the last car of the train was getting smaller and smaller as it rolled down the converging rails, still glistening in the feeble afternoon sun. The crossing bell stopped clanging, the red lights quit, and the barriers wobbled upright like stiff, wooden zebra tails.

Crossing over, Ryan was between the rails watching the train shrink into the distance when he noticed a dog in a corner of the station platform. White, with irregular coal-black patches here and there, the dog stood out against the gray-green walls. He'd never seen this dog before and he'd been growled at or chased by every one in town. He decided the stationmaster must have a new dog and he went on his way.

Ryan was the middle in age of the three Gaillard-Brady children. He lived on Belmont Street with his mom; brother, Pete; and sister, Callie. He was average height for his age, with blonde, curly hair leaning toward brown, and blue eyes that would start to smile before his lips. His daily contact made him friends with nearly everyone in town. Strength from carrying a full bag of papers almost every day gave him an advantage; he was a pretty good in-fielder on the high school baseball team.

Delivering one hundred-twenty papers, six nights a week went fast in summer when he could ride his bike. Winter was tougher. Walking in the snow, cold, and early winter darkness was a pain—literally. Often he curled up his hands in his homemade mittens and stomped his feet to get the freezing ache from fingers and toes.

Sometimes, passing Harold's restaurant where his mother worked, he would stop briefly to say hello and warm up. It took him about an hour and a half to deliver on Main, Church, Lambert, and Seneca before going back across the railroad for another half hour to do Factory, Walton, and finish up on his own street, Belmont.

Crossing back over the rails to Factory Street that Tuesday, he saw the lights were out at the station. The stationmaster had gone home, but the black and white dog was still sitting in the same place.

Ryan went over and let her sniff the back of his hand. She wagged her tail. Despite her long hair, she was cold and shivering. He thought, *She looks like a Newfoundland. Her nose is medium-length, broad, and her mouth has generous jowls like a Newfoundland, but she's small. Maybe she's young. Her fur's clean and she looks healthy.* He held her in his arms awhile and the shivering decreased.

With only twenty more stops to go, he put her in the canvas bag with the remaining papers. Putting the broad strap over his head to his opposite shoulder, he lifted her, supporting the bag from the bottom with his left hand. The extra weight made him sink deeper in the snow banks to reach front porches and slowed his pace, but she stayed quietly in the bag. *She likes my body heat,* he decided.

At home, he called out, "Look what I found!" and put his canvas paper bag on the floor so the dog could get out. He told his mom, brother, and sister how he found her. "I think she's a young Newfoundland."

His mom petted the dog gently. "I think you're right, Ryan. She looks like Newfoundland, but she must be a crossbreed. Isn't she beautiful?"

The dog was docile and went to each person, obviously glad to be out of the cold and with people. She ate the food and water provided rapidly. It was clear she'd been suffering. The next day on his paper route, Ryan asked people in town, including the stationmaster, if anyone was missing a dog. No one had even seen her before. He wrote a description of her and where she was found and put it up in the post office, and he watched for "lost dog" ads in the paper.

Daphne, Ryan's mom, saw the happiness the dog brought her children. "She can stay as long she wants, and forever, if no one claims her."

No claim was made. She was a keeper: and what a keeper she was. She became a cherished family member: especially for Ryan. They had an unbreakable bond. Admitting to his teasing siblings he was a creative dunce, Ryan named her Bandit because one of her black spots circled one eye, half her face, and one ear like an askew mask.

Ryan didn't care what breed she was; she was gentle, playful, smart, and rarely barked: unless he was slow throwing a ball for her to retrieve. She would follow him anywhere.

Every night when he came home from school, Bandit would be hunkered-down trying to hide behind a fence post at the corner of their lawn. As soon as Ryan came past the post, she would jump out at him and they would roll around in the grass, leaves, or snow like they'd just met for the first time. He never tired of it, nor did she. She knew the exact time to be there, too. *How does she know what time I'll come?* he wondered.

Ryan didn't let Bandit go with him on his paper route. He was concerned a car might hit her. But hiking down to the Indian River to fish or going up the hill to ride down on the toboggan, she would run in circles around them, barking, hurrying them on. At the swimming hole on West Creek, it was a different story. She had to be urged to jump in, even on white-hot days, probably because she knew Ryan had soap and would give her a bath.

By the spring of 2007, big changes had occurred in the county. A large military base was under construction and the surrounding community was in a growth phase: new housing, new schools, new stores, and new service centers. The railroad no longer carried passengers. Passenger service profits had been gobbled up by buses and motor vehicles on the new four lane highway running north from New York City to the bridge crossing the St. Lawrence River to Canada. Harold's Restaurant, near the highway, was busier than ever.

Daphne, the chef, kept her usual hours of 9 a.m. to 3 p.m., despite the increased workload. She hired three part-time sous chefs, all mothers in the community. She prepared the lunch and evening menus and the sous chefs prepared breakfast. They also served the evening meals as she directed. Being home when her children returned from school was important to her and, by this arrangement with Harold's restaurant, she was able to make some of their ball games and other events.

Daphne Gaillard-Brady, mother of Peter, Ryan, and Callie Gaillard-Brady, had divorced Brady after she and the children were abandoned. She preferred to use Daphne Gaillard as her business name.

Neatly dressed in a doubled-breasted chef's white coat and hat, she was trim and tall, a feature accentuated by the hat. At thirty seven, with an easy smile and truth-seeking, no-nonsense blue eyes in a face that made people look at her twice, Daphne didn't need to ask for attention when she spoke; she already had it just by being there. Her light-brown hair was pageboy short and peeked out from under the hat.

On April 3, 2007, a Wednesday, John Henry Andrews stopped for lunch at Harold's. He was surprised by the quality of service and the food. In fact, the Philly Cheese-steak sandwich was the best he ever had, including ones in Philadelphia. He asked Betty, the waitress, to tell that to the chef.

Two weeks later, he was back. He ordered a Julienne salad, and was surprised once more by the presentation, freshness, and flavors. Again he asked

Betty to tell the chef how much he enjoyed the salad. Betty mused, *Maybe he'll ask her out. He sure is good-lookin'.*

While Betty cleared John's table, she said, "You should tell her yourself. I'll send her out," and she went to the kitchen. Winking at Lois, another waitresses, she touched Daphne's arm. "That tall, good-looking guy is here again. Now he likes your Julienne. He wants to talk to you."

"Really?"

"Really. Go talk to him."

Daphne looked in a mirror, took a smudge of flour off her face, and straightened her cap. As she approached the table, John stood up, all six feet four inches of him, and extended his hand. Despite her chef's hat, he was still taller. "John Andrews. I just wanted to tell you the food you prepare is excellent."

His grip was strong, his compliment and expression sincere, and his opinion had the ring of experience. Wearing a gray Armani suit and an expensive shirt, collar open, he was not the typical lunch customer at Harold's. "Daphne Gaillard. Thank you. Are you a chef?"

"No, but I'm on the road much of the time and eat in many restaurants. I'm kind of a hotel troubleshooter. I pass through here often on my way to Montreal."

"It was kind of you to stop here. I hope you'll come again." Daphne didn't see a wedding ring or a tan line to suggest one recently removed.

"May I ask where you learned your cooking skills?"

"That's a long story. When you come again maybe there'll be more time to talk," and she stood to leave. She was surprised that he stood too. *I like his face. He looks steadily into my eyes and he's a good-looking guy, just as Betty described.* John's chin made a strong curve below his mouth. His narrow, straight nose didn't dominate his face, and his green eyes were inquisitive and searching. Carefully trimmed dark-brown hair, lightly tanned skin, a friendly smile, and the broad shoulders of an athlete didn't escape Daphne's notice.

"I have more time a little later in the day, when the noon push starts to wane, say 2:30."

"I'll come at that hour next time, Chef Gaillard." He gave Daphne's hand a quick shake and waved to Betty.

Two weeks later, at 2:30 on a Tuesday afternoon, John finished his lunch and was waiting for Daphne to make an appearance. She knew he was there; Betty told her.

He stood as she approached and she thought, *His mother taught him manners.* "Hi. Sorry to keep you. Busy day." She was carrying four large boxes and set them on the table, with John's help. "You wanted to know how I learned to cook." She was peering around the boxes.

"Right." He smiled at her forthright manner.

"My father started this restaurant, and my brother Mike and I worked here with him and my mom as soon as we could walk. Actually, it was probably cheaper than a babysitter. We even did our homework here. After high school, I went to Pace in Manhattan, took general courses and then slid into the Culinary Institute. I went to the Paris Culinary School as an exchange student for a year, but had to come home. My dad was ill, and my brother and I both came home to help. Our parents are deceased now. Mike runs the bar and I run the food service."

"Is Harold your husband?"

"No." Daphne made a faint smile. "Do you want to continue this conversation on the move? Pete has a lacrosse game at three, and I'd like to be there."

"Sure. Should I put the boxes in your car? I'll need to follow you. I don't know where the school is. Is Pete your son?" He said, as he noticed she wasn't wearing a wedding ring.

"Yes, Pete is my oldest. I don't drive to work. It's only a half-mile walk home." John thought, *There's no laziness in this woman. She carries these boxes half a mile.*

"I'll put them in my car and give you and your son a ride home after the game."

On the way, Daphne continued. "Harold's and I have an agreement. They buy the produce needed for the restaurant from me at the going market price. My children and I, with the help of a local farmer, grow most of the vegetables needed. The greens for the salad you had came from our garden. The other part of the agreement is in those boxes. I cook a little more than the restaurant needs daily, and take it home for us, so I don't have to cook twice."

"That's smart!" His compliment created a subtle Daphne smile.

As they watched Pete's lacrosse game, Daphne heard John's insights on the action. "Did you play lacrosse?"

"Yep, Cornell. Still play some. Many of my co-workers at Templeton Hotel Group are former lacrosse players. We have scrimmage games nearly every week."

After the game, Pete came over to them. Daphne introduced him. "Pete, meet Mr. John Andrews."

"Mr. Andrews, this my son, Pete Brady."

"Please, call me John. Pleasure to meet you. Enjoyed your game."

"Hi. How do you know my mom?"

"We met at the restaurant, so I gave her a ride here. She has many boxes to bring home. I can give you a ride, too."

"Pete, John played lacrosse at Cornell." Pete looked puzzled, then suddenly smiled.

"I know who you are. You were Most Valuable Player in the Atlantic Coast Conference. I saw your picture and jersey last summer in the gym at Cornell."

"Well, it was either wash it or pin it up. They took the easy way out."

Pete laughed.

Callie arrived from school as they were talking. At age nine, she resembled her mom in many ways. She was taller than the other girls with her; her hair was more blonde and curlier than her mom's. John thought, *She has her mother's engaging smile.*

Daphne worried about Callie. She had taken the absence of her father harder than the boys. They seemed able to use sports to fill that gap in their lives.

Daphne presented her daughter. "Callie, this is Mr. John Andrews."

Callie looked up briefly at the face of this man who towered over her, stood back, and softly, without confidence said, "Hi," and gave him a quick wave.

John surprised Daphne, Pete, and Callie by dropping to a knee in the dust. He looked into Callie's eyes, and said, "Hi." He took her hand in his huge one and shook it gently. Callie blushed, making Daphne smile.

Arriving at the house, Pete and John carried the boxes from the car. Daphne's garden was partially visible near the house and John was asking her questions about it. Inside the house, Bandit was barking non-stop. Daphne, Pete, and Callie looked at each other in surprise. She often barked briefly when she recognized their voices, but only once or twice.

As soon as Daphne opened the door, Bandit raced directly to John, circled his feet twice, then sat in front of him wagging her tail. Daphne was startled, *Bandit recognizes him. I'm sure of it. And from the look on his face, he knows her.* John put down the boxes he was carrying and went on his knees to pet her gently. Callie told her mom later, "He had tears in his eyes."

Daphne was mystified. *How is that possible?* Suddenly, Bandit's ears went up, and she bolted away, to crouch down near the corner post on the lawn. Daphne motioned for John to watch Bandit. "Wait till you see this."

Ryan reached the corner, leaned his bike against the post, and Bandit jumped on him. They both went down on the grass wrestling each other, Ryan laughing and the dog making fake growls. Daphne explained, "They've done that, rain or shine, at the same time every day for two years." John was mesmerized.

Daphne told herself, *There's some kind of connection between Bandit and this man. What is it?* She made a quick decision. "You better stay for dinner, Mr. Andrews."

"Please, just call me John. Can I call you Daphne?"

"Sure. Ryan, meet John Andrews."

Ryan grasped John's hand, "Hi." What John felt was a tough hand, strong and accustomed to hard work. *How could this be at his age?*

John's eyes met Ryan's. "I think I saw you at the restaurant one day."

"Yeah, I stop there sometimes to see Mom and Uncle Mike, especially if it's freezin' outside and I need a shot of Jack Daniels." He laughed when his mom gave him her raised-eyebrows-sans-smile glower, meaning, "You're in trouble, Ryan Patrick Brady."

Daphne took food from the boxes and put some in the oven to warm and put others in the freezer. "Okay, everyone. Pitch in. Set a place for John. Give him the red plate."

"Are you sure? I don't want to impose," John stuttered.

Daphne replied, "The plates are up there." She pointed to a cupboard. "You can reach them best. Let's go, people."

Getting the plates, John asked Ryan softly, "Is she always like this?"

"Only around food." He grinned.

Not only was the meal delicious, the interaction between the children and their mother fascinated John. Daphne pointed toward John's plate. "Callie, tell John about the red plate and what it means."

"Whenever one of us does something special, like have a birthday or graduation, we get the red plate. See how it says on it, 'You are Special Today?' You get it because you're our guest."

"Thank you!" He had a flashback to times with his parents. Sitting down for a meal with a family had been a rarity for him since starting the troubleshooting job for Templeton. *I'm missing something important in life and only I can fix it.*

Daphne broke into his daydream by asking, "Bandit seems to know you. Why?"

John took a deep breath; it was a tender subject. He was uneasy about how the story would be received. "The winter in 2004 was really tough. Remember?" Heads nodded, especially Ryan's. "A colleague from Templeton Hotels and I had to go to Montreal. I brought my dog, BW, because we'd be there a week and I didn't want to put her in a kennel. Her name, BW, means black and white. ... I know, it's lame. When we reached Syracuse, the storm was in full swing and driving was treacherous. We decided to take the train.

"While we were in Montreal, my office called and asked me to fly to San Francisco right away. Elaine Mitchell, my colleague, took the train back to Syracuse. The train stopped at many small towns. At one, Elaine took BW out for a short walk. BW bolted after a squirrel or something, leaving her broken collar attached to the leash. BW ignored Elaine's calls to return.

"The stationmaster couldn't delay the train, and it left with Elaine on board, but not BW. My friend was distraught about leaving her behind. She didn't know what to do, didn't recall the name of the town, and she wasn't dressed for the cold. I'm certain BW is the dog you call Bandit. I'm very grateful you saved her and took care of her."

"Ryan saved her." Daphne turned to Ryan, her mother's pride obvious. "Tell John about that night." Ryan described the cold and bringing the dog home in his newspaper bag.

"You're a special man, Ryan Brady, and I'm honored to know you." Ryan blushed. Bandit was lying on the floor at his feet.

Callie spoke so softly John had to lean forward to hear her, "Are you going to take her away when you leave?" Silence filled the room. Even breathing seemed to stop. Daphne pulled in a breath, *Please, God, don't put another loss in her life.*

John hadn't even considered it. BW and this family fit each other. "No, she belongs with you. Will it be all right if I visit her?"

Callie got out of her chair, ran around the table, grasped John's sleeve, and pulled him down to kiss his cheek.

"Wow! I have to come back often. I won't wash that cheek for a week, maybe never." Callie laughed. Daphne studied John's face. *I just had a glimpse of a real and caring man. Somehow he knows Callie is sad, not shy, and wants her, and all of us, to be happy.*

"Thanks for inviting me to dinner. You're very gracious. I am envious of BW, uh … Bandit."

Daphne walked with John to his car. "Do you have a family, John?"

"No. Not married. Only child. Parents are deceased. I was engaged once to Elaine, the lady I mentioned earlier. It didn't take. How about you?"

"Divorced."

"I'm traveling most of the time. From here, I'm going to Houston, Miami, and Atlanta. Hope to be back this way in three weeks. Would it be all right if I stopped to see you?"

"Sure. Here's my cell phone number and email address." She handed him a card.

"Callie really misses a dad, doesn't she?"

"Yes. How did you realize that?"

"I don't know. I just felt it."

"She never really knew her father. He left soon after she was born."

"Who is Harold?" He was petting Bandit as he spoke.

"That was my dad's name. When you come back, I'll introduce you to my brother, Mike. You'll like him."

"If he is like you, I'm certain of it." He shook her hand. "Bye."

"Bye."

When Daphne returned to the house Callie asked, "What did John mean, he was envious of Bandit?"

"I think he likes being with us, just like Bandit does."

Three weeks later, John appeared at Ryan's baseball game. Daphne and Callie were there. "Sorry, I'm late. Hi, Callie! I just saw a pretty young woman driving a car as I came into town. Was that you?"

"I can't drive yet. I'm nine." The ruse made her smile.

"Oh."

"How was your trip?" Daphne was surprised, not by the question, but that Callie asked it.

"Hot and muggy. What's the score?"

"Four to three. We're ahead."

"How's Ryan doin', Daphne?"

"Pretty well. No errors. Strong throwing arm. No hits though."

"Wonder if I could help him. I used to be a pretty good hitter. I played baseball before deciding lacrosse was my game."

"Why don't you ask him later?"

"Okay. Is Pete a junior or senior?"

"Junior. Why?"

"Coach Clark, my friend at Cornell, wants to follow his lacrosse stats. May want to offer him a scholarship someday. You think Pete would be interested? Where is he?"

"He's at practice now. You mean play college lacrosse? Of course he'll be interested."

"Better not mention a scholarship because the number is limited and the competition is fierce. I'll just tell him Coach Clark knows his coach here and is going to follow his progress."

"Good idea."

Daphne turned to Callie. "Don't say anything about a scholarship to Pete, please." Callie nodded, she understood.

John handed Callie a small package.

"What's this?"

"You'll only know if you open it."

Her eyes sparkled and a delighted smile took over her face, unlike any Daphne had seen from her in a long time. She lifted a gold charm bracelet from the box. It held two charms: one engraved with her name, another with Bandit's face. She looked up at John, grabbed his sleeve, and pulled him down to kiss his cheek.

"Now I have two cheeks I can't wash." Callie laughed, and John continued. "Every time you get the red plate, you get a new charm for the bracelet to show what you did."

Daphne's gaze was locked on John. *This guy's somethin' else.*

Ryan, his game over, walked up, breaking into her thoughts.

John turned toward Ryan. "I was late and only saw two innings, but you're a good in-fielder. I'm certain I would've caught a couple of those hot grounders in the mouth."

Ryan grinned. "Thanks, John. No hits though."

"Are there any batting cages around here? We could practice some. I used to play baseball. Maybe I can help. Can you read the blackboard okay in school?"

"Yeah. There's a cage at the golf driving range. I can see the blackboard; I'm not nearsighted."

They were walking toward John's car. "Why do you have a bike rack on the back?" Ryan asked.

"I bought this mountain bike awhile back, but I never use it. I thought you could. It has a gearshift, so it is easier going up hills and stuff. I really don't know how the shift works. You can figure it out better than me. Could we put a basket for papers on it, you think?" Ryan just looked at him, his mouth open.

Daphne prompted Ryan, "I think the stare and open mouth mean, 'Thank you, John.'"

"Man! That's a sweet set of wheels! Thank you, John," Ryan blurted.

"John, you're invited to dinner. Let's go, people." Daphne was smiling as she spoke.

"I was hoping you'd say that, otherwise I'd have to find another girl for these." He reached into his car and brought out a bouquet of yellow roses.

Daphne was speechless. *How did he know I like yellow roses? He must've asked Mike or Betty.*

"Thank you! They're perfect." She almost took a cue from Callie's gift-response, but held back.

Pete saw the rose presentation as he arrived, lacrosse stick over his shoulder. With a broad grin he shrugged his shoulders and looked at Daphne. "I didn't tell him."

They piled into John's car, boxes, lacrosse sticks, roses and all, laughing and teasing each other. John was thinking, *I have to get a life. I've been missing something really important.*

At the house, Bandit also got a gift: one dog treat, and to everyone's surprise, John unloaded a huge bag of dog food from the trunk of his car. It was the variety they fed Bandit. Daphne was astounded he'd noticed that subtlety and stared at him in disbelief. John made an I-can't-help-it face, raised his shoulders, and threw up his hands.

Daphne passed boxes to the boys. "Pete, put the food in these boxes in to warm. The others go in the freezer. John and I will pick some spinach in the garden for the salad." She picked up a colander in the kitchen and led John out the backdoor.

She showed him how to pick the spinach leaves without injuring the plant, so new ones would grow. "John, thank you for all the gifts. They're very nice, but please don't raise the kid's expectations. A chef in a small restaurant doesn't make enough money for three college tuitions or expensive gifts. One may go to college, but not all. Mike has kids, too, and I can't take money away from him, even though I know he would offer."

"Daphne, I did those things as much for me as for the children. I've been living a well-paid life for the last twenty years. I have many friends, but no family. It makes me feel terrific to see the sincere smiles and happiness in your eyes and the eyes of Callie, Ryan, and Pete. I'm sorry for causing you worry by doing these things without asking you first.

"All of you put your heart into saving a freezing dog, *my* dog, and I guess I was carried away with my thank you. I won't do it again without asking. I don't have your knowledge of responsible parenting. Will you forgive me?"

Daphne smiled. "You're forgiven. Let's feed those hungry kids."

Before he left that day, John asked Daphne, "Harold's is closed Mondays, right?"

"Yes."

"Would the children be able to manage alone if you and I went to dinner on Monday, three weeks from now?"

"You're asking me to dinner?"

"Yes."

"I'd like that."

"Good. I'll pick you up at four o'clock. There is something I want to show you in daylight on the way."

"What is it?"

"That's a secret."

Before leaving, John took Pete aside. "Your mom and I are going out to dinner in three weeks. Do me a favor. Don't say anything to her, but be sure she has her passport with her. Secret. Okay?"

Pete, nodded, and grinned; he liked secrets, but more than that, he was happy someone appreciated his mom as much as he did.

There were multiple telephone calls between Daphne and John in the next three weeks, but try as she might, she couldn't wrest the secret from him.

On Monday afternoon, John arrived on time and stuttered to Daphne, "You-you-you're stunning." She was wearing a subtle flower-patterned cocktail dress, a necklace and bracelet with the same pattern, and brown shoes to pick up the brown in the dress. John thought, *She's going turn every head in the place, male and female. The models we use for the Templeton literature aren't as pretty as she is.*

"Thanks. I like your tie and Cagney handkerchief. They blend with the blazer. Very GQ."

"Are the children going to be okay?"

"Pete's taken charge. I don't know what sparked that. Usually he hangs back when it comes to watching Callie and Ryan. Where are we going? This isn't the direction for any restaurant I know."

"We're going to the airport. We're having dinner in Montreal at the Frontenac, one of my company's hotels."

"Really?" *That's why Pete asked about my passport. He knew.* Daphne studied John's face. *I hope he doesn't have funny ideas.*

He anticipated her thoughts. "I'll have you home by eleven or eleven-thirty, don't worry. You're going to have the night out you deserve."

The flight followed the St. Lawrence River northeast. John had Daphne sit at a window and pointed out details to orient her. The lights on the bridge to Wellesley Island and Canada arched across the water and a large ship with green and red navigation lights was passing up-river through the narrows. "Watch the shore where the river narrows. Look for a large open area that extends right up to the water."

"I see it. It looks like a park. Rocky shoreline, but a small bay extends into the park."

"That's it. I want to take you there someday. We may build a hotel at that site. We're working on land purchases now. The engineers and architects are making plans. I have some plans, too. Also secret."

"Why is it a secret?"

"That's secret, too."

"You're teasing me, John Andrews."

"A little."

The Frontenac Hotel limousine was waiting for them when they arrived in Montreal. The driver lifted the brim of his hat in a motion of respect. "Good evening, Mr. Andrews. Nice to see you again."

"Thank you, Paul. Meet Ms. Gaillard."

"Pleasure, madam." Paul made a shallow bow toward Daphne, and held the door for them.

Daphne smiled. "Thank you."

It was nearly six o'clock as they approached the hotel. "Your company owns this hotel?"

"Yes, this is our only one in Montreal. We bought it five years ago. I was on my way here when I stopped at Harold's—my lucky day, as I call it now.

Daphne smiled. *I like that he knows the driver's name and the driver is respectful. Maybe I worry too much.*

The desk clerk greeted them. "Good evening, Mr. Andrews."

"Thank you, Renée. The same to you. Meet Ms. Gaillard." Renée made the same shallow bow as the driver. "We're not staying overnight. Paul will take us back to the airport around ten. Are they ready for us in the restaurant?"

"Yes, sir."

John took Daphne's arm. She was gazing about at the chandeliers, decorations, paintings, and expensive furniture in the large, impeccable lobby. *This is an elegant hotel.*

They entered the restaurant through a door off the hotel lobby. John passed by seated diners, receiving and acknowledging greetings in French from some customers, several waiters, waitresses, and busboys.

They marched right into the kitchen. The size, equipment, and number of people at work impressed Daphne. A large man, his back to them, was talking in French to a group of six people, all in kitchen garb. John, with Daphne on his arm, stopped just behind him and made a throat-clearing sound. The large man turned to them and his face, looking tan against his white chef's jacket and hat, burst into a smile as huge as his broad face could produce. "Daphne!"

"André! What are you doing here?" Daphne managed to say over his shoulder, as he embraced her, lifting her feet off the floor. They moved to a table in the restaurant. John sat quietly, reveling at their delighted faces and the repartee as they caught up on friends and classmates.

John ordered white wine, Daphne's choice, and Scotch for himself. André refused a drink. John assumed he was being cautious in front of him since he was his boss. While Daphne and André were talking about friends he didn't know and their year together in Paris, his mind wandered through past events. *Strange the way life tumbles. Lovers in France, separated by family illness, both divorced, working only a hundred fifty miles apart, and my lost dog gets them together.*

After an hour John was irritated. *This evening is a mess. Daphne's choices of veal francaise and other dishes are excellent, but André is in and out of the kitchen to talk to us and every time he appears Marji, the new black-haired sous chef, comes to the kitchen door to watch. I hope Daphne doesn't notice. If André was Daphne's former, passionate lover, he seems a little aloof. Maybe my hotel authority worries him. Every time Daphne and I start to talk about something he interrupts us.*

He decided to take Daphne's attention away from the unanticipated intrusions. He asked her to dance, and despite her claims of being rusty, she blended smoothly into the music. "I've been giving my boys some lessons," she explained.

"You are a marvelous dancer, and very beautiful, I must add." *She just glides and her subtle perfume is great. She laughs at the same things I do, and means it. She isn't phony or pompous. I could dance with her all night. Holding her makes me feel important. I'd like to leave with her right now. The hell with André. But, if she loves him, she'd never forgive me.*

While they danced, Daphne started to asked details about the hotel. He teased her about inability to put work aside. The paso doble music proved her rusty claim wrong. Daphne matched his dancing skills and took it up a notch. Forgetting André, they laughed and danced and laughed some more.

"Thank you, John. Not just for the compliment, but the dinner, the dancing, and the adults-only time."

"Your welcome. *She didn't mention André. Is that good or bad? I'll have to wait and see, I guess.*

When it was time to leave, André accompanied them to the hotel exit. Daphne hugged him quickly. "Keep in touch." Her voice lacked enthusiasm. John, his face stiff and emotionless, gave André a brief wave.

By the time they were airborne it was after eleven o'clock.

"John, don't you have something better to do?"

"What?"

"Here's what I think happened tonight. Are you listening?"

"Of course!"

"After we first met, you told André about me. He told you we were in love in Paris. You gave him my phone number. He never called. Why? He didn't remember me, at all. André Surette was in my class at Paris Culinary. He hit on every girl in the group, and nailed a couple, not including me. He was thrown out of the class.

"My guess is he's in Canada to escape French alimony and child support. The last I heard from a friend, he'd been married two, maybe three times. I'll bet his job at the Frontenac is the third or fourth one he's had since coming to Canada. The black-haired sous chef who watched his every move is probably his current squeeze."

"Daphne, I'm- I'm sorry." He was astonished. *She knows more about my employee than I do.*

"Don't be. Actually, it was pretty sweet."

"What?"

"You wanted me to be happy, even if it meant unhappiness for you. I saw the sadness in your face. I have experience with it." She took his head in her hands and gave him a full-Monty kiss, no peck on the lips. Pulling back, she said, "Can you come to dinner Friday for Pete's birthday? He'll be seventeen."

"Of course I'll come. What would be a good gift for him? Maybe a laptop?"

"You have one lying around you're not using, right?" and they laughed, a laugh more about mutual understanding than humor.

John's heart was pounding; he could hear it in his ears. He pulled Daphne to him and kissed her back. The feelings that rolled over him—like a wave at Waikiki—were new, strong, and permanent. Of that, he was certain.

"Daphne, we've only known each other a short time, but I feel you're the person I've been waiting to meet for a long while. Does that make sense?"

"It does to me. I feel the same way." She smiled, took his hand, and put her head on his shoulder. "But we have to go slowly and get to know each other, not just for you and me, but for my children as well. I can see they already like you, and not just because of the gifts."

"They're grand people. I'm proud of Ryan. Not many grown-ups would've carried Bandit home in those conditions. You may have a veterinarian in the family."

They held each other, content to listen to the hum of the plane's engines, enjoying a feeling of relief knowing the years of loneliness and searching for someone to love who would love them back might be over.

"There is more to the secret, you know."

Daphne straightened up, studying his face. "What do you mean?" He was trying to be nonchalant, but his eyes were serious.

"I told Templeton I'm tired of traveling. They offered me the job of manager and part owner of the new hotel on the river at the site I showed you on the flight north. It's twenty minutes from your house. I have approval rights on the plans, construction, everything. I'll probably have to take a small cut in salary, but not much. My Uncle Ralph and Aunt Violet are the majority stockholders in Templeton."

"Why didn't you tell me?"

"I was waiting, watching, worrying. It would've been too painful for me to be around you, or even see you on the street, if you loved André. If you and André had gotten together, I would've taken the hotel in Los Angeles offered to me by Templeton."

"John Henry Andrews, are you keeping any other secrets from me?"

"Yes, but I'm reluctant to tell you. They're more questions than secrets."

"Why don't you want to tell me?" She could hear the worry in his voice.

"I'm afraid it might affect our relationship."

"Nothing you have done for me or the children has been disappointing. It would be out of character for you to do something without our best interest in mind. Tell me what worries you and let me decide?"

"Okay. … Would you help me by working with the architects of the new hotel to design the ambiance, kitchen, and plan the food service for Daphne Gaillard's Restaurant at Templeton's Saint Lawrence Hotel? Can we meet with your brother Mike and talk things over?"

Daphne was staring at him—speechless—her eyes wide and fixed on his face.

The air was suddenly heavy and he was afraid to take a breath. "See, I knew it would change our—" the rest of his words were smothered by her lips on his.

Daphne was flushed and what she wanted to say couldn't come fast enough. "I wanted to ask you about the hotel but couldn't find the courage and thought

I might be interfering. I've dreamed about designing my own restaurant since I was fifteen. I have so many ideas!"

John laughed at Daphne's excitement, enthusiasm, and the flood of concepts that burst from her like air from a punctured balloon. *What a joy she is. Her smile alone lights up my life.*

Will You Go Out With Me?

"Mr. Mullen is expecting me for an interview at two o'clock," Sofia told the burly, uniformed guard. He looked her up and down, his eyes lingering on her breasts. He called somewhere, hung up, and turned to look at her chest again. With a knowing smile, like he was in on some caper, he pushed a button. The huge steel-bar gate swung open. She stared right back at him, wondering, *Does the warden sometimes order in girls for purposes other than job interviews?*

A wheezing officer shaped like a bowling ball with a smaller, expressionless bowling ball head to match, escorted her to another door and spoke on an intercom to a female officer on the other side. She checked a list, pushed a button, and the door slid open, groaning and clanking. After Sofia stepped through, it closed with a resounding, no-nonsense crash and a loud snap of locks.

The officer looked Sofia up and down. "I need to pat you down, look in your purse, and record your photo ID or driver's license." It was Sofia's first time being felt-up by a woman. After the search, she was handed off to a tall, skinny male officer with tufts of red hair bordering his forehead. He pointed directions at corners they would travel instead of speaking.

After going through two more locked doors, they passed along a corridor with waist-to-eye-level windows on the left wall. The thick, greenish glass had embedded wire mesh in it, and allowed a subdued, possibly one-way, view into each room. Sofia felt she was being escorted out of the real world a step at a time, perhaps never to return. Hank's opinion surged in her mind. He'd tried to talk her out of applying, but she was determined. They needed the money.

Mrs. Sofia Natasha Backus—twenty-four, tall, blonde, trim, with lips in a near-permanent smile, arched brows, blue eyes, and a body straining to push through her clothes—graduated from York University in January of 2001 with a master's degree in English literature. Unable to find a teaching position in a college or high school after trying for three months, she answered an ad for an English teacher at the Weiner Maximum Security Correctional Facility—the place she was currently walking through.

Ushered into one of the rooms off the corridor, a short, stocky man seated with two other people jumped up to shake her hand and say, "Mrs. Backus, thank you for coming in. I'm Warden Edward Mullen." A black wig was perched on his head like a bird's nest surrounded by a wreath of steel wool. The hair in his nose and ears matched the wreath. He added, "Please meet Mrs. Alverna Lloyd, Head of Education and Mr. Harold Wiley, Head of the Language Department in the state penal institutions."

Sofia decided Mrs. Lloyd looked like a gray-haired Meryl Streep. She often related faces to celebrities. It helped her remember names. She couldn't do it with Mr. Wiley. A celebrity wearing a screaming-tweed sport coat and hiking boots just wouldn't come to mind.

Each shook her hand and began taking turns asking her superficial questions about teaching and English. Actually, teaching English seemed to be of minor interest to them. They probed more into whether she had ever been arrested, used drugs, or associated with known criminals. Since her background was pretty bland, except for smoking weed once at party and throwing up all the way home, she had little to tell them. She saw papers labeled background search on the desk and suspected they were about her.

Fifteen minutes into the meeting, Joel Bradshaw, a psychologist, arrived and was introduced. Tall, angular, smelling like tobacco, and clean-shaven with piercing brown eyes, he took over the meeting. "Mrs. Backus, most of the inmates are at an eighth-grade education level or lower. They're here for the long term, so, if inmates elect to get some education, like English, their motivations vary. Some want to learn to read legal documents to appeal their sentence, some are trying to avoid physical work, and others just want to see outsiders. I'm sure there are many other motives, but these are the most common. Many gave up on education long ago. Most inmates are clever verbally and can talk someone out of their better judgment in minutes, but they're weak at reading comprehension and writing."

Mrs. Lloyd asked Sofia, "Do you think you can tolerate going back to teaching at an eighth-grade level?"

"It will be difficult, but teaching is mostly about challenging students to learn. Isn't it? If I can get them to try at any level, they'll be better off," Sofia replied. For the first time, she saw smiles flicker in the room and she was dismissed soon after.

The hand-talking officer led her back through the corridor maze. After another pat down, she was passed off to other guards, then finally into fresh air and freedom. She went lightly over the interview highlights with Hank when she got home, omitting details that gave her shivers and she knew would worry him.

Two weeks later she was offered, and took, the job. The orientation was simple: a photo identification card with a barcode to be worn on a strap around her neck at all times and details on forbidden actions such as bringing in medications, drugs, metal objects, or messages in or out for inmates. The tour was concluded by a view of her classroom and the library.

Knowing testosterone was as thick as toothpaste in prison, Sofia tried everything she could think of to dilute it. She even used the "before" picture of a "before-and-after" ad for miracle plastic surgery as a template. Putting on a baggy sweater; loose black slacks; low-heeled black shoes; cheap drugstore glasses with thick, black-rims with plain glass she didn't need; an ugly yellow blouse; and a minimal amount of makeup: she still felt uneasy.

Piling her hair on her head in a chignon, she asked Hank's opinion.

He hugged her. "You look awful!" But, from the look in his eyes and smile, she knew he didn't mean it. Still, for what would perhaps be the only time in her life, his "awful" response made her feel better.

Her first class had ten students. They came in assorted sizes, colors, attitudes, and intellects. Kurt, the classroom guard told her, "They're just trying to avoid work in the laundry, kitchen, or shoe repair shop." The need for a six foot-three guard weighted down with a pistol, club, handcuffs, and mace outside the door gave her more anxiety than reassurance.

"Good morning, class." Sprawling in their chairs, the students suddenly sat up straight as she entered. They'd expected a female neo-Nazi wrestler.

"My name is Mrs. Sofia Backus. I'm your English teacher and I'm here to help if you have reading and writing difficulties." They all laughed.

"What's so funny?"

"Teach, we speak 'street,' so we all have trouble with English, except Prof. He graduated high school. Name's Squeaky."

"Thank you, Squeaky." Sofia had decided earlier that there was one thing she wasn't going to ask about—their reasons for being in a prison known for sentences of thirty years to life, or more. Immediately she added another item—do not to ask for an explanation of their nicknames. "Raise your hand if you can read a newspaper." Slowly ten hands went up.

"Please say your names when you speak, like Squeaky did, until I get to know you. Here's my plan. To start, I'm going to read a short story or chapter from a book at the beginning of class each day. Afterward, we'll discuss it for half an hour. The next hour, one of you will read a selection from a book of your choice for discussion. A different person will read each day, so watch the list I'm posting to see which day you'll read."

She paused to see if this initiated questions. No response. She continued, "During discussions, no one may interrupt the person speaking. Everyone will get a chance to talk. If someone is taking time away from others, I'll hold up my hand. That means the speaker should stop. I'll ask questions, not only about the subject of your story, but also about the punctuation, sentence structure, and the meaning of words. So, you'll need to think about those things too, and look them up in the library. We'll correct pronunciation as we read."

She looked at each man. "Those are my rules. Do you agree to honor them?"

Spook said, "I'm Spook. We can choose any book?"

"Yes. I look forward to hearing what interests you. We'll try to build on that. Are you okay with this plan?"

"Plan's good." The others nodded in agreement.

That first day Sofia read from *The Adventures of Huckleberry Finn.*

Shade was troubled by what he heard. "Man, I know where that dude's comin' from: drunk dad, no mom, can't read. Don't like the black man bein' sold like a dog."

Gabby looked at Shade. "When I had a mom, she told me her grandma was sold as a slave."

Freedom to choose their own books made the discussions lively, and sometimes sexually explicit. Their street-talk often required them to explain the meaning to Sophia. Since this made them "dress-up" their English for her, she frequently played dumb to urge them along. She discovered that talking about the thoughts and actions of people in the books often gave them a window into their own lives, a psychiatrist's laboratory.

When Sofia didn't flinch, or even comment, on their initial choices of erotic literature, their attitudes changed. About three weeks into the class, even duck-in-doors-tall Hulk joined the discussions. "Books with all the sex stuff are boring. They all say the same thing over and over. The players change, but the words are always the same. Teach, I learn somethin' new from books you read. They tell about different places or different kinds of people."

To Sofia's surprise, Pug, Spook, Squeaky, Gabby, and Stud all nodded or murmured agreement. None of the others objected. They began to read and talk about the courage, skills, and endurance of the men and women. They spent hours talking about the bravery of the men and the photographs in the book *Endurance,* about Shackleton's expedition to Antarctica. They'd never heard of Antarctica.

Whenever Sofia went to the library, one or two of her students were there. Prof was usually there. He took the book cart to prisoners in lock-down cells and helped re-file returns. The librarian, Mildred, told Sofia, "Since your class started, I've had more questions from inmates than ever before."

Mildred, Denise, the filing clerk, and Sofia chatted whenever possible. Denise didn't say much, but when she did, Sofia thought her native tongue was Basque or Spanish. When Sofia got to know her better she found Denise's parents, like many Basque families, had immigrated to Guatemala. Mildred was intelligent, pleasant, but reticent. Denise was small, wiry, and constantly moving. With dark-brown eyes and clear, light-brown skin, Sofia put her in the Salma Hayek category in her memory system. In the mostly-male enclave, their camaraderie at first was safety-in-numbers, but it quickly blossomed into friendship.

Sofia's limits were tested by a few high school tricks, like the garter snake in her desk drawer. She'd calmly picked it up and carried the wriggling reptile to the door and handed it to the officer. The class howled, watching the classroom guard do the impromptu dance they'd expected from Sofia. She had their respect and, with time, every one listened, asked questions, and made an effort to do as she asked.

Prof, a soft-spoken, small white man with narrow shoulders and delicate features, looked a few years older than the others. Her husband Hank would label him a "milquetoast." To Sofia, he seemed incapable of violent crime. Prof was also suitably named. He was more educated than others in the class and read law books and historical texts.

The other students had a subtle respect for him. They asked him questions and he always answered patiently. The accuracy of his nickname reinforced her decision not to initiate nickname explanations. She decided it could be painful or embarrassing, for her and for them.

Over the next six months, Sofia noticed Prof getting thinner and thinner. So much so, that his prison uniform was becoming much too large and hung on him like a deflated balloon. She worried he was ill, but it didn't seem to prohibit him from doing his library job, so she didn't feel it was her place to ask him about it.

In mid-January of 2004 Sofia told the class, "I'm pregnant and won't be returning after the end of the month."

Shouts of disappointment came from everyone, except Prof. "I'm very happy for you," he said, and all the others followed his lead. Each one congratulated her and thanked her for teaching them. *It's amazing,* Sofia told herself, and later Hank—*these men with such terrible, vicious lives can still build sincere feelings, every last one of them.*

On her last day she encouraged them. "You've been excellent students. I'm proud of you. You're like Shackleton; you never quit. You've proven you can learn. Now do it, and do it, and do it. You can travel the earth and the universe through books, and you should. Now I have to go and teach my little one to do it, too. Thank you for helping me help you."

When Denise, the library clerk, left work on March 16, she had a leather tote to hold her purse and lunchbox. As usual, everything was emptied out on a table to be examined by Charlene (nicknamed "Patty" for her infamous pat-downs). Charlene asked, "Where did you get this tote?"

"The guys in the shoe repair shop made it for me as a birthday gift. You like it?"

Charlene examined the tote inside and out. "It's really made well. Clever how they put all the little pieces together. Happy birthday, Denise!"

Denise began to wear make-up she hadn't bothered with before. Rouge, lipstick, and eye shadow became her routine and the guards teased her about having a new boyfriend. She always wore a bright colored bandana to cover her short, black hair.

Every workday, Denise carried her things to and from work in the tote. On Tuesday, June 5, and again on Wednesday, in addition to the usual items, she had small boxes of tampons and tissues. Charlene said, "That time of the month, huh?"

"Yeah. Think I'm getting a cold, too. May take a day off." Denise replied. "Even my hands feel cold." She had on soft cotton gloves.

At noon on Thursday, June 7, the doorbell rang at 734 Orchard Lane. Sofia was slow getting to the door. In her third trimester, she had really packed it on. At first, she made excuses to herself saying, *It's my first child.* Then she would get angry, *Damn. I'll never be able to play tennis or run again after this. I'm not goin' through it again—for sure.* The bell rang a second time before she could get to the door. Opening it, she was surprised to see Denise holding a package.

"Denise, how nice to see you. Didn't you have to work today?"

"Hi, Sofia. No. Took a day off. Your class asked me to deliver this. We all say good luck with the baby."

"Can you come in? I'll make some tea. Do you have a cold?" Sofia thought her voice was hoarse.

"No. Thanks. Lots to do. Have to run."

"Thank you for delivering the package. I'll write a note to the class," she called to Denise's back as she hurried off in her usual small, quick steps. Denise waved over her shoulder. Sofia mused, *I think she shaves her upper lip. I didn't notice that before. Maybe it was the dim light in the library.*

Unwrapping the package, Sofia found a tote made by stitching together small, brown pieces of leather. She laughed seeing "Weiner Maximum Security Correctional Facility" stamped on some of the inside pieces. In the bottom was a note:

Dear Mrs. Backus,

We made this tote for you to carry around the baby necessities. Good luck with the baby. Thanks for teaching us to appreciate the world through books.

Your English class

Sofia knew Prof had written the note. The spelling, punctuation, and wording were too perfect for anyone else in the class to accomplish. She put the note on her desk, as a reminder to write a thank you. Having the baby intervened, and she forgot the obligation.

At dusk that same day, a man parked a car on a side street and walked a block to a high-rise building where the J. Richard Burton Company kept a condo for the use of visiting clients. In a black coverall and mask he was invisible in the dark. He crouched behind a low wall and bushes near the entrance.

An hour later a BMW screeched to a stop at the curb and a pretty, giggling, young blonde woman bounced out of the passenger seat into the light of the building's entrance. The driver followed her, took her arm and kissed her neck as they entered the building. As anticipated by the masked man hiding behind the wall, the driver was J. Richard and he smiled. *My scout was right. Her second-job vacuuming and cleaning the building lobby paid off.* He settled down behind the wall to wait.

About nine o'clock, J. Richard emerged alone, late enough to enjoy himself, but not late enough to make the excuse of "working-late" sound suspicious. As J. Richard unlocked the BMW, he was pushed down hard, facedown, against the car and ordered to be quiet. A sharp instrument against his back prompted compliance.

His nose was bleeding. Sliding to the ground, he lay facedown beside the BMW, out of the light from the building. The masked man, astride his back, took his wallet, cell phone, and car keys, saying, "You start counting when I say so and don't get up before you get to 500," then poked him in the back with something sharp.

J. Richard could feel warm liquid on his skin. *Am I going to bleed to death?* he wondered.

The man in black pushed down hard on J. Richard's back and jumped up hissing, "Start countin'," then disappeared.

The mugger made a stop at a refuse-burning plant where he once worked. He put Burton's wallet, minus the driver's license, into a cardboard box along with his cell phone and car keys. He added a handmade map, a list of names and descriptions, his gloves, the black balaclava and coverall, and a sharp, bloody stick. Slipping into the building, he threw the box into the furnace while the bucket operator had his back to him, and stood in the shadows to see it buried in the fire by a fresh bucket of trash.

Back at the apartment, wearing new gloves, he put a bloodstained handkerchief and the driver's license in sealed plastic bags. Depositing the plastic bags, plus a letter, in an addressed, pre-paid USPS Priority envelope, he taped it shut and walked to the mailbox on the corner. Just as he was told would happen, the young neighbors ignored him and he returned the favor.

On Friday morning, he was up early to wipe down everything and get into Denise's work clothes and make-up. He added the minor clothing variations she suggested. He loaded the new tote Denise had selected and left on a chair for him with her purse, lunch bag, and partially emptied boxes of tampons and tissues. As he started to leave, he turned back to put some black pepper in a pocket.

Driving carefully, because his skills were rusty, he parked in Denise's designated spot at the prison. He shredded the cotton gloves he was wearing and threw the pieces down a storm drain, while bending over to do a fake tire inspection for the benefit of surveillance cameras.

Sneezing and coughing vigorously into a handkerchief while entering the prison, he didn't speak to anyone and acknowledged the guards with a simple nod or wave. His uneasiness about the make-up made him sweat and helped him look ill. Emptying the new, colorful canvas tote on the table, he greeted Patty with a gesture and nod. Patty said, "You got a new tote. I like it."

In a hoarse voice smothered by coughs and a handkerchief with subtle lipstick stains, he mumbled, "My friend liked the leather one. Goes with her brown coat, so I gave it to her."

Patty, anxious to avoid catching the cold, started to pass him on through without delay. As he turned to move on she said, "Wait," and his heart almost stopped. She scanned the barcode on Denise's identification card. "Okay. Hope your cold gets better soon." Then she turned to wash her hands.

"Thanks," he said weakly offering a brief salute with his gloved right hand. He was really sweating now and the red-haired, hand-talking guard walking him through to the library stayed a safe distance away.

Starting Denise's book routine in the library but anxious to see her, he forced himself to remain calm. At the expected ten o'clock time, draped in Prof's prison uniform and wearing his shoes, Denise pushed the tall cart of books from the isolation cells into the library. She parked it in the usual place at the end of the stacks between the surveillance camera and the supply closet door. In the closet they switched clothes quickly and silently. Denise helped remove Prof's makeup, and put on her own. A wink and momentary touch of lips said much more than conversation.

⸎

While feeding the baby the next morning, a newspaper item briefly caught Sofia's eye and was promptly forgotten:

Daily News: June 8, 2004

J. Richard Burton was robbed as he was leaving work last night. The attack occurred in front of a building on Adams Street where his company owns a condominium. He suffered a minor cut on his back, a broken nose, and his wallet was stolen. He could not identify his attacker. Burton was in the news twelve years ago when his pregnant secretary was murdered by her husband. The husband is serving a life sentence.

⸎

On a Tuesday morning late in August, Sofia was out for a walk in the neighborhood with Hank Jr. in a stroller. She was surprised to see Denise walking toward her. "Denise, great to see you. How are you?"

"Nice to see you, too. Is this the special little guy? Oh, isn't he beautiful? Look at that smile."

"Do you live around here?"

"On Valley Road, about five blocks down," Denise answered.

"How have you been?"

"I'm fine, Sofia. How about you? You look great—back to your old self."

"I am back in shape. In fact, I got a job teaching English at Lincoln High. I'll start in September. How come you're not at work today?"

"I quit in June. Budget crunch at the prison. They cut me to three days a week. Couldn't get by on it, so I work for an office cleaning service in town.

Pay is good, but I have to work nights. Don't like goin' home at one in the morning."

"Denise, Hank and I have been looking for a nanny for Junior. We don't want to put him in daycare until he's potty trained and a little older. Would you be interested in the job? You'll have to tell me how much you need to make so I can talk with Hank. I don't know if we can afford it. You wouldn't have to work evenings, unless my husband takes me on a date." Sofia rolled her eyes and chuckled.

"I'd love to do that," Denise answered and they walked on, talking. By the second time around the block, Sofia, Denise, and Hank, Jr. were smiling. Hank, Sr. didn't stand a chance of refusing the deal.

Over the next few months Sofia discovered Denise had a year of practical-nurse training in Guatemala before she became an American citizen. Only four years older than Sofia and never married, Denise and Sofia shared the joys, anxieties, thrills, and learning involved in raising Hank, Jr.

Denise was trying to get Hank, Jr. to say words in Euskara. Sofia, still in awe of how she could instantly love a little person she'd never met before, glowed with happiness, and most events outside her circle of life were irrelevant—that is until October 21.

That day, Sofia and Hank, Sr. heard the following local news:

> WXYR: October 21, 2004—*New evidence was announced today in regards to the murder of pregnant Alice C. Guerra twelve years ago. Materials tested at the time of the murder did not match anyone, including her husband. The routine entry of a blood sample from a recent mugging into the police DNA database triggered a match to the unexplained samples from the previous murder scene and Mrs. Guerra's unborn child.*
>
> *Mr. Guerra is in his twelfth year in prison for the murder. Bruce Staller, his attorney, has petitioned for a re-trial of Gilbert T. Guerra based on the new information. He stated, "Mr. Guerra has always proclaimed his innocence." The police have not released the name of the person identified by the match.*

Sofia told Hank, "Gilbert T. Guerra was the man called Prof in my English class at Weiner."

"Maybe he's been in prison for twelve years by mistake. That's cold!" Hank grimaced.

The evening news two days later gave Sofia a jolt:

WXYR: October 23, 2004—*Mr. J. Richard Burton's wife found him unconscious in his garage earlier today. Emergency technicians were unable to revive him and he was pronounced dead on arrival at Memorial Hospital. The medical examiner declared the cause of death to be suicide by carbon monoxide asphyxia. There was a note. The police have not released its contents.*

Suddenly, Sofia recalled what Hank said: the class gift, her failure to write a thank you, the delivery of the tote, her question about Denise shaving her upper lip, *That wasn't Denise!* "Oh, My God! Oh, My God!" she yelled to herself.

Sofia tore through the items in her closet looking for the tote. She didn't see anything special about it except, turning it inside out, the leather pieces stamped with Property of Weiner Maximum Security Correctional Facility seemed to be aligned peculiarly in one section. Parts of the words were obscured by the sewing technique.

In some places the words were upside-down or backward so a 'p' became a 'g' or a 'd' and a letter 'y' turned over resembled an 'h'. Moving it about, she studied the words, then gasped—the first letters of the altered Weiner title made new words, like a vertical tweet. She wrote them down:

"to our SPecial teacher tanx For curing our louSy reading
look in handle"

She found tightly rolled pieces of paper stitched into both handles. One had a note:

Dear Teach,

Thanks for helping us see the world by reading, instead of teachin us to avoid dangling particles. We put the pieces of leather in the totte stamped Property of Weiner Correctional inside so you wouldn't be embarassed to use it. Ha!

Denise, the liberry clerk lady, will be in Prof's cell for a night. He's got somethin' he needs to take care of. He got thinn to wear her clothes. He'll be back fore her shift after a day out. We'll take care of her fore him. He looks like her, don't you think?

Just before Prof leaves there will be big excitement here. A sewer pipe will get broke in the garage above where the warden parks his convertible. If it ain't cleaned up before he gets back from vacation, there will be hell to pay. It is his own fault. He should keep it at home, or at lest put the top up. Watch the news. Please just read and listen. Stay mum. Even to your husband. Burn this.

The hole english class wish you and your baby health and happiness. Give the baby lots of love so he or she won't end up like us.

—Squeaky Waters, for Shade, Hulk, Spook, Gabby, Stick, Stud, One-Tooth, Pug, and Prof

"Oh, My God!" She yelled this time.
Hank called from the kitchen, "What did you say, love?"
"Nothing." Sofia followed the class instructions.

When Denise arrived the next morning, Sofia brought out the tote. Seeing it, Denise's world, and knees, buckled. She swayed and tears welled up only to change from tears of fear to tears of joy. Sofia took her in her arms. "I think you're the bravest person I ever met." She hugged her long and hard. Nothing more was said then, or ever, on the subject. The shredded tote followed Burton's wallet and the tote note into oblivion.

When Gilbert—Prof—left Weiner Correctional for the second time, he held a letter of apology from Governor Wells and a check. His ears were still ringing from the cheers in Cellblock #4.

Eight months later, Gilbert Teodor Guerra and Denise Evadine Zumaran were married. Sofia, Hank, Sr. and Hank, Jr. were there as surrogates for the friends and family Gilbert didn't have. Each member of Sofia's English class used their one-call-a-month to congratulate the happy couple.

A Conversation on Female Abuse

—*The 'Y' Factor*—

"**H**ow do you think the Equality parade went today?"

"Pretty good. Rain didn't help." She tried to hold her smile, but it slid away, like a movie fade-out.

"Most of the marchers don't know what they want, do they?"

"What do you mean?"

"Who do they want to equal? Men? Do they think there are more ugly guys than ugly women, and want to even-up the ugly bin?"

"Now you are being ridiculous." Her eyebrows went up, a sign of annoyance he knew well. "You know they want equal salary for equal work, or an equal chance to be the boss. Lots of things. Most of all, they want the same respect given to men."

"You mean, like the gal on the side street with limited upholstery trying to solicit the guy in the limo? He has no morals. She's putting her life at risk. Does she want to equal him?"

"Cut it out. You know what I'm saying. In many nations women are treated like dirt. Men beat, rape or kill them just because they can; and they get away with it. In some creepy cults they cut the clitoris of young girls with an old, rusty razor blade." She stared at him, her eyes on fire.

157

To relieve her anger, he spoke softly. "Yeah. I know. I agree with you. But, how do you stop it. In some places, women think they deserve beatings and abuse. I read the other day about a mother who killed her teenage daughter by throwin' acid on her because she looked at a boy goin' by on a bicycle. It's the cruelest thing I've ever heard. Her own mother, for God's sake. It's worse than stoning someone to death." He grimaced and shivered, shaking his shoulders.

She sighed and looked away, her flash of rage fading. "Something has to be done. …We have a lot of work to do abroad, and at home, as you point out with the street-girl."

He wasn't quite sure what to say, but started anyway. "The problem is, women have been kept in ignorance by biased laws, dominating family mores, or males who considered themselves religious authorities. No benevolent God would want women to be inferior or subservient to men. That has human design written all over it. Their self-confidence is in rags."

"Not everyone," she replied. "Mary Walker graduated from medical school in 1855, and was a surgeon in the Civil War. She was the first woman to receive a Medal of Honor for Meritorious Service. That was 162 years ago. As half the people on earth, you'd think we would be further ahead by now."

"It's not women's fault, you know. It may not be the fault of men either."

"What?" —*What's he talking about?*

"I'm not sure you can talk or train someone out of inherited characteristics."

"You have to explain that. Are you saying men inherit the right to mistreat women?"

"No. Not 'the right', the personality and physical strength; just like women inherit the tendency to be more docile, flexible and patient."

"Oh. When did that difference start?"

"It goes way, way back. Charles Darwin said fitness helped all species survive. Years later William Hamilton and Richard Dawkins decided it was an adaptation of animals to warn others of danger so some could survive."

"Really?"

There are Canada Geese near my house that produce five or six chicks every year. When they move around the neighborhood, the goslings stay with the mother, and the father follows behind. When the mother and little ones come to some obstruction where she can't see what is ahead, she and the goslings stop, and the father goes first."

"Is that right?"

"Every time. Later, Hamilton and Dawkins changed their opinion. They decided behavior, camouflage-coloring, size, strength, and many other adaptions, are all gene changes aimed at survival. This applies to people, as well as plants and animals."

"You mean we have survived 300,000 years because those who went before us passed on how get food and protect ourselves from weather and predators?"

"You got it! That, and how many kids we produce, plus luck. The more offspring, the better the chance some will make it. It's kinda like a poker palace. The more people playin', the more winners there are. There's much more to understanding equality."

"Man, you are a cold dude." —*Is he makin' excuses for men's lousy behavior?*

"Do you know what cloning is?"

"Yeah. They cloned a sheep or goat named Dolly in England a few years ago. It's like makin' a copy."

"Right. The Whiptail Lizard that lives in Arizona, New Mexico and California clones itself. No male of the species has ever been found."

"All females?"

"Yep. If people were cloned like them, the 'equality' we are talkin' about would be a shoo-in. Cloning was probably the first way most organisms reproduced. There are other organisms that clone: for example, dandelions, blackberries, and cockroaches. Did you ever see bees or butterflies in a field of yellow dandelions? You won't, at least not many. There's no sweet sap to attract them. They don't need pollination to reproduce. On the other hand, bees are all over apple blossoms. The farmers count on them for a good crop."

"I never noticed the bees don't go to the dandelions…"

"There are advantages to cloning. It's easier than sex: no flirting, no coitus, and no sexually transmitted diseases. Having offspring is just a pop. Cloning has hang-ups though. A long time ago a change occurred and we are one of the beneficiaries."

"Man, you are really into this. You want another soda? I'm buying. This is getting interesting. Your not as dumb as you look." The declaration was softened by a laugh.

"Yes, and you are dumber than you look. I'm only doin' this for the drinks, you know."

She faked a hurt look, then smiled, knowing he didn't mean it. "Okay, … enough with the clever repartee, what happened 'a long time ago'?"

"It may have started about 220 million years ago, and it is still going on. Did you ever see the videos of sea turtles laying eggs in the sand?"

"Yes."

"Then you remember; if the sand is cold, all the eggs hatch into males. If it is hot, they are all females. The 8-degree difference between 26°C and 34°C changes the lives of the whole brood. It still does for sea turtles, and in reverse, for alligators. Temperature makes a difference."

"What's got to do with humans?"

"Way back in Earth's history, a gene mutation created a sex region on a chromosome, now called *the Y*. It directs development of an embryo to produce a male instead of a female. The Y chromosome may actually be a converted female X. If that happened, females were here first. In any event, it did us a great service."

"Why so great? You men aren't so special." She couldn't hide her skepticism. It wrinkled her brow.

"Whoa! Wait a minute, will ya? Whole cell splitting, as in cloning, has limits. Any mutations, like the survival protector genes, are only passed to direct descendants of that one plant or animal. Sexual reproduction is a whole new ballgame."

"You makin' this up?"

"No! In sexual reproduction the new genes from the father and mother join."

She yawned. "I know, if the Y from the father joins an X from the mother, the child will be a boy."

"Not right away. Two important things happen first. Just before the female egg goes haploid(half), that is fertile from 46 to 23 chromosomes, the two halves hug briefly and long strands of DNA and genes are traded. Think back a generation. Those genes came from her mother and father. This 'hug' is important. It causes a trade of new and friendly genes of the mother to mesh with those from the father. So, a whole new person is created. A person never before seen on Earth."

"Wow!" This is deep!" He had her attention.

"Girls have their lifetime quota of eggs in their ovaries before they are born and produce fertile eggs each month. Boys are manufacturing millions of sperm every day and keeping them in the cooler. Maybe it's the reason why—to women—men always seem to be in heat."

She grinned and poked him in the ribs. "For the first six weeks of gestation all embryos are girls."

"Right. That's the second important thing. You knew it? Go on." He was surprised.

"If the baby is going to be a boy, at the 7th week of pregnancy, the sex gene of the Y chromosome switches on for a few a hours and starts pouring in testosterone and other stuff to change the girl embryo into a boy embryo."

"I'm impressed. You really listened to the bio prof."

"I have a vested interest." Her voice had its smile back and she gave him a proud glance.

"Let's move a little. I'm tired of sittin'." He walked the perimeter of the room, stretching.

She threw the critical question at him. "If females were somewhat responsible for creating male genes, why did they make men so big and loaded with lust for power, money and position?"

"Good question. Maybe they needed them big and strong for protection, to hunt for food, and carry equipment as they followed the migrating herds. When it was discovered seeds would grow food 10,000 years ago, migration slowed. Families formed and claimed land that produced food, and wealth."

"Your a Wikipediac."

"You won't like this part. Wealth brings crime. Ferocious, violent men massacred the weaker men, confiscated their land and valuables, even enslaved their women and children. These ambitious Y chromosome kings skewed the gene pool away from the gentler people. The attitudes of powerful men toward women still haunt us today, world over."

"I don't think men's attitudes toward women have softened much in my lifetime."

"There are reasons. Human mutations occur on an average of once every 20,000 years. And the quickest, most important ones all occur in mitochondrial genes of women to be passed to their children, male or female. The male mitochondria are shot down by the female at fertilization, so only their nuclear genes get passed, and they take twenty times longer to mutate. Sykes says, '*If the average baby-producing time for women over the course of human evolution is twenty years … this is the equivalent of roughly a thousand generations*'. Expecting to separate men from their aggression genes by mutation is like expecting water to run uphill. It is strange though…"

"What's strange?"

"There are authentic matriarchal societies."

"See! I knew it. You're holding out on me."

"You better listen to this before you start flying around the room. There are clans lead by women in Tibet, Indonesian, Ghana, Costa Rica, and India. In many of these cultures the woman own all the property, manage all the money and any family business. Men are the chiefs and take care of political matters, however, the women select them."

"My God! The women are in control."

"Right. There's a Native American example. The Iroquois Nation of Mohawk, Oneida, Onondaga, Cayuga, Seneca, and Tuscarora Indian tribes, was a matriarchal organization, and the first democracy in North America. The women are greatly respected in the tribes. We can go there to meet the men and women, and ask about their society. They have excellent records."

This isn't fiction. He has studied this! "Great suggestion. How did you get so smart?"

"It came with the bolt in my neck. If I looked like George Clooney you would have noticed it long ago."

She chuckled. "Okay, Professor, continue."

"What I don't understand though, is why men in matriarchal societies are more conciliatory. Maybe their genes came from our ancestors the barbarians missed in their pillage. Could be the men just use their aggression a different way, say, by playing lacrosse. The Iroquois invented the game, you know."

"No they didn't. It originated with the Algonquin in my home area in Canada. I knew you were going to bring it up. Our girl's team is better than you clods."

When he rolled his eyes and changed the subject. "Do you think marchin' in the streets in funny clothes carryin' signs and shouting will accomplish anything as far as equality is concerned?"

"Probably not." Her voice wilted.

"Survival, survival, survival! That's what brought the existing species, including us, through four and a half billion years to where we are. But, right now, we are our own worst predator. We are killin' each other and ourselves. How dumb can we get?"

They fell silent. Even the voices and shouts bouncing off the walls from nearby rooms failed to invade their thoughts.

After a long pause, she put her face close to his, "Do you think women will ever escape being pushed around by men?"

"I hope so. Men enjoy winning a fight or a deal, whether it is with a man or a woman. It's built-in. There's another possibility to consider. A mutation could go too far and make women like men are now. *Survival is nature's goal—not sentiment—*. It's clear the creation of the Y chromosome probably improved the odds for survival. But, so far, survivorship has ridden mostly with the bold, belligerent, and adaptive members in species. With the long duration of male attributes, it is unlikely punishment, education or gene mutation will eliminate all the lubricious libertines in our lifetime.

Women can't continue to accept misogyny as they did in the past. As women achieve greater wealth and power, they will crush sexual harassment, if they are strong and brave. I will help them every way I can. But, what do I know?"

"Don't put yourself down. You understand the issues better than most of us. I'm proud of you. We don't want either gender to dominate, right? It's better if both men and women have input and influence. *It's fairness that's important, not equality.*"

"Exactly! Now you are showing me talent." A broad smile affirmed his feelings for her. "In 1980 Milton Friedman said: *"A society that puts equality before freedom will get neither. A society that puts freedom before equality will get a high degree of both."* Notice he didn't say, '100% of both'. My interpretation: usually, the person who is hired should be the one who can do the job. The only other characteristics needed are honesty and loyalty. Nothing more, nothing less. So, what do you want to happen?"

"Aha! You led me through this whole diatribe just to ask this very question. Didn't you?"

He nodded yes and his smile held, gentle and sincere.

She stood up and walked in a circle talking and waving her hands. "Here is what I think. In general, women understand compromise better than men. They find more joy in work and accomplishment. We have to bring every woman to this level, according to their ability, as the Walker family did with Mary. That is the goal! They must be as aggressive as men at times, but in a better way. Nothing takes the bluster out of an arrogant, angry windbag better than a soft-spoken, electric, carefully crafted solution to a problem. If we do it well, and we are honest, we can make the rules, or at least, have a major say in their creation. How am I doin'?"

"Milton would be on his feet applauding. It will take time though. I'd add 'persistent and patient' to the necessary female characteristics. There may be times you need to use males for their aggressiveness, so learn how to exploit their native trait, too. Some guys don't like takin' orders from women. In the military, a man may be boiling mad when a female officer gives him an order; however, failure to follow the order, or talkin' back, means cleaning the latrine, KP or a ten mile hike. Now, as I think of it; adopting military discipline is a good idea. Yeah! I like it. I can picture guys doin' push-ups in offices. Just kiddin'." Her grin made him chuckle at his own joke.

As the grin faded, a brush-stroke of worry crossed her face. "When I ask you to do something for me, do you resent it?"

"Never. I have a special reason and I hope you know what it is." She put her arms around his neck as he spoke. "Political effectiveness begs for good management, common sense, strength of character, cooperation with others and diligence reading the public needs. Women do it better than men. I think they listen and remember better. They have deeper empathy. We need their ability now more than ever."

"Right. The good-old-boys network should keep their mouths shut, brains open and alert, and listen to the female half of the workforce." She was on a roll.

He held up a hand. "But females need to organize their thoughts, too. Sometimes my sister starts a sentence in the middle, like I already know what preceded it. It drives me nuts. Men like linear, sequential presentations, and the multi-directional approach of women is confusing to them. I don't think this male attribute will change. Women need to adapt to this brain-twist given to men."

She sighed. "We're talking 'ideal' here; as if everyone is decent, sincere and respects one another. But all kinds of cheating, pay-offs, stealing and other felonies, even murders, slide under the radar in many places. Getting men to treat women fairly seems impossible."

"Setting a good example and inviting people from wayward countries to observe the results, are probably the best training tools we have right now. If visitors see the benefits and take them home, it can work. Don't expect a rapid change. If fairness and full respect between women and men can be achieved any place, it will happen in America where religion and government are separated by the Constitution, and—at least part of the time—in real life. I'm against financial assistance to countries where Mary and Joe are not equally valued people. This sort of change has to come by example. You can't buy it. I'd donate to help anyone who wants to learn the value of gender fairness. I'd push for it big time. How about you?"

"Me too. You said, "*usually the person who is hired should be the one who can do the job*". What's that mean? If you were a politician, how would you decide which way to vote, say, on a bill giving women the same opportunities and pay as men?" She was testing him and he knew it.

"The equal pay is a no-brainer, but I'm ambivalent on opportunity. That's why I said 'usually'. There are certain professions I don't believe women should enter, not because they lack courage or are incapable, but because size, strength and endurance may be a handicap for success against male adversaries. I'm thinking about military units like the mountain, infantry, underwater and air-borne divisions. I'm not sure women should take on such a role. It may be too dangerous for them. This issue needs study to see if their skill can nullify the physical differences."

He paused, thinking, then said, "Here is my way of finding the truth. Do you remember Daniel Patrick Moynihan's statement: *'Everyone is entitled to their own opinion, but not to their own facts'*. Facts are critical. We have myriads of experts with facts from studies on women and men. Quiz them. When they present results, ask them for the study power. The higher the power number, the more effective a study is at proving the conclusion." He paused.

She was leaning forward, her eyes fixed on his. It encouraged him to go on.

"One more thing, don't let anyone carelessly extrapolate information. For example, if a study proves something concerning people, the results apply only to people similar to the ones in the study—not to all people. When experts disagree, I would seek out more experts. Often the best professors to consult are those without big reputations or titles. The backroom profs are more immersed in seeking answers and less interested in science-politics. They would be my choice. What's most important is: listen, question, and verify answers. As one's experience grows, so does their sense of who is telling the truth. Were I a politician, I would expect people to disagree with my decisions and press me to change my votes, maybe even offer me bribes. If I've done my homework, I'd rest easy. Opinions don't count."

She sighed, "That's heavy."

"We all make decisions based on our experiences and those of others. Moynihan's advice works everyday in every way. Imagine you are waiting to cross a busy street and the guy on your left says, *'We should be able to make it,'* and the woman on your right adds, *'We studied 100 accidents on this highway. If you can run the 100-yard dash in 12 seconds, you have an 86% chance of making it across safely. It's better to wait for the light to change'.* Which one would you believe?

"Moynihan was so smart! Man, you are gettin' to me. Why didn't you tell me all this before?"

"You never asked me. I don't think the topless parade for Equality was such a good idea."

" Runnin' out of the crowd tearin' off your shirt to cover me and resisting arrest didn't help."

"I never saw an officer take an hour to write a one page report, like he did with you; or, see so many other officers come into a room to help him do it. You're probably goin' to make the front page of *The LA Times* tomorrow. I'll be the guy in the picture kissin' the cement with a 300-pound cop sittin' on him. At least nobody at work will see my face. It's a good thing we're married. If we had been goin' together when this happened, it might have been a deal breaker."

"I'm sorry." She started to laugh and he joined in. Every time they looked at each other, another burst started. Down the hall a door opened. Struggling to control the mix of laughter and speech, she pointed toward a woman approaching their cell. "We're out of here. Here comes our lawyer. Where do you want to go for dinner?"

"Home."

REFERENCES:

1] "Cutting Young Girls Isn't Religious Freedom," by Kristina Arriaga; *Wall Street Journal* 8/25/2017.

2] "When Love Turns To Fear," by Ginny Graves; *REAL LIFE,* Everett Collection March 2016.

3] "Parents Kill Teenage Daughter For Looking At Boy;" *Post Standard,* Syracuse, NY 11/6/2012

4] "Play Celebrates Medal Winner Once Arrested For Wearing Pants," by Marnie Eisenstadt; *Seneca Falls Convention Days/Post Standard,* Syracuse, NY 7/11/2017.

5] *Scientists Find Earliest Human Specimens,* by Robert Lee Holts; *Wall Street Journal* 6/8/2017.

6] *DNA USA; A Genetic Portrait of America,* by Bryan Sykes, ISBN 978-0-87140-412-1. ©2012; Liveright Publishing Corp (Division W.W. Norton & Co.), New York.

Also see the following Bryan Sykes' books:
  a) *The Seven Daughters of Eve,* ISBN 0-393-32314-5. Publisher: W. W. Norton Co. NY & London 2001;

  b) *Adam's Curse,* ISBN 0-393-32680-2. Publisher: W. W. Norton Co. NY & London 2004;

  c) *Saxons, Vikings & Celts,* ISBN 978-0-393-33075-5. Publisher: W. W. Norton Co. NY & London 2006.

7] *Women After All,* by Melvin Konner M.D. ©2015; ISBN-13: 978-0393352313. Publisher: W. W. Norton Co. NY & London, March 2015.

8] "Tech Opens Up To Sexism Debate," Yoree Koh; *Wall Street Journal* 8/25/2017.

9] "Matriarchy on the March, " by David Barash; *Wall Street Journal* book review, 3/28-29/2015.

10] "Pakistan Debates Religious Role," by Saeed Shah and Qasim Nauman; *Wall Street Journal* 7/24/2016.

Gotcha!

The Exposé

It was a clear sunny day in Beckett's Bay in the summer of 2015, and the village was bustling, as it always did in the season. The population quadrupled then, with city dwellers there for the cool breezes.

Jed Dawkins was in the Main Street Barbershop waiting his turn. Next to him, Barry Birkholz was reading the *Times*. They were barbershop friends. Barry's daughter was in Dawkins' math class at the high school.

John, the barber, was having a lively conversation with postman Ed Roe, who was in his chair, and Pierre, the women's stylist. Pierre was sitting in one of his salon chairs, awaiting a customer and half hidden behind the door that usually separated them while he was working.

John was sure he was right. "I tell ya, BMW stands for British Made Wheels. It's an England car."

"It's a Goimen car. Da 'B' is a Goimen name, like some kinda beer." Pierre was adamant.

Jed turned to Barry. "I think Pierre has a Brooklyn accent. Did you hear him? What is a city guy doin' here?"

"You just noticed it? You musta been here thirty times. You don't know the story?"

"What story?"

"Look, the statue of imitations has run out so I'll tell ya, but in confidential. An armored truck bringin' money to the bank next door was robbed fifteen years ago. The thieves took over five million dollars. The cops couldn't find the money, or the crooks, so the bank offered a reward.

"A city-guy from Brooklyn workin' in this building for contractors found the robbery money. It was hidden somewhere here. He got the reward and bought this building with it. He rents this shop to Pierre and John. Pierre's from Brooklyn. It's all there in the book." He pointed to a bedraggled, hard-cover book on the table titled *Gotcha!* by T. A. Powers.

"Next," John announced.

Barry got in the chair. "Fix me good, John. Tonight's karaoke night at the bar and I'm lead singer."

John took a step back. "Can't work miracles. Maybe you should let your eyebrows grow long and comb 'em back." He wasn't kidding. Barry's hair had long since gone south leaving only a halo of gray. John trimmed the hair remnants struggling to hide Barry's sail-like ears and charged him the same as everyone else, mostly in retribution for messing up a good story on the robbery.

Jed Dawkins had picked up the book and was reading when it was his turn in the chair. After John finished cutting his hair he asked, "Can I borrow this book?"

"Sure."

"Thanks." He was reading as he walked out of the shop…

Gotcha!

By T.A. Powers©2015

Chapter 1

Born and raised on Melrose Avenue in the Bronx, John Michael Donovan struck out on his own after the third beating from his alcoholic, second stepfather. Mary, his mother, took him to Urgent Care for stitching of the laceration on his head where it hit the kitchen table. He lied to the social worker about the cause of his injuries and his age so they wouldn't create trouble for his mother.

Late Sunday night, he wrote a note to her to say the beating was his fault for just being there. He thought if he weren't there, maybe Jake wouldn't be so angry. But, if Jake hurt her, she should immediately call the police. He added he was taking $20. He put the note in the mayonnaise jar in the kitchen cupboard where Mary hid money.

Packing an extra pair of shoes and clothes in a small bag, he pocketed the credit card obtained from Joey Sanchez in exchange for his baseball glove. It belonged to someone named Steve Moore, so he knew the card was stolen, just as he knew he had to leave home or he would be killed.

Monday morning, he kissed his mom and went out the door as if he was going to school. Crossing over the Harlem River at 3rd Avenue, he stopped often to rest. He was sore and stiff. Walking south without any destination in mind, he sat on a bench in front of a Harlem school, watching the children on the playground and thinking, *I could go to Aunt June's house in Brooklyn, but she'll call my mom because she's a good sister. I musta gone thirty blocks. Nobody's gonna accept this credit card for food. My twenty bucks won't go far.*

❖ ❖ ❖

It was nearly five o'clock when he came to a gray stone building on 122nd Street where a steady stream of people was entering. A sign over the door read "Palladia." He'd never heard of the place. A woman pushed past him. She was wearing a heavy brown coat, a knitted red cap and boots, despite the hot day. He asked her, "What is this place?" She didn't answer. He walked along beside her and asked again, "Why are you going there?"

She scowled at him, as if he was the stupidest person on earth, and growled, "It's a shelter."

"Can anybody go there?" She didn't reply and kept moving. He followed her in.

A pretty black lady wearing a flower-patterned apron greeted him. "Well, hello there. Have you been here before? I don't recognize you."

"Is it all right I come in? I'm awful hungry."

"Of course you can. What happened to you? You're all bandaged up, with stitches and everything."

"It's a long story."

"It usually is. What's your name?"

"John."

"John, I'm Cassandra. Glad you came in. Sit over there by Frank." She pointed to an empty space at one of the long picnic-like tables filling the room. There were twenty-five or so people already eating. "Do you like spaghetti and meatballs? We've got salad, too, and ice cream."

"Yes, Ma'am."

"John, will you stay with us tonight? You look tired. We'll have a nurse here tomorrow and she can change those bandages and see if you're healing up okay. Would you like that?"

"I don't have any money to pay her."

"John, John, John. You don't need any money here. After you eat, one of us will show you where you can wash up and sleep. Don't worry, son, things will get better."

What a nice lady. I sure lucked out tonight. She didn't even ask my age.

❖   ❖   ❖

And so, John Michael Donovan started his adult life. He was fourteen. Short on education, short on self-confidence, short on skills: he built the best life he could. Cassandra gave him a job washing dishes to pay his room and board, all the time trying to get him to tell her his age, family history and education details. Every time she tried, he lied. Since he was taller than most boys his age, she accepted his lies as truths.

Soon, he moved up to helping the cook, and Cassandra was proud because she was sure he had more ability than he realized. In fact, with her recommendation, John took on a second job. As a mid-town courier he was on time, fast and courteous—all characteristics to put him in demand and lift his confidence. He found a small walk-up room in Harlem he could afford.

By fifteen John was six feet tall and strong from riding a bicycle successfully around Manhattan as a courier, an accomplishment surprising even to him, given the traffic hazards. Emilio Angelo, an artistic friend, made him general education development and birth certificates and he joined the Army.

❖ ❖ ❖

From basic training at Fort Benning, Georgia, he was sent to a military base in Stuttgart, Germany. In the Quartermaster Corps with a cook's MOS number (military occupational specialty) based on his work history at Palladia, he learned, hands-on, how to cook for 150 hungry soldiers, and even received a commendation. In mobilization drills, he learned to drive a loaded truck and improved his marksmanship. Covering all the needs of the soldiers in his regiment, he qualified to give haircuts.

Refining his social skills at USO dances was tough. The USO people were friendly; but he was younger than everyone here, and, except for army things, he couldn't find much to talk about with the hosts.

He wrote to his mother and sent her $50. His letter was returned "No such person at this address." Writing to his Aunt June, he learned his abusive stepfather was dead after alcoholism led him into a fight with a speeding taxi, and his mother was living in Florida. She provided her address.

John re-sent his letter and check with some additional text. Receiving a reply laced with love, happiness and gratitude, he continued to write and send money every month. At first, his mother asked how he could be where he was at his age, but didn't repeat the question when he told her not to be concerned.

After four years of Army life, and still a teenager, he was homesick. He rebuffed Army attempts to make him a career soldier and was sent to Fort Dix, New Jersey, where he received an honorable discharge and $150 in back pay.

❖ ❖ ❖

John made his way back to Harlem. Finding a job was more difficult than he expected. In Morley's Bar & Grill he met old acquaintances. They'd solved the scarcity-of-jobs problem: some sold drugs, some were thieves, and others were on welfare. The courier service had no position for him anymore. Email and fax communications had reduced the need for prompt document transportation.

At the St. Nicholas Avenue Library in Washington Heights, John used the computers for job searches. An assistant librarian, Tina Powers, helped him find employment information. She was professional and stiff at first, but actually smiled a little at his quips and military style "yes sir, no sir" when she corrected his computer errors. He began going to the library more and more often. Tina attributed this to his job anxiety.

At his tenth trip back she asked, "Any luck yet?"

Donovan's reply startled her. "Are we talking about my getting up the nerve to ask you out, or getting a job?"

Tina paused, looked at the floor, then at him, and a stern expression clouded her face. Donovan saw fear in her eyes. He took her left hand and just held it, saying nothing. Tina whispered, "Job."

"I've had a job since the second time I came here." Tina's eyes widened with surprise. "I'm not in the Longshoreman's Union yet, but they needed extra help, so I'm drivin' a forklift on the docks. Pay's pretty good. Enough for me to take you to dinner."

He continued to hold her hand and she didn't try to withdraw it. Her feelings were in a tumult of fright and pleasure, and she admitted to herself, *I never thought this would happen for me.* When she looked up at him, the anxiety in her eyes had softened and then glistened with gratitude for the unexpected offer. "Thanks. I'd like that."

❖ ❖ ❖

During the next month, they met almost every evening for a meal, movie or just to talk. Tina was eager to hear details: how he cooked for so many men, what Germany looked like, and what he did on the docks. Near the end of the month she asked, "Do you have brothers or sisters?"

As she said it, John's mouth opened as if he was about to speak. Then his head dropped from looking at her face to stare at the floor. Tina saw the hurt she caused by the question and took his hand. Slowly, he described the beatings, his fears, the helplessness, the shelter, even the fake birth and high school equivalency certificates to achieve army enlistment just before his 16th birthday. She put an arm around his shoulders. "You're not alone, John."

When he looked up, there were tears in her eyes. The thoughts of his own despair fell away and he asked, "Why are you crying?" He took both her hands, kissed the back of each and held on.

Tina spoke softly. "I left home in Hackensack after my mother's boyfriend hurt me. I was thirteen. My mother wouldn't report it to the police and ordered me not to either. I knew it would only get worse, so I left."

She described how she took a bus over the George Washington Bridge and spent several nights in the bus station in Washington Heights. She found the Palladia by chance after talking to a homeless person, just as he had. John turned his head so she wouldn't see the tear on his cheek, but she did. Tina took a deep breath, *He knows how I felt. He's been there.*

She paused, and then spoke again. "I was really lucky. Michelle, the social worker at Palladia, got me a job re-stacking books at the library. I hid in the janitor's storeroom and slept there at night. I was crying in the bathroom one day and Emily Lowe, the librarian, heard me. She took me to her apartment that night, gave me dinner, a room of my own, and we talked and talked and talked."

"Emily never married, and lived alone. She asked me if I would like to finish high school. I did. The principal at the Community Health Academy on 158th Street was her friend and she gave me an evaluation test. I got in. When I graduated from high school, Emily gave me a permanent job at the library, not as a librarian, just an assistant. You need to go to college to be a librarian." John was listening to every word, so she continued.

"I lived with Emily until she died two years after I graduated from high school." She didn't mention Emily had posed as her mother when they first met and helped her get an abortion.

From that day on their respect for each other deepened. They understood each other's worries.

❖ ❖ ❖

A week later, John was walking down 158th Street when Marty Fucillo, a friend he met in Morely's, stopped the car he was driving to offer him a ride. John got in. "What a beautiful car! I didn't know you had a Mercedes."

"You want to drive it?" The car was still at the curb. "Come on." He got out and switched places with John.

John asked, "Where are we going?"

"The Bronx. Just drive, I'll tell you where to turn." They stopped at a used car lot on 138th Street. A man and woman were strolling among the cars, apparently shopping.

As they exited the car Marty yelled, "Run!" Before he could say anything else, the tall, lean male shopper in a gray sweatshirt and black pants had him pushed face down on the car's hood and was applying handcuffs.

John got the same treatment from the woman. "What did I do?" he asked.

The woman spoke in the raspy voice of a chain smoker. "You're both under arrest for grand theft auto."

Any explanation by John and his court appointed lawyer proved useless. A guilty plea, and his clean prior record, sent John to Lyon Mountain Correctional Facility for six months. Before leaving, ashamed, he called on Tina to explain.

"I'll be here when you come back, John. Will you write or call me?"

"Yes. I'm sorry, Tina." Too disgraced to look into her eyes more than a few seconds, he bowed his head and walked away.

❖ ❖ ❖

At Lyon Mountain Correctional, John's history gave him two choices: work in the kitchen or the barbershop. He chose the barbershop. Joshua, a lifer and expert barber, helped him improve his skills. They discussed the cutting methods needed for hairstyles they saw in magazines.

After a couple of months, Joshua suggested John apply for New York State barber certification and gave him books to study. The penal system actually brought in a barber from outside to test him. Joshua served as the guinea pig for the practical part.

John passed and wrote to Tina trying to explain the examination details. His letters made her frown and smile; they revealed his stunted education, but silently she applauded his effort. Her letters were full of details on library activities and titles of audiobooks she believed he would like, but evaded personal feelings.

Does she like me? he wondered. He had an empty feeling in his gut.

John never missed a chance to call Tina. She was his anchor. "Tina, that audiobook *The Ten-Cent Boy,* it's your voice, isn't it?"

"Yes."

"I knew it. I've listened to it three times already." Tina was smiling, even laughing. John added, "I can understand stories better in audios. I don't have to look up the definition of so many words. Thank you."

"You're welcome. Do you have some paper and a pencil? Here are two more to look up. ... John, the city's boring without you in it."

His shoes had sponge-rubber soles on the return to his cell.

❖ ❖ ❖

As soon as John was released, he went to the library. Tina's happy but restrained greeting dashed his lofty dreams and hopes a little, but he understood her caution, given her past experience with men and his stained reputation.

Tina had news. "I have a new and better second job. Listen to this. I was doing my usual Children's Hour at the library and one of the mothers heard me reading to them. Her husband runs a sound studio in Brooklyn and she got me an audition there. They record audio books for authors. They liked my voice and pronunciation. I've already narrated three books. You heard the first one."

The excitement in her voice made John smile. *I like to see her happy.*

They discussed narration and pronunciation. They talked for an hour and would've talked longer, but Tina had work to do. They agreed to meet for dinner at Tarbet's. By the end of the evening, they were sharing their thoughts and worries, as they had done before, and decided to block their pasts from future conversations.

John found work on the docks again and saw Tina every day. Six months later, they decided to have a trial relationship, and he moved into her apartment.

❖ ❖ ❖

A fight on the docks between union longshoremen and non-union laborers resulted in the death of a workman who fell, hitting his head.

John actually tried to break up the fight but was in a group of four men arrested and charged with involuntary manslaughter.

Again, he had to explain and apologize to Tina and tell her he was ashamed. He was on his way to Rocky Shores Correctional. Tina had attended some of the trial and heard John's friend from the docks, Mike O'Neil, tell a lawyer, "John really was trying to break up the fight. He didn't mean to hurt anyone. Why won't they listen?"

❖ ❖ ❖

Chapter 2

It was early in the spring of 2000 when John Michael Donovan shuffled along a sterile, gray-walled corridor toward the warden's office, accompanied by two uniformed Neanderthals. An orange prison-issue scrub suit, leg irons and handcuffs fastened to a leather belt at his waist defined his position in life.

He was asking himself, *What did I do? It was only a little argument. The dumb ass was askin' for it. He shouldn't have told me he wanted a Mohawk if he didn't know what a Mohawk looked like.*

His barbering skills at Lyon Mountain Correctional were highlighted on his record, and noted by the prison staff at Rocky Shore Correctional. Warden Gelky insisted on free haircuts, but let John collect fifty cents each from his prison guard "clients." For John, getting anything from them was like a mini payback.

He enjoyed the work. Talking with people made time move faster. It also gave him an "in" to outside and inside scuttlebutt, and a sense of personal worth, something most other inmates couldn't claim. It was a status thing. He had eight months to go.

Entering the warden's office, Donovan was surprised to see two men and his so-called lawyer with the warden. "So-called" because she was appointed by the court at no cost to him, and was worth exactly what he'd paid. In his opinion, trying to talk sense to her was like trying to get a used car salesman to give back your money after he sold you a lemon.

Instinct told him, *These other men aren't lawyers. Their clothes and shoes are from Sears or K-Mart; they have lousy haircuts and no briefcases. Greta Schwartz is shined-up as usual. Tall, slim, with frosted blonde hair, in a light-green suit fitting her like an under-sized condom, and a fancy, high-priced manicure. She has a briefcase.*

The warden interrupted his assessment. "Mr. Donovan," Warden Gelky said, in his political-speech voice garnished by his political smile, both used to plug the hole in his sincerity, "we asked you to come here today for a special reason."

Donovan growled to himself, *Like I had a choice. Was the monkey I gave the Mohawk the mayor's son?*

Gelky was an ex-policeman whose height of six feet five and loud voice coming down from above gave the impression God was talking, or so he thought. This possibility didn't occur to listeners. High pitched, his voice sounded as if somebody had tromped on his gonads in a football game. He had gray hair, including a mustache, gray skin and was in a neat gray suit. Only his tie had life: red stripes alternating with, you guessed it, gray.

The warden continued: "The prison is overcrowded and the penal commissioner has instructed us to find prisoners nearing the end of their terms for early release. The Parole Board, with Attorney Schwartz's help," he waved elegantly in the direction of Schwartz, "has selected you as one to be considered for the program."

❖ ❖ ❖

He had Donovan's attention. His mouth was hanging open and Greta stifled a laugh. The warden added, "Your attorney and I," he looked toward Greta to be sure she appreciated his blessing, "agree you're a good candidate and she's found you a job. It is near a halfway house where you can stay for six weeks, then continue mandatory parole supervision to finish your sentence. Do you have anything to say?"

"...That's great. What's the job?"

Greta said, "Working for a building contractor."

"Doin' what?"

"You'll be trained in all kinds of jobs: painting, carpentry, sheetrock installation, shovel work, any type they need you to do."

The warden added, "The job will be here in Beckett's Bay. We chose this location purposely to isolate you from old, say, *temptations;* to try to keep you from returning to our hospitality. The halfway house is near this facility and your supervision will be transferred to our parole department."

For a year and four months, Donovan's only thoughts were of the past; it was real. The future wasn't. Here was a break, and his mind suddenly plunged into what was ahead.

The warden introduced the Amorsetti brothers, owners of Amorsetti Construction. No handshakes were offered or attempted. They sat there like funeral directors at a speech on embalming fluid. The warden explained, "Joe and Frank Amorsetti have worked with us for five years rehabilitating men coming out of prison. They'd like to give you an apprentice job at their company."

Donovan looked at Sears and Kmart. Both were burly, barrel-chested men with broad, beard-shaded faces and flat noses. They stared back at him, unsmiling, as if it was an imposition to even be there. The one on the left, Joe, was the tallest; his vertical growth arrested at five seven. Both had tanned skin and shag-rug hair, graying at the temples and together they overlapped two chairs with their strong-looking arms crossed on their chests. He decided, *They look like Army drill sergeants with attitudes.*

❖ ❖ ❖

Donovan, age twenty-three, always made an effort to keep an erect posture. He thought it showed the prison guards, and tall cons that they didn't intimidate him. He made a quick effort to square his shoulders. His strong, serious, chiseled face favored a tough image; which was only semi-true. He wished he were braver.

The orange prison garb clashed with his black, self-administered buzz-haircut. His dark eyes darted from face to face searching and questioning, trying to identify the significance of what he'd just seen and heard. He was good at it. Since he was fourteen, and on his own, he'd studied people's actions and motives, both the spoken and unspoken. Now he was shaking the rust from those skills and tingling with their reemergence.

Long ago he tagged his first prison trip as being dumb and the current one to bad luck.

"Okay. I'll do it," Donovan said, and saw Frank Amorsetti give Greta a quick wink. *What does that mean?*

"Fine." Warden Gelky gave him a condescending smile. "We'll get you transferred within a week. The parole office will take over getting you set up in a halfway house and on a supervision schedule. Good luck to you." He shook Donovan's hand, making the chains attached to the handcuffs clatter like marbles in a tin can.

Greta approached. "John, I'll pick you up when they release you, give you a tour of the town, and get you settled at the halfway house. The state will give you a hundred dollars for food and lodging. It should keep you okay until your first paycheck. Amorsetti Construction is going to pay you five dollars an hour. Okay?"

Donovan stared at her. *I know people who can heist a car and sell it at a chop shop in twenty minutes for nine hundred bucks.* He gave her a limp smile, so she could feel proud of herself. The Kmart-Sears brothers gave him the evil eye and he smelled trouble. *This isn't going to be a picnic.*

As he shuffled from the room with the two giants, he saw the warden put his arms around the shoulders of the Amorsetti brothers, and they all stared at Greta's cleavage. It was clear they were a team and she was giggling with the attention placed on her major attraction.

Chapter 3

Two weeks later, John Donovan was ushered into the Rocky Shore Parole Office. One of the hacks removed his cuffs and leg irons. He rubbed his wrists and ankles and sat down to thumb through a tattered magazine.

It was thirty minutes before the parole officer entered and introduced himself. "Mr. Donovan, I'm Roan Gates, your parole officer here. Can I call you John?" A short, bald man with glasses so thick his eyes seemed to have shriveled, he stood behind a desk, looking down at the sitting Donovan.

Apparently looking down at prisoners makes him feel superior, Donovan mused. *I'll bet he keeps the desk between us the whole time. He would run if I said boo.* Donovan nodded at his request.

"I've read your file and the early release program seems to fit you. I'll need to see you, or hear from you, every week for the first six weeks. Since you don't have a car, I'll come to where you're working, or we can talk on the phone.

Amorsetti Construction will keep me informed of your whereabouts.

"You'll need to find a rooming house or apartment after six weeks and should start looking for something you can afford. Your sentence may be shortened a little, if you follow the rules I give you.

"The mandatory supervision visits will be less frequent after the six weeks is up, but you'll need my approval to leave this area. I'll transfer you to a local parole officer if you move after six months. Do you understand?"

John nodded again, thinking, *The Amorsetti brothers are grinning. They're getting free labor out of me for six months.*

❖ ❖ ❖

Chapter 4

The next morning, Greta arrived in a yellow Corvette to drive Donovan and his duffle bag around town, and to at 434 Main Street. His total assets consisted of a check for one hundred dollars from the New York Penal System, forty-nine bucks from cutting hair, two changes of underwear, jeans, three shirts, the brown shoes he was wearing, a pair of sneakers, four pair of socks, and a windbreaker. Except for the check and the haircut money, it was exactly what he'd brought to the prison a year and a half earlier. Everything fit him better now, except the money. He'd lost twenty pounds.

At the halfway house, a stone-faced Salvation Army officer in a hand-me-down uniform with cuffs three inches too short, showed them to a room on the second floor. "You may get a roommate if we get overloaded. The house rules are on the back of the door."

After the officer left, Greta jumped on the bed and kicked the door closed with one foot, giving him a peek under her skirt as far north as bikini-land. "This isn't bad, John."

He didn't say what he thought, *I'm going to work my way out of this and I'm not going to be your tool or anybody else's.* Instead he gave her his best concrete look. "Thanks for getting me the early release."

Realizing he refused her invitation, Greta got up and pushed the sheet of rules and the parole officer's phone number against his chest. "Be sure you call Gates every week. Frank Amorsetti goes to the prison the last Friday of the month and will take you with him for a face-to-face with Gates.

"Make sure you call him. My ass is on the line if you screw up. Good luck," she added over her shoulder, her voice cold as dry ice. She cursed to herself, *Damn! I can't even get a dude in bed who's fresh out of prison. Either he's gay or I gotta get a makeover or somethin'.*

❖ ❖ ❖

Chapter 5

Throwing the duffle bag on the bed, John looked around at the scarred desk, three drawer dresser, green chair with stuffing peeking out here and there, and a floor lamp just barely holding to a vertical position, and life. The walls were gray and bare except for a few nails and a poster of a scantily clad girl named Lila. The window was nailed shut. *It doesn't make any difference; there isn't any fire escape.* The shredded curtains were so faded the color was indeterminable.

It was his first time living as a civilian outside the five boroughs of New York City: lower than an eighth floor; in a building without an elevator; and in a place where there was no street noise, even at noon.

From the window of his room, he could see the red, crumbling asphalt shingles of another building eight feet away. An old black Toyota sedan, near death, was parked behind it. The room didn't have a bathroom, but he found one three doors down the hall. Another stairway at the back of the building provided access both down and up.

He walked outside, unrestrained by barbed wire for the first time in more than a year. He had a strange feeling, like he was a dog whose freedom was defined by the length of a leash, and the leash had just broken. He hadn't done anything without asking permission for a long time.

Most of the buildings on both sides of the street were three or four stories high, hugged the sidewalk and had diagonal parking lines in front. All had small shops or eating-places on the ground floors and curtained windows above. Neatly painted storefronts with small patches of manicured grass or trees lined the street. The river came almost to the back of the buildings on the opposite side of the street from the halfway house. He could see decks at several levels stretching out toward the water on the backsides of some buildings.

The green, choppy water of the St. Lawrence was alive with the whine of boat motors. They flashed past his view through the gaps between buildings. The bow of a huge red ship lumbered along, followed by an endless red steel hull and finally a stern with a flag he didn't recognize. It dwarfed the motorboats. *It's too close to shore. It's going to hit something,* he thought. The deep, throaty throb of the engines surprised him and the pavement vibrated a little under his feet. He'd seen big ships roped to docks in the New York harbor, but never this large, and moving.

In New York City, he could rely on street signs to tell directions, but here he had no clue. *Which way is east? I wonder where this monster is headed. Which way is upstream? Maybe I can get on one and get out of here. Naw, they'd catch me. It moves like a turtle.* The ship passed on by and he marveled at how it fit in the narrow strip of water between the buildings and the rocky islands off shore.

He watched to see if anyone else on the street was concerned this monster sliding by meant trouble and decided after a few minutes, *You can tell the locals on the street from the tourists by who looks at the ship. Only the tourists in fancy shorts give it a glance or point it out to their kids.*

❖ ❖ ❖

It was almost noon and he was hungry. He walked into Allenburg Bank on the river side of the street, a block from the halfway house.

"I need to cash this check, please." He handed the paper defining his networth to the teller.

"You need to endorse it on the back, Mr. Donovan," the young woman said, smiling, and pointing to the line for his signature. "Do you have identification, like a drivers license?"

John gave her his license. "One moment, please." She walked to a neatly dressed man with glasses sitting at a desk behind her and showed him the check and license. He looked at both, then at Donovan, and gave him a stiff, sterile smile. He whispered something to the teller.

She returned to her window. "Did you know your license has expired?"

"Yes. I have to renew it, but haven't been able to yet. I'm going to start a new job Monday."

"We can use it for identification today since the photo is still good. Good luck with the job." She gave him a hundred dollars in fives and tens, and a professional, wary smile that said, you're a felon and I'm glad to be on this side of the bulletproof glass.

John knew the source of the check labeled him a former convict. The operative word "former" made him smile back at her, his confidence rising gently to the surface. "Where can I get my license renewed? Do you know how much it costs?"

"The motor vehicle office is in the court house. It's four blocks down that way," she said, pointing, "and six up the hill from the river toward the highway. It'll cost about seventy dollars."

"I guess it will have to wait. Thank you." He turned away.

❖   ❖   ❖

Chapter 6

Two blocks from the bank, on the uphill side of the street, a sign for O'Toole's OT Bar & Grill flashed a neon arrow at an entrance. Inside, the bar was dim and coming in from bright sunlight, Donovan had to hesitate until his pupils dilated. There were people at tables along the right wall, all the way to the back. The bar on his left had brighter lighting.

Four men on barstools near the entrance were engrossed in discussion, boisterous at times. All had gray coveralls with Highway Department stamped on the back and wore leather work boots. The mahogany bar was clean and shiny. The bottles on the back bar were in order, like soldiers at attention.

Donovan looked around, and, judging by the customer's clothes, decided the bar served both vacationers and local workmen. *It's not a fancy, expensive place.* Since he didn't fit in either category yet, he selected a stool at the distal end of the bar. The bartender approached and Donovan asked, "What does OT stand for?"

"O'Toole's or Over Time, whichever you like. What can I getcha?"

"Can I get a sandwich?"

"Sure. Today we have BLTs or BLTs."

"Then I guess it's a BLT, and a Bud."

"You got it. You new around here?" He opened a door a crack at the back of the bar and yelled, "BLT. Make it a double."

"Goin' to start work for Amorsetti Construction Monday."

"Just get out of the slammer?"

"Yeah. How'd you know?"

"Been there, done that. Most of the guys they hire are ex-cons. Me too, until I married up and got this bar. Name's Bud Gigantelli," he extended his hand. A stocky, medium-height man with a strong, confident voice and bushy black eyebrows, his head seemed to sit directly on his shoulders. His wide smile fit his broad face and nose, and invited conversation.

"John Donovan." He shook the offered hand. "I'm in the halfway house for six weeks. Know any place I could afford to rent nearby?"

"You're in luck. Rita and I bought a house in the country. I'm not sure why, except she said it'll be better when the kid comes along. We are goin' to move there in four weeks. Our apartment upstairs will be vacant. Keep in touch. As soon as we move out, I'll show it to ya."

"Thanks. How much you askin'?"

"Have to think about it. I know what you're up against; ever tend bar?"

"Some. Know the simple stuff."

"It's mostly beer, gin and vodka except in the summer when the fancy boats dock. Then we have to get out the funny little umbrellas and stuff for the girls the dandies bring in. It's not hard to learn."

"Can I have some mail sent here?"

"Sure. I'll tell my people to hold it for ya if I'm not here."

"Thanks." *Good bartender,* John decided. *He's a pro. Probably hears everything and remembers nothin'.*

Chapter 7

Leaving the bar, Donovan walked about ten blocks east to the Walmart, using Bud's directions. He bought a burner phone for $9.83 and called Tina while walking back to the halfway house. "Hi, doll. Everything okay?"

"John, happy to hear your voice. I'm fine, how about you?"

"Great. You're my first call from the outside. Got some good news. How would you like a seaside vacation?" He described his release, new digs, the conditions and job to start Monday. "I have a lead on an apartment for after the six-week halfway house tour is done. Hope you'll come up after I have the place."

"How long will it be before you come back to the city?"

"Six months, maybe more."

"I'll be up. Give me your number. I'll call evenings. John … I miss you." They exchanged some pleasantries and hung up. Tina smiled, *He called me before anyone else and as soon as he could. He has me on his mind.* She danced around the room.

In John's life, there were phone taboos. You only said things understandable to the person you called. Nobody wrote anything down. Identity was by first names or nicknames, even if you used a burner phone. He struggled to recall Emilio Angelo's number. Emilio took 'Angelo' as his last name because it advertised his creative abilities in the Italian section of Brooklyn. John finally remembered it.

"Emilio? John."

"John, haven't heard from you for a while."

"Been away."

"I heard. What you need?"

"The usual. Mine expired. I'll send ya the old. You at the same address?"

"Yeah. How soon you need it?"

"Couple weeks. Send it to the address I give ya."

"Gonna cost ya three big ones."

"I know. Can't pay right now."

"I know you since we was in fourth grade. Pay when you can. Glad you're eatin' out. Bye."

❖ ❖ ❖

Chapter 8

John arrived at the Amorsetti Construction Company office at six o'clock on Monday morning. It was along the main highway at the south edge of town, a fifteen-block walk from the halfway house.

Joe Amorsetti was surprised John was there on time and offered him a cup of coffee and a donut. "You'll need a hardhat," and took him into the equipment repair building to try on a few. "We do some new houses, but most of our work now is remodeling commercial buildings for businesses or conversion to apartments or condos. I'm going to have you work with Sam Wolcott today tearin' off wallpaper and fixin' sheetrock. Ever done it?"

John shook his head no slowly. He didn't have a clue how it was done.

"That's okay. Sam will show you."

On the first day, John met two employees also tethered to Amorsetti Construction via the parole office. John recognized the name Abe Waverly. He was one of those men known more by reputation than business, a type of notoriety he preferred. Abe always had a black cigar in his mouth and rolled it from one corner of his mouth to the other, lit or unlit. The tougher a price negotiation, the faster the roll.

In the help-yourself market of other people's autos, price was the only subject open to discussion. He had owned, and claimed he still did, the busiest chop shop in the Bronx. He bragged about a special metal shredder just for MD license plates. His popularity came more from prompt cash payments than personality. A large man covered with black hair, he was advertised in his youth as the Bronx Bear, or

BB, and wrestled for money and fame. When the fame went out, his second love—automobile plastic surgery—took over.

The Amorsetti brothers pounced on his mechanical skills and taught him to use a crane. At six three and stocky, Abe cursed daily getting in and out of the cramped control cabin on the crane, but, once he got in, he savored the power. In there, he was in command of the foot pedals and levers like Billy Joel at a piano.

Near the time Donovan started work there, Abe had verbally agreed to stay with Amorsetti Construction two more months, even though his time there was finished and he could report to a parole officer elsewhere. Beckett's Bay didn't fuss with crane operator certification like the city, so he accepted the Amorsetti brothers offer after they upped his pay to $15 an hour.

Donovan also met Ed Lightfeather, better known as Shadow. Shadow was slim as a toothpick and short. Walking behind the bar at O'Toole's he disappeared. Later Donovan learned he used this attribute, plus his sleight of hand, to get free beer from the tap when Bud's back was turned. Often he startled people by appearing unexpectedly. Soft spoken, quiet, and smart, Shadow dressed neatly, polished his shoes, kept his brown hair combed and presented a countenance that made him look distinguished, like a Shakespearean actor or a life insurance salesman.

When he was young he worked as a riveter on the high steel, but gave it up after a fall left him dangling in his safety harness eighty stories above 5th Avenue. As a night-school trained bookkeeper, he felt grounded. Borrowing $80,000 without permission from his get-rich-quick customers went unnoticed until he hit a losing streak at Yonkers Raceway and gaps appeared in their holdings. His only admission was, "I shoulda read the spread better."

Rocky Shore Correctional had been his home for two years. His innovative income tax skills and cheap service fees pleased the guards. They were his guardian angels and, despite his diminutive size, nobody inside dared touch him.

Shadow had been working for the Amorsetti brothers for two months when Donovan arrived. The contractor saw it was useless to expect heavy labor from him and started him painting. By the time Shadow met Donovan, he'd become the firm's expert on paint, wallpaper and color coordination.

Every week, for ten hours a day and five on Saturday, Donovan tore out old plasterboard, paneling and nails. Each night he was coated in dust, sneezing non-stop, and had a major backache. Each Saturday he received a check for two hundred-fifty dollars, minus the usual deductions.

❖ ❖ ❖

Chapter 9

Bud handed Donovan an envelope at O'Toole's ten days later. "You got mail."

"Thanks, Bud. You know where I can lease, or buy on time, a secondhand motorcycle in good shape?"

"Sure. Jack Wiltsie has 'em. He's pretty fair. I know bikes. I'll go with ya. The price will be better."

The following Saturday afternoon, with Bud's help, John made the first month's down payment on a 1986 Harley. "It's only been in one minor accident," Wiltsie proclaimed. Donovan smothered a laugh, *That's the best fake look of absolute honesty I've seen since leavin' the city. This guy musta lived in Queens.*

Wiltsie reduced the price by two hundred dollars when Bud told him, "We know where to find ya."

Three weeks later Bud asked Donovan, "You wanna look at the place upstairs? We moved two days ago."

They went up the inside stairs to the third floor. The upper floor was one big apartment. Windows in the front gave a view of Main Street below and the river beyond the businesses across the street. It wasn't fancy but it was clean and had a sofa, kitchen table, desk and a double bed. Bud explained, "Rita bought new."

"Can I afford this?"

"Tell you what, you help me at the bar Saturday nights, I'll give it to you for two hundred a month. You can put the Harley in the shed out back."

"Done," Donovan said.

He called Tina that evening. "I found an apartment. Will you come up?"

After he described the details of his job, the apartment, and Beckett's Bay, Tina said, "Yes. For a visit."

"Great. I'll call you when things are settled. May have to fix it up some."

"I'll help you."

"You're the best. Bye."

❖ ❖ ❖

Chapter 10

John Donovan was becoming an expert at tearing out sheetrock, but didn't believe would it have value at a future job interview. He was getting better at installing it, too, but didn't think it was worth bragging about either. He'd also done some painting and rough carpentry, and the Amorsettis seemed pleased with his work.

The foreman, Sam Wolcott, in his fifties, was a reasonable guy who didn't share the Amorsetti penchant for cheap, untrained, ex-con labor, but he was a reticent man of unlimited patience and took pride in seeing people without skills improve. Long ago, he'd given up trying to change the Amorsetti mindset.

Sam was strong. His broad shoulders and tall, sturdy body let him match any of the young ex-cons in tough jobs, and he had the efficiency of experience they lacked. He would give a man a job to do and walk away. Watching unseen from a distance for a short time, he would return and join him in the task. Sam was better at it, and faster. He didn't scold or make fun of the man's skill, or even speak, unless he needed to explain something.

If a man was repeating the work in another area and using his techniques, Sam smiled. His motto was, actions are better than words. They called him Grandpa because of his gray hair and teased him for never even getting a parking ticket.

❖ ❖ ❖

Chapter 11

Donovan called parole officer Gates every Friday at noon, hoping it would interrupt his lunch. If he was at the Amorsetti Construction office, he called from the phone there. Out on a job, he asked to use one of the Amorsetti brother's cell phones.

At three in the afternoon, on the last Friday of the month, and two weeks before Donovan's halfway house time ended, Frank Amorsetti approached him. "Come on, Donovan. You gotta see Gates today. I'm goin' over there. I'll take ya. I gotta stop at our office on the way."

"Okay."

When they reached the Amorsetti Construction office Frank said, "Stay in the truck. I'll be right out." Coming out of the office, he carried a scuffed-up brown briefcase and slid it behind his seat in the truck.

This was the second time Frank had taken Donovan for his Friday visit to the parole officer. Each time he brought the same briefcase. Donovan was curious. *I can't believe he does much paper work. Maybe Sheila, the secretary, has to send in reports.*

Frank Amorsetti was in an unusually talkative mood on this Friday. "You know the red brick building on Main with the shoe store?"

"I think so."

"You know, there's a little park between it and the bank with a black iron fence along the sidewalk."

"Yeah, I know the one."

"We just bought it at tax auction. We'll make four apartments in there, maybe five. We'll start on it as soon as we can. Have to tear down a lot of partitions and stuff. I'm aimin' to get the demolition done this fall. You could walk to work."

"I found a place to live upstairs over O'Toole's after I leave the halfway."

"Good. That's even closer. Bud's a good fella. Worked for us when he first came out of Rocky. I'll wait and give you a ride back after you're through with Gates."

"Thanks."

Donovan gave officer Gates his new address and got the okay to move after the halfway time was up. He didn't bother Gates with the details about Tina coming up, the apartment being over a bar, that he made extra money as a bartender, had his own phone, and owned a motorcycle.

He moved to the apartment on a Saturday and talked to Tina for an hour in the evening.

Chapter 12

The following Monday morning, there was a meeting at the Amorsetti Construction Company office with Joe, Frank, Sam and eight parolees, including Donovan. Joe Amorsetti did the talking. "We got a big job downtown, turning the upper floors of the old Hockmeir Building into condos. If we get the demolition and debris disposed of while the weather's good we can work indoors all winter." This brought a cheer from the group.

"There are some hitches. We have to get the tenants out. The bank owns the small park between the buildings. They agreed to let us get a crane in there to lower the debris from the upper floors. I'm glad, because, if we try to load trucks on the street, we'll have to pay a bundle to take the wires down, put them up, and listen to all the bitching concerning the power shut-offs and the trucks screwing up traffic.

"So, we're going to anchor a barge in the river behind the building to take away the junk. Abe, you have to be careful getting the crane under the utility wires, so go down and check it out. See if you can get in there and let me know if you see problems. When you're ready to move the crane in, we'll have the utility people standby."

Abe nodded he understood. "If I can move it to the river edge, the boom will reach the upper floors."

"Okay. We have to restore the park after we're done. The bank wants a new sidewalk in front of their entrance and the park. Any of you ever use a jackhammer?" Getting no response, he turned to Donovan. "You're low man on the pole, John. You're gonna learn how to break cement." This brought a group hoot, and John rolled his eyes.

Amorsetti chuckled. "Four of you will push our other jobs along and the other four will get started in September at the building, as soon as all the tenants are out."

❖ ❖ ❖

Chapter 13

Donovan explored the community on his Harley. When Tina called to say she'd be there Thursday on the 7:15 bus, he was in a quandary. The bus station was twenty miles away and he knew she'd have at least four suitcases.

He approached Bud at the OT and explained the situation. Without hesitation Bud said, "Take my pickup. It's out back. Just fill the tank. Looking forward to meetin' her." He tossed John the keys.

Donovan wasn't used to such generosity, except from Tina, and did a double take. "...Thanks."

On the way to the bus terminal, he mulled over Bud's conduct, *Either he's a generous man who's really gone straight or he's a mole. Got to ask questions. I wonder who his friends are. The Amorsettis?*

In the city, Donovan knew people by their skills, time served and nicknames. In any job, a fair share of the profits was the limit of friendship. Most men he knew didn't hang around together. The police could show up at any second and you wouldn't want to be there.

Tina was special. Generosity reigned between them. It was unspoken love. Tina bounded off the bus and saw John's arms thrashing the air to get her attention. It told Tina everything she needed to know. She waved back while moving through the crowd, and leaped into his arms.

He kissed her quickly and studied her face. Her smile was gold to him. She knew John disliked public affection, but hugged him anyway. To the unknowing observer, the brevity of Donovan's greeting might have seemed a little cold. It'd been over a year since their last time together, but their written correspondence had been steady. His greeting was more than she expected; a sense of belonging and a strange, tingling feeling washed over her.

She had five suitcases, not four. Donovan could feel his heart thumping. He loaded her bags into Bud's pickup and, in the cab, gave her a kiss that confirmed her decision to travel there was the correct thing to do. And, even though she'd never been to Beckett's Bay, she felt like she was home; she should be with John.

Slim, shapely, page-boy black hair, sparkling, dark eyes, smooth skin, narrow lips, delicate nose and sweet smile: her beauty shouted at him because it wasn't just on the outside, but imbedded in her personality. Donovan had marveled for a long time at how Tina, from a God-awful family life, had come to him without a prior marriage, drugs or a streetwalker's history.

Within a week, Tina had the apartment in shape, and Bud had become a first name friend. She also had a lead on a cashier's job at a supermarket.

After ten-hour days of hard labor, coming home to hot showers, meals prepared with a purpose, and Tina, Donovan was a happy man. He told himself, *Only the parole time is hangin' over me now, and I will clean it up. Tina deserves to be with a good man.*

Tina smiled into the mirror every morning. She wasn't sure why, but couldn't help it.

Chapter 14

Bud initiated a weekly poker game at the OT Grill. A corridor extended from the barroom to the back of the building. Doors along the walls of the corridor were branded with make-your-own-signs from a hardware store and defined their internal functions as Kitchen, Machos and Maidens. Near the end of the hall an unmarked door opened into a large unkempt room with beer and liquor cases stacked by supplier names along three walls. At the end of the hall, a door opened into the back alley. It provided access for supplies and shy poker players.

A helter-skelter array of empty cases surrounded the back door. In the storeroom, a single, oversized light bulb in a dented, green metal shade the size of a tire hung over a sturdy round table with scars from age and abuse. Ventilation was achieved by leaving the alley and room doors partly open; a choice disapproved of by the majority but necessary when cigar smoke hid the cards from view.

Garage sale chairs and a multi-colored, torn settee faced the table. The first poker players to arrive, out of habit, chose seats facing the hall door. It was instinctive. It was good to know early if a person entering the bar was a player or a cop so there was time to get out the backdoor. The settee was reserved for Abe. He didn't need help filling it. Nobody argued about his choice.

The game, with paltry winnings potential, was set at a quarter a bet. It was more for recreation and camaraderie of men with similar life experiences, and ex-cons filled the chairs to share thoughts, ideas, gripes and the reduced price of beer, thanks to Bud.

Two weeks after Tina's arrival, on a Thursday night, John and Tina hosted the poker game in their third floor apartment, a decision that pleased Bud. Shifting locations made the game less likely to be discovered by the law and relieved his worry concerning the bar's liquor license.

205

Tina met Rita, Bud's wife. Rita was raised locally but, at nineteen went to Vegas to be a line dancer and later a blackjack dealer. When she found her husband in bed with one of her friends, she returned to Beckett's Bay, leaving him with nothing more than his underwear. Bud had been her high school sweetheart.

At thirty-one, Rita still had the pretty face of her youth but was struggling to avoid the softer physique created by having a baby. She was a foot taller and eight years older than Tina. With an easy smile, she was past the age of foolishness. She could relate to a young woman who wasn't afraid to work. They became instant friends.

Later, she often asked Tina to help her run the bar for a few hours, while Bud went fishing. Their relationship was cemented when Abe first saw Tina and said to John, "Donovan, how did an ugly bugger like you get this cute girl?"

Tina didn't give John a chance to answer. "He didn't get *me*. *I* got him. And by the looks of you, I did damn good."

A "Whoooooha!" and roar of laughter filled the room, with Rita leading the pack.

John was still laughing as he introduced them. "Tina, meet Abe Waverly, the Bronx Bear, or just BB. Greg Waters' nickname is Gomer. He's from Flatbush. Ed Lightfeather, sometimes called Shadow, used to work in Manhattan."

Tina put a cold beer in each extended hand and gave each face a smile. "If you're John's friend, you're mine, too."

Gomer(Greg), age twenty-six, whose voice and body had been on separate maturation schedules since puberty, was a bookie for three years. He found supplying vehicles to a chop shop more profitable, until a bum near a drop-off turned out to be a New York City Police detective. Tall, with an angular hooked nose, his ferocious appearance masked a genial, quiet personality and a body with surprising physical strength. Donovan had been amazed at the weight he could lift. He'd started work at Amorsetti Construction at the same time as Donovan.

Bud grinned. "Because of your skinny paychecks, I'll supply the beer tonight. Let's keep the stakes at a quarter, too. We'll go big time if we get one of the Amorsettis in here. Then maybe we can get some of our money back."

Donovan looked at him. "What do you mean?"

"You don't know?"

"Know what?"

"They are payin' you $5 an hour and chargin' the New York State Penal System $15 an hour for your work. They're making $10 an hour off each of you, plus your labor, except for Abe. Maybe more. The numbers may have gone up since I was in your position."

Donovan studied Bud's face. "How do you know?"

"You know Sheila in their office?"

"Yeah."

"We dated for a while before Rita came home. I walked in the office one Thursday after work and she was stuffing cash in a briefcase. She was a little flustered. Later, she told me one of the brothers took the briefcase filled with cash the last Friday of every month to pay bills, and she had to have it ready. She'd asked for a counting machine, but they wouldn't get her one; she had to do it by hand.

They cashed the check from the state and brought the money to her. After putting the amount they requested in the case, she put it in her locked file cabinet with the accounting books. She then locked half of the remainder in each of their desks. This information stays in this room, by the way."

Shadow(Ed) cleared his throat for attention. He knew numbers. "If they're chargin' the penal system fifteen an hour for your work and payin' the eight of you say, 8k a month, they're skimmin' at least 15k a month for themselves." Everyone at the table stared at him.

"Really?" Bud sputtered. "That much? I know they got two sets of books. I helped Sheila with the regular one, but she left the cheat book on the desk one day and I went through it. She doesn't know it. Don't say nothin'. She has two kids, no husband, and needs the job." Everyone agreed with his request.

John lost $2 in the game, but, along with the others, gained a new opinion of Amorsetti Construction.

❖ ❖ ❖

Hosting the poker game at Tina and John's apartment became a weekly habit. Tina opened the windows for a breeze to flush out the cigar smoke. It made her nauseous.

Abe's long-time girlfriend joined him in mid-July for a break from the city heat. Jadlyn Jezek, was tall, like Abe, but better proportioned. She had tried modeling but found it boring. Interested in action, she worked as a stunt driver in movies filmed in NY for a time.

She'd met Abe after one of his wrestling matches. She was into kickboxing back then. It was an enigma how she kept such a beautiful face. Abe said it was because she was so good nobody could touch her. Her face, figure and athletic prowess opened many doors for her. Abe made her laugh and they'd been together ten years.

Running Abe's business while he was 'away', she gave it a feminine touch by moving the chop shop to Harlem and 'fronting' it with a women's clothing store. The original site became a productive used car lot with an assortment of vehicles with VIN numbers supplied by her friend in Spain.

When Jadlyn came north at Abe's suggestion, she drove a converted bus-like recreation vehicle and towed along a red Honda sports car for short runs. Abe found an RV park with amenities near Beckett's Bay and gave up his room at the boarding house.

After getting to know everyone, Jadlyn subsequently invited her friends Lloyd Yarwood and his common-law wife, Janet Sacket, to visit. They managed a marina owned by a group of wealthy boaters. Lloyd was a fishing guide on Long Island Sound. On arrival, he quickly became Bud's river fishing companion.

Lloyd and Janet met in the Navy during the Gulf War. He was an explosives tech and armed planes on a carrier. Janet, who was in a rescue unit, pulled Lloyd from the ocean after he jumped in to avoid being killed by an incoming plane with disabled landing gear.

❖ ❖ ❖

Chapter 15

By the first week of August, Amorsetti Construction had its smaller jobs nearly completed and was ready to start work on the Hockmeir Building in downtown Beckett's Bay. On Friday, the foreman, Sam Wolcott, took Abe and John to the worksite. Abe's job was to assess the crane and barge access. They found cutting the electrical wires along the street was unnecessary. The crane would fit under them, and, once positioned close to the river, the boom would reach the top floors of the building without risk of damaging them.

Sam decided the best way to protect bank patrons, windows and doors from flying debris during demolition of the concrete was to make a frame for the whole front of the bank and cover it with canvas. By extending it out from the bank wall above the first floor windows and doors and down to the ground, there would be a narrow passage along the bank front. Customers would have safe access from both north and south.

Joe Amorsetti, Abe, Sam and John were at the Hockmeir Building to start preparations early Monday morning. By Tuesday afternoon, the crane was in place, the barge had been delivered and secured, and the protective covering for the bank entrance was complete.

Sam taught Donovan how to use the jackhammer. They decided to break the concrete closer to the curb first, and then move closer to the bank later. He showed Donovan where to pile the broken concrete in the park so Abe could reach it with the crane. They removed and stored the park fence in the Hockmeir Building for re-installation later.

By Thursday, everyone within two blocks was tired of the noise and dust, and avoided the area. Gomer fed load after load of broken sheetrock, paneling and other debris through a fourth floor window into Abe's crane bucket for deposit in the barge.

Using the jackhammer for a day left Donovan vibrating well into the night. Tina gave him aspirin and pushed him into a hot shower as soon as he arrived home.

❖ ❖ ❖

Chapter 16

F riday morning, August 16th, at 10:30, Donovan, ear protectors and hardhat in place, was busy breaking concrete when a Surety Company armored truck drove up in front of the bank. Donovan didn't hear it and looked up surprised as it moved in right next to him. Seeing the construction mess, Stan, the driver, backed the truck up to the sidewalk next to the jackhammer air compressor instead of parallel parking in front of the bank as he usually did.

The Surety Company rented the whole basement of the bank for its counting and vault facility. The entrance was down steps to a steel door on the park side of the bank building. The guard, Mike, jumped out of the passenger's seat and waved to Donovan. He didn't wave back. It was foolhardy to take his eyes off the hammer pummeling the cement at his feet, or lift a hand off the handle to wave.

Mike walked behind the truck on the side away from Donovan. Stan waved to John, too, but kept his window closed, defending himself from noise, dust and flying chips of cement. John didn't see him wave.

Stan stayed in the truck confident Mike could unload the delivery and, as per protocol, to guard the rest of the load. All the while, Donovan pounded away at the concrete like a hungry woodpecker on a tree, throwing chips in every direction.

Mike pulled five canvas bags from the truck to the sidewalk quickly. He was closing the rear doors when the whole truck convulsed. The steel doors flapped back and forth rapidly, making him duck to protect his head. A loud screeching, metal-ripping sound briefly overwhelmed even the jackhammer noise.

He rushed around front to see what happened. Stan had already exited the truck and stood staring at a large white Cadillac. The heavy bumper of the truck had protruded a little into the narrow driving lane, and the Caddy had a bumper-high, metallic tear along the right side from front to back, decorated with streaks of black paint.

A tall, comely young woman with blonde hair in an expensive black suit and lots of jewelry, jumped from the driver's seat, leaving the door ajar, and joined them to stare at the side of her vehicle. "Oh my God!" she shouted. She searched her pockets for a tissue and started to cry. "Oh my God! There was a car coming the other way and the space was narrow. I thought I could get through."

She was really crying now and one of the Surety guards took her elbow and guided her to the side of the truck, away from the jackhammer noise and dust. Mike and Stan, stunned and helpless, looked in unison back and forth at her then at the car as she wiped her eyes and sobbed.

❖ ❖ ❖

Finally, to be heard over the jackhammer noise, Stan shouted, "Do you have insurance?" He felt he had to say something.

She nodded yes, wiped her tears and screamed back. "Is your truck damaged?"

Both men went into the street with her to look at the front of the truck. Stan yelled, "Nothing. Just a little white paint on the bumper." Unsure if she could hear him, he made a baseball umpires "safe" motion with his hands and yelled, "I'll get our insurance card," and started walking around the front of the truck toward the driver's side door.

"I've got to get this fixed today! My husband's gonna kill me!" she shouted and ran to the open Caddy door, jumped in, and roared off down Main Street. All Stan and Mike could do was stand frozen in place. Their eyes followed the Caddy as it made a screeching left turn and disappeared from sight. They looked at each other, bewildered and speechless.

Mike finally closed his mouth, and then opened it again to ask, "Did you get her plate number?"

Stan was walking in a circle putting his hands first on his hips, then in his pockets. "No. I think it was Canadian. Did you get it?"

"No. I thought it was a Florida license with an orange on it, but maybe it was a peach."

They looked at each other again; both gave short nervous laughs, shrugged their shoulders and went back to the truck. When the five canvas bags weren't on the sidewalk, Mike panicked and yelled, "Stan! Stan! The money's gone!" He looked in the truck, thinking, *Maybe I didn't pull the bags out yet.* When they weren't there either, Mike raced down to the bank door, his feet just grazing the steps on the way. Fumbling with his keys and the lock code, he talked to himself, *"Maybe one of the people from inside came out and took the bags."*

Entering, he shouted, "Did any of you bring in the bags from the truck?"

Everyone looked up.

Victor, the counting house manager, walked over to him. "We didn't know you were here yet. What's wrong?"

❖ ❖ ❖

Outside, Donovan went on breaking the cement. A deputy sheriff walked over, trying to peer through the cloud of dust surrounding him by waving his hand back and forth in front of his face. Finally, only a few feet away, he yelled at Donovan.

But John, his gaze fixed on the concrete, only noticed Deputy Rudall when his feet appeared near his own. He looked up and saw, but did not hear, Rudall yelling. Donovan shrugged and made a quick motion with one hand to point at his ear protectors, clearly anxious about even a momentary release of his grip on the machine. Rudall decided speech was useless and made several quick thumbs-down motions. When Donovan stopped the jackhammer, he asked, "Did you see anyone near the Surety truck this morning?"

Donovan, still shaking from the jackhammer, raised a hand palm up and shrugged his shoulders. Then, realizing his ears were still covered, he took off his hard hat and the hearing protectors. "What did you say?"

The deputy repeated his question.

Donovan's hearing was slow to recover. "What's wrong? Did I break somethin'? I can't help it if chips fly around."

The deputy started anew. "What time did you start work?"

"Six. But couldn't start the jackhammer until eight. People complain if I start too early. Is it break time?"

"Did you see anybody around the Surety truck?"

"I didn't even see the truck until it backed in right next to me. Dust covers my goggles and I can't hear anything while I'm workin'. What happened?"

"Surety was robbed."

"Really?"

"Really. Did you see anybody new around?"

"There was a white car in front of the truck for a minute or so. The two uniform guys were talkin' to a lady."

"What did they say?"

"Are you kiddin'? When this thing is goin' I can't even hear myself sneeze."

"Did the Surety guys give anything to the lady?"

"Not that I saw. I don't look around much using this jackhammer. I'd like to keep my toes."

Chapter 17

Since the start of work in the morning, Abe had been steadily moving debris down from the fourth floor window near the back of the building and into to the barge. When Gomer had the clamshell bucket of the crane filled with broken boards and sheetrock, he would signal Abe with a wave of his hand. The control cabin where Abe sat rotated with the machine, and his back was usually toward the street.

He would swing the bucket around and lower it at the same time. Depositing the debris in the barge, he squashed it down with the bucket to make room for more.

On one pass, he saw a young woman with curly blonde hair and black-rimmed glasses watching him from a second floor window of the bank. He waved and she returned his wave. He stopped the boom's motion in mid-swing, pointed at her, made an imaginary circle around his face with his right hand, then gave a thumbs-up sign. She grasped the meaning of his sign-language compliment on her appearance and smiled. He tipped an imaginary cup up to his lips, and then pointed to himself, and then at her. She held up her left hand and pointed to the wedding ring on her finger. Abe put his hand to his heart. The woman laughed and walked away from the window. It was 10:36 in the morning.

Abe resumed his routine until a sheriff's deputy suddenly appeared on the ground nearby and motioned for him to shut down his machine and come to him. The deputy watched as Abe struggled exiting the metal and glass control cubbyhole much too small for his huge frame. "You see any strangers near the armored truck around 10:30?"

"I'm lookin' toward the river or the window up there most of the time," Abe replied, pointing at the fourth floor window. "I watch Gomer at the window for hand signals for whether the bucket's full or I'm near the building or wires. What happened?"

"Something was stolen."

"Whew! I thought the bank manager reported me for flirtin' with one of his office girls." All the while he was talking, his big black cigar was rolling back and forth from one corner of his mouth to the other. The deputy was mesmerized and, coupled with Abe's Bronx accent, he was uncertain of some of the words Abe delivered.

Convinced Abe couldn't have jumped down from the crane to seize the money, he decided to leave the conversation, and climbed up to look in the crane's cab. Coming down, he watched the cigar make a couple more runs, shook his head, and walked away.

❖ ❖ ❖

Chapter 18

Deputy Sheriff Collins found Shadow studying the building plans in the old shoe store on the first-floor of the Hockmeir Building. Collins glared at him. "You got a name? What time did you come to work?"

"I do. Do you?

"Don't be a smart ass."

"Rightbackatcha. Ed Lightfeather. Got here at six, like always."

"You stay here since six?"

"Mostly. Sometimes, I go upstairs to take measurements when they finish clearin' a room, or go for coffee, if Amorsetti asks me to."

"Where is Amorsetti?"

"Frank's in the back, I think. He has an office in there. He may've gone to the diner." He pointed to the former store storage room where the men had assembled some old furniture left in the building by the former tenants.

Collins walked to the room, saw it was empty, and returned. "Is there an elevator?"

"Are you kiddin'? This is an old building." Shadow motioned, "The stairs are over there."

Collin's stomach hung jiggling like Jell-O over his thick, black leather belt, same as the neck rolls over his collar. The belt was draped with handcuffs, a firearm and a truncheon. A radio near his left shoulder spouted unintelligible squawks sporadically.

Collins checked each floor and found no one until he reached the fourth. Arriving there, breathing had priority over police work, and his face was tomato red. After a few minutes of hanging on to the banister with both hands, he looked around the room. Some walls were only wooden two-by-four skeletons with wires running through; others held remnants of sheetrock, paneling and an occasional steel beam. Gomer was frosted with dust as Deputy Collins approached him. "What time did you start work this morning?" he wheezed.

"About six. What happened?"

The officer stared at him, didn't answer, and then pointed at Sam. "Who's he?"

"Sam Wolcott, the foreman."

Collins waddled over to Sam. "What time did you and your men start work?"

"Six. What's wrong?"

"Robbery. Cash from the Surety truck. You see any people you didn't know outside as you came to work?"

"Some of the bank people comin' into work around eight. They all had keys or people inside opened the door for them."

"How about later, near ten o'clock?"

"I don't go to the windows much. I'm tryin' to be careful getting these partitions down without damaging wiring or bearing walls."

"What are the work hours?"

"Six to six weekdays; six to noon Saturdays."

❖　❖　❖

Collins turned like a loaded logging truck and shuffled to the window again where Gomer was pushing debris into Abe's crane bucket. For a minute, he studied the view of the money truck and the pile of concrete Donovan had accumulated, mostly as a delay to suck in more air. He turned and squinted at Gomer. Standing between Gomer and the open window he blocked most of the incoming light.

"Did you see anybody by the truck around 10:30?"

"Just Donovan bustin' the sidewalk and there was a lady talking to the guards for a few minutes. How much money did they get?" He had heard what he told Sam.

This time Collins did a double take when he heard Gomer's high-pitched voice. *Is he mocking me? That can't be his real voice. Is he one of those guys who used to be a woman? Thinkin' of him with long hair and heels makes me want to puke.* "Don't know yet. Did you go downstairs for anything this morning?"

"Just to the third floor to get a crowbar."

❖ ❖ ❖

The state police were on the scene by the time Sheriff Wiley and his deputies had interviewed Mike and Stan from the Surety truck, Frank Amorsetti, and his work crew. Frank told them he wasn't in the building when the Surety truck arrived. "I was talkin' to Mary at the Columbus Diner." Wiley believed him because Frank was hitting on her every time he went in there, but he would check with Mary anyway.

Wiley gave the state police a summary of events. "The Surety men estimate there was nearly a million dollars in the five bags. They didn't see anyone around except the man runnin' the jackhammer and the crane operator. The little fella who is working in the building arrived with coffee from the diner down the street at the same time the guard discovered the money was missing. He didn't see anyone near the truck. The men workin' on the fourth floor didn't leave the building or see anything either. We have to consider the Surety guards. The girl in the Caddy could've been a set up and the money went with her."

A forensic team arrived to dust for fingerprints and collect samples of the white paint on the truck bumper, along with any other materials the detectives suggested. The detectives searched the Hockmeir Building, the bank next-door, other nearby buildings, and set up roadblocks to check vehicles leaving the area. They stopped and searched suspicious vehicles on outgoing streets, too. Even the crane cab was searched and the rookie cops had to dig through all the debris Abe had put in the barge.

Abe's crude sign language "conversation" with the pretty blonde at the window was the only detail offered by anyone at the bank. Two tourists passing down the other side of the street to avoid the dust and noise confirmed the white Caddy, but didn't recognize the driver. Mike and Stan sat in the Surety truck cab with their ears attached to cellphones. Their faces were pale and they were wrestling with nausea.

Mr. Theodore Wilson, the bank president, was on the sidewalk behind the Surety truck, frowning, pacing, and pulling at his collar. Embarrassment and anger twisted his usually calm, professional banker's-face as he confronted Donovan. "You covered the God dammed surveillance cameras. I told you not do it."

"Sorry, Sir. I just do what they tell me." Donovan struggled to keep a serious, concerned appearance, standing straight like a soldier at attention, but thinking, *This is more fun than I expected. It isn't even his, or the bank's money. His face reminds me of Tony Canaletto's the day he dropped a $2,000 wedding cake.*

Joe Amorsetti arrived and listened to State Police Lieutenant Baxter's report. "Have you talked to all my men?"

Baxter said, "Yes. And so has the sheriff. Send them home so they don't disturb the area. The forensic team is here."

Joe called Sam over. "Send everyone home. We can't do anything today. As soon as we get clearance, we'll call them back. What the hell do you think happened?"

"I don't have any idea. Everything was going along great. I was on the top floor rippin' out partitions and Gomer was feeding Abe's bucket through the window. Donovan was right in front of the bank and never saw or heard a thing except the Surety truck backin' in and a lady with a white car."

❖ ❖ ❖

Oblivious to the excitement on land, jet-skiers churned the water off shore and a few small boats with fisherman plowed slowly through the aquatic turmoil toward places on the river where fish would be more interested in bait.

Chapter 19

That night conversation was limited at the poker game. Abe growled, "They're gonna try to pin this on us. We got the rap sheets and they're going to pound on us, hard. Tina, they'll get warrants and tear this place a part; same where each of us lives."

Tina had a lilt in her voice. "I know. Nothin' we can do." She smiled. "Don't worry." Everyone looked at her and realized she wasn't blowin' smoke and was truly confident. The seasoned men had a tough time accepting advice from a young woman and hunched over the poker table, staring at their cards.

Shadow heard more than Tina's words and knew she was trying to lift their spirits. He joined in. "They won't find nothin'. Did you hear the big cop wheezin' and puffin'? He asked me if there was an elevator. I'll bet he stopped to rest six times goin' to the fourth floor. The sheet-rock dust all over his uniform and the trip back down didn't make him happy, either. I shoulda asked him if he wanted Abe to give him a ride down in the bucket." This got chuckles from the group.

Donovan dealt a blackjack hand. "Don't be cocky with these guys. Be serious and leave them thinkin' we want to help. Don't get in their way. Abe's right, they'd love to drop this on us. We're easy marks. No resistance or we'll all be back behind the wire. Don't say any more than you have to." He looked at each player as he dealt the cards and got agreement all around.

The game was less fun this time. Bud kept the beer coming and Rita and Tina supplied sheets of pizza. The girls even got into a few hands of poker. When Abe suggested they change the game to strip poker, Rita broke the sour mood by saying, "I don't like to gag!" The game broke up early.

Chapter 20

It was three days before the police let Amorsetti Construction back on the job. Nine hundred thousand dollars were stolen, according to the newspapers. The press couldn't extract the "who and how" from Sheriff Wiley. They got the amount from a leaker at Surety.

No valuable information came from tests by the forensic teams. There were fingerprints of the ex-con employees everywhere, except on or near the Surety truck. The police questioned anyone with a past police record who lived within a mile of the bank, even if it was just a parking ticket.

The Amorsetti workmen were grilled and re-grilled by detectives. They repeated what they'd already told them. Mike and Stan, the Surety employees, were given desk jobs. As Donovan expected, the police, armed with search warrants, tossed his apartment and the rooms of all the ex-cons.

Tina stood her ground and blocked their exit as the police tried to leave. She insisted they put everything back the way they found it before they left. She had "before" photos on her cellphone. One of the officers was a female, and agreed with Tina. They restored some order before exiting.

After a month-long stalemate, the Sheriff and State Police declared the robbery "professional." The community knew what this meant— they didn't have any idea who did it, or how. They'd visited all the auto repair shops in a sixty-mile radius and couldn't find a white Cadillac with a damaged right side, an invoice for one being repaired, or even a repairman's description of a damaged one driven by a blonde woman. Surveillance cameras at toll bridges and customs checkpoints failed to disclose any damaged white Cadillacs with female drivers entering Canada after the robbery, destroying a popular police suspicion.

The only positive help came from the managers of Wal-Mart and Target. Machines at both stores recorded serial numbers on all bills of ten dollars or above before the money was given to Surety for transport to the bank. The sheriff didn't release this information to the newspapers.

Store checkout clerks in a fifty-mile radius received lists of the stolen bill numbers. They were instructed to give a subtle signal to the surveillance camera if they spotted any bill on the list. They were warned to avoid confronting anyone. The facial recognition ability of the cameras was tested in each store. The first week, so many false reports came in that Sheriff Wiley's operating budget was in shreds. Normally a jovial man, his patience was shredding also.

❖ ❖ ❖

Chapter 21

The investigation was as active as a mime in a cast three weeks after the robbery. The bank and the Surety Transport insurers offered a reward of $25,000 for recovery of the money or information on the perpetrator, or perpetrators, leading to arrest. When the inquiry was still going nowhere at four weeks, they upped it to $50,000 then eventually to $60,000.

The first clue came the on the fifth week. A clerk at a convenience store spotted a bill on the missing-money list. The surveillance camera produced a photograph of a well-dressed woman with blonde hair.

Detective Mullin knew her. He'd seen her in courtrooms. He was going to ask Judge Pugh for a search warrant when another call came in. A hardware store clerk reported a similar encounter, this time with a tall, well-dressed man. When Judge Pugh saw the photographs he gasped. "That's Greta Schwartz and Warden Lewis Gelky!" He had to sit down. "Are you sure these are photos of the people who passed the stolen bills? If you're wrong, I could be in big, big trouble issuing a warrant. Can you check it somehow?"

Detective Mullin offered a choice. "What if we follow their cash transactions for a while to see if this happens again?"

"Yes. Yes, do it. There has to be some mistake. Let me know what you find as soon as possible. Not a word to anyone about this!" His glare was piercing and dead serious.

Detective Mullin passed his stern warning on to the uniforms. "We have to be sure we're right. Pick up every bill these two put down for the next week or so. Also the bills their wives, husbands or children pass, if you can. Do it like it's a random search, so the store clerks and managers don't get suspicious and blab to the press or something."

Chapter 21

Marge Rothman, Warden Gelky's secretary, and Greta Schwartz had been friends since high school. They had lunch together at the Blue Moon every Tuesday. Like many well-organized mature women in business, Marge did most of the work and Warden Gelky took all the credit for the successes and blamed her for the failures.

At age 50, her children were out of the house and in college. Her husband, a traveling salesman, didn't come back from a trip to California eight years earlier and it bothered her for a week, until the Goodwill picked up his clothes and other accouterments. Greta found her attractive because of her take-charge attitude and physical strength from running in Iron-Girl races. They chose to live separately, but got together often in addition to the Tuesday lunch.

The missing-bill discovery was still a secret when Marge met Greta the following Tuesday. Marge was in a jovial mood. "Gelky has been walking on air the last month. He finally explained why. You know how he always brags about his investments? Last Friday he said he'd made $1,000 this month." She looked up from her plate. "Why is your face all white? You sick?"

"That son-of-a-bitch!"

"What's the matter?"

"He's stiffin' me. Half the money's mine."

"What do you mean?"

"I can't tell you right now. I don't want you to get hurt."

"Hurt? How?"

"I'll tell you someday, but not now. I've got to go." She jumped up like there was a tack in her seat and hurried out, leaving Marge staring at her back and floating in a fog of confusion.

Chapter 22

One week later, Mullin faced Judge Pugh with his report. The judge sat apoplectic at his desk. "The Warden and Schwartz? Oh, my God! Well, ... do what you have to do." He signed all the search warrants. The bombshell hitting him was a scratch compared to the ones about to hit Warden Lewis Gelky and Greta Schwartz.

Detective Dave Stokes went to the Amorsetti Construction Company main office hoping to talk with Frank Amorsetti. Sheila Dupree, the secretary, said, "Frank's at a jobsite." He wasn't disappointed. Stokes liked talking to women. Tall and broad-shouldered, with a gentle smile and a celebrity-magazine face; women responded to him. They offered him information more readily than men did.

Much of Sheila's youthful beauty remained, but in a softer package. Since getting divorced, her solitary existence and responsibility had left her looking a little worn around the eyes, but she wasn't immune to a good-looking man.

He held up his badge. "Ms. Dupree, how long have you worked for the Amorsetti brothers?"

"Four years." She pushed a wisp of her light brown hair behind an ear. She thought, *He's a lot better lookin' than Bud Gigantelli.* She was still angry at Bud for dumping her for a barfly years ago.

"What do you do?" Stokes was walking around the room trying to be non-threatening. He picked up a framed photo of two children and added, "Are these your children?"

Her straightforward manner masked apprehension. It had been a long time since she had talked with a handsome man her own age. "Well, I answer the phone, type letters and forms, or put in construction material orders Mr. Amorsetti gives me. Yes, those are my children, Alisha and Mark." Stokes put the photo gently back on her desk.

"Do you handle any money?" He was looking at framed certificates and awards.

"I make out the employee's checks for Mr. Amorsetti to sign, then hand them out to the men. They come here to get them, usually Saturday morning after work."

"Do you handle any cash?" She looked away. The discussion had changed and Stokes saw it. Pausing, she fidgeted with things on her desk. "I'm not supposed to talk about it."

"About what?"

"The end-of-the-month money."

"You can tell me. I'm a policeman."

"Well ... the last Thursday of the month, either Joe or Frank brings in payroll cash. They ask me to count out some and put it in a briefcase so one of them can pay Friday bills. They insist I double-check to be sure the amount is correct. I lock it in my file with the— until Friday morning."

"With the what?"

"Nothing."

"So, the amount is the same every month?"

"It went up a little a year ago. Some increase came from the state."

"How long have you done it?"

"Three years."

"How much each month?"

She paused, then leaned forward and whispered, "Eight thousand eight hundred dollars. "

"Every month?"

"Yes."

"What is it you lock in with the cash?"

"The special-payments book."

"Oh. You've been very helpful. I'll try to catch Frank Amorsetti another time. Thank you." He smiled at her, not just for her help, but because he was amused by his own words, *Catch him another time. I sure as hell will. Wait 'til Charlie hears this!*

Sheila smiled back. She noticed he didn't have a wedding ring or a white mark on his tan finger where one would go.

Dave winked at her. "Better not mention to either of the Amorsetti brothers that you told me about the money. Let's keep it between you and me." He gave her his friendliest grin.

"Okay," she replied, sheepishly.

❖ ❖ ❖

Chapter 23

Charlie Mullin was in the precinct office when Dave arrived. "Wait 'til you hear this. The Amorsetti's are pocketing an extra $8,800 a month."

"How do you know?" Mullin asked.

Stokes described his interview with Sheila. "She wasn't lying. There was no reason she should, and it just popped out. They told her not to mention the cash, and get this, there's a second set of books she has to keep."

"We gotta look at their financials."

"I'm on it. Oh, Sam Walton, the foreman, and two workmen, told me the ex-cons are paid $5 an hour. Somethin' isn't adding up."

Mullin got up from his desk. "I'm goin' to meet with Warden Gelky at two. Do you think some of the briefcase money came from the robbery and was goin' to him? How else would he get stolen bills?"

"Could be. Maybe Schwartz, too."

Mullin's planned visit with Gelky came to a sudden halt. He received a call from Sheriff Wiley and covered the mouthpiece to tell Stokes, "Somebody found the Surety money! Let's go."

Chapter 24

Sheriff Wiley met them at the door of the Hockmeir Building. Mullin was skeptical. "Are you sure it's the Surety cash?"

"Certain. Dead certain." They were walking on the ground floor toward the storage room of the old shoe store.

"Who found it?"

"One of the workmen. I can't tell you which one. They won't tell me. He's afraid the Amorsettis will drop him in the river in a barrel of cement. He told Bud Gigantelli he found it, but not where it was located. Bud talked to Ted Wilson, the bank president, and he, Surety and the insurance companies agreed: the finder will remain anonymous. Whoever he is, he's no dummy. He made them put it in writing and notarize it."

Wiley kept talking. "The bank and insurance people have been all over Bud to make sure it isn't a scam. He agreed to take a lie detector test. He wasn't lying; he didn't know where the money was hidden. We went through every place we could think of, again. Bud refuses to tell us who found it.

The reward money has to be deposited in cash in a safety deposit box at the bank with the signed agreement. Bud has to hold the key and, get this: Surety or the insurance companies have to pay any taxes on the reward. Once Ted had the agreement from Surety and the insurers, he signed the paper. After the cash and notarized statement were in the box and Bud had the key, the unnamed guy told Bud where he found the money. Bud brought both Ted and me over here and showed us what's going to knock your socks off!"

They passed through a doorway without a door and into the old shoe company's storeroom. It occupied a third of the first floor. Windows and four evenly spaced light bulbs hanging from the ceiling were the only sources of illumination. Partially dismantled wooden shelves were against the front and side walls. Near the windows, a stained, sagging sofa, three wooden chairs of different colors, a reading lamp and an office chair with wheels circled an old-fashioned dining room table covered in papers and blueprints. An old television in a scarred wooden cabinet was on the left as they entered. The opening below the screen held only an old shoe catalog.

Another television in a larger, handsome, cherry-wood cabinet was against the wall behind the table. This TV was turned at an angle, away from the wall. The doors of the cabinet below the screen were open and it was empty. Three dusty magazines were on the floor nearby.

Sheriff Harold Wiley was unhappy. Both his forensic team and the State Police lab people had searched this room after the robbery and found nothing. His bad mood surfaced and he spoke louder than necessary. "Don't touch anything! The forensic techs are on their way. You may look only."

He went to the larger television cabinet behind the desk. The plastic cover that usually housed the old-fashioned cathode ray tube protruding from the back was on the floor along with four screws. The "guts" of the television were gone. Neat stacks of money filled the space where the tube had been. Wiley gestured at the money, a look of disbelief still clouding his face. "A workman found this when he tried to repair the television."

As Wiley spoke, Frank Amorsetti walked into the room. "What's goin' on, Harry?"

The sheriff took his arm, turned him around, and walked him out, avoiding his gaze and loaded question. They'd gone to high school together. He ordered everyone except the detectives out as well, and instructed Deputy Collins to seal off the room.

"We found some money, Frank. It may be stolen. Stay out of there until I say you can go in. The tech people have to go through their song and dance, and I don't want to screw up anything."

"How would stolen money get in there?"

"That's what we want to find out."

"I'll call Joe. He's gonna be upset. This project is behind schedule already because of the robbery."

Mullin saw the disappointment on Wiley's face as he returned from escorting his friend out. He thought it might reassure Wiley a little to say, "I think it's all here."

Sheriff Harry Wiley hit his forehead with palm of his hand, indicating he thought Mullin was right. Stokes disagreed. "Not quite all. You may find $8,800 is missing, if the Friday delivery of "payroll" Sheila Dupree described came from this cash. I'll bet the money Gelky and Schwartz passed came from here. We'll know after we match up the bills. Harry, I didn't get a chance to tell you. You know Sheila Dupree. She told me Frank and Joe had her put 8.8k in a briefcase and give it to them the last Friday of every month. She didn't know where it was going. We don't either, yet. They told her it was for payroll or bills. The strange thing is, she's been doin' it for three years, maybe more."

Mullin changed his opinion. "Holy Toledo! Harry, Dave may be right. The financials should be interesting. We better go through them with a microscope and talk to Gelky's secretary and Schwartz before we approach Gelky, Frank or Joe."

Sheriff Wiley was looking back and forth from Stokes to Mullin. "Damn! Damn! Damn! I better call the DA. This thing's getting into FBI territory. Dave, you take the warden's secretary. You better go to her home after work. We don't wanna start a stampede. Charlie, you do the same with Schwartz. I'll get the search warrants updated."

Chapter 25

Dave Stokes was waiting when Margaret arrived home from work. "Ms. Rothman, I'm Detective Stokes from the sheriff's office." He held up his badge. "I need to ask you a few questions. May I come in?"

"Sure. What's up?"

"Do either of the Amorsetti brothers come to Warden Gelky's office?"

"All the time. We have this early prisoner release program to rehab eligible men, and they give many of them jobs."

"When do they come there?"

"At meetings if new men are entering the program, and the last Friday of every month one of them comes to give the warden a progress report on the men. The warden gives it to me, I file it, and make an annual report for the State Penal Commission in December."

"What does the report from Amorsetti look like?"

"It's just one or two spreadsheets. They could just mail it, but I guess they feel more comfortable delivering it. Roan Gates, the parole officer, tells me they sometimes bring a parolee with them. He has to meet or talk with each man every month."

"Are the Amorsetti brothers carrying anything else when they meet the warden?"

"They always bring the reports in a briefcase. I don't know why; the sheets would fit in a folder. I guess it makes them feel important or something."

"How long have you worked for Warden Gelky?"

"Since he came here, ten years ago. I worked for the warden before him for three years."

"Has Warden Gelky seemed irritable or stressed lately?"

"Not at all. Like I told my friend Greta the other day, the last month he's been happier than usual. Said his investments were doing great.

She got upset when I told her about it. I don't know why. They're friends. Seems like she should be happy for him."

"Thank you, Ms. Rothman. You've been very helpful."

"You didn't tell me what's goin' on."

"Can't right now. You'll hear soon, I think. Goodbye."

She closed the door wondering, *What's this all about? I hope none of the parolees tried to escape or got shot or something. Should I call Gelky? Better not. He's probably upset. He'll call me if he needs me to come in.*

Chapter 26

It was getting dark and raining lightly as Charlie Mullin knocked on the door at Greta Schwartz's house. No one answered. After several tries, he decided to wait. He fell asleep in his car parked in front of her house, only to be awakened abruptly near midnight by the lights of a fast-moving vehicle coming straight at him. Ten feet from a head-on collision with his vehicle, a Corvette swerved into Greta's driveway and screeched to a halt, inches from the garage door.

He took a couple of deep breaths and wiped the sweat from his face. A few minutes went by before the garage door went up, then the Corvette made two quick lurches into the garage, hitting a trashcan in the process. He took a time-stamped photo of the car and garage. It was raining harder now and the wind drove it against the windows.

Mullin got out of his car, pulling on a baseball cap with "Sheriff's Office" written in capital letters on the front. The wind whipped his raincoat as he moved toward the garage. No lights had come on in the house. As he reached the garage entrance, the Corvette's door was flung open, banging a white Cadillac in the other stall. Greta swung her legs out and stood up, then clutched the door as she crumpled toward the floor. Mullin caught her in mid-crumple.

"Thanksss. Who the hell are you?"

"Detective Charles Mullin, ma'am. From the sheriff's office."

"Was I speedin', off-fficer?"

"Yes. But speeding is not why I'm here. I would like to ask about your work at the prison."

"Oh, that. Gelky screwed me. Marge Rothman told me." Her legs gave out and Mullin caught her again.

"Who are you?" She looked at him again, as if he'd just appeared out of nowhere.

He helped her inside and she dropped like a rock onto a couch. She was already asleep by the time he found a glass to fill with water and put on a nearby table. He took a few more photos as a precaution, put the coverlet from the back of the couch over her, and left via the garage, ducking under the door as it closed.

On the way out he inspected the white Cadillac. *It doesn't look like it's been repaired. If it was, the repairman is a genius.* He called Margaret Rothman. "Mrs. Rothman, I'm Detective Charles Mullin from the sheriff's office. Do you know Greta Schwartz? Is she a friend of yours?"

"Yes. Is she all right?"

"Just inebriated, I believe. I helped her into her house just now, and she's asleep on the couch now. It would probably be best if you looked in on her. There's no one else at the house. Your phone number was on her calendar. I'll need to talk with her tomorrow. I'll call at nine. Can you go over to her house?"

"Yes, of course. What's going on?"

"Can't answer right now. Still investigating. Thanks for your help."

Chapter 27

Mullin called Greta at nine o'clock the next morning. He had information from the forensics team. The money found at the Amorsetti worksite office was from the Surety truck robbery—and it was all there—except for $9,800; close to what Dave Stokes predicted. No fingerprints could be found on the money or cabinet. They'd been wiped clean. Fingerprints on the table, doorknobs and pencils matched the Amorsetti brothers and Ed Lightfeather. The forensic technicians said some of the money was wrinkled, like it had been wet.

Greta's voice on the phone didn't give a suggestion that the previous night's episode had left her incapacitated, or even that she remembered it. "Detective Mullin? What do you want?"

This is going to be a tough one, he thought, before saying, "Ms. Schwartz, I'm on my way over to talk with you concerning some recent events."

"I'm leaving for my office."

"Do you want me to come there? I'm trying to be as discreet as possible." There was a short silence.

"Were you here last night?"

"I was."

"Is this about last night?"

"No."

"I'll wait for you."

"Thank you."

The front door opened as Mullin approached. He was impressed with the way she looked. After the previous evening's events, he expected a major hangover. Instead Greta looked clean and attractive in a pressed, tan business suit, her blond hair combed, and cosmetics skillfully applied. Opening the door, she shielded her red eyes from the light with a hand and Mullin smiled. *She's still feelin' last night a little, but she's a bulldozer!* Greta ushered him into her living room and pointed to a chair.

"Ms. Schwartz, money was stolen from an armored car a few weeks ago. Do you know anything about the robbery?" He watched for hesitations or other signs she was lying. There were none.

"I read the newspaper story. Why are you asking me about it?"

"Is this your picture?" Mullin slid a photograph across the table.

"Yes. That's me checking out of the grocery store."

Mullin slid another print across. "Is this you at Harlan's Liquor Store?"

"Yes. Why was my picture taken?"

"You paid the clerks with bills from the robbery."

Greta was wide-eyed, pale, and not breathing. She blurted, "That son-of-a-bitch!" She jumped up and began pacing back and forth across the room muttering.

Mullin watched her for a minute. "Which son-of-a-bitch are we talking about?"

She whirled and stared at him. He could almost hear the wheels grinding in her head and stared right back. "We found most of the money, you know."

"You did? Where was it? How much was missing?"

"I can't tell you. Well, maybe I could, if you tell me who the son-of-a-bitch is."

"Come on. We're going to the sheriff's office. Call the sheriff right now and tell him to be there. Call the DA and get him there, too."

Mullin did as he was told, all the while bubbling inside. *I think I struck oil! She's going to try and save her ass.* He had a difficult time keeping a straight face while driving Greta to the Municipal Building in his cruiser.

He didn't ask any more questions; concerned she might change her mind about talking. She sat rigidly looking straight ahead. She didn't fidget or sigh, or seem to see anything around them. He had to admire her calm. *For a country lawyer, she's one tough cookie. She's been around. I wonder if she has a rap sheet?*

Chapter 28

Sheriff Harold Wiley was there when they arrived. He gave Mullin a questioning look, but didn't speak. Greta marched right past him. Mullin, following her, gave Wiley a subtle thumbs-up and escorted her into a conference room. "I'm sure the District Attorney will be here shortly. Can I get you anything?"

Getting an acerbic, "No," he said, "I'll be right back," and left, closing the door behind him.

With his back to the conference room's one-way window, Mullin spoke to the sheriff. "Harry, she's got something to tell us and she's mad as hell at somebody."

Just then District Attorney Allen Roberts came in and loudly asked, "What the hell's the hurry? Sometimes, you guys are a pain in the ass." Tall, neat, abundant gray hair, and a bloated face: he was always ready with a joke if speaking to a voter; but wasn't in that mood right then.

Roberts was a vote getter at election time but a bombastic know-it-all the rest of the time. His grasp of the law was dependent on the quality of his lowly paid subordinates who he treated, like the police, with disdain. In Sheriff Wiley's opinion, he needed a turnstile in his office for the turnover of assistants.

Once Roberts was convinced there was notoriety to be had in a conviction, he was like a bulldog and whipped his staff into finding conviction-winning information. Wiley didn't like working with him. He was glad local judges understood his character and made him prove his facts.

Wiley wasn't sympathetic. "Shut up, Al. Keep your voice down. Greta Schwartz passed some cash from the robbery list and we're trying to find out how she got it."

"Oh! Greta? I've known her five years. Are you sure?" Astonished, his voice dropped to whisper and his forehead wrinkled in disbelief. He moved to look around Wiley at Greta in the conference room.

Mullin nodded. "We're sure. She asked me to bring her in. When we go in, let us do the talking." It was an order, not an option, and he paused to be sure it reached the DA's brain. Roberts gave his acquiescence with a nod.

Roberts and Wiley shook Greta's hand and thanked her for coming in.

Mullin faced Greta across the table. "Ms. Schwartz, when I spoke with you at your house earlier and mentioned the robbery money you used for purchases, you asked to come here and meet with Sheriff Wiley and District Attorney Roberts. Why?"

"Because the money was given to me in return for all the pro bono work I do for the prison, and I don't want to go to jail."

"Who gave you the money?"

"If I tell you, will you give me a pass?"

The District Attorney spoke up despite the earlier warning. "Greta, you're a lawyer. You know we can't do such a thing unless we know the whole story. Who gave you the money and how much was it?"

"Gelky. He didn't tell me it was hot money from some half-assed robbery."

"How much money did he give you?"

She hesitated, fidgeting with her rings and avoiding their eyes. Mullin broke the silence. "Your financials show you deposited about $4,000 at the end of every month for the last two years, and nearly the same each month the year before. Where did it come from?"

Greta's face was leaking confidence like a goalie who suffered a hat trick in the first five minutes of a game. "I got half of the monthly payment for the parolees' re-training program."

Detective Dave Stokes, who was listening and watching through the one-way glass, made an emphatic swing of his fist toward the floor and hissed, *"Yes!" Greta got half the money Sheila put it in the Amorsetti briefcase and Gelky got the other half. After the robbery the Amorsettis must've added some extra bucks as a bonus. Gelky kept it all and she knows it. If we can find the bills, I'll bet they add up to the missing $9,800.*

He knocked on the conference room door, entered, and whispered to Wiley. "Sheriff, I need to talk to you a minute." They went out and closed the door.

"What is it, Dave?"

"Remember Sheila Dupree was putting $8,800 in the briefcase once a month for at least three years? If Schwartz and Gelky each got an extra $500 last month, we may have all the heist money back. The numbers on the bills they passed will tell us. I'll bet Greta is mad at Gelky because he kept her extra $500. I'll bet she's gonna roll on him. But, forget the robbery. If Gelky, Schwartz and the Amorsettis were pocketing 4 or 5k a month for three years, that's over half a million bucks. Somebody's gettin' screwed big-time. Oh ... There's also a white Caddy in her garage."

Returning to the room, Sheriff Wiley asked for clarification. "Ms. Schwartz, I thought you said your work at the prison was pro bono? Exactly what were you doing for the re-training program?"

"I helped to select prisoners who would be most likely to benefit from re-training, did the paper work to make it happen, and found them jobs. The money was mostly a donation for my efforts."

"According to the records it looks like all the re-training candidates for the past four years have worked for Amorsetti Construction."

"That's true. They've done a good job training men and cooperating with the program."

"I'm told the prisoners working for this company make $5 an hour. Correct?"

"I don't know." She squirmed a bit and broke visual contact with the sheriff.

She's lying. She knows, he thought. "How much did you say the 'donation' was you received monthly?"

"I didn't say."

"Would you please tell us?"

Greta stood up. "I'm done talking. I want my lawyer present." The angry, pugnacious look on her face said asking more questions would achieve nothing.

District Attorney Roberts advised her, "Greta, stay in town. We will need to talk with you and your attorney again."

❖ ❖ ❖

Chapter 29

After Greta left for home in a police cruiser, District Attorney Roberts, Sheriff Wiley and the two detectives reviewed her statements. Roberts advised the officers. "She won't dare call Gelky. She wants to drop everything on him and is sure he cheated her somehow. Go ahead and question Gelky. You better ask him to come here. I suspect he'll clam-up and you won't get much.

"You better look at his financials closely before the interview. Do it tomorrow and let me know what he says before I contact the state penal department. New York State Penal will want to do their own investigation. The penal system union is tough and they're going to be all over us to protect Gelky.

"Don't make threats or be rough, just ask for facts and explanations. And, for God's sake, keep good records. Back up everything, especially the details on the briefcase, who saw it, when and where.

"Get warrants for his home and office." Roberts added, "Tackle the Amorsettis after you hear what Gelky has to say. Maybe he'll roll on them."

Wiley was writing notes and sweating. The robbery was solved but it had dumped an even bigger problem in his lap. Some of the people involved were in law enforcement, friends, powerful— and noisy—and he was up for re-election in a year. Wiley sighed and put down his pencil. "We have a warrant for Gelky's home but the judge wouldn't let us go into his office. Something about state owned land. Penal will have to do it. Dave already talked to his secretary at home. She doesn't seem to know anything of value."

Stokes interrupted. "Harry, don't forget she said one of the Amorsettis brought a briefcase to his office on the last Friday of each month. She can identify it."

"Get the briefcase before somebody wipes it down. You think Sheila has it?"

"I think so. I'm on my way." Stokes ran out the door.

Chapter 30

Tall and impeccable in gray, Warden Gelky looked coldly down his nose at Sheriff Wiley as he was ushered into the conference room by a uniformed officer. His lofty position and physique brought his respect for the sheriff up only as far as tolerance, not even close to an admiration level. He resented being urged to come in for an interview.

Sheriff Wiley pointed toward a conference room chair, then motioned toward the detective. "Lou, thanks for coming in. You know Dave Stokes, don't you? You want coffee?"

"No, thanks. We've met a few times. Nice to see you again." Gelky bowed slightly at Stokes and shook his hand without a trace of enthusiasm. "What's this regarding, Harry?"

Wiley slid a photograph across the table. "That you?"

"Yes it is. Why do you have this? What's goin' on?"

Wiley pushed a second photo toward him. "How about this one?"

"Yes. That's me."

"Lou, you passed stolen bills at these stores. They were from the Surety truck that was robbed six weeks ago."

"What? ... *What?*" The crescendo was accompanied by a jump to his feet, knocking over his chair.

Sheriff Wiley and Stokes ignored his reaction. "Sit down, Lou. We have witnesses who say one of the Amorsetti brothers brought a briefcase to your office every month. What was in it?"

Warden Gelky was starting to sweat. "Just reports concerning the parolees they're re-training."

"Are you sure there was no money in the briefcase? Because we have several witnesses who've identified the briefcase independently, and one of them put money in it every month. We have the briefcase and it has your fingerprints on it."

"Yes, some money was exchanged. Not much. It was a gift for helping with the ex-con re-training program."

"We have a warrant. Your financials indicate you've deposited $4,000 each month over the last three years. Where's the money coming from? You keep it in an account separate from your direct deposit salary. How do you think money from the robbery got into your hands?"

"I don't know. I need to talk to my lawyer."

"Probably a good idea. The DA feels obligated to contact the state penal department. All the salary money penal is paying for re-training ex-cons isn't getting to them." Warden Gelky stood up, pale and unsteady. He didn't seem as tall as he had when entering the room.

Wiley took his arm and walked with him. "You're not the only one who passed the bills," he said, trying to soften the effects of their talk, and subtly passing a warning. "Lou, I wouldn't ask Greta to be your lawyer, if I were you. Oh, and stay in town."

Gelky's eyes flicked toward him, wavering and afraid. His face was as gray as his suit.

Chapter 31

Joe Amorsetti arrived at the precinct at nine o'clock, as Mullin requested. "Charlie, what's this pertain to? I'm in a hurry. I already told Harry Wiley, I don't know how the robbery money got in our office at the Hockmeir Building."

Mullin wasn't intimidated by Joe's fierce stare. "Something else has come up and I need some answers from you. Like, who was the blonde drivin' the white Caddy creased by the Surety truck bumper? Was she one of your bimbos? Did you have her put on a crying act and pull the guards around the other side of the truck while you put the money in the Caddy's trunk?"

"I wasn't even there."

"Then Frank did it. He was there. You passin' the blame to him? But that's not your big problem, you putz. I've known you since the fifth grade. You were a pain in the ass then, and you're pain in the ass now."

Joe had a smirk on his face. "Yeah, I punched you in the nose and you cried."

"You're not goin' to feel so goddamned cocky in a few minutes. Sheila told us you and Frank told her to put $8,800 in a brown briefcase every month, and half the same amount in each of your desks. Gelky's secretary, Rothwell, described the same briefcase being brought to Gelky's office every month by you or Frank. They both recognized it by the scratches and grease marks.

Two of the ex-cons saw you put it behind the seat in your truck on several occasions. We have the briefcase and it has your fingerprints on it, and your brother's as well. We also found your second set of accounting books. Were you takin' money to Gelky every month?"

Joe's smirk began to wilt. He swallowed hard and began tapping the desk with a pencil. His eyes were on fire as he turned toward Mullin. "It's a share of management fees we receive from the NYS Penal Department for the parolees' re-training program."

"I read the agreement. There isn't any payment coming directly from penal to your firm for management, only for salaries for the apprentices. You only provide work-time data to the prison parole office so they can make a report. That's their job. But, you give the ex-cons $5 an hour for their work and penal gives you $15 an hour to pay their wages."

"It was more a ... donation to thank Gelky and Schwartz for letting us run the program and to pay us back for our training expertise." His voice had lost its bluster and he began to sweat.

"The DA talked to the state penal business department this morning. They thought you were paying the ex-cons $15 an hour for their work and that they were getting a bargain in today's labor market. They have programs all over the state, some paying more because of the local living costs.

"Checking your financials, we found you've been depositing $4,000 a month in an account separate from your direct deposit salary account. You been doin' it for nearly four years."

Amorsetti's face was getting red and he tapped the pencil faster and faster.

Mullin continued. "There's $9,800 missing from the robbery money found in your office at the Hockmeir building. You have any idea where it went? It's almost the same amount that was put into the briefcase every month."

"Somebody set us up!" Joe's eyes blazing.

"You mean somebody told you three or four years ago the salary money for the ex-con laborers supplied by the penal commission was partly yours, even though the agreement specifies otherwise? Or you think somebody robbed a Surety truck and put the money in your office just for the fun of it?"

"Stokes has Frank in the other room. Maybe he made a mistake and put robbery money in the briefcase. Or maybe he was gonna stiff you and take a double cut this month. Either way, the stolen money blew you right out of the water."

"Doesn't matter. The robbery problem is solved. We have the money back. What we don't have is any legal reason why you withheld money from the workmen. I'll bet you twenty bucks Frank is gonna roll on you.

Maybe Gelky, too. He didn't sound very happy when we talked—losing his job and all."

"The way I see it, you were getting money from New York penal to pay the ex-cons $15 an hour. Instead, you paid them $5 an hour, got nearly free labor, and shared the extra $10 an hour with your brother, Gelky, and Schwartz for three or four years. That correct? It totals more than half a million dollars in three years. You wanna tell me if I'm right?"

"I ain't saying nothin'. I want my lawyer. Now!" He broke the pencil in half and threw it against the wall.

"I thought so. Probably a good idea. The DA says State Penal may bring in the FBI. You were a bully in the fifth grade and you're still one. You're also a horse's ass. Come with me. I'm going to put you in a holding cell and you can call your lawyer from there." Mullin cuffed him.

❖ ❖ ❖

Chapter 32

Sam Wolcott, Donovan and the other men continued work on the Hockmeir job for five weeks after the robbery. The work came to crashing halt when the indictment of the Amorsetti brothers, Gelky, and Schwartz pushed the robbery screed out of the newspapers.

Two days later, Donovan, Abe, Gomer, Shadow and the other ex-con employees of Amorsetti Construction were summoned to Rocky Shore Correctional to meet with Parole Officer Gates. As usual, he stood behind his desk, staring down at them with his tiny eyes. "I asked you to come in today because there are major changes in your re-training jobs. Amorsetti Construction will no longer be able to employ you. You'll each get any unpaid wages as of today. We're looking for other employers in the area to take on the re-training program, but it may take some time to check their qualifications."

This brought a big laugh from the men. They'd seen the morning newspaper headlines: *"Prison Warden, Lawyer and Construction Firm Indicted for Stealing a Million Dollars."*

Flustered and red-faced by the laugh innuendo, Gates was slow to continue. "Mr. Abe Waverly, your parole time here has been completed and you may leave the area. You'll need to make contact with the parole officer in New York, as described in this letter." He handed Abe an envelope.

"The rest of you need to stay here, so I suggest you look for new jobs. You still have two months before you can leave. I'll be looking for jobs and will contact you if I find something. Because of this sudden disruption, the penal system is going to give you each $200 a week until you find work. Report to me every month, like before, and tell me if there are changes in your addresses or phone numbers, or if you find a job. Questions?"

Just for the fun of watching Gates squirm, Donovan asked, "What the hell happened?"

His face, now bright red with sweat-beads glistening on his brow, Gates sputtered, "It's a legal problem needing correction."

Abe was grinning like he'd won the lottery. "Don't fool with us, Gates. This place has crooks guardin' the crooks. And the ones on the outside are bigger crooks than the ones on the inside."

"That has *not* been proven. You're dismissed." He retreated further behind his desk as he spoke, then relaxed as the men went out like boys leaving school on a Friday afternoon, laughing, bumping each other and passing out playful shoulder punches.

Chapter 33

At the poker game that night, Donovan asked, "What're we going to do now? How will we find jobs? Employers don't think much of parolees. Two hundred a week won't pay for rent and food."

Everyone was there, including Abe's steady, Jadlyn, who'd decided to stay until he was ready to leave. Lloyd Yarwood and his wife, Janet, were there, too. They'd come up from the city in their RV for a weekend of fishing with Bud.

Bud Gigantelli was ready for Donovan's question. "It'll be months before they bring this to trial and soon most of you will be done with the part of your parole keeping you here. Abe can't go now. The New York penal people and FBI will probably interview each of you."

He added, "They mistrust Schwartz, Gelky and the parole officer, and they'll be suspicious your release into the work program wasn't legit. Just answer their questions, and don't give them anything to chew on. They'll transfer you to a parole officer in the city when your time is up here, or maybe sooner."

Shadow looked at Donovan. "You think they bugged this place?" This drew a startled look from everyone. The thought hadn't occurred to them.

"No. But they might try." Bud got a pad and pencil. He wrote, "I don't think so, but let's check around." Pointing, each took a room and scoured for the devices. They were familiar with their appearance and the common locations in phones, under tables or in cracks.

Nothing was found, but, as a precaution, Donovan printed on the pad, "Poker talk only tonight. I'll find another meeting place for next time and let you know where. If they come to search your place and question you, check your clothes, and near the bed or the phone afterward. If you find one, don't throw it out. It lets them know you're onto them. They can track the location of it. Just put it in a glass of water so they can't record what you say. Later, you can flush it down the toilet after they back off. Tight lips though, everywhere."

They muttered their agreement as he burned the paper.

Chapter 34

Steve Stojak from the FBI and Martin Dalton from the New York Penal System Investigation Unit came to John and Tina's apartment with a warrant the following Friday. Tina told them straight out, "This place has been searched before. If you move something, put it back where you found it. If you break anything, you *will* pay for it. I have photos, so use your head."

Stojak smiled. "We'll be careful, Mrs. Donovan." This caught Tina by surprise. No one, not even John, had called her Mrs. She smiled at John who, close to saying something, changed his mind and returned her smile.

Dalton said, "We need to talk to you both after we look around."

After examining the premises Stojak asked, "Mr. Donovan, were you told by the parole officer how much you would be paid while in the re-training program?"

"No, sir. But Greta Schwartz said it would $5 an hour."

"Do you think you were a good candidate for re-training?" Dalton was studying John's face.

"I think so. I'd been giving haircuts to the prisoners and some staff six days a week for over year. I wasn't against working."

"Were you in any trouble while at Rocky Shore?"

"No, sir. I thought I was when they took me to Warden Gelky's office to give me the early release choice and training."

"Why did you think that?"

"I gave a guy a Mohawk. He got mad and took a swing at me. I thought he knew what a Mohawk looked like because he asked for one. He didn't like it."

Both Stojak and Martin choked back a laugh.

"Well, I think we're done here." Stojak shifted his gaze to Tina. "Is everything back in place all right, Mrs. Donovan?"

"Yes. Thanks. You can't believe how the last guys left it."

Dalton asked, "Mr. Donovan, how do you think Warden Gelky got bills from the robbery?"

"If I knew the answer I'd apply for your job."

Stojak and Martin laughed, and left.

❖ ❖ ❖

Chapter 35

As a precaution, the poker game the following week was squeezed into the storage room in the back of O'Toole's. Bud had scoured the place for listening devices even though the police hadn't served a warrant or been in O'Toole's.

It was raining hard. The wind whistled through the cracks around the windows and pellets of rain rattled against the glass. The single light bulb over the table dimmed with lightning strikes a few times, but they didn't pay attention to it. It happened often when George, the cook, made toast in the kitchen next door. Rita, Jadlyn, and Tina were in and out of the storage room, but mostly in.

Shadow, Abe, and Gomer were reporting visits from Dalton and Stojak as Bud entered. "I heard from a court attendant today that Greta blew the whistle on the Amorsettis and Gelky. They all pleaded guilty. Greta tried to bargain, of course. I don't know how it will work out, but doubt she will be out on the street. They're awaiting sentencing."

This brought a military-type "Hooo-raaaa" from the group.

Bud continued. "The penal people are still pawing through things, so keep a lid on it, even with people you think are trustworthy. They keep checking up on Parole Officer Gates to see if he was in on the scam. They may watch where you go and how much you spend, so be cool.

"Ted Wilson, from the bank, told me there are questions floatin' around his bank board concerning Amorsetti Construction defaulting on their job loan for the Hockmeir Building. If that happens, we may have first dibs on it."

Rita was standing behind Bud sitting at the table and had her hands on his shoulders. She looked from person to person. She knew Abe's time there was up and Shadow, Gomer, and Donovan only had a month or two left on the parole requiring them to stay in Beckett's Bay. "If we get to buy the Hockmeir soon, all of you will have jobs with us until it's move-in ready, if you want to stay here awhile. Maybe some of you will want to stay permanently."

❖ ❖ ❖

Chapter 36

Over the next few weeks, cash was a tight for everyone. Lloyd and Janet went back to their jobs in the marina on Long Island Sound. Gomer and Shadow weren't lucky finding work and the $200 a week from the parole office didn't go far. Tina had them come to their apartment for supper many nights.

The second floor apartment above O'Toole's was vacant and difficult to rent because of the bar noise. Bud let Shadow and Gomer park there for free. Tina worked at a grocery and with Donovan at O'Toole's some nights.

They were both there one October evening when Bud and Rita came in with their baby, Elle. Bud wasn't as talkative as usual. "Your *buddies* are on the roads to Danemora and Bedford. There's a lock on their assets. Some bad news, though. The lawyers are in a hassle. The bank may auction the Hockmeir building again. We may not get it. I heard some outside investors are after it."

Rita was contrite. "Sorry for getting your hopes up over a job."

❖ ❖ ❖

Chapter 37

On a Sunday in mid-October, O'Toole's closed at seven o'clock. A final meeting of the group was planned for the second floor apartment above the bar. Before going downstairs from the third floor, Tina was uneasy. "John, everyone will want to discuss details, especially the things not involving them. Do you think it's safe to give out the information?"

"I think so. They already know enough to cause trouble if they wanted to, but they all know it's a team game. We can ask them to stay mum. You can't always trust people to do what they say, but I think they'll stick together. You worried?"

"Some."

"Why?"

"Even though all the money was recovered, the company paying the reward and the district attorney will want to know who received it. They may try to get the reward back and lean on the income tax people for a name. The taxes had to be paid by the insurer, and I'm sure they don't like that. The newspapers would love to have the information, too. Do you think there's a statute of limitations?"

"I don't know. We can ask Bud. He might know. I don't think the tax people will care about a name as long as they were paid. Let's just see what happens tonight. "

"Okay. Don't bring up the limitations thing. It might stir up trouble." She was worried.

At eight o'clock, the six men and four women were seated around the dining room table in the second floor apartment. Ed "Shadow" Lightfeather, always cautious, was checking under the table for listening devices.

Bud sat back in his chair, put his feet on an old, stained futon with tiny volcanoes of stuffing sticking out here and there: a cold beer in one hand, a cigar in the other, and a big smile on his face. He was looking forward to fleshing out details and laughing at their success. "I know we talked around what we were going to do with Gelky and the others, and I knew what I had to do. But I don't really know how some of you did your parts."

"For example, I don't have a clue why the bank cameras didn't see what happened, or how Abe knew when to move the bucket, how Jadlyn decided when to smash into the truck, or what Janet did underwater. And that's only scratchin' the surface. So, Tina, you were steering this boat, tell me how you made it go!"

❖ ❖ ❖

The Ruse

At home, Jed Dawkins stared at the book in his hands. *Gotcha!* just stopped. The next page had no words! Just when Bud asked for details on the Surety truck heist—the pages went blank. He flipped through them looking for clues, but found none, just wordless paper! He talked aloud to himself, *"Damn! I was just gettin' to the best part."*

The next day he was carrying the book as he entered the Main Street Barbershop. Hayden Wiggins, his dentist, was in the chair and Jared Bingham was waiting. The door separating John's barbershop from Pierre's beauty parlor was wide open and no one was in there. Jed waved to Hayden and Jared. "Hi, Doc. Nice to see you. Jared, I like those lures you sold me. John, how are ya? Pierre sick?"

Jed got a brief smile and "hi" from all three.

"Pierre had to take care of some family business in the city. He'll be back Monday," John replied.

"My wife, Annie, told me he worked on television soaps once and was in some kinda scandal. She says he's gay?"

John never stopped cutting Wiggin's hair as he replied. "People say it because he does women's hair. He's a good man and creative. Women like him. He always asks them, *Got any gossip?* They love it. He has a steady business. He knows all the inside celebrity buzz and the new hair designs.

"Your wife's right. In New York he was the wig-man on the soap opera *Laurel Hill,* until he got fired for hitting on Dee Ibarra, one of the stars. He opened a shop near the Barclay Center in Brooklyn and was doing well there, but he gave a dye job to one of the mayor's girlfriends and her hair fell out. Turned out it wasn't his fault. She had somethin' called allo pizza."

"His real name is Jake Spicer. His wife, Celeste, is from Beckett's Bay. Nice lady. She's independent, the kind of woman who can deliver her own baby with a kit. They have five girls."

"No kiddin'. I'll tell Annie. Here's the book I borrowed. Part is missing. The last pages are all blank? It just stops when it gets into the good part describing the robbery." He was startled by the bursts of laughter from Wiggins, Bingham and John.

"What's so funny?"

Trying unsuccessfully to stop laughing, John went to a glass-front bookcase at the back of the shop, returned with a new copy of the book, and handed to Jed.

"Thanks. Can I borrow this?"

"Nope. I'll sell it to you though, for $29. I know the author."

"Okay." Jed pulled out the cash. "What's the joke?"

Wiggins finally stopped laughing, dried his eyes, and turned to John. "John, how many you sold?

"Now, five hundred forty-six. Jed, no offense. My wife wrote the book and I'm helping her sell it. Sorry for the scam, but the fact that you came back to get the missing part means it's a pretty good read. She is gonna be pleased an educated man like you enjoyed it enough to ask for the ending; and, was willing to pay for it."

"The guys weren't laughing at you, just laughing because they all read it and fell for the same scam. Pierre has sold six hundred eighty. Women love it, too. He has four copies with missing last pages, and they're out all the time. He's ordered more."

"When you laughed, I thought the story was unfinished, or somethin'. Your wife is a fine writer. Give her my congratulations. Has she written anything else? Look, she signed it. Why is her name different than yours?"

"It's her writing name. T.A. Powers is a pen name, a nom plumb, or something like that. She chose the name so publishers wouldn't know whether she was a man or a woman and would have to judge her on the quality of her work, not her gender. Apparently some of 'em are biased."

"It was published eight months ago. There's an audio book version, too. I'll sell you a copy if you want to listen to it in the car. She recorded it herself at the Bianco Sound Studio in Carthage. She used to narrate books for a living. She only does her own stories now. An audio book of short stories and another novel will be coming out soon."

"I'll take the audio for my wife. She likes to listen to stories while driving." He thumbed through pages until he found Chapter 38, read all through the haircut and on out the door—

Chapter 38

Tina spoke in a distinct, gentle voice. "When I first arrived here, Rita became my friend." Rita's smile confirmed it was mutual. "Working together we discussed the scam Bud described and how the men were at risk if they tried to do anything about it."

"The more we listened to all of your opinions of the Amorsetti brothers, Schwartz, and Gelky, the more we were convinced to do something. Rita knows the Amorsetti brothers from their visits to O'Toole's, and considered Joe a wife-cheating rat. He brought in many young women, but never his wife. She heard him bully his older brother Frank, too."

"We didn't know Gelky, but from your descriptions, we pegged him as a self-centered, arrogant man. Schwartz had been in O'Toole's. She seemed to be a woman of the world, independent, and a person who would fight back if mistreated. We planned just how to use their relationships." Not one face showed a sign of disagreeing with her.

She went on. "After Jadlyn came to town, Rita and I asked her to meet with us, and she was wonderful. So up-beat, so much experience, so strong: she set our plans on fire. She has many skills and loads of ideas."

"After we got from the 'this-is-impossible' stage into 'this-is-possible,' thanks to her help, we got down to details. Jade suggested we include Janet in our meetings, which was a winner of an idea. Janet knew specifics none of us had ever imagined."

"We each concentrated on separate issues, then met to polish the plan, and finally, to go over it with you for input. At first, I know you thought we were nuts." ...

She was enjoying the grins around the table. "But gradually, you joined in, slipping in things we overlooked or actions we didn't understand, like Abe and his crane. By then you were on-board 100%."

She stopped. The next subject worried her. "As we go along, we'll explain who did what, but remember to keep quiet until the statute of limitations runs out. We think it's five years, but it may be less since the money was recovered. Let's use five years to be safe." Everyone nodded or gave a verbal "Okay".

Tina knew men were linear-thinkers and liked details in an orderly manner, especially when it involved them. She directed their attention to Rita with her hand, inviting her to start filling in the blanks.

Chapter 39

Rita stood up and walked around the room as she spoke. She felt more confident standing, like she was at a table in Vegas. "We watched the Surety truck every day. We could tell if it had a heavy load. The tires were a little flatter and it sat down on the frame after a busy-store weekend, or a holiday. The truck always got to the bank at the same time, give or take five minutes."

"When John told Tina he was ordered to cover the bank windows to prevent breaking them with flying cement, she suggested covering the surveillance cameras at the same time. Sam soothed the bank manager's concerns by emphasizing the jackhammer's tendency to throw cement chips and the need to protect the windows, their customers, and employees, temporarily. He didn't know he was helping us."

Rita put her hand on Donovan's shoulder. "John wasn't too happy runnin' a jackhammer, but admitted the dust, noise and inconvenience made a great distraction, and kept people away."

Donovan laughed. "I coulda lost a foot."

Rita grinned and gave him a thumbs-down sign indicating he was a wuss. He laughed louder. She went on. "We watched how the armored truck men unloaded the money. One man always stayed in the truck. The other unloaded all the bags he could carry, closed the truck doors, and took the bags downstairs to the basement door of the bank. He set them down again and punched in a code to open the door."

"We decided the best time to snatch them was while they were on the sidewalk behind the truck. Then we got lucky. After John started tearing up the cement in front of the bank, the driver had to back up to the sidewalk just south of the bank and right next to the jackhammer compressor. Voila!"

"That's where Ed came in. As you all know, Ed can appear out of nowhere and disappear in a flash. At O'Toole's, he slips behind the bar and uses the tap to get free beer." Everybody was laughing and looking at Ed, who was shrinking into an overstuffed chair. Rita added. "You thought I didn't know. Look at his face." She joined the guffaws and slowly Ed joined in, realizing there was no ill will intended.

Smiling, Rita continued. "He was the man for the job. We had him walk slowly down the street in front of the bank watching for Jadlyn in the Caddy 'borrowed' from the Harlem chop shop. Abe's seat in the crane cab was high and he and Greg had a view of the back of the Surety truck. They had the signals worked out."

"Jadlyn crashed the truck bumper, shaking it up like a pro. Nobody could've ignored the noise if they were within a block, if John hadn't been poundin' the cement. As soon as the guards ran around front to the accident, Abe lowered the bucket near the ground by the bags, but didn't touch the ground, to avoid leavin' a mark. Ed threw the bags in the bucket, and kept on walkin'."

Donovan was laughing and pounding his thigh, but didn't interrupt her. "John was right there, knew it happened, but never saw it, and never tried to. To stop work would have drawn attention and he played his part perfectly, just like we discussed. Only Ed, Abe and Greg saw what happened. Jadlyn, in her blonde wig, fancy clothes, and ripped-up car put on a real show." Rita sat down as she said, "Jade, explain what happened next."

❖   ❖   ❖

Jadlyn had the poise and confidence of a professional actress and speaker. Tall, beautiful, and calm, it was easy to see she loved a good story. "After putting the bags in the bucket, Ed walked straight on down the street to meet Tina who was walking toward him with a cardboard tray with four cups of coffee. He took the tray, turned around, walked slowly back up the street toward the armored truck, and turned into the Hockmeir Building, timing his arrival so the Surety men would see which direction he was walking coming from and what he was carrying."

"All this time, John was tearing at the sidewalk with the jackhammer. As soon Abe had extend the crane bucket up to the fourth floor window and Greg's white handkerchief appeared, I took off in the Caddy."

"A mile south of the village, there's a boarded up bowling alley. I drove the Caddy into the empty parking lot behind the building, and right into the open end of a dumpster and locked the brakes. I wiped everything clean, put on gloves and crawled out a window."

"I stripped off the blonde wig and fancy clothes in favor of my underlying jeans and blouse, and put them in the Caddy's trunk. I pulled out the chocks to stuff behind all the wheels."

"Abe's nephew, Zach, was waiting in his truck and jumped out to help. We stacked empty palettes on top and behind the car and strapped down a tarpaulin over the top. Zach reassured me the car would be crushed and on the way to Pittsburgh as scrap by six o'clock."

"He showed me a signed invoice for a palette delivery in case he ran into a truck inspection stop on the way back to Buffalo. As soon he loaded the dumpster on his truck and started off, I walked a short distance to the next street where Abe's run-around car was parked, and drove back to our RV, stopping for groceries and calling Tina on the way. Janet should take it from here." She smiled and extended a hand toward her.

❖ ❖ ❖

Proving Tina's observation men like detail order, Abe interjected. "Wait. You're leaving Greg and me out," He wasn't one to be left out of anything.

Jadlyn deferred to him. "You're right, Abe. Sorry. Go ahead."

Earlier Abe had noticed Tina chose Shadow (Ed) and Gomer's (Greg) real names. The first time she did it, he realized they were childish nicknames, weren't funny, and might be hurtful. He saw a change in Greg's manner and how he listened carefully to everything she said. As Abe used his real name, Greg smiled, something not one person there had ever seen him do before.

Chapter 40

"Greg and I knew what we wanted to do, and that it had to be fast and precise. A mistake could mean ten years in the slammer for us, and maybe all of you, too. We talked a lot. Everything depended on whether the disturbance Jade created made the guards abandon the moneybags for at least a minute or two."

"I did a dry run with the boom a few times, and Greg put up markers to show me wires and other obstacles to avoid. We also went over the machine several times to make sure it was in good working order."

"Jade, Greg and I set up signals because I wouldn't be able to see her on the other side of the truck after the 'accident.' Greg could see her. Standing in the fourth floor window, Greg wiped his face with a white handkerchief to tell me the money was out the guards' sight. He planned to use a red kerchief if it wasn't.

"Jade watched for the bucket to go toward Greg in the window. Once it was there, he flashed the white handkerchief again to tell her we had the money bags and she should go—and she did, in a hurry."

Abe paused to see if there were questions. None came. Everyone was leaning forward, eyes fixed on his face.

Greg's smile grew larger as Abe went on. "Well, you all know the rest. Jade put on a performance that had the driver and guard stumblin' over each other to help her out. I think she could've kept them away from the money for a week." The group laughed and Tina patted Jade on the back.

Jade bowed. "Thank you."

Abe continued, "I had the crane bucket at the window in seconds, so Greg could load it and cover the money bags. You already know the bank girl watching-from-the-window-story. The bags were in the bucket when she saw me bringing it down to the barge.

"Greg made the pieces of sheetrock large enough so I could put the edges on the barge, lower the bucket into the water to raise one side a little from the bucket to make it easier for Janet to pull the money bags out. If she was having trouble getting the bags, she'd let me know by letting a block of wood float to the water's surface. If necessary, I could lower the bucket into the water more and tip it down."

"Greg's sizing was just right; she got them out quickly and gave me the 'go' signal, an air-filled bottle popping to the surface. I raised the bucket slowly, deposited the debris in the barge, and tamped it down.

"Now I pass the story to my waterlogged friends, Janet and Lloyd, who followed up by doing something I could never, ever, do."

Abe put his huge arm around Greg's shoulders and his rare smile was even larger. Laughter followed.

❖ ❖ ❖

Chapter 41

Behind her youthful appearance, Janet was a mature woman of intelligence and ability. Wiry and slim with blonde hair in a pageboy cut, she was invariably asked for ID in bars. She met the disbelief head-on, and after it was discovered she was a Navy veteran, she received a lot of apologies.

"I was in my scuba-gear waiting under the debris barge and could see the shadow of the crane bucket as Abe lowered it. I was puzzled when he hesitated for a minute and learned later he was flirting with the girl in the bank window, to distract her, he says." She laughed, and looked at Jade. "I'm just givin' him a zinger, Jade. It was pretty quick thinkin' on his part."

"As the sheetrock caught the edge of the barge, it was lifted off the bags. Lowered a little more, put the bucket into the water and I could see the canvas bags. I passed a rope through the handles of the each one, tied a bowline, and pulled them out of the bucket. As per our plan, I released the bottle signal."

"Abe lifted the bucket to push the sheetrock on the barge, then moved it away. I gave the rope a yank to let Lloyd know I was ready, and he began to move the boat slowly out toward the channel. The rope was tied to the bow of the boat. I took my end with the bags down to twenty feet to avoid the boat propellers, any yahoos on Ski-Dos, and to stay out of sight of any helicopters."

"Lloyd dragged the bags and me across the main navigation channel to the north side of a huge rock, fifty feet long and protruding ten feet out of the water. Lloyd had been going there for several days to fish, but mostly to make his presence there routine to any watchers."

"Once there, I opened the bags one at a time underwater letting the blue dye flow away with the current. I passed each bag to him and he put the contents into the big cooler in the bow of the boat. Lloyd passed each bag back to me with a big rock in it."

"If a helicopter was around, Lloyd signaled me to wait and stay out of sight under the boat by dropping his bait can over the side. After I had all the bags back, we moved out in to the main channel where the water is 300 feet deep. I made sure there were no air pockets, released the bags and watched them drift down out of sight. We started down river toward the dock at the RV Park. I still had half an hour in my tank, so I stayed under the boat. The helicopter was circling overhead."

Captivated, everyone was silent. "When we got to the dock, Lloyd took his fishing gear to the RV and brought back a waterproof bag that was large enough to hold the cooler. Making sure no one was watching, he tied a rope on it and slipped it to me in the water."

"I tied the bag to one of the dock posts, underwater, and out of sight. I got out of the water just as my air tank signaled 'empty.' People in the area were used to seeing me dive there. I'd been doing it every day for nearly a week, under the guise of looking for shipwrecks."

"There you have it." She bowed to a round of applause and pointed at Lloyd. "It was a two-person operation. Couldn't have done it without my partner."

Lloyd was beaming. Six feet tall with sun-bleached hair and deeply tanned skin, exaggerated by the white shirt he was wearing, he had the straight posture of a sailor. The way he looked at Janet, it was clear he loved her. His voice was brusque, with the remnants of the military leaking through. "The Long Island Sound Amphibians thank you for your praise, good cheer and camaraderie. It's always good to be able to say, 'mission accomplished'."

❖ ❖ ❖

Chapter 42

G reg, always embarrassed by his strange voice, rarely spoke, but couldn't contain his curiosity. "But how did the money get to Amorsetti's office in the Hockmeir building?"

Tina, the coordinator, was just as efficient at delivering the story as she was at planning it. She took the question. "Once the forensic teams from the sheriff's office and the state police completed their work at the Hockmeir and moved on, plan five kicked in, and it was in the hands of Ed and Bud. They should tell about it. Ed, you first." She had always called him by his real name, Ed Lightfeather, not Shadow or Fast Eddy, as others did. This little gesture had gained his respect and admiration when he was skeptical whether a woman could plan such a job.

Ed fidgeted and took a deep breath. He wasn't an in-the-limelight person. "Well, it was pretty simple really. I was working in Hockmeir all day long every day, planning what colors to paint walls, ordering materials, and putting them on Frank's laptop for his decisions to purchase stuff.

"I got bored and tried to fix the old TV. I had it all apart, then found the cathode tube was cracked. I knew they didn't make them anymore. I broke it into small pieces and sent the guts of the TV to the dump in the town trash pickup."

"Tina and I talked over where to hide the money and decided the best place was where everyone could see it. That TV came up in the conversation. She realized it was the perfect place, and asked if it had enough space. I knew it did.

"She suggested spray painting the inside of the glass gray, to match the color of a screen when it's off, and screwing the plastic cover back on with the electrical cord dangling out in its usual place. I did it a little at a time. I was right, the money fit inside with room to spare."

"I bought the paint for the re-modeling. It came in gallon cans, four to a box. Bud helped me and we put the money in the bottom of the paint boxes, covered it with cardboard and put the paint cans back in. It only took five boxes."

"I was a little worried one time, though. Frank Amorsetti was there when I carried in a box one day. He looked through it and took a can of pink for his kid's room."

"I worked late that night and got all the money socked away in the fake TV, except for the bucks Bud kept for the briefcase."

The transfer being done right under the Amorsettis' noses sparked laughs and Ed was grinning because everyone appreciated the subter-fuge. What he liked most, however, was that everyone followed Tina's lead and dropped his nickname. He'd never felt as close to anyone, even his family, as he did with the people there.

❖ ❖ ❖

Chapter 43

As one of the ex-cons who saw the Amorsetti brothers bring the briefcase along on rides to the parole office, Donovan asked, "How'd the robbery money get in the briefcase?" He thought he would be able tell who did it. *It'll be the one who smiles. ... Nobody's smiling.*

Everyone was silent: then suddenly the women burst into laughter. They'd heard him bragging how he could read people's motives just by watching them. Donovan saw Tina's impish look and knew she'd coached everybody to keep a straight face. *She knew I'd ask that question. She's so smart.* He gave Tina a fake fierce look, and then joined the laughter.

What surprised him most, it was Bud who spoke up. "Remember, now, this all happened long before Rita came back to me." He tried to catch Rita's eyes but they couldn't be caught. "I had a key to the Amorsetti office. The locked file drawer, too. Sheila didn't know. I made a clay impression when she left the room.

"I used to help Sheila count the money for the briefcase on Thursday nights at the end of the month after everybody'd left. We'd fill the briefcase with the cash and lock it, along with both ledgers, in her file drawer. We'd put the rest of the cash in the locked drawers in Joe and Frank's desks. Occasionally I would skim two or three hundred from Frank's share and give it to Sheila. He never counted his money. He can't count to a hundred anyway."

"I kept the keys. They were kind of like insurance. I wanted to be sure I could get to the money or the books if somethin' went wrong. The keys are gone now. I dropped them in the river while I was fishin'. I like havin' things when you need 'em and not havin' 'em when cops thinks you do."

Smiles from the men confirmed they liked his philosophy.

❖ ❖ ❖

Bud continued. "So I exchanged the briefcase money one Friday at 2 a.m. and wiped the place down. You know the rest." He looked at Rita again. *She is smiling this time. Thank God.*

Bud stood up. "Okay. There's something I need to do." He went to the old books on a nearby shelf and extracted nine brown envelopes, each with a name written in the corner. "The reward money from the bank and insurance people was $60,000 cash, given to an anonymous finder and kept in my safety deposit box at the bank.

"The bank, insurance company, and the newspapers are frothing-at-the-mouth to know the name of the 'anonymous' finder. In case they marked the bills to find out, I took the money, $2,000 at a time, to a guy at the casino business office across the river in Canada. He exchanged our American dollars for American dollars they took in at the casino. Believe me, they know forged and marked bills."

"My friend there didn't know, or care, where the money came from. All he cared about was his accounts balanced at the end of the day. Anybody lookin' for marked bills is gonna run into hundreds of names, none of them yours. Because of the exchange rate, we even got a little bonus."

"Wow! Smart." Donovan was impressed.

"I know. I can't take the credit though. Rita used to be a dealer and told me how to get the best exchange value." He squeezed Rita's shoulders and she grinned. "Rita and I decided to take just one share between us to give you guys a little more of a head start."

He handed out the envelopes. "If I counted right, you should each have a little more than six and a half thousand in these. If I made any mistakes, tell me. Use it wisely. I gave half the switch-money from the Amorsetti briefcase to Sheila, and the other half to you. It was supposed to be yours in the first place. I cleaned it up the same way I did with the reward money."

"Sheila thinks it is severance pay because she lost her job when the company went belly-up. She may be all right though. Detective Stokes brought her in the bar the other night and they seemed really happy."

❖ ❖ ❖

This prompted a toast and lots of cheers. They parted, agreeing to meet the following week, before going their separate ways.

On his way out, Bud took Greg and Ed aside. "Sam Wolcott has purchased a larger workshop. Cabinet making is his favorite work. He says you both have talent and wants to talk with you about working for him. With all the new buildings going up because of the military base, he's behind and could use your help. Here's his number." He gave each of them a card.

Ed didn't believe him. "He really said that?"

"He did. He says you are the best color coordinator he ever saw and Greg is a born woodworker. You should talk to him."

Greg was smiling like never before. "Thanks, Bud."

Chapter 44

Sunday afternoon Tina and John took a walk along the beach near Beckett's Bay. Fall color was at its peak and reflections in the water doubled the beauty. Perhaps the meeting that night would be their last with many in the group. They were grateful, not just for their skills and knowledge, but for the team they had become when it mattered. Donovan wasn't a sentimental person. His early life experiences had seen to it; but an unspoken feeling was jostling him and was both strange, and unexpected.

"John, do you like it here?" Tina asked gently.

"Well, it's not exciting like the city with all the sirens, traffic noise and people jamming the streets. I'm not sure which worries me most, the possibility of gettin' mugged or steppin' on a snake. I'm beginning to enjoy the quiet and seein' fields, trees and water instead of scroungy old buildings. It's kind of like livin' in a huge Central Park, where the streets are so far away you don't hear the traffic."

Tina laughed. *He's good at seeing things from a different angle. Love it.* "Me, too. I like the serenity of this small town. It's refreshing to meet people on the street I actually know."

John smiled. *She's smart. In her delicate way she slips ideas into our conversations knowin' they'll interest me. She's tryin' to polish my lousy education. When I ask questions she says, "I think I have a book on it." Then she finds the book and, after I read it, we discuss it. Sometimes she helps me and I don't even know she's done it. I want to be the person who deserves to be with her, always.*

Then it hit him like a fist in a bar fight, *We aren't the ones who were nuts and needed treatment. It was our parents. We just followed their terrible examples. We're in charge of our own happiness. Actually—not 'we'—me. Tina's already decided. I can see it in her face.*

Tina turned to look at him and was on the verge of speaking. The admiration and emotion in his face brought her to a quizzical stop. His eyes embraced her and he put an arm around her waist. Not sure what was happening, she decided to go ahead with what she wanted say. "I'm happy here. It's a simpler life. It's like we've been given a second chance. I think I can write here. The schools are excellent and there aren't all the distractions, like in the city."

"But how do we make a living here? Small towns don't have many jobs."

"You're an excellent barber. There is always a need for a barber. The money isn't great, but it is steady. It costs half as much to live here as in the city, and I can work, too."

"I *do* like being a barber. What do the schools have to do with us?"

"There's something I need to tell you."

"What is it?"

"There's going to be a new Donovan and I don't want to complicate the baby's

life before it even starts."

"... What? ... *What?*"

Tina was watching his face anxiously. As she saw a grin spreading across it like a sunrise, the worry pressing on her lifted away. She felt weightless and life took on a whole new meaning. She was free of the past and with a companion who really loved her.

John raised her off her feet and danced around on the sand. Then he stopped suddenly. "You all right?" He put his hand on her belly.

"I'm fine." Tina laughed. *With our family histories it's a miracle he can be this happy.* It gave her a rush of self-value—and joy—unlike any she had ever known.

John had many questions, including some she couldn't answer. "When did you find out? Is it a boy? What will we name him?" Tina bathed in the glow of his happiness and answered the questions she could.

"I'm going to be a father! Wow! Do you want me to carry you?"

Tina laughed. "No, silly. I'm fine. Let's go."

"I gotta go to the bar and get some cigars."

❖ ❖ ❖

Chapter 45

Rita and Bud were in a booth talking as John and Tina entered O'Toole's. John interrupted. "I'm going to be a father! Can you believe it?" Rita jumped up to embrace Tina. Bud started shaking John's hand and patting him on the back at the same time.

Tina whispered in Rita's ear as she held her. "And we're going to stay here in Beckett's Bay."

Rita stepped back, holding Tina's arms and looking into her eyes. She saw Tina was serious. She pulled her back into her arms. "Bud, they're going to stay here!" The hug became a four-person huddle.

Donovan had a warm feeling unlike any he had experienced. *Rita is the sister Tina never had, and from day one, Bud has treated me like a real brother.*

John didn't have to get the cigars; Bud beat him to it. "These, my boy, are the real Cubans. We're celebrating Elle and Child-to-be-Named!"

Rita and Tina were already in baby-talk mode as they started up the stairs. Rita stopped. "Bud, we can have a barbershop and beauty parlor on the first floor next door to the restaurant. There'll be plenty of room."

"You talking about the Hockmeir?" Donovan asked.

Bud grinned. "Yep. We bought it last night. We took out a mortgage on O'Toole's and Jake Spicer, from Brooklyn, has already promised to lease space for a beauty parlor. His wife's from Beckett's Bay and her father is on the County Board of Directors. The word will get around that the reward money got put back into the community. Rita's right. We'll start on the ground floor. You can work on the renovations with Sam Wolcott. Greg and Ed are going to stay here, too, and work in Sam's cabinet business. We'll have you cuttin' hair there by spring."

Chapter 46

That night Jadlyn, Janet and Rita smoked cigars with the men. Tina did not. She took her motherly responsibilities seriously and opened all the windows. Tina and John's decision to stay in Beckett's Bay puzzled Jadlyn. *Havin' a baby wouldn't make them stay here. There's got to be more to it. Do they know something I don't?* She asked, in a slightly petulant voice, spitting out the word 'here' like it was bitter. "Why are you staying here?"

Tina looked at John. He smiled and nodded yes, as much as to say, *Go ahead. You can do it. You should tell them.* They had talked non-stop the last few hours and hardened their decision. Tina spoke almost in a whisper. She liked making people strain to hear. It made them listen and she wanted them to consider her words.

"We're poor and from screwed up families, but look at Gelky, Schwartz and the Amorsettis. They're educated and wealthy, yet couldn't tell right from wrong. I don't think it's the wealth or the intelligence of the family you're born into that teaches you to know the difference. I think it's the support and example the family sets, the love, and maybe not just the family love, but also the love of the place and the people in it." She glanced toward Rita and saw a smile as wide as a slice of watermelon.

She paused. *Please, God, let me say this right so they understand I'm not judging them, but trying to help.* "I think we're gettin' a chance to change our future for the better." The sincerity in her face couldn't be questioned.

"Greg and Ed have found skills they didn't know they had. Abe is a magician with a crane. Jadlyn, you're the coolest person under pressure I've ever seen. You can choose any job you want and do it to perfection. Lloyd and Janet, you know water better than the fish. Look what Rita and Bud have done in business. They're great at it. What I'm sayin' is this: every one of us has skills, not fancy skills from education, but good skills, skills worth wages—and not one of us needs to see the inside of a jail again—ever. We are better than the Amorsettis, Schwartz, or Gelky!"

Tina stopped and looked at the floor. When she lifted her head, she hesitated, then looked at each person before speaking. "I'm sorry for preachin'. I love you all. I want you to be safe and happy, and hope you'll come to visit us here often."

❖ ❖ ❖

John gathered her in his arms. Looking at the faces over Tina's shoulder, he was surprised that even hardboiled Abe, Ed, and Bud had watery eyes, and Greg was outright crying. He thought, *Even though they're not kids, it's as if Tina's their mother and steerin' them down the correct path. They're really feelin' what she's sayin'.*

Silence followed—several minutes of silence.

Janet was the first to speak. Even her military discipline had succumbed and she was blinking back tears. "Tina, you're going to be a great mother. I think everything you said is right. We had a real life lesson here and it's time to move on. We'll be back whenever the fishing's good. You can count on it. We heard what you said." Lloyd smiled in silent agreement.

Ed hugged Tina long and hard. Greg, with tears still streaming down his face, took her right hand with both of his and lifted it to his lips. Tina hugged him.

Abe, the Bronx Bear, was an ingénue with sentiment. He turned away and opened three bottles of champagne so fast the popping corks made everyone jump, dispelling the weighty feeling in the air.

Filling glasses for everyone, he stopped, facing Tina. "You, young woman, are a person to know and have as a friend. You speak the truth and we'd be fools if we didn't listen."

Jadlyn kissed Tina on the forehead. "Abe's got it right. We'll be back."

❖ ❖ ❖

Separating that night, each was a different person from when they arrived in Beckett's Bay. The effect wasn't the same on everyone because it sat atop their varying experiences. But there was something new in each one; and it was welcomed; it was positive; and it was honest.

The End

The Karma

In early October of 2015, business was steady at the Main Street Barbershop and Beauty Parlor. John was grateful none of the barbershop friendships had been torn asunder by the impending election, yet.

The river water was holding the temperature up and the weather was warmer than usual. The leaves of the hardwood trees were in full fall finery: brown oaks scattered among the red and orange maples, yellow birches, and the green hemlocks.

At the usual time, 3:30, the school bus stopped out front and Ryan flew out the door, a backpack and lacrosse stick over his shoulders. His younger sister, Cali, followed him more discreetly.

John made a mental note, *I've got talk to Ryan so he takes care of his sister and respects girls.* "How'd lacrosse practice go today, Ryan?"

"Okay. Coach gave us a routine to use in the gym all winter so we aren't mush in the spring. He's good."

John pointed to the man lying back in the barber chair his face covered by a hot towel. "Say hello to the mayor."

Ryan rolled his eyes. "Hi, Mayor." The right hand of the man in the chair rose up, paused, and flapped back down. John looked at Ryan and they both bent forward smothering laughs.

John lifted Cali up to give her a hug, and her arms wrapped around his neck. "How was your day, young lady?"

She smiled, her nose against his. "Fine. I have a new friend, Chloe. Her mommy and daddy are soldiers. She's black like me. I got a hundred in math."

"No kiddin'. Wow! Say hello to the mayor."

"Hi, Mr. Mayor." The right hand went up and down again. John made a face and Cali couldn't resist laughing, nor could John.

"Go see Mom, get started on your homework, and I'll be there shortly."

A door at the back of the shop opened into an enormous room with large windows overlooking the river. Greg, Ed, Sam, and John had made this special lounge for the employees of the barber-beauty shop and restaurant when they refurbished the building. A second door opened to a deck with lounge chairs and a grand view of the sunsets.

A third door opened into the kitchen of the restaurant next door. Furnished with two desks, a sofa, overstuffed chairs, and a dining table for eight by the windows, it had become a quiet place for Ryan and Cali to have dinner with their parents or, on alternate days, for Rita and Bud to do the same with their daughters, Elle and Darcy.

Rita and Tina alternated the late shift at the Casa Rita Tina Restaurant. That night, as they did every other day after dinner at the restaurant, Tina, John, Ryan, and Cali walked home together.

Cali and Ryan were running on ahead, exchanging challenges on who would be first getting to a tree, or a swing, or who could walk the top of a low wall without falling.

As they walked, Tina took John's hand, making the usual comforting thrill run through him. "Those people called again today, offering to buy the movie rights to my book."

"You better talk to Blanche Martin at the Bianco Sound Studio. She knows legal stuff on music and books. You may need a lawyer to help you. We should have the Martins over again, anyway. I'll bet Ken would like to go fishin'."

"Where would we put them all?"

"We'll set up a tent in the backyard for the boys, one for the girls, too, if they want to camp out. Or we could rent a camp for the weekend at Spicer Bay. The season's over. They'll rent cheap. We'll get one with a fireplace and have an old-fashioned marshmallow roast."

Ryan heard this part of the conversation. John added, "Ryan, Patrick Martin is into lacrosse like you. He might have some new tricks."

"I know. He's good. His dad played at Cornell. If we go fishing, can we go to Eel Bay? Lots of bass there."

"Of course. Maybe Bud will go, too, and take his big boat."

Cali looked up at John. "Can I go, Daddy?"

"Sure. But maybe you won't want to go with us. You're hostess for this visit. I suspect Grace and Kaitlyn Martin would like you to take them shopping. What do you think?"

"I'm hostess?"

"Yes, you are."

"I'll go with you some other time."

"Okay."

Tina squeezed John's hand and they exchanged smiles. No words were necessary.

The Riff Raff

My first stop is the bar of the Diggs Hotel. That's where most of the village gossip, fights, rumors, lies, jokes, nicknames, hurt feelings, and advice-to-the-president originate in our village. I deliver the local newspaper to businesses and a few houses. It only takes an hour. They use 'em as perks for their clients.

It isn't exciting work, except for the people. Especially the people. A daily visit to the Diggs' bar makes me an honorary regular, according to the regulars. "Honorary" because I'm only fourteen.

The Diggs has been getting less popular since 1827. Its claim to fame is a poker game played there in 1864. The son of an American president put courting rights of his girlfriend in the pot and lost to a local. If she was smart, she'd have told 'em both she was going to be washing her hair or out-of-town for the next ten years.

I ignore warnings of damage to my soul by associating with bar riff raff, mostly because I don't know what the words riff raff mean, and all the perils described tweak my curiosity. Many "upright" citizens avoid the Diggs Hotel as if it's coated with Ebola virus. I think their real fear is being labeled with an innovative, spontaneous, or funny nickname.

At the hotel they call me 'Yogi,' after Yogi Berra. I like it. A bar patron saw me throw a rolled up newspaper from my moving bicycle and hit a front door thirty feet away on a windy day. He carried this news back to the regulars, and they tagged me. It doesn't matter if I miss most of the time.

But the silent, military-bearing, eyes-straight-ahead minister who refuses to return the "hellos" of patrons sitting on the hotel porch when he walks by, they call "Icicle" to his face. He crosses to the other side of the street now to avoid passing in front of the hotel.

Six days a week I hand *The Bugle* to Jake or Nicki, the Diggs' barkeepers. Jake Olmsted, shaped like an outhouse, has the breath to match. Challenged about this by a new patron, he asks the regulars' opinions. "It's not that bad," they lie. It's worse. He has the personality and voice of a kitten. His height allows him to reach the highest shelf in the place, but bending for something under the bar elicits a litany of curses. The majority of the hair on his head is black, and confined to his upper lip. His nose goes left, then right. The tattoos on his arms resemble watercolor paintings left out in the rain.

In high school he was center on the football team and eager for an athletic scholarship. The dream evaporated one day when a 285-pound lineman from Worthington knocked him on his ass and marched over his legs, belly, and head to sack the quarterback.

Jake has three things going for him: he can remember the favorite beverage and tab of every customer, calculate in his head the odds on any Phillies game at warp speed, and he is married to Nicki.

The Diggs wraps around the corner of Main and Byrnes Streets in the center of town. Next door, by a driveway width, is a funeral parlor run by Fred Mason, who doubles as a barber, and a bank is just beyond. Across the street, a hardware store, meat market, dinky post office, and grocery all belly-up to the sidewalk in what we call "downtown," if we're there, or "uptown," if we're going there.

The hotel shows signs of age, neglect, and irrelevance. The paint is faded and peeling on the dark-yellow siding, brown trim, and sign. Repairs on the porch railing remain unpainted, gray with age in some places, and even older in others.

Foot-traffic gouges in the wooden steps and barroom floor attest to the wood's age. The gouges are garnished daily with new snow or mud, depending on the season. In fair weather, the front door is open and loud conversations from inside mingle with, or join, those on the porch.

A flimsy, almost rectangular screen door on the front entrance slaps closed with a squeak and a smack as customers pass through. The screen itself has bulges top and bottom created by patrons who don't notice it's there, usually when they're leaving. The porch chairs are a garage-sale collection of types and colors in various states of destruction.

To the left of the front door, behind a window with an admirable coating of dirt, there's a blue and red neon "Bud...iser" sign, the "we" flickering on and off whenever it feels like it. If the neon light shows any life, the bar is open.

Customers' cars face the hotel at haphazard angles, leaving only the sidewalk between their front bumpers and the porch. Only a seriously deaf passerby can avoid hearing, and maybe taking part in, the conversations of patrons on the porch.

On a day in April 2009, the regulars are in consultation as I enter. I raise a hand in greeting. All wave back, but don't speak. They're too engrossed in the subject *du jour*. Pabst (nicknamed for his favorite beer) is saying, "Did you ever try fly fishin'?" Murmurs suggest this is a topic of great interest, and something to know about.

Bud Lite asks, "Why do you want to catch flies?"

"They eat 'em in some countries. I saw it in *National Geographic.* They dip 'em in chocolate," says Red Wine.

"What do they taste like? Don't say chicken. Everybody says that, even about snakes," Bud Lite replies.

Labatt joins in, "I seen pictures of guys fly fishin'. They use these long fishin' rods and whip the line back and forth. Must be a real art to catchin' flies like that. Those sticky things I put up in my barn work better. They must be pretty tasty flies to go to all that trouble." I move on and don't hear the conclusion. Reaching one often takes hours.

Delivering the paper one early spring afternoon, I see a tall man sitting at the far end of the bar. He has broad shoulders, a sunburned face, and scraggly brown hair sticking out from under a dirty baseball cap of indeterminable color. Hunched forward, solitary, he is staring at a coffee cup. His unkempt brown mustache and beard look as if they started at puberty and had been on their own since.

His black chinos and green shirt are creased in multiple directions, like he slept in them. The cuffs and sleeves are frayed. Ankle-high, scuffed-up leather boots with worn soles finish setting him apart from the usual patrons with bib overalls and rubber boots. I judge him to be fifty years old, or close to it.

As I hold out the paper to Jake, he points at the new man with the glass he is drying. "Give it to Tom." When I hand the paper to Tom, he wiggles his mustache at me in a quick half-smile, makes an upward salute with the folded paper, and mutters, "Thanks." His voice comes out weary. His hands are large and strong looking, with prominent veins.

After a few such encounters Tom asks, "You want a soda?" I have to lean in to hear him. The regulars are making up a song at the other end of the bar; and he talks softly. I give a "yes" nod.

He motions to Jake for the drink, then points at the Phillies logo on my t-shirt. "You play baseball?" He looks me in the eyes with his blue ones, his voice slightly stronger. He doesn't smell as bad as I expected—more like Ivory soap.

"Yes."

"What position?"

"Short stop."

"First. Used to."

"Where?"

"High school in Cambria County, College in Gettysburg, Pro for the Phillies."

"Wow! You played pro ball? That's awesome! … What are you doin' here?"

"Long story, kid. Finish your route. We'll talk more another time. Okay?"

I'm surprised. Here's a guy who understands my job, talks to me like an adult—except for the "kid" thing I write-off as not knowin' my name—uses teacher-quality English, and is at a bar drinkin' coffee.

It's Friday the next time I see Tom. Nicki is there to help Jake. She brings me a Pepsi, leaning over the bar to demonstrate her cleavage, as usual. The new guy turns his head away as she approaches, as if he has a sudden interest in the corner of the room. Nicki's not hard to look at and she knows it—tall, trim, blonde hair piled on her head, smooth skin except for a few pock-marks on her cheeks, matching rouge and lipstick, fetching smile, and big boobs—she's second only to alcohol as the bar's main attraction.

She asks Tom, "More coffee?"

He shakes his head.

His response puts a twist in her panties and she gives him a stern, quizzical look. I could tell from past encounters that she expected at least an ogle to confirm her good looks. She sniffs and turns away.

When she's gone, Tom turns toward me. "When does she work here?"

"She helps Jake Fridays and Saturdays, or subs if he's away. She's Jake's wife. Their daughter goes to my school."

"What's her name?"

"Samantha Olmsted. We call her Sam." When I say that, Tom's head suddenly drops toward the bar and a shiver shakes him. After a minute or so he straightens his back, then stands up, and walks out of the bar without a word.

I don't know what I said wrong. I shout, "Thanks for the Pepsi," after him.

Tom isn't in the Diggs again until Wednesday, two weeks later. I'm runnin' late. We played our first league baseball game that afternoon and lost.

The regulars are having a serious discussion on what Joe Lacombe should do about the heifer that keeps getting over his pasture fence. Joe's there, and so is the heifer. The captured heifer is waiting in Joe's old Buick out front. You remember the big ones with four doors, a long hood with a vertical radiator made to accommodate eight cylinders, and a fancy Buick ornament on top?

Well, Joe's Buick is missing the ornament and about everything else including paint, but does have a fresh coat of mud to vouch for his description of the heifer round-up.

The heifer replaces the missing back seat with its ass against the back window on the driver's side and its face sticking out the open window on the other. She seems unconcerned, but considering the complexity and duration of the discussion, I thought she ought to be a little worried about the ride home.

Handing the paper to Tom, I say, "Give me the ten-minute version of why you're here."

He smiles a little and motions for Jake to bring me a Pepsi. "Okay, kid. What's your name?"

"Mike. Mike O'Malley."

"Tom Black." He offers his hand. I can feel calluses that don't go with his city clothes.

"Tell me."

"Okay. A friend offered me a job here at Baum Engineering."

"I mean, why aren't you playing ball?"

"I was injured and the team let me go."

"Oh. ... Are you all right now?"

"Yes, but I can't play anymore."

"... Would you be interested in coaching our summer league team? We don't have a coach." I give him some details about our twenty players, their ages, who we play, and where.

"Tell you what, I'll come to some of your high school games this spring and think about it."

"Okay. Gotta go. Thanks for the Pepsi." I get a bigger smile from him this time. He has a full set of real teeth, all white. His blue eyes kinda sparkle, but there's something missing. They seem sad.

It's a week before I see Tom again. Our high school team already played an away game at Latrobe and lost 4 to 1.

As I enter the hotel that afternoon, the regulars are discussing Ray Holmes' accident. The night before, driving home from the bar at 1 a.m., he missed the bridge and ended up in Pleasant Creek.

On my way to school that morning, I saw his pick-up truck nose down in the water, as if it was thirsty. The creek is only two feet deep but it's at the bottom of a steep bank. The back of the truck was pointed toward heaven and the driver's door was open.

Ray's telling the regulars he walked home. I'm sure it wasn't a straight-line stroll. I wasn't astonished by what I saw—he'd done it three times before. I wouldn't have noticed the new dents in the truck either, if the Highway

Department hadn't put white paint on the guardrails when they fixed them the last time.

Ray, better known as Molson, is explaining, "I tell you, the bridge moved just as I got to it."

Pabst is skeptical. "Bridges can't move! Did you have both eyes open?"

"What do you think, dummy?" Molson fires back.

"That explains it then," says Pabst. "You got crossed eyes, right?"

"Yeah. So what?"

"With crossed eyes you see two of everything, but one's real and the other's fake. You were just lookin' at the fake bridge instead of the real one."

"Oh. That explains it," says Molson, and the other regulars nod in agreement. "Jake, give me another."

"I saw you at our last game," I say to Tom, handing him the paper. I don't mention he looks a lot better with his hair, beard, and mustache trimmed, and a baseball cap that isn't terminal. I'm way off on my age-guess. Cleaned up, he looks Dad's age.

"You have a game Friday?" Tom asks.

"Yeah. We're probably gonna get beat again. Connellsville is tough."

"I'll be watchin'. You're good with your glove, Mike, but you have to get faster with your feet. Get in front of the ball if you can. Then you can stop it and, even if you can't catch it, there's still time to make the throw."

"Thanks. You thinkin' of helping us?"

"Yeah."

"I told Coach Roy about you. I'll bet a quarter he'd like to have help coachin' at the high school. Teachin' history is his big thing. He coaches because he has to, I think. What did you graduate in at Gettysburg? He wants to know."

"Phys Ed."

"Have you ever coached?"

"I coached the new players comin' up to the Phillies from the minors for three seasons."

"Mr. Roy is gonna like that. I'm runnin' late because of the game. Mom'll be wonderin' where I am. Gotta go. Still 36 more papers to deliver. See ya at the next game."

We lost to Connellsville 8 to 6. Afterward I introduced Coach Roy and Tom. They talked a long time.

Tom is at every game and practice the next two weeks. He and Coach Roy seem to get along. I hear Coach askin' him questions.

The next time we meet is at our game with Uniontown. Tom hadn't been at the bar all week. Giving me a big smile he says, "Mike, your school's getting my college and pro-ball information together. They may use me as a part-time assistant coach. I don't want you to be disappointed if it doesn't work out, so I need to tell you something."

I kinda stare at him. "What's wrong?"

"I was beaned—had a fractured skull and blood clot in my brain. It's called a subdural hematoma."

"Are you sick?"

"No. Not anymore. But I was in a coma. When I came out of it, my job was gone and no team wanted me. I told Coach Roy. They may not want to take me on. I'm damaged goods."

"Do you think you can help us play better baseball?

"Yes."

"That's enough for me."

"You made my day. Your mom and dad must be proud of you."

"It's just my mom now. My dad was killed in Afghanistan three years ago. He's a hero."

Tom looks away, pauses, and then looks back at me. "He certainly is, giving up time he could've been with you, and trying to make things safe for all of us."

"See you at practice," I respond and leave to finish my paper route. When I get home, I tell my mom and sister, Katelyn, what Tom said. For some reason, my mom goes in her bedroom and stays quite a while.

Tom's at every baseball practice and home game the next three weeks. He tells me, "It's kind of a try-out." At practice, he gives us pretend-game situations, sometimes with teammates as base runners, hits fungoes, and lets us decide how to play the ball.

He doesn't say anything if we drop the ball or mess up the throw; just has us try again. If our play decision is wrong, he calls us onto the mound and quietly explains a better choice.

Gradually, he increases how hard he hits the ball at practice. Sometimes he talks with individual players about ways to improve. He's good at showing us what to do.

I can feel a change. Our team-talk shifts. It's more and more about baseball, even when we're just goofin' around or between classes. To our amazement, parents begin appearing at games.

And something happens to Tom, too. He's wearing clean, pressed jeans, clean shirts with button-down collars, and Oxfords. A fresh Phillies' cap replaces the scroungy one, his hair and eyebrows are trimmed, and the beard and mustache have been shaved off to reveal smooth, tan skin.

His lively smile; searching, inquisitive eyes; full-attention listening; and thoughtful questions mark him as a man to know. It is kinda like the butterfly comin' out of a chrysalis we saw in biology class. He hasn't been at the hotel for weeks.

My mom and sister came to our last high school game and I introduced them to Tom.

Mom says to Tom, "Thanks for helping Mike and the boys. You're a major subject of discussion at our house. This is Mike's sister, Katelyn."

"Hi," Katelyn says, taking her eyes off the ground to look up at him for a second. She's ten years old and shy. I tell her all the time she's pretty, and she is: curly hair that's more blonde than mom's, mom's delicate nose, smooth skin, and green eyes.

She wasn't shy when Dad was home. He'd tease her, saying, "You walk like a girl," and she'd give it right back to him, "Your nose smells." I try to take his place, but it doesn't work coming from a brother.

"Pleasure to meet you, Mrs. O'Malley and Miss Katelyn," Tom says shaking their hands. "Glad you could make the game. Coach Roy is pleased with the boys' enthusiasm and improving skills."

Mom looks him straight in the eyes. "I heard you had a lot to do with the change."

"Well, maybe a little," he replies, his face going from tan to red.

I tell him, "My mom played basketball in high school and college."

"Wow." Tom turns to her. "Where?"

"Greenburg High and Cornell." Mom is tall, very pretty, smart, and kind. She loves Katelyn and me. She's a nurse and works in the hospital operating room with the bone doctors.

"College basketball? Wow! I like basketball. It's fast."

Mom asks, "Do you have family here?"

"No. I found a job at Baum Engineering through a former teammate. My minor at Gettysburg was business statistics. I like the work."

"Well then, you'll have to come over for supper some night. You should be welcomed to the neighborhood. I'll let you and Mike work out a time."

"Thank you. That's very nice of you." Then he turns to me, kinda talking out of the corner of his mouth like he is sayin' a secret, but loud enough for Katelyn and Mom to hear, "Mike, you better tell Katelyn to watch out for Billy Stephens, our left fielder. He keeps lookin' at her."

Katelyn blushes, looks up at Tom, smiles, almost laughs, and moves closer to Mom. Tom had done what Dad would do, and I couldn't. He made her come back to life for a moment.

I glance at Mom. She has a look on her face I haven't seen in a long time. It's as if something special happened.

Samantha Olmsted walks by as we're talking and gives me a flat-of-your-hand-waist-high wave, which I return. I say to Tom, "That's Sam Olmsted." His eyes follow her, and when we say goodbye he seems to only half hear us.

The school baseball season is over, but not final exams or the paper route. Katelyn and I both pass all our classes, but she just squeaks by. She used to get A's all the time.

I see Tom around town five or six times. Often he's talking on the street or in the diner with Sheriff Tompkins. The sheriff's son, Dan, is on our team, so I suspect they're talking baseball.

Tom came for dinner on Friday night the week school ends. Mom put out the best table stuff and made her specialty: spaghetti and meatballs.

She gets out the "Welcome" placemat, the one she uses when someone new visits. Mom, Katelyn, and I talk it over and decide it's a good idea to give it to Tom.

Arriving with a half gallon of chocolate-marshmallow ice cream, Tom shifts it from one hand to the other like it's too cold to handle. He hands it to Katelyn, who laughs when she finds it's in an insulated bag and not cold at all.

During dinner, we talk mostly about our town, the school, and the summer baseball league. Tom suggests, and Katelyn and I agree, that the three of us should do the cleanup, since Mom did everything else. Mom protests, but Tom insists.

As dusk settles in, we sit on the back porch, listening to the frogs, the soft coo of an owl, and watching the lightning bugs. About half an hour later, Katelyn is asleep, her head in Mom's lap. As Mom tries to get up without waking her, Tom says softly, "Let me."

Gently, he picks up Katelyn. Her head against his chest, she opens her eyes briefly and mutters, "'Night, Daddy."

Tom looks at Mom, who seems frozen in place, and whispers, "Show me where to go." They take Katelyn up to her room and return.

Tom says, "Thank you for dinner and letting me be in your family tonight. I haven't had such a pleasure in a long time."

After he leaves, I ask Mom, "What did he mean?"

"I think he has no family of his own and likes being with us."

* * *

Our summer boy's baseball team is having a good start. We've won three games so far. Billy Stephens and Dan Tompkins have sisters on the girl's softball team coached by Mr. Stephens. When Mr. Stephens sees how well we're doing, he asks Tom to help coach the girl's team after work on the days he isn't with us. Tom agrees, and encourages Katelyn to join the team. She does.

Both teams are having fun and learning. The boys, girls, and parents like Tom, and it's obvious he likes us. He brings out the best in us and keeps the game a game, nothing more.

When I watch the girl's team play, I notice Sam Olmsted is their leader. She's the best player, by far. She talks to Tom and they understand each other, sometimes without even talking. She knows all the baseball hand signals. I think she's a better player than some of the boys on our team, maybe even me. When she sees I'm watching her, she flips the palm of her hand up at waist-level in an aborted wave and smiles. She seems happier than usual.

Tom is a frequent and welcome visitor at our house. Often, he brings food, sometimes pizza, or cooks on the barbecue. He helps us fix broken windows, loose doorknobs, and many things. He shows me how to do it, too.

One day while he, Katelyn, and I are playin' catch and watching the burgers cook on the grill, he says, "Your mom's doing two jobs—work, and home-making. I'm proud of you. I see you help her by cleaning your rooms, the bathroom, and putting away your own clothes. ... You know, if you always do more than you're asked or expected to do, like you're doing now, you'll be a valuable person, not just to your mom, but to any person who gives you a job someday."

At Katelyn's request, the three of us paint her room. She wants pink and white walls. While we're working, Tom asks, over the soft radio music, "Do you like playing softball, Katelyn?"

"Batting scares me. I'm afraid I'll get hit by the ball."

"You can measure how brave a person is by what they do when the going gets rough, whether it's softball or in life. Anybody can give up. The person who tries even harder is special, I think. What do you think?"

Katelyn puts her paint roller in the tray and looks up at him on the ladder, "I want to be brave."

"You already are. So are your mom and Mike," says Tom. Katelyn starts to sing as she paints, like she did helping Dad.

Back in school after a fine summer, I continue my afternoon paper deliveries. On a Wednesday, early in October, I notice something strange is going on at the hotel. The 'Bud…iser' sign is off. There are no cars in front except Sheriff Tompkins' cruiser, and he's never there unless there's a fight.

The sheriff is inside talking, as I approach the screen door. I enter quietly and slip into the coat alcove. He's speaking to Jake and Nicki. "Family Court, ten o'clock, next Thursday. Bring Samantha. You'd better bring all your birth certificates, including Samantha's. Oh … also your wedding licenses to each other, and to anyone else, plus any divorce papers."

Jake asks, in the little voice that doesn't fit his huge size, "What's goin' on, Sheriff?"

"I'm not sure Jake. I'm just serving you the papers, as I'm told. If you got a lawyer, you may want him or her to come too. I forgot—bring any papers you have on buyin' the hotel, especially on how you paid for it, or a mortgage schedule."

Nicki, looking pale, plopped down in a chair like her legs gave out.

Deciding to get out of there before I got caught, I open the screen door gently and left the paper on the porch.

Tom came to our house for supper the next evening. He's quieter than usual and his mind seems elsewhere. He doesn't hear questions and asks for them to be repeated.

After eating and cleanup, we sit on the porch. An early frost has started the leaves changing color and dropping, but it's a warm, Indian Summer day. The special smells of fall fill the air.

Tom's face is serious. "I have to tell you something. I hope you won't hate me and will try to understand." All eyes turn to him. "My name isn't Tom Black. It's John Patrick Quinn." Mom draws in a quick breath. Katelyn and I are fascinated. This is like a movie.

Tom, now John, looks at Mom. "When I came out of a coma about six months after my head injury, my house, my money, my job, my wife, and my daughter were all gone. Gone!

"While I was unconscious, the court appointed a guardian for me. My wife submitted divorce papers and my guardian signed them, since I couldn't. It took me six years to track down my wife and child.

"My former wife is Nicki Olmsted from the Diggs Hotel and Samantha Olmsted is my daughter. Her real name is Emily Grace Quinn."

I take in a quick breath; I might as well, my mouth is hanging open.

"I got a sample of her hair and some chewing gum for saliva and had her DNA checked against mine. She's my daughter. And I'm going to get her back." John's teeth are clenched, his jaw muscles rippling, and the words come out partly squashed.

His voice sounds determined, but I think it's tinged with uncertainty, or perhaps a little fear. His eyes water up a bit. I remember seeing this look before, when I first told him about Samantha. Mom takes his hand and squeezes it tightly.

John, after a short pause to stiffen his resolve, continues, "I just wanted you to know, Family Court is going to hear the case next Thursday and it'll probably be in the papers or on TV. I didn't want to deceive you, but I couldn't risk Nicki taking Emily and running again."

I'm thinkin', *This explains a lot: how he turned away from Nicki at the bar, his lousy clothes and hair at the beginning, the sheriff at the hotel, the way Samantha is a softball whizz and a nice person.*

Mom turns to Katelyn and me. "Why don't you go finish your homework, brush your teeth, and go to bed? John and I need to talk." She kisses both of us.

Katelyn gets up, goes to John, gives him a hug, and kisses his cheek. He says, "Thanks, Katelyn. I needed that."

I tell him, "I don't care if you're called Tom or John, you're still one of the best people I know."

"You keep making my days better and better, young man," his voice kinda choked up-like.

As I leave I hear Mom say, "Does Samantha have any idea who you are?"

"No. I'm worried about that. She was only three when they left."

They're still talkin' when I fall asleep.

"All rise," the bailiff says. "The Murray County Family Court is now in session, The Honorable Judge Margaret Holmes presiding." I'm surprised. I recognize the judge; I take the paper to her office. I didn't know she was a judge. The bailiff continues, "Be seated."

Jake, Nicki, Sam, and a man I don't know sit at a table in front of a railing across from us. John and an unknown woman sit at similar table in front of us. Sheriff Tompkins is behind them and the railing. Two other men I don't know are with him.

Mom, Katelyn, and I are behind the sheriff. Mom took a vacation day and got morning school passes for us. She said, "John needs our support."

As soon as we sit down, the unknown man beside Jake jumps up and says, "Your Honor, I move that this case be dismissed."

Judge Holmes demands, "On what grounds?"

"Mr. Quinn has only been a resident of this county for eight months."

"Counselor, I have before me a copy of Mr. Quinn's birth certificate. He was born in Cambria County, Pennsylvania and has been a resident of this state since then. There are no county residency requirements applicable. Are you trying to tell me I don't know the laws of this state?"

"No, Your Honor."

"Then sit down. Mr. and Mrs. Olmsted, are you married? I have no record of your marriage in this state or any other."

Jake squirms in his seat. "No, Your Honor."

"Mrs. Olmsted, is the young lady sitting next to you your biological child?"

"Yes, Your Honor."

"The birth certificate I have here says she was born in Philadelphia on June 28, 2001. Is that correct?"

"Yes, Your Honor."

"Who is the father of this child?"

The lawyer jumps up again. "Your Honor, I object. Mrs. Olmsted should not be forced to divulge that information in front of her child."

"Counselor, the child should know her father. She has a right to know. It's her life. It's written right here on the birth certificate. Would you prefer I hand the birth certificate to her and let her read it herself?

"I want her mother to tell her the name of her father. It's not embarrassing to have a father. Objection overruled. Mrs. Olmsted, you may answer."

"John Quinn, Your Honor." Samantha looks at Nicki, who stares straight ahead and won't look at her, even when she pulls on her sleeve.

Samantha looks at me and silently mouths, "Who's John Quinn?" I'm afraid to say anything aloud, so I point at Tom. She leans forward to look at him, but he's partially hidden from her by his lawyer. I can't tell what Sam's thinkin'.

"What name was given to this child at birth?"

"Emily Grace Quinn, Your Honor."

Judge Holmes says, "Mrs. Olmsted, you divorced Mr. Quinn while he was in a coma. Is that correct?"

"Yes."

"Since Mr. Quinn could not sign the divorce papers, who signed for him?"

"The guardian appointed by the court, Attorney Harrison Bradshaw."

"Mr. Wayman, as counselor for Mrs. Olmsted, have you read the divorce papers?"

"Yes, Your Honor."

"Are there any visitation rights in the divorce agreement allowing Mr. Quinn to see his daughter?"

"No. Mrs. Olmsted told me she did not expect Mr. Quinn to survive his injury."

"Mrs. Olmsted, what is your maiden name?"

"Nicki Louise Bradshaw."

"Is Attorney Harrison Bradshaw, guardian *ad litem* for Mr. Quinn, related to you?"

Wayman, the Olmsted's attorney, looks at Nicki in disbelief. Either he';s a good actor, or he never thought of this possibility.

"Yes. He's my uncle."

"Mr. Olmsted, do you have papers indicating you adopted Emily Grace Quinn or that her name was changed legally to Samantha Olmsted?"

"No."

"A little louder, please, Mr. Olmsted," says the judge.

"No, Your Honor."

"That's better."

"Mr. Quinn, are you gainfully employed at present?"

"Yes, Your Honor. I have been doing business statistical work for Baum Engineering since arriving here eight months ago. I'm working on a master's degree in business sponsored by my employer, and coaching baseball and soft-ball part-time at the school."

"Are you married? Do you have other children?"

"No, to both questions, Your Honor."

"Are you certain Samantha Olmsted is your daughter?"

"Yes, Your Honor."

The lady sitting next to John stands and says, "Your Honor, I'm Mr. Quinn's attorney, Casey Phillips. May I speak for Mr. Quinn on this subject?"

"Yes. Please do."

"When Mr. Quinn discovered the whereabouts of his daughter after a six-year search, he entered this community somewhat disguised and using an alias: Tom Black. He feared Mrs. Olmsted would flee with his daughter if she recognized him.

"Mr. Quinn collected a sample of hair from Samantha's baseball helmet and her saliva from discarded chewing gum. These samples were sent to laboratories used by the FBI and State Police." She hands a copy of the report to the bailiff for him to pass to the judge. "Both laboratories confirm independently there is a 99.9% chance Samantha is Emily Quinn, his daughter.

"Furthermore, Mr. Quinn says Emily Grace Quinn has a birthmark: a light-brown patch of skin that roughly resembles a daisy on her right-lower back. It is approximately the size of a half-dollar."

I'm watching Sam. Disclosure that Tom is not Tom makes her sit up straight. The significance of the hair and gum tests she doesn't understand and frowns, but at mention of the birthmark, her eyes pop open wide. She looks quickly back and forth from Nicki to John. She clasps and unclasps her hands nervously, then turns her whole body trying to see John around Attorney Casey Phillips.

John has been leaning forward, watching her constantly since declaring she is his daughter. She pauses, studying his face. He smiles at her. ... Slowly, Sam's face breaks into the biggest grin I've ever seen on a girl. Their eyes are locked on each other.

She hesitates a moment, pondering something, then quickly, in sequence, she runs her left hand down her right forearm, pinches her right earlobe with her right hand, and touches her nose with her left index finger—softball talk on her team meaning, "Hit away, you're doin' great." But she adds a final motion; she puts the palm of her right hand over her heart.

John's face is flushed, he's smiling, and he has tears in his eyes, all at the same time. He can't sit still and automatically lifts a phantom baseball cap by the visor. This is baseball talk for, "I understand the signal."

Attorney Phillips grabs his arm as much as to say, "Calm down; it's not over yet. Don't upset the judge."

Judge Holmes asks Sam, "Would you be willing to show us your back? You can show it to me, your mother, and Attorney Phillips in my chambers, if you're embarrassed."

"No. It's okay. You can look," she replies and she pulls up the back of her sweater. On her lower back is a pale, milk chocolate freckle-spot with scalloped edges like flower petals and a slightly darker center. Mom squeezes Katelyn's hand and mine. I look at her face. *Why is she crying? This is a good thing.*

I can tell by the judge's face she is having a difficult time trying to look stern. I know this because, when I stop to be paid for the paper at her office, she always teases me. "My, this paper is getting expensive," she says, with the same stern look. I know it's fake because then she starts laughing and hands me an extra quarter.

Judge Holmes asks, "Does anyone want to add any information? Counselor Wayman?"

"No, Your Honor."

"Counselor Phillips?"

"Your Honor, I would like to point out Emily is living with her mother and mother's boyfriend in a hotel where they tend a bar. Mr. Quinn plans to remain in this area and wants to provide a more home-like atmosphere for her. He has rented an apartment in the village. It's a short distance from the school and Emily would have her own room. In view of the anguish and duration of his separation from his only child, he asks for her full custody."

The judge says to Emily (Sam), "Please come up here," patting the seat next to her. Emily sits down and the judge says, "I know this is confusing, but you need to help me here. It's not likely your mother, father, and you will be together again as a family. This means you'll live with the one I appoint to care for you. You'll be able to visit the other parent. I'm going to appoint the one I think will be best for you, given the history of your family. Do you understand? I want you to be happy, but I must do something."

Emily says, "Yes, I understand." She takes the judge's hand, pulls her down to whisper in her ear. Judge Holmes starts to smile, then remembers who and where she is, and quickly puts on her sober face. Later when I get to know Emily better, I ask what she said to the judge. "I told her, 'I trust you and John,'" she says.

"You can go back to your chair." The judge turns to the bailiff and motions for him to help Emily down.

Judge Holmes looks at Emily's mother. "Mrs. Olmsted, the records show the bank accounts held by you and Mr. Quinn at the time of the divorce totaled about two hundred thousand dollars and were in both your names. Is that correct?"

"Yes, Your Honor."

"You withdrew all that money when you divorced Mr. Quinn. Is that correct?"

Her face is pale and she whispers, "Yes." It is heard easily. There isn't another sound in the room.

"The will of Mr. Quinn's parents, Mr. and Mrs. Patrick Quinn, indicates their house was to be given to their son and daughter, John Patrick and Mary Elizabeth, upon their deaths. I understand Mr. Quinn bought his sister's share since she lives in California, and you and Mr. Quinn lived in that house about three years before his injury. Is that the house you sold after you divorced Mr. Quinn?"

"Yes," Nicki replies, scowling and biting her lips.

"Mrs. Olmsted, did you or your uncle sign your husband's name on the bill of sale and the deed transfer for this property?"

Mr. Wayman jumps to his feet, "Judge, that is none of this court's business."

"Counselor, I see we agree on something. That's why, as per my obligation, I'm turning this information over to the District Attorney for investigation. Release of bank funds, sale of the house, and the appointment of Mrs. Olmsted's uncle as guardian *ad litem* for a helpless man will be of interest to him. Forgery is a serious offense. Undoubtedly, he'll want to talk to you and your clients. You may sit down now. We will take a fifteen minute recess."

John, Mom, Katelyn, and I are in the hall when Emily comes over to us. John takes both her hands in his. "Emily, I'm so sorry to put you through all this."

She doesn't say anything, just moves in to give him a long hug, her face against his chest. She takes John's hand and smiles up at him. I'm certain John's heart is racing; I know mine is. I introduce her to Mom. Katelyn already knows her from the softball team.

Mom says, "I'm so glad to meet you. I hear about you all the time. Your dad is very proud of you."

"Really?"

"Really," Mom and I say together.

The bailiff calls us back in and says, "All rise."

Judge Holmes waits until the room is quiet. "After reviewing the pertinent documents, the answers to questions by the parents, the genetic studies, the home conditions assessment provided by Sheriff Tompkins and Social Services, and Mr. Quinn's work-ethic confirmed by his employer, I conclude Emily Grace Quinn should be in the custody of her biological father. I believe her health, happiness, and future will be best served this way. I add, this arrangement is acceptable to Emily. I, therefore, place her in the custody of John Patrick Quinn as of this date."

She continued, "As should have been done at the time of the original divorce of Mr. and Mrs. Quinn, a visiting schedule will be made so Emily has opportunities to see her mother. Mr. Quinn and Mrs. Olmsted, I leave it to you, or your attorneys, to prepare such a plan for the future. Submit it to me for approval within four weeks."

"Court is dismissed."

Emily and John stay at our house that night. Mom insists. We have Mom's spaghetti and meatballs and talk about the day's events while sitting on the back porch. John and Mom answer our questions about the court proceedings.

Hesitating and seeming unsure whether to ask, or perhaps afraid to hear the answer, John looks into Emily's eyes. "Emily, do you remember anything about me from when you were little?"

"I remember your clothes were white with stripes; and not like ones other people were wearing. Must have been your baseball uniform. You used to read me stories at bedtime. I liked that."

He starts to ask another question. I see Mom give him a signal to slow down by slightly shaking her head. I think she meant he shouldn't go so fast and Emily is tired.

John reads Mom's signal, stands up, and kisses Emily on the top of her head, and Katelyn, too. He tousles my hair and grins. "Goodnight team. You better get some rest: school in the morning. Being with you makes every day special for me."

Emily looks up at him and sighs like a great weight has been lifted from her body.

John sees this. "Tough day, huh, Emily?"

She takes his hand, pulls him down, and puts both her arms tightly around his neck. She whispers in his ear and his smile echoes around the room. All of us are smilin' too—it's contagious. Softly he says, "I love you, too."

Mom's eyes are glistening and her voice sounds odd. "You guys go up and get ready for bed and we'll come and tuck you in."

"Wait 'til you see my poster of Taylor Swift," Katelyn tells Emily, as they start upstairs. I start up, and then turn back for a glass of milk.

I hear Mom say to John, "Welcome home, John." He leans in and kisses her cheek, then pulls back and looks into her eyes. She kisses him back.